ASA

ASA

Donna Bender Hood

Library of Congress Control Number: 2009912543
ISBN: Hardcover   978-1-4500-0166-3
               Softcover   978-1-4500-0165-6
               Ebook   978-1-4500-0167-0

This is a work of fiction. Names, characters, places and incidents either are the
product of the author's imagination or are used fictitiously, and any resemblance to
any actual persons, living or dead, events, or locales is entirely coincidental.

This book was printed in the United States of America.

To order additional copies of this book, contact:
Xlibris Corporation
1-888-795-4274
www.Xlibris.com
Orders@Xlibris.com
70954

Contents

Prologue

He concentrated on putting one, worn boot in front of the other. It was the only way to walk home and not think about how far he still had to go. Asa James Bennington had already trudged several hundred miles and many more lay ahead. Going home depended on swollen rivers, food, and people in general. It was his feet that worried him now. He had a long way to walk and this boots were old and wearing thin. He did have another pair in his pack, but he did not want to wear them. Over a year ago, he had taken them off a dead soldier. True, the man had died in his arms. The man knew he was dying and told Asa to take anything he wanted. Asa had taken only the footwear, which was in little better shape than what he was currently wearing, but boots were boots. Other people would come along and strip the body of anything and everything. Asa only removed what he knew would help him walk home. From Virginia to Ohio and home to Catherine seemed like a dream, and what protected his feet was the key to making that dream come true.

The War Between the States was finally over. Asa felt either dammed lucky or blessed to be alive and not even injured. During the first part of his duty, he had served in the front. He had seen the men on either side of him killed or injured. Twice cannons down the line from where he was crouched had exploded killing the soldiers standing next to them. It wasn't that he hadn't seen dead men before, but the war carnage and the sounds and smells of that carnage would stay with him the rest of his life.

Because it was too hard to lose friends, Asa tried not to make any. The man you shared your evening meal with could be dead beside you in the first skirmish the following morning. He didn't want to hear nighttime, campfire talk of wives and sweethearts and mothers and see the mangled body of the speaker dumped into a stinking, mass burial trench the following evening.

For the first time in his life, he regretted knowing how to read and write. He wanted to be left alone, a loner. However, because he could read and write, men came to him with their letters from home. He could not turn down their requests. Asa knew how much letters from Catherine meant to him so he never refused to read their letters or carefully write their answers. It was this behavior that brought him to the attention of some officers and that caused him to be ordered to the rear.

This evening was like any other evening, hot food of a sort, discussion of the day's engagement and sorting out the various rumors that always circulated. At the moment, not everyone was in agreement about their location except probably the western side of Virginia. The last community they passed though was called Boone.

Somewhere a soldier played a harmonica, and the conversation died down a little as men's thoughts turned toward home. The moment was spoiled when an unfamiliar sergeant appeared. Looking around he saw Asa, "You, Bennington, come with me." Vaguely Asa wondered what he had done to be singled out and decided he had not done anything wrong.

The sergeant took him to two saddled horses and indicated that Asa should mount. The officer led him back to the command post, which was only a little different from where Asa had left the regulars. Well, maybe a little better. There had to be a real latrine some ways away and things smelled better. He could even smell cigar smoke. There were assorted tents and bigger fires. The whole area seemed a little more spit and polish.

Inside one of the tents, a harried captain was smoking the cigar. There was a glass of whiskey on the desk. Hardly looking at Asa, he handed over a sheet of paper. At first Asa thought it was a letter. In fact, it was a military dispatch.

"Read," was all the officer said. He could read it well and that seemed to satisfy the officer.
"You write as well as you read?" was the officer's next question.
"Yes sir."
"Fine, you are now a company clerk." Asa was dismissed to go fetch his gear and then returned. He would be assigned a cot, a tent, and his duty location. Later he would learn that dysentery had killed two clerks. Asa was filling one of those vacancies. He was kept busy. Asa would spend the remainder of the war as clerk, and he was now thankful he had learned to

read and write. He wrote to Catherine as soon as possible. Maybe knowing her husband was assigned to a place in the rear and away from the fighting most of the time would make her feel better.

A month later Catherine received the letter and she did feel better. At the moment, she was watching the postman come up her lane. She was hoping for another letter. Instead, the man removed his hat and solemnly said, "Miz Bennington, I have sad news." She felt as if her heart had stopped beating. She gripped the gatepost so hard as to drive splinters into her hand.
"Your uncle and aunt, the Hurleys, they've been dead for almost two weeks."

"Not Asa. Not her husband," she thought. Old Mr. and Mrs. Hurley had taken her in after the loss of her own family. Catherine had been living with them the whole year Asa courted her. After her marriage to Asa, she did not see them much as they lived in town. Even her infrequent visits seemed to be unwelcome which was not much change from when she lived with them. Now they were dead.

The old mailman explained. There had been influenza in the town and with so many missing from the Sunday morning service no one thought much of the Hurley's absence for a while. When the pastor did go to the house, he found them passed away in their bed. They had been dead for a while, and it seemed expedient to put them under as soon as possible.

Despite the fact she and her aunt and uncle were not close to her, they were her only blood relatives and it saddened her to think how they died and how they were buried with no family present for the reading of the proper words. The mailman was speaking again, "Buried in the church grave yard and for that reason Pastor Wright would like you to come into town as soon has the roads are passable. He wants to talk to you." "Also," the mail carrier continued, "There is the matter of the house, and something has to be done about the pigs. At least that is what Judge Pimm said so he desires to speak with you too. When you came to talk to Pastor Wright, if that is convenient for you."
The man was now silent and Catherine was confused. "What house and what pigs?"
"Please tell both Pastor Write and Judge Pimm, I will come to town straight away." The man bid her good day completely forgetting that he was supposed to deliver a letter for her from her husband. It would be three more days before she could make the trip because of more rain and the end of the week before she received the newest letter from Asa.

In Glennville, she sought out the pastor first. He was a kindly man, and Catherine knew his wife because they were both part of the local quilt circle. He expressed his condolences and showed her the two graves in the cemetery. He spoke slowly, "I was wondering. What kind of markers are you planning? As you see all the graves here at the church have head stones or at the very least a wooden marker." In her heart, Catherine thought the truth was more like markers and a donation to the church. Perhaps that was right. She would sort that out later. Saying she would have to think on it, she bid the pastor good-bye. She left to find the judge.

In his office and just like the pastor, the judge expressed his condolences after ushering her into the chair opposite his large desk. He adjusted his poor fitting reading glasses, then opened a leather-covered book in front of him, "Of course, Catherine, you know that you are your aunt and uncle's only living relative."

Catherine thought the man was slick and not sure what he was leading up to so she answered his question honestly, "As far as I know, I am."

"Well you might find this pleasant news, at least as pleasant as it can be under the circumstances. You inherit their house and all it's contents." His statement was such a surprise that later Catherine would wonder if her mouth had fallen open.

"I have the front door key here. If you will sign these papers, you can take possession of your property immediately. Of course, there is the matter of the pigs."

"What pigs?" she asked.

"Your uncle was raising pigs. There are eight I believe. A neighbor, Mr. Bertolli had been feeding them following your uncle's demise. You will have to make restitution to Mr. Bertolli for the feed." Bertolli was not a name familiar to Catherine, but she thought it should be. Standing in the street, Catherine considered the last the few hours. She had become a woman of property, not that that was unheard of, but she was a young woman of property and already in debt for pig food and responsible for finding money for two head stones.

The Hurley house looked just like it did seven years ago, gray, weathered, and in need of a coat of paint. With the big key, she opened the front door to be greeted by the smell of mildew and dust. It did not take long for a house to go to rack and ruin with no care. The inside was much the same as the outside, but before she could make an inspection of her new property there was a polite knock at the door.

Standing just to the side of the door with hat in hand was a small man with a large, black, drooping mustache. He tipped his head and asked, "Signora Bennington?" After that, he spoke rapid Italian with a few words of English added. There was just enough English that Catherine felt she was talking to Mr. Bertolli, the pig care man. Communication was going to be difficult she thought. Mr. Bertolli motioned to someone out of Catherine's range of vision. A small boy appeared.

To the boy's embarrassment, Mr. Bertolli removed his hat for him, folded it into his small hands and began speaking to both Catherine and the boy. The boy listened carefully nodding at times then translated, "My grandfather apologizes for his poor English. He asked me to tell you that he and Mr. Hurley had an agreement about the pigs and it is his earnest hope that you will honor this agreement."

It was Catherine's turn to apologize, "I have no knowledge of this agreement. Perhaps your grandfather could tell me the terms?" There was more conversation between the grandfather and the boy.

"My grandfather says your uncle agreed to raise the pigs till fall then sell them to us." The boy corrected himself, "To my grandfather. We smoke hams and bacon and make sausage," the youngster added rather proudly.

Now Catherine knew why the name was a little familiar to her. Bertolli Hams were becoming famous in the area surrounding Glenview. She had never been able to afford the bacon let alone a ham. "Ah," she said and gave the worried looking Mr. Bertolli her best smile. Catherine reasoned if she chose not to sell the pigs to him, there would be no (or at least fewer) items from the Bertolli smoke house and that would hurt his family's income.

"Please tell your grandfather that I have no way to care for the animals. If he would agree, I will give him the pigs outright, today. I only ask in return is a ham and some bacon." The boy translated. From the grin that spread across the old man's face, she felt she had made a good suggestion. She almost jumped when the man grabbed her hand in both of his and shook it vigorously. Turning to the boy, he rattled off more Italian and then bowed his way off the porch.

The boy was also grinning. "My grandfather says your ham and bacon will be the best ones. My grandfather also says you are very pretty." The boy had embarrassed himself, and he quickly followed his grandfather.

Now she thought, I will take note of the house. Another knock at the door brought her back into the living room. This time it was Pastor Wright. She had only left the man a few hours ago and had not had the time to think about grave markers yet. She invited him in and apologized for not even having tea or something to offer.

He was not here about the grave markers. For a man who could preach fire and brimstone on Sundays he was having difficulty in relating the reason for the visit. After several starts, he began. "I am here on business for the church. You see, the personage is truly falling down around our ears. It is in need of extensive repairs. The deacons have told me that I must move my family during the repair work. They have authorized me to ask you if you might rent this house to the church for the duration of the repair work about two years they think." He paused, "As you know Mrs. Bennington our congregation is not wealthy, but we could offer you a small monthly sum plus we would do any upkeep on this property." To Catherine it was a perfect plan and she accepted his offer. Pastor Wright was very relieved. Secretly so was she.

"I would like to come back on Friday," she said. "I will try to find a wagon and remove those items that I wish to keep. Anything I don't take I would like to donate to the church. When I leave Friday, I will bring you the key." He immediately offered her the use of his wagon and the services of his son to help her load items and drive her home. She watched him depart and thought, "Another happy man has just left my door, but they are all the wrong man."

It was noon. She was hungry. Because she hadn't known how the day would go she had a lunch with her. She pulled the old rocking chair onto the porch and was just about to eat when she saw Mrs. Wright, the pastor's wife, heading toward the house. Martha Wright was a portly woman and that was being polite. The pastor himself was thin as a rail. Every time Catherine saw them together, she could not help but remember the nursery rhyme about Jack Sprat. "Jack Sprat could eat no fat. His wife could eat no lean and betixed them both they licked the platter clean."

Now that Martha Wright had huffed and puffed her way up to the gate, she stopped to catch her breath. Again, Catherine apologized for having nothing to offer a guest.

"No bother, child," Martha said when she could finally breath. "I only wanted you to know that now that the weather is again fair we will be starting up the quilt circle again. Same as last year, the last Thursday of the month. We hope you come."

"I shall," answered Catherine.

"We have two baby quilts and one wedding quilt to work on." The smile left Martha's red face. "Two ladies want to start stitching mourning quilts." Martha wiped her brow with a huge handkerchief. She waved it at Catherine and whirled off in the direction she had come from. Despite the recent rains, her long skirts made dust puffs in the dirt behind her.

Having no more visitors, allowed Catherine to wander through the house. Most of the furniture she would leave. She would take the rocking chair and the pewter candlesticks on the mantle. In the bedroom, the bed linens were gone except for a comforter folded in a corner. It was wool tied together with red yarn. She recognized the pattern as "Lightening Strike." Probably the wool rectangles were scraps from the Hurley men's Sunday-go-to-meeting suits. She would keep the comforter. A Bible rested on the dresser. Catherine was going to leave it as she and Asa already had two. She changed her mind when she opened it and found the carefully written birth dates and death dates of long gone Hurleys.

In the closet, hung her aunt's four dresses, one brown, two gray, and one black. On a top shelf wrapped in tissue paper was a funny, old, black hat. Perhaps it was a Sunday hat from when her aunt was younger. On the softly pleated hatband was a velvet rose with dewdrops of black jet beads. Catherine put the hat in her to-go-home pile. She wanted the soft, velvet rose even if it was black.

In the kitchen, she selected some pots and pans, a washboard and two flat irons, and the dishes. Catherine had forgotten about her aunt's dishes, not fine china but to Catherine they were beautiful. Some were chipped, and there was only enough for four people with some odd serving pieces. The small blue-flowered pattern on the white rim would look lovely on her wooden table. She would make or maybe even buy a tablecloth. In a cupboard, she found an assortment of table linens and it included a tablecloth and matching napkins. When Asa came home, she would be able to set a proper table, well almost.

For Catherine, the best find was her aunt's sewing basket containing a thimble, needles, spools of thread, two pairs of scissors, and cloth. Her aunt was not a quilter but like many thrifty women kept every scrap and any length of cloth that might be used later. On her way home, Catherine thought it felt a little like Christmas.

Martha's mention of the mourning quilts brought a little sadness to the otherwise bright day. Mourning quilts were always stitched in dark colors. Usually, there was a good-sized square or rectangle in the center. This represented the cemetery. Around the center would be stitched a small border some fancy, some just plain. It was the fence around the cemetery. On the wide, outer border the quilter would select a shape or object stitching on one for every member of the family. Often these were shaped like small coffins. With each family death, a coffin was removed from the outer border. Careful stitches added deceased's name onto the coffin piece, which was then stitched inside the cemetery fence. Would the war never end?

"Too sad," she thought. Tomorrow she would write Asa and tell him of all about today's adventures, how for a few hours at least, she had been a pig farmer. She could post the letter on Friday. On her doorstep, she found a letter from him, how often their letters crossed.

A month later, Asa had that very letter in his pocket. He had gathered as many newspapers as he could find and hoped this evening he just might have time to read. In his capacity as a company clerk, he often had access to newspapers. Asa skimmed over the war articles. He searched for information about the states and territories out west. Even before Asa was called up, he had thought about selling the farm and moving west. It had been only a small idea, but more and more he was giving it serious thought. He had never mentioned it to Catherine. Reading the newspapers made him worry that time could be running out. The great wagon trains of the 1830s and 1840s were over. The California Gold Rush was sixteen years ago. He was not interested in gold. Besides he was smart enough to know that the precious nuggets did not jump out of the earth into your gold pan. He wanted a farm, a good farm with rich soil. He didn't want to deal with rocks that heaved up out of the ground every spring thaw.

Asa's captain was a good man but not really a military man. Everyone knew he had received his commission because his father was a New York banker. Asa was in the army because the powers that be decided they needed more men and Asa and all the others like him had been called up. Asa didn't know, that in the eyes of the Captain, he looked a little different from the rest of the enlisted men. That was because during slow times in the day and in the evenings, the captain observed Asa reading newspapers, many newspapers. The captain wondered why.

It was evening and as was his habit, Asa was scanning the papers first and saving Catherine's letter for last. An orderly approached, "Bennington, Capn wants you." Generally in the evening, a rider coming in would alert Asa that a summons to the Captain's tent would be forth coming, but tonight he had heard no rider. He gathered his writing supplies and reported.

The captain was not at his desk, but sitting outside the tent in a make shift camp chair. He had his boots off. Asa suspected the man had a foot problem, and the boots caused him pain. Motioning Asa to take a chair the Captain said, "Tell me about yourself, Bennington."

Asa really didn't know what the captain wanted to hear except he most likely did not want war talk.

Asa began at what he felt was a reasonable beginning. His grandfather, whom he did not remember, had planted the apple orchard in an area that was now called Glennview in Ohio. Asa had been born on that farm and until the war had not traveled much beyond Glennview, but he did know about other places and he knew about the great migration west. He hoped he was not too late to make the move but would his wife, Catherine, consider the idea?

His mother died when he was eighteen. She went out to the hen house, as was her morning custom to gather fresh eggs for breakfast. When she didn't return, Asa went out to find her. She was dead on the floor amid the broken, freshly gathered eggs. He and his father wrapped her in a blanket and buried her along side the twin brother Asa never knew.

His father slipped away before the apple trees bloomed, another grave on the little hill on the east side of the orchard. Spring did come. The trees did bloom. He planted the garden. He took care of the orchard, and the land just as his father had done. Because Asa thought the Captain might be asleep he concluded his history with his courtship of Catherine and their marriage some six years ago. The Captain was not asleep. He opened his eyes. "So you think you want to sell the apple farm and move west? Not sure your wife is open to the idea?"

"No sir. I've not mention this to her, and there are many memories attached to our home."

Thoughtfully, the captain commented, "Women are funny that way."

Before Asa thought about the wisdom of his question he asked, "Are you married, Sir?"

"I was when I received my commission. I'm not so sure now." Picking up his boots, the Captain entered his tent and closed the flap.

Back in his own tent, Asa read about Catherine's pig-farming adventures. Asa laughed out loud and hoped there would be a hams and bacon in their little springhouse when he returned probably not considering he did not know when the war would end. There was never bad news in her letters, and he wondered whether there was anything she was not telling him.

There was worrisome news, but she didn't tell him about the poor apple harvest. In the spring, she thought she had noticed the lack of buds on the trees. First, she hoped it just might be her imagination. Walking to town on Thursdays, she saw other orchards looking much like hers. When the buds opened, there were fewer flowers and she knew the harvest would be small. This had not happened in the years she had lived on the farm with Asa. Listening to snatches of conversations in town, she learned everyone had the same concerns. The solution to this year's crop was a wait and see attitude about the next year's crop. Hopefully, Asa would be home.

Catherine did include in her letter, that thankfully, while in town she had met up with old man Pike. This meant she did not have to go to the Pike's home to see if he was planning to buy the apple crop again this year. She wrote that he was prepared to buy the crop with the same agreement as last year. Asa was relieved to read this. Considering what he knew about the Pikes, he didn't like the idea of Catherine alone with any of them.

The whole Pike's family was a rough, coarse lot, and consisted of the father and his six sons named Mathew, Mark, Luke, John, Isaac, and Jacob. The fact that all the Pike's boys had biblical names was a source of local humor since none of the family came close to any of the teachings in the good book.

Catherine sat on the porch. The evenings were now chill. Shortly, there would not be enough light or warmth for her to sit and sew outside. Tomorrow she would put up jars of applesauce. She had already made apple jelly and berry jam. There were hams in the springhouse. She had potatoes and onions, and dried peas and beans. She had flour and corn meal. She even had sugar, cinnamon, and dried fruits. She didn't expect to be baking a Christmas cake. She would be alone again.

Today she had been in town for the quilting circle. Even that would be coming to an end soon because of the weather. She pricked her finger and stuck it in her mouth. "Time to go inside," she thought.

She put away her thread and the thimble. Looking at the thimble made her think about her mother. It was one of the few items Catherine had of her mother's.

Catherine could remember as a little girl sitting on the hard horsehair sofa next to her mother. They each had sewing. Her mother's fingers moved quickly, and they created tiny stitches while Catherine's fat child's fingers stumbled along leaving a trail of long, uneven stitches. In Catherine's mind, it was the magic thimble worn by her mother that made perfect stitches, and now and then her mother would let Catherine wear it. Always it would fall off her small finger, tumble down her apron front and bounce across the floor till it lodged in the bumps of the braided rug. Her mother would pretend to be very distressed. The thimble was lost. Could little Catherine find it? Of course, they both could see it, but Catherine on her hands and knees would make a great pretence of searching. If she were very lucky that day, her mother would join her and the floor. Together they would find the missing thimble. Amid a flurry of skirts, aprons, bloomers, and petticoats, her mother would hug and praise her. Catherine was a young woman before she realized that only happened on days her father and brothers were not at home. Looking into the western sky, the light was totally gone and a few stars shown above her. Catherine went inside, locked the door, and went to bed.

There was a gap in Catherine's letters, and Asa worried about her. Ever since the evening conversation with his captain, newspapers appeared on his cot with articles about the country's westward expansion circled. With no letters from his wife, he reread old ones and studied over the newspaper articles. When at last a letter arrived from her, he knew that somehow one had gotten lost in the mails. She was canning applesauce and making jelly. He could tell she was lonely.

His thoughts turned inward. His father died a year after his mother. Asa knew in the late winter of that year his father would probably not live to see the spring. He did everything he knew to do. His father continued to cough and lose weight. Asa kept the fire banked high. Only warm dry air might help the old man and that kind of weather was a long way away. Most of the time his father was lost in old memories and told the same stories repeatedly. Asa listened with half an ear.

One night the old man startled Asa by saying, "You need to take a wife." This was not something they had ever discussed so Asa paid attention. "Having a full-time woman in your bed is not a right as many men say. Your wedding night will be one of the most important nights of your life . . . not because you can satisfy your needs, but because how your wedding night goes so goes the rest of your married nights. You need to be slow, tender, and gentle with your woman. Your mother was a good woman, and she did enjoy our marriage bed. Loving and being loved in that way is not a sin as some would say. It is part of a good strong marriage." His father did die in the early spring before the apple tree budded.

Asa cared for the orchard. He planted a garden. He reshingled the cabin roof. He harvested the apples. He sold the crop to old man Pike as his father had every year before. And just as his father had done, he took one bottle of Applejack and the rest in trade or cash for payment. By the beginning of the year, he knew he was lonesome and he remembered his father's words about a wife.

Years ago Asa's father saw that many a town girl had set her cap for his son. Father reasoned young Asa was a hard worker, sober, and probably going to inherit a paid for farm. With his light brown hair and his bright blue eyes, mothers told their daughters that he was a nice looking man. If Asa Bennington had a drawback, it was the Bennington temper, a family trait. The Bennington men simply could not stand to see ill treatment of an unfortunate person or an animal. Asa never knew any thing about the girls or the comments of the parents. In fact, he had decided there was no girl in Glenview that interested him. He was wrong.

March turned the roads to muddy mess, but Asa still managed a long, awaited trip to town. That was the first time he saw the young woman walking with old Mrs. Hurley. Asking a few quiet questions, he learned she was the niece of Mr. Hurley. Her name was Catherine, and she had come to live with her aunt and uncle after loosing her family in some kind of accident. He knew he had found the woman to be his wife and he began a courtship. Early on, he understood that the Hurleys were not happy about having the girl in their home, but it was their "Christian Duty" to care for her since they were her only kin. One evening after Asa and Catherine were married he said, "I think your aunt and uncle would have been happy to see me take you away instead of courting you proper."

She laughed and replied, "You are right and I would have gladly gone with you."

He didn't take her away but did court her for the traditional one year. At first, the Hurleys were not happy about having him there either but he tried to win their approval with gifts of honeycomb, fresh caught trout, and vegetables from his garden and over the winter, seasoned firewood. By the spring wedding, he knew they would have liked to prolong the engagement just so he would keep bringing courting gifts.

The young couple's wedding day came. They were married in the town church in the presence of many neighbors and the dour-faced Hurleys. After a wedding lunch and amid much laughter and well wishes, the new Mr. and Mrs. Asa Bennington were allowed to drive off in his wagon loaded with her small amount of personal possessions, which included a trunk. In the trunk was a quilt she had been stitching on for the entire year of their courtship. Traditionally, a girl was supposed to have twelve everyday quilts plus one special one. With help of friends and neighbors, she had the one special quilt finished just in time to be her wedding gift to him.

In preparation, Asa could not have made the cabin any cleaner. He placed wild flowers on the rough wooden table. He was touched when after he moved her trunk into their bedroom she opened it, took out the quilt and spread it on their bed. She said, "It is called Ohio Rose."

He looked puzzled so she explained that quilts and quilt patterns almost always have names. She added, "If I had selected yellow fabric for the flower blossoms it would be called Texas Rose." All he knew was that the red flowers and the dark green leaves on the white background were very pleasing and brightened up the small dark cabin bedroom. He loved her all the more for her work. He remembered everything his father had said about the wedding night. He was slow and gentle and when they did finally consummate the marriage, her passion was as deep as his own.

His thoughts came back to the present. The campfires were burning low, and men were settling in. The troop was moving out tomorrow. The telegraph was done again. Asa looked at the stars and wondered if Catherine saw the same ones as he did.

In the spring of 1865, it was thought the war was finally winding down. In Glennview, the farmers watched the apple trees and were concerned again. For Asa and his detachment, the news of the war's end was two days late in coming. The telegraph was still down, and it was a rider that brought in the news of Lee's surrender. After the initial excitement and celebration came a time of some confusion. No one knew exactly what to do. Did they remain a military unit? Most of the enlisted men said no. The war was over. That meant they could go home and some even slipped away that night. Others thought they should be mustered out with the proper papers. At this stage, they did not want to be thought of as deserters.

Even the officers could not agree, and the discussion went on the next day. Whatever was decided Asa knew they would be moving somewhere and not for the first time. He also thought about leaving during the night. In preparation for moving out, Asa was packing his few belongings when the sergeant appeared, "Capn wants you."

In the command tent, the Captain handed him papers. They were discharge papers. "Go home to your wife and your orchards. If you do go west, good luck." The man rose and offered his hand to Asa. Before Asa exited the tent flap, the Captain added, "Asa be careful. The war maybe over on paper but not necessarily in men's hearts and right now we are in the south." Back at his own tent, Asa was packed and on the road in short order before anyone could change the order to go home.

Yes, he was on the road and worrying about wearing the dead man's boots, "What the hell," he thought. He was going home. However, he was watchful just as the Captain had suggested.

Chapter One

Going Home

Inside his shirt and wrapped around his waist he carried most of his military pay, all Catherine's letters, and the discharge papers. The pay, he thought, would help with the trip west or the purchase of new apple trees if Catherine should not want to leave. In his heart, he now understood that he truly wanted to make the move west.

As a married couple they talked freely about all manner of things. The absence of children in the home was the one subject that they did not discuss. He knew she had sought the advice of the local doctor and several of the midwives in the area.

He thought back to spring and their third anniversary. They were in the orchard looking at the blossoming trees, which they often did. A warm breeze caused petals to drift to the ground. Clover bloomed in the new spring grass. It seemed the most natural thing in the world to pull her down onto the grass and make love with her. Just as they were complete in their lovemaking, they heard the sound of a wagon coming down the road. She became embarrassed and ill at ease, but he laid her back in the tall grass, covered her with his shirt. Together they listened to the sound of the wagon as it rolled slowly past their lane. Kissing him softly, she laughed. They were covered in a snow of pink and white apple blossom petals.

Spring turned to summer and blossoms turned into little apples. In August, it was hot and they were sitting on the porch in the evening, as was their habit. As usual she was busy with needlework, and he asked, "What are you working on?"

She smiled broadly and said, "It's called Double Irish Chain and it is a crib quilt for the baby." It took him several minutes before he comprehended just what she was telling him. He could hardly believe it.

All he said was "When?"

"January, I think," was her answer.

It was not to be. She delivered at six months. The baby was a perfectly formed girl child born dead. Asa dug a small grave along side the graves of his twin brother and his parents. He laid the wrapped baby in it and covered the fresh dirt with the ever-present rocks. If his sorrow was deep, Catherine's was deeper.

He hid his grief and cared for her till she began to heal both physically and emotionally. He had some comfort in that he had not lost her as well as the child. The cradle went into the attic, and the quilt went into her wedding trunk. He harvested and sold the season's apple crop. Winter came followed by Christmas and with the advent of spring she was almost herself and their life returned to normal.

Two years later, she conceived again. He would not let Catherine work in the garden or carry the wet wash or anything that might hurt her or the child they both wanted so desperately. This time she carried the baby full term. She worked on another crib quilt just for this baby. She said the quilt pattern was called Double Nine Patch. Another daughter was born in the spring. Asa held the baby in his arms and knew why some people said new babies were like little pink rose buds.

He was slightly alarmed when the baby's breathing seemed to become labored. As the evening wore on his worry became real. The baby struggled for breath, turned blue, and died. He could hardly contain Catherine in her grief. She cursed herself and sobbed deep racking sobs. He held her tightly. He rocked back and forth and let her weep till she exhausted herself. She told Asa to take the dead infant, wrap her in all the baby quilts and bury then, burn the cradle.

He did not. He would not bury those quilts on which she had worked so hard. As far as he was concerned, his daughters were wrapped in the arms of God and to bury all Catherine's fine handwork did no good whatsoever. It took more time, but she did recover. There was always a little sadness about her, and it was because of the two small graves that Asa was thinking she might not want to leave the farm.

On the road, he looked like any other returning soldier. He kept to himself because he did not want to be slowed down. He tried not to spend much money. But last night, it had rained. He was wet and was cold. He decided at the next town, if he found an inn or a tavern he would purchase a hot meal. He was near the Ohio Virginia border. Perhaps Southern sympathies did not run too high this far north. He had been ten days on the road. It was afternoon when a town with a tavern came into view. Inside the smoky room, he ordered stew and corn bread and applesauce. He found a chair as near to the fire as possible as most of the tables were occupied mostly by men, and the bar was nearly full. Eating the hot food, feeling the heat from the fire, and letting the conversation wash over him felt good. He savored the applesauce though it was not as good as his wife's.

Asa felt like taking a nap except one large man at the bar was talking too loudly and had been ever since Asa entered the room. Next thing Asa knew the man was in front of him and now speaking loudly to him.

"Well gents. Looks like we have one of our brave, blue belly boys right here. On your way home are ye?" There were some low murmurs from the drinkers at the rough bar.

Asa nodded. "We think you should have a drink on us. Don't we boys? Several men at the bar mumbled yes. Better yet, as you blue bellies won the war maybe you should buy us drinks." This time there were not as many responses from the listening drinkers. However, Asa was having a bad feeling about the whole thing.

"Thank you for the offer, but I am on my way home. I need to be getting on my way," Asa said this as politely as possible but it did no good.

The big man became surly and men at the bar were looking sideways at the two of them. "You too good to drink with me, are you?" The man wore a Bowie knife at his belt. He was fingering it. With his fists, Asa was probably better than most, but when it came to knife fighting he knew next to nothing. Drinkers within earshot of the conversation had picked up their drinks and moved away. Asa thought, "They know this man. He has done this before. No one is going to intercede." The drunk was weaving slightly, and his hand was still on the knife. Asa's temper was bubbling to the top. He tried to tamp it down.

The door to the tavern banged open. "They've shot the president. Mr. Lincoln is dead!" The speaker was motioning to a lathered horse and excited rider outside. The room exited in mass to hear all about Ford Theater and about the hunted assassin, John Willks Booth. Asa followed the group picking up chunks of corn bread from the forgotten plates and stuffing it in his coat. Asa listened with the rest. Some in the crowd were pleased, but not all. No one noticed him in the milling throng of listeners or when he departed and made his way out of town. Like most folk, Asa liked President Lincoln and thought that without him the Southern States would have a more difficult time rejoining the union. Two weeks would pass before he learned of the capture and resulting death of the assassin.

Asa had run out of the stolen corn bread yesterday, and he was thinking about finding food. A yelling, cursing old woman stopped his thoughts about hunger. Asa did not know such words could come from a woman's mouth. The object of her anger was a mule, which walked just ahead of her so she could not catch it. Asa easily caught the animal and returned it to the woman. She thanked him and then eyed his uniform. "On your way home, are you?"

"Yes ma'am."

"You been on the road long?"

"Since the war ended," he replied because he did not know the dates.

"You're not a deserter, are you?"

"No ma'am. I have papers," he answered.

"You hungry?"

"Yes ma'am."

"Can you fix my fence so that son of a bitchin' critter can't run off again?"

"Yes ma'am."

"I'll show you the tools and the fence. You come to dinner," and she handed him the rope on the mule.

He repaired the fence and the gate. He chopped firewood. He drew water from the well for her. When he thought she didn't see him, he tried to wash up as best he could. The old woman hadn't seen a young man naked from the waste up in along time. She watched. It was a pleasant sight.

She fed him chicken and biscuits and a salad of greens from her yard. Dessert was more hot, buttered biscuits with homemade berry syrup, and real coffee. He told her about the farm and Catherine. She guessed there were no children so she didn't ask. As the daylight stole away, she handed him a lantern and said, "You can sleep in the barn. Breakfast is at first light."

She was good at her word . . . bacon, flapjacks, and more coffee. And as if that were not enough she handed him a whole roasted chicken wrapped in a towel, a sack of biscuits, and a small mason jar containing a clear golden liquid. Holding the jar up to the sunlight she said, "Best sippin' liquor you will ever have."

Hours later, he was still thinking about his good fortune. He figured he would be home in two weeks at the most. He was admiring the big roadside bushes . . . dark, green leaves and covered in giant pink, and pale lavender blossoms. If Catherine were beside him, she would find the flowers beautiful. He was not prepared for the small child careening out of those bushes, crashing into him and crying while she wrapped her little arms around one leg.

"Papa, Papa! Mama won't wake up." She was crying harder now. The girl was maybe six or seven he thought. Despite the morning chill, she wore no shoes, a long calico dress, and a muslin pinafore. She had released his leg and stepped back. This tall man with the brown beard was not her father.

Asa watched as she twisted her pinafore in her little hands. He could tell she was trying to decide if she should talk to a stranger. Asa squatted down and quietly as he could he asked, "Is you mama sick?"

She was not crying now, but she only nodded yes.

"Is she sick in bed?"

"No sir. She is on the floor by the kitchen stove."

"If you take me to her perhaps I can help her." The girl thought it over then took hold of his hand and headed into the bushes from which she had first appeared. There was a small path.

For such a little one she moved quickly and the branches slapped Asa in the face. Once she stopped and asked, "You know my papa? He is blue like you."

"The uniform," Asa thought. "Her father is in the Union Army."

"What is his name?"

"Joshua," she answered. Asa shook his head no. Ahead of them was a cabin surrounded by field that had not seen the plow in at least a year. No garden patch was tilled and ready for spring planting. In side it was sparse but clean. The child was right. The mother lay on the kitchen floor. Asa could see she was breathing.

Putting down his pack he said, "What is your name?"

"I'm Lizzy and I'm six," she said proudly.

"Lizzy, can you fetch me water from your well? I expect your mama will be thirsty when she wakes up." Lizzy was pleased to help. While the child was out of the room, Asa examined the mother. She appeared to be in a faint. Neither his mother nor Catherine had ever fainted so he was not sure just what to do. If it were a man on the floor, he would douse him with water but that did not seem the thing to do to the young mother. He looked around the kitchen. For mid-morning, there should be at least remnants of the morning cooking fire. The stove, in fact the whole house, was cold. There was not even any smell of a breakfast.

Lizzy returned with the water. "Lizzy, what is your mama's name?" The child gave Asa a look that meant she thought the question silly.

"Mama. Her name is Mama," stated the child.

Asa tried again. "Your name is Lizzy, Lizzy what?" Asa prompted.

"Adams. My name is Lizzy Adams."

Clearly the child and the woman were mother and daughter. Besides the family looks they were both very thin and pale with dark smudges under their eyes. "Lizzy, what did you have for breakfast?" Asa asked.

"Nothing. We ain't got no food," she replied.

"Did you eat last night?"

"Yes sir," she nodded.

"Did your mama eat last night?"

"No sir."

"Ah, hell," Asa thought. "They're starving."

"Well Lizzy Adams would you like some chicken and a biscuit?"

"Oh yes." Lizzy was bouncing up and down. He put her at the table and gave her a drumstick and a biscuit out of his bag.

In the bedroom, he found the bed heaped with blankets and quilts. Probably the only way they were keeping warm. He took a pillow and a quilt and made Mr. Adams as comfortable as possible. Looking at the quilt, Asa thought if Catherine were here she would know what to do and would be telling him the name of the quilt pattern. Asa waited.

Mrs. Adams came around slowly. When she first saw Asa she said, "Joshua?"

"No ma'am. My name is Asa Bennington. Your daughter fetched me from the road. I think you need to eat something." She did not argue. All the chicken and most of the biscuits were gone in no time.

Mrs. Adams had recovered some of her color so Asa said, "Ma'am, you cannot stay here." She started to argue then her shoulders slumped and she said nothing.

"Don't you have family or someone? Somewhere you and Lizzy could go?"

The woman started to say no, but Lizzy was faster. "We could go to Granma's. We can take Minny." Asa was not happy to hear that there was another mouth to feed. Instead he said, "How far is grandma's house?"

"My parents are three days from here but how will my husband find me?"

Asa was a little irritated, "Mrs. Adams, if you were not here wouldn't your husband look to your family first?" She didn't answer him but stared at her empty dish.

"Who is Minny?" was Asa's next question.

"He is our horse," Lizzy answered waving in the general direction of the back of the house. A horse? Asa hoped the animal was in better condition than the mother and the daughter.

Minny was in fairly good condition having had the run of the whole pasture. She did not want to be caught, and it took Asa over an hour to coax her into a bridle. At last with the horse in the barn, Asa looked over everything. Not many tools, but there was a small cart. He thought the horse could manage the cart with the mother and child. He would continue to walk. Off to the side was a wooden barrel. Lifting the lid, he discovered a bag of oats. He smelled them. They did not smell rancid. Sure they were horse food but boil them enough, he could make oatmeal. They would start out in the morning.

Returning to the house, he told them his plan and suggested they pack so they could all start early. He was able to find some wood. He cut it and built a fire saving enough wood for a morning fire to boil oats. By bedtime, the house was fairly warm. She offered him a pallet on the living room floor. He declined saying he would sleep on the front porch. Should the missing husband arrive home in the night, it would be better he find a stranger on the porch rather than in the living room or so reasoned Asa.

The morning went just as he planned. He boiled enough oats for a hot breakfast and cold for lunch. He took a pot and the remaining oats for them and the horse. The first day and night and the second day were uneventful. Mrs. Adams was quiet, but Lizzy's happy chatter filled the void. At a fork in the road, Mrs. Adams pointed right and Asa's heart sank. Home and Catherine was the fork to the left.

That night, after Lizzy was sound asleep, Mrs. Adams approached Asa. "I ain't got no way to thank you, Mr. Bennington." She was undoing the buttons of her dress. "If you were wanting to lay with me I believe I could do that for you." He was stunned. Just briefly, he thought he had not had a women in over two years. Not that he hadn't thought about it. "No," he corrected himself. He had not enjoyed his wife in over two years.

"No, no ma'am. I'm a married man, a happily married man. No." He was stammering. She was clearly relieved and returned to the other side of the fire with her buttons all done up.

"Lord," thought Asa, "Would Catherine ever find herself in a similar situation?" He hoped not. He would never let that happen.

However, he was not there to protect her when Catherine heard the wagon in her lane that very morning, she would never forget the visit of the two Pike's brothers, Luke, the oldest and Jacob, the youngest. She walked out to the gate along with the barking, growling dog. The brothers tipped their grimy caps, and Luke said, "Howdy, Mistress Bennington. We were hoping you was planning on selling us your apple crop this year and if you don't mind we would like to have a look at your trees." She did not recall that the Pike's brothers ever looking at the orchard before but she did not want to be rude. She needed them to buy the crop.

She smiled and nodded her head. Looking at the still angry dog and with a tone of worry in his voice, Luke suggested, "Maybe you should chain up your pooch. He seems mighty serious about protecting his ground." Jacob was looking at her with a thin, sly smile on his face. As she chained up the dog, she tried to remember what she knew about the Pike's family. All she remembered was the old man has suffered some sort of a stoke recently. The boys under Luke's direction were running the business. Of the six brothers, three were missing, the rumor being they were up north either in jail or had been hanged.

When she returned to the front gate, the wagon was empty. She saw Luke walking into the trees, but Jacob was walking toward her from around the other side of the wagon. He was near enough she could see his broken teeth. He reminded her of a rodent. He moved quickly and quietly. He grabbed for her.

Ripping open the bodice of her dress, buttons went everywhere and she could hear fabric tearing. He shoved her to the ground. He was on top of her. His breath was foul. He tried to fondle her exposed breast and at the same time work his way under her skirts and petty coats. She was screaming. With his weight, she would never be able to throw him off. Her hand searched the ground next to her head for anything to use as a weapon. She found the row of rocks bordering the flowerbed. Her fingers closed firmly around the biggest one she could grasp. Catherine clouted Jacob soundly in the head over his right eye.

He yelled and cursed. He rocked upright still effectively holding her down by his weight, but now his hands were trying to stem the flow of blood down his face. He was yanked off of her. Big brother Luke stood over both them. Luke sent Jacob sprawling into the grass. He kicked Jacob and yelled, "You fool! Get your ass in the wagon."

Luke grabbed Catherine up by her shoulder and with his face close to her he hissed, "You tell anyone about this ever, Mistress, and I will come back and finish what my little brother couldn't." He dropped her. Catching the gate, she fell. The gate came loose from the hinge.

It was almost noon the following day when Hiram Glick saw his daughter and Lizzy coming down the road. They were in their cart. He recognized the horse as belonging to his daughter, but the man leading the horse was not Joshua Adams. He called for his misses. Together they watched the approaching group. Lizzy was waving and calling her grandparents. Up close Mrs. Glick was appalled at the sight of her daughter and little Lizzy. She hustled both of them inside the house. Asa introduced himself and told Hiram the whole story omitting the fireside conversation of the night before.

"We are much obliged. We didn't think much of Joshua when they married and my daughter has always tried to make things look better than they were. We're glad you brought them home." In the barn, the old man watched Asa care for the horse. "You can take that horse iffin you think it will get you home faster. I got my own horse and not enough feed for two."

Asa was pleased with the offer but said, "You think Miss Lizzy would let me take her horse?" They agreed to ask her during dinner. "You a drinking man, Mr. Glick?"

"When I can get it and the bills are paid which ain't to often," replied the older man. Asa handed him the mason jar of whiskey. He studied the golden contents, unscrewed the lid and smelled the liquor. "Ah" was all he said. He put the lid back on the jar and hid it behind a stack of rusty hinges on a high shelf. Next morning Asa left the Glick farm riding Minnie and carrying a sack of food that just might last him the week he figured it would take him to be home . . . if he didn't eat much.

And it was just a week later he road slowly through Glenview. Not much had changed. Well, some things had. Just as Catherine had written in her letter the parsonage was still being repaired. The Hurley's house had a fresh coat of paint. There were more head stones in the cemetery. Two elderly men sitting on the bench in front of the Post office doffed their hats to Asa not because they recognized him but in respect for his travel stained uniform.

No one recognized him. He was thinner and he was bearded, and no one knew the horse he rode either. There was one new shop, and in the window, there was a display of fancy bonnets. Asa suddenly wished he had a gift for Catherine. He was too dirty, and he knew smelly to go shopping so he rode slowly on.

Outside of town, he began to notice the orchards . . . not many buds on the trees. Tomorrow he would walk his own orchards with Catherine. Right now he turned the horse into the woods where he knew the stream widened into a small pond. He washed as best he could and thought maybe, just maybe, he would have a hot bath before the end of the day. As he dried himself off, he remembered the time he brought Catherine to this very spot. He was going to teach her to fish. It had not gone as he had expected. She would not touch the worm and wouldn't look when he put it on the hook. Once he caught a fish she wouldn't touch the wriggling, slippery fish either and turned away when he thunked it on the head to kill it. This was the woman who could slip a flour-coated, gutted, and cleaned fish into a hot fry pan and served up a gold-brown treat. It had made him smile. Out of his pack, he took his only clean clothes and started the last mile home leading the horse.

The first part of home he saw was the rock wall at the southern end of his property. The wall seemed to be in good repair. Further on he could see part of the cabin roof. It did need repair, but nothing he couldn't do himself. He looked at the apple trees as he walked up the lane. He was concerned about what he saw. He tied the horse to the fence and made note that the gate was off one hinge. He could repair that, too. He saw there were flowers near the front porch steps. He picked a few. He saw she had started the vegetable garden.

Around the corner of the house, he found his beloved wife at the clothesline. He stopped. He wanted to drink in the sight of her. She was taking down the clean laundry, folding it neatly, and placing it in a basket at her feet. The dog saw him first. The animal began to growl and its hackles came up. She dropped the clean clothes, missed the basket, and turned toward him. Even at this distance, he could see the fear on her face. The dog's growls turned to yips of joy. Catherine saw the flowers in Asa's hand. She was running toward him with apron strings streaming out behind her. Catherine was in his arms. Asa felt at home.

Chapter Two

Going West

He kissed her hard, probably harder than he should. She drew back and fingered his beard. "I've never kissed a bearded man," she said.

"I should hope not," he replied and kissed her more softly this time, but he saw his beard left red markings on her face.

She did heat water for him to take a bath. He noticed she averted her eyes from his nakedness. After two years alone, she was shy with him. He thought it was going to be their wedding night all over again. He shaved his beard. She trimmed his hair and gave him clean clothes from the dresser. That night she would express concern about his thinness and he would comment about the bruise on her shoulder. All she said was, "The front gate gave way with me." He had no reason the doubt her, and she never said more.

The next morning she fed him a huge breakfast. It was as if she was determined to put some weight on him all at one meal or maybe he thought she just missed cooking for him. Both were true. Over breakfast he told how he learned about the death of President Lincoln, about the old woman and the mule, and about Lizzy and Mrs. Adams. He omitted the part about Mrs. Adam's offer of payment, and he never mentioned selling their farm or going west. Not yet, but he had not forgotten.

After breakfast, hand in hand, they walked the orchard. The apple trees were beginning to bloom, but again the bloom was sparse. "It was that way last year. I think it is worse this year," she said. Asa had never seen this actually happen to the fruit trees, but he had heard his father talk about it. It was a wait and see proposition. Maybe next year, the trees would come back.

"I'll have to go talk to the Pike's brothers and see if they will take whatever crop we have," he commented.

She looked past him into the trees to avoid looking directly at him. "Two of the brothers, Luke and Jacob, stopped by a week or so ago. Said they would take the whole crop same agreement as last year." Asa was thinking ahead to harvest and did not notice the worried expression on his wife's face.

The whole valley was looking ahead to the harvest. Everyone waited. Asa and Catherine like everyone else planted their vegetable gardens. Spring edged into summer. Catherine put up berry jam. She dried peas. Asa repaired the cabin roof and made a stall for Minnie. Minnie was turned loose in the orchard and she cropped down the weeds. She looked better and so did the orchard except for the small amount of ripening fruit. On Thursdays, they drove to town. Catherine participated in her quilt circle. Asa talked to other farmers about the apples. He purchased and read newspapers searching for any information about moving west but said nothing, yet. Catherine was sure Asa was stewing about something more than just the coming harvest.

It was as bad as they feared, not just their trees but all over the valley, as was expected. Asa loaded what crop he had and drove to the Pike's. It was true what Catherine had told him. Old man Pike had suffered a stroke. He simply sat in a rocking chair in the dirt outside the house where he could chew and spit trying to hit an ancient hound, which was smart enough to stay just out of range. When Asa returned home with his pay, he related to Catherine how strangely the bothers acted. "Jacob has a new angry scar about his right eye and seemed to be jumpy. Luke could not seem to complete the deal fast enough as if he wanted to get rid of me. In fact," Asa continued, "Luke was surprisingly generous in his dealing with me. I think he gave us a better price than some of the others in the valley and I am not so sure our apples were any better." Asa was satisfied but worried about the next year's crop. Catherine remained quiet.

For the next several days, Asa was preoccupied with his thoughts. Catherine wondered and even worried a bit. The evenings were cool now. They sat inside by the fire. For no other reason than to keep her fingers busy, she was making a pillow for her aunt's rocking chair. Asa was making her uncomfortable as he again related his visit with the Pikes and his concern with the orchard.

She did not comment but watched him. Just as he had when he proposed, he was tapping his foot as he always did when he was about to say something he deemed very important. "I think we should sell the farm and move west," he blurted out. This was not the approach he had practiced over and over again. It certainly was not what she expected to hear.

Later he would decide she understood him better than he thought because her answer, after a pause was "I agree but won't it be hard to sell the farm?" He nodded his head. He feared it probably would be.

In the end it was not hard. The Pikes offered a more than fair price saying it was in their best interest to own the orchards and cut out as many middlemen as possible. Asa was not about to debate their logic. He just wanted to be gone. The spring of 1866 came early which pleased Asa, It meant they might be able to find a wagon train sooner which was better than later considering they had to cross the Rocky Mountains and the Sierra Nevada. Loading all their positions into the wagon, they hitched up Minnie and headed toward St. Louis, "The Jumping off Place" as it was still called.

Traveling with Catherine was almost like being on a long picnic or maybe a holiday. She took delight in everything. She complained little. They followed the road west camping off the road at night. With the spring weather it was pleasant. It seemed to Asa that Catherine was relieved to put the cabin and Glenview behind them. For that he was thankful.

Asa figured they were about three quarters of the way when the weather turned ominous. He needed to find some cover for them and their belongings. He picked a grove of trees he felt would offer shelter and thought about the big canvass army tents he once hated. Catherine caught his eyes, and she nodded back toward the road. A man on foot was approaching. "You fixing to spend the night?" he inquired.

"If we are not trespassing," answered Asa. The man was about Asa's age and dressed like he worked the land.
"You're welcome to stay here if that is you choice, but I can offer you and your misses a shed and a lean-to for your animal."
"We would be obliged. My name is Asa Bennington. This is my wife Catherine."
"I'm Leman Cooper." He held out his hand. By the time they made their way to the house, Leman Cooper's offer had changed to a pallet on the living room floor for Asa and Catherine, which was good because the skies opened up and poured rain all night. The Coopers were nice people with two boys ages

eight and two. Asa watched Catherine holding the baby. Mrs. Cooper was a quilter and for the two days they remained with the Coopers while the roads dried out the two women talked about cloth and patterns. To Asa it sometimes sounded like a strange langue. Asa helped shingle the leaks on the shed and lean-to roofs. As they prepared to leave the Coopers, Leman shook Asa's hand, wished them good luck and then quietly so his wife could not hear said, "I wish we were going too."

Nearing St. Louis, Asa began to wonder if he should have thought this through a little more. Just how did one find a wagon train headed to California? As he often reminded himself the big trains of the 1840s and 1850s were over. Famous mountain men like Bridger, Carson, and Fitzpatrick were all old and ill. There was even talk about a transcontinental railway, but that was some years away. As if in answer to his worried thoughts, they began to find handbills advertising the Dunston and Fishburn wagon train. These handbills made it clear that the Dunston and Fishburn train was the last train leaving St. Louis in time to be in Sacramento before the Sierra snows.

The address of the Dunston and Fishburn offices was printed across the bottom of the handbill. Asa had trouble finding the location. It was not a building as they expected, but rather an army tent on a vacant lot wedged in between a barn and a warehouse. A small but neatly lettered sign told them they had at last located the offices of Dunston and Fishburn.

Asa helped his wife from their wagon. He was not optimistic about the office being in a tent. Before Asa could reconsider, a thin man emerged from the tent. Later Asa and Catherine would remark about Mr. Fishburn's coloring . . . his gray hair, gray coat, and gray complexion made Asa think the man might be ill. Mr. Fishburn was pumping Asa's hand and smiling at Catherine. At the same time, he managed to look over her head and before Asa could say anything the man was talking about going west . . . yes indeed that is where the future of this great land lay, unlimited opportunity for those that were not afraid of a great challenge.

"Natural born drummer," thought Asa.

Inside the tent, the desk was a single, wide plank held up by two barrels. Three mismatched chairs and a coat rack on which hung Mr. Fishburn's top hat was the sum total of the furniture. Fishburn offered the best chair to Catherine. On the plank desk, Asa saw assorted papers, a good many maps, and official looking ledgers. He didn't need to say they might want to go to California. Mr. Fishburn launched himself into a long well-rehearsed speech.

"The wagon master and my partner is William Dunston. Will is a well-respected wagoner. Why, he has already made this same trip several times over the past few years. Not only that but also the scout for this trip was none other than the famous Zeke Flowers. Surely you have heard of him?" Fishburn paused. Asa knew with the beaver almost gone, some of the younger mountain men were giving up that life to become scouts and guides. Maybe this Zeke Flowers was one of them. Asa nodded politely and Fishburn continued talking. "Yes, Zeke was part mountain man, part plainsman, a good hunter, and thoroughly familiar with several routes west. You and your Misses," he gave Catherine a big smile, "Have nothing to fear with men like Will Dunston and Zeke Flowers guiding this train."

In general, he told them that usually twenty-five to thirty wagons made for a good-sized train and many members were already encamped just up river a few miles only waiting for a the last few wagons to sign on. Otis Fishburn could recommend a stable where they could trade their wagon and the horse and with a little money obtain a covered wagon and oxen. Otis had a list of required supplies and, not so surprisingly, Otis could recommend a general store for those items.

Lastly he read over the rules of the train, which he added Mr. Dunston would not hesitate to enforce. Asa could find no fault with any thing the man said. The price was acceptable and by nightfall Asa and Catherine found their small amount of personal possessions greatly increased in size and all piled inside a covered wagon drawn by a team of oxen. Asa and Catherine even had some money remaining. Later as they drove in the direction of the camped wagon train, Catherine surveyed the collection of supplies in the back of the wagon. All she could say was, "My, My, My!" Asa smiled to himself. He felt such love for her that some times it hurt.

For Asa, handling team of oxen was a new experience. Once they had concluded the deal, the stable owner turned them over to a young man whose duty it was to show Asa how to harness and drive the team. It seemed to take a great deal of cursing, yelling, and snapping a whip because the young man thought oxen were the dumbest animals God ever put on the earth. The animals seem to be agitated and unresponsive. Secretly, Asa was hoping that this was not the way it would have to be all the way to California.

On their way to find the encamped wagons, Asa stopped in an empty spot on the road to check the animals and the harness arrangement. He talked to the animals, stroked their big heads and rechecked everything he could think of before resuming his seat next to Catherine. When he said to her that he must have been getting the hang of driving the animals because they were behaving better she said, "Oh Asa."

"Oh what?" he asked, not understanding her remark.

"Asa, don't you know you have a gift?"

"A gift?"

"Yes Asa, animals like you. They respond to you," she explained. He knew that there were people that seemed to have an easier time, a gift, as some called it, when it came to animals but he only did what his father had taught him and he told her that. "I suspect he passed it on to you" was all she said. He would remember this conversation later when he saw other men still struggling with their teams long after the train was on it's way.

They found the encampment with little trouble and were met by William Dunston himself. They heard him before they saw him. Dunston was riding a big black horse and tooting a small brass horn. In the months to come, they would learn to hate that horn. The mount, named Black Jack was the most beautiful horse Asa had ever seen.

If Otis Fishburn seemed to be wrapped in gray, his partner William Dunston was just the opposite. A barrel-chested man, he had reddish hair and a red face that made Asa wonder if he was a drinking man, especially when one of the wagon train rules was no spirits. However, he seemed clear eyed and articulate as he welcomed them with enthusiasm. He pumped Asa's hand and dipped his hat to Catherine all the while talking about the great trip that lay before them. Black Jack pranced and side stepped as if he too was excited about the upcoming trip. Dunston escorted them into a wide grassy area containing the other wagons by tooting on a small brass horn the entire way. People waved and shouted greetings. Older children ran along aside. Asa and Catherine felt very welcome.

There were not twenty-five to thirty wagons as Fishburn had led them to believe. Their wagon brought the count up to eighteen and that included Dunston's own wagon. Asa noted that despite the large size of the campsite, there was not enough grass to keep the animals fed for many more days, especially if more wagons with teams arrived. Hopefully that meant they would move out soon. The camp was situated along the edge of a small river, which did provide unlimited water.

The site also bordered on a marsh area. Asa's suspicions were realized when at sun down clouds of biting, stinging insects rose out of the marsh, crossed the river and descended on the hapless campers and their animals. Beside the limited amount of feed, this was another reason that Asa hoped they were not long in this spot.

Not even the insects could dampen the enthusiasm over the coming trip. Will Dunston showed Asa where to camp. "Get yourselves setup. I be back shortly. We will go round, and I will make you acquainted with the other fine folk already here," Dunston promised. He was good for his words, and Catherine found herself alone in the cluttered wagon with a pile of unfamiliar items to deal with. She knew they would sleep in the wagon and she needed to put some order to the crates, boxes, sacks and her own chest with all her quilts, the Bibles, the pewter candlesticks, and her aunt's dishes all packed in straw.

One at a time and in family groups, the woman made their way over to the Bennington wagon. They came by to say welcome, to visit and since they all had been through it before they offered ideas about arranging the jumbled interior of the wagon.

The smell of roasting meat permeated the camp. One of the Patterson women said, "Mr. Dunston is having a pig roasted. We all bring side dishes. It's been that way most evenings."

"Oh," Catherine worried aloud, "I'm not sure I can have anything to contribute so soon." The second Mrs. Patterson patted her hand;" It's understandable since you are only newly arrived." The two Patterson women were sisters-in-law and to Catherine's mind a little elderly to be starting this trek. Despite their assurances about not bringing any food, Catherine managed to find a jar of apple butter. The other woman that left Catherine wondering was Mrs. Shelton. She informed Catherine that she was usually called Sister Shelton and that her husband would be asking grace before they ate. Mrs. Shelton made a point of saying, "We do hope you and your husband will join in."

"Odd and unnecessary remark" was Catherine's feeling. She could hardly wait to tell Asa what she had learned about their traveling companions.

Asa, for his part, was being introduced by Will Dunston to the other men on the train. He met the Patterson brothers. Later he would agree with Catherine they seemed too old to beginning such a trip. Asa met the Shelton men, a father and a son with a new wife. Although they were overly polite Asa felt they could be a problem and he was not sure why. He made other observations, which he looked forward to sharing with Catherine as soon as they had time alone. Looking around Asa thought being alone could be difficult.

The evening meal was the best Asa and Catherine had enjoyed since they left the Cooper farm. Brother/Mr. Shelton did ask grace. It seemed to run on too long and many of the hot foods cooled. Some fiddle music and some dancing ended the evening. The Sheltons returned to their wagons with the start of the music. If the food, the music, and the dancing set the tone for the nights to come it was going to be pleasant. The last campfires died down. Men smoked their last pipe. Mothers took sleeping babies and complaining children off to bed. As a whole, the camp retired for the night.

Despite what Catherine had done with the interior of the wagon, they had a miserable night. It was not because the quilts and comforters were not soft enough. Even the biting bugs had left. It was the lack of privacy that made them uncomfortable. Having spent all their married life in a cozy cabin where the nearest neighbor was two miles away, seventeen families, in such close proximity, made them feel like they were not alone. Dogs barked. Babies cried. One couple had a spat loud enough for everyone to hear. Catherine was embarrassed for them. Asa thought it funny, especially when someone hushed the arguing couple. They never did know who it was they over heard.

In guarded whispers, Asa and Catherine exchanged their thoughts and observations. The train consisted of all families. With the exception of the Benningtons and several newly married couples, the families included children of all ages. Catherine told Asa two of the young wives confessed that they might be pregnant. They were fearful about the trip ahead. Four couples stood out in both Asa and Catherine's mind. The Patterson brothers and their wives were all elderly. They both agreed on that. In Asa's mind, they were too elderly to be starting such a long and probably hard trip. Catherine agreed. The other two families were the Sheltons. In one wagon were the elder Shelton, his wife, and their younger children. In the second wagon were the oldest son and his new wife. The Sheltons were religious people and seem to want everyone to know that. The father and son expected to be addressed as brother as Asa had been told. "Mrs. Shelton wants to be called sister," Catherine said.

"Did the other Shelton wife visit?" asked Asa.

"There's a second Mrs. Shelton?" questioned Catherine.

"Yes the son has his own wagon and a wife. By the looks of her, it is not a happy marriage." Thinking of his own marriage, Asa pulled Catherine close to him. Briefly he thought about slipping his hand under her gown but decided against it. Too many ears and she was already asleep. Sleep for him did not come right away. He had much to think about.

It was Asa's observation that only three men were farmers like himself, the rest being shopkeepers and tradesmen. Most of the men did not own a gun and of those who did he was skeptical they were proficient in the use of their weapons.

Overall nothing could dampen the excitement felt all over the camp. Catherine, he decided, should learn to drive the wagon and handle the team. Resting in his hand was her small hand. His hand was tough and calloused. Her's was not a lady's hand but would still need serious gloves. He wondered if there were gloves small enough for her. Dunston would know.

Dunston did know and the next day Asa and Catherine walked back to town in search of gloves. Taking a day to walk to town was also a way of achieving a little privacy. The gloves were purchased and there was no reason not to return to the camp when Catherine stopped Asa on the boardwalk and pointed to a business establishment. She was looking at a business that advertised photography. She wanted to know if they could afford to have a photograph taken. To her it seemed the thing to do before beginning their new life. He allowed that they could and they did.

The resulting picture would be small and grainy. It would show her seated with her hair escaping its bun not only because of the walk to town, but also because they had slipped off the road and made love in the shade of an old weeping willow. For the picture, he stood behind her looking stern with his hat in hand. They would return the next day to pick up the photo and maybe revisit the willow tree. They did both. She thought the photo a treasure. Catherine's pleasure in the photo pleased Asa.

That was on Monday and Tuesday. There was still no famous scout arriving in camp. Dunston's answer to the whereabouts of Zeke Flowers was, "Mr. Flowers will be joining the train several weeks out on the trail. After all, with so many wagon trains preceding us, following the trail is going to be easy." Didn't need a scout for that. On Wednesday, Otis Fishburn came to camp and spent much time talking to Dunston out of earshot of the of the train members. On Thursday, there was not much to do and Asa and Catherine decided to walk up the stream bank with a picnic lunch. From the looks of some of the men as he and Catherine left the camp area, Asa knew what they were thinking. His bundle did not contain a blanket. It contained towels. Catherine wanted a real bath and to wash her hair even if the water was cold. Water for bathing was probably going to be in short supply.

Returning in the afternoon, they found the camp in an uproar. Dunston had made the announcement that they would depart at sunrise on Sunday morning. The Sheltons said as God-fearing souls they would not travel on the Sabbath. Dunston showed them the paper they had signed. The document stated clearly that the train could travel seven days a week, including Sundays, if the wagon master felt it necessary. Apparently, the argument had continued for some time.

In the end, both Shelton wagons left the camp saying they intended to find Otis Fishburn and demand their money be refunded. Asa thought it unlikely that they find him or have their monies returned.

Sunday, with the rise of the sun, the Dunston and Fishburn wagon train of 1867 began the long trip to the California. Dunston blew his horn. Asa thought that Black Jack might calm down if Dunston would just stop tooting the damn horn. There were shouts and whistles, a few gunshots. Asa hugged his wife. She winked at him, and he wondered just where had she learned to do that? In return, he gave her that crooked smile that made the pit of her belly go warm. In later years if history books even mention this particular wagon train it was described as "ill fated."

The first three weeks were pleasant enough. The train followed the clear track of the trains headed out before them. The track meandered along the great Missouri River so that water was never an issue, not even for bathing if a person could find a spot of privacy. Any firewood someone might have brought along was quickly used. Dunston explained to the parents and children alike that it was everyone's duty, especially the children and women to gather all the cow chips and any wood they might come across. Those few women that were finicky about the cow chips usually decided that a good fire was worth the effort since wood was turning into a rare find. Dunston did warn them to watch for snakes in the long grass and for Indians on the skyline.

Dunston determined the placement of the wagons. As no one wanted to be the last wagon because of the dust, Dunston rotated the wagon positions. Asa noticed quickly that his wagon was always behind the two Patterson wagons. To him, that was a clear suggestion that Dunston expected him to help the elderly Pattersons if necessary. Asa felt it was a wise thing, and he didn't mind. Catherine and the Patterson wives were good for each other and generally in the evening the three couples shared a fire. All three women had needlework of some sort, which they worked on after supper until the light failed. On the evenings when chores permitted more women joined the little sewing group. The husbands gravitated to one of the other fires to smoke their pipes, discuss the events of the day and especially venture guesses about the missing Zeke Flowers. Asa was thankful that no one in the group wanted to refight the War Between the States.

The euphoria of the departure was gone. It had been replaced by a comfortable routine as the miles rolled under the wagon wheels. Somewhere near the Missouri Kansas border, Dunston headed the train in a more westerly direction along a tributary of the Missouri River. The train began to follow the smaller Kansas River.

When that river turned north, Dunston continued west and for the first time water became an issue. Zeke Flowers had yet to make an appearance. One evening, Asa lead Catherine away from the group just to put some space between them and all their fellow travelers. Always watching for snakes and trying to stay out of the wind, they crested a small hill from where they could see the wagon tracks disappearing over the tops of the most distant hills. The gently waving grass reminded Asa of the ocean, or at least the pictures he had seen of the ocean. "Is there worry because Mr. Flowers is not yet with us?" asked Catherine.

"Yes," Asa replied, "some of the men are worried, especially since we are now away from the rivers and must depend on finding streams or water holes which is something I believe is the duty of a scout."

"And your thoughts?" she asked.

"I have more than one concern," he said slowly as if thinking over the situation.

"Fresh water is a valid issue. Also it seems to me the graze for our animals is becoming less. It is comforting to see that we are following other trains but because of the animals that went before us the feed is eaten down. The days are getting longer and warmer. I do not think the grass will come back till next spring. This land confounds me." He waved his hand to indicate the same view in all directions . . . waving grass with seeming no end. "I do not recognize the grasses or the other plants. At night, the stars are not in their right places. I know Mr. Dunston consults his maps, but I do believe we should be moving in a more northerly direction." Asa picked a small flower and placed it in her hair.

The train was eight weeks into the trek. The daily routine started with Dunston blowing he horn early each morning, followed by a quick breakfast of whatever was left over from the night before they headed west. If they were lucky, there might be some hot coffee. The nooning occurred when Dunston found a likely spot and then, they continued till sundown and hopefully water.

Dunston saw that Catherine Bennington was now driving their wagon and doing a fair job of it. He complimented Asa about this and said, "I want you to take Black Jack and ride ahead of the train. Scout the trail. Look for water. Also you might just keep and eye out for Zeke. Expect him any day now." Asa was also to bring down any game that he might find. Some times in the distance he could see buffalo, mighty fine eating he had heard, but he was never near enough to take a shot. Asa liked riding the fine horse, but there was not much need to scout the trail. Every time he looked ahead from the top of some small rise, he could see the trail disappearing into the empty horizon. As he had told Catherine, the land bothered him. From time to time, he saw high clouds of wind-driven dust or was it smoke from a lightening strike wild fire? Dust he hoped. They could never out run a prairie fire.

Dunston was right about one thing. The trail was easy to follow. There were clear tracks and in the sandy bottoms even ruts. They passed dead campfires. Each day seemed longer and hotter. The grasses were not growing back as Asa had suspected. The water became in short supply, as he had feared. Some streams were too small to top off the water barrels. Some water holes were just mud.

Besides the old campfires, the women began to notice the graves along the way. Some marked with rough crosses. Others were just unmarked mounds. As first they did not talk about what they saw. Too many of graves were small, the graves of children. The mothers gathered their children close by and warned them to be careful. When the first death occurred it was a child.

As they had since almost the beginning of the trip, the children went out to gather the needed cow chips. Because of the buffalo, there were more patties to pick up and they were bigger. The little boy did not see the snake coiled under the sun-warmed chip. The snake struck him in the throat. Screams of the other children alerted the adults. Asa was out on Black Jack. He heard faintly the children's screams. He watched as the adults rushed from the wagons toward where the children had gathered in a tight circle. By the time they reached the now silent little group the boy lay dead on the ground.

Only then did Asa note a rider coming in from the opposite direction. The stranger dismounted and approached the children and adults. As the weeping mother cradled her dead son, a thin man with a long drooping mustache, made his way through the crowd, looked at the small lifeless body and said, "Snake bit." Zeke Flowers had joined the train.

Flowers wore greasy buckskins. His long hair was tied in the back with a thong. From too many years in the weather, his face was dark and he had a permanent squint. When Asa shook hands with the scout and saw the narrowed eyes he hoped the squint was from the sun and not a vision problem. With the arrival of the Flowers, spirits should have been high but the dead child and the subsequent burial saddened everyone. The grieving mother pleaded with Dunston to let the train stay camped near the grave for just a day or so. Then, she asked if just she and her family could remain behind to grieve. They would catch up later. To both requests, the answer was "No." The train moved out.

The wails of the mother could be heard the length of the train, and their wagon lagged behind till Flowers rode back and spoke to the husband.

Asa observed that Dusnton and Flowers talked and pondered over maps. It seemed to Asa that they did not always agree. In one of their frequent evening walks away from the others Asa said to Catherine, "I do not believe that Mr. Flowers and Mr. Dunston are of one accord."

"Could we be lost?" she asked.

"Why do you ask?" was his reply.

"Because," she said. "Some of the women say so and that must be what their husband think."

"It has come up with some of the men. However, we are still following the tracks of earlier trains" was his answer. Asa didn't say that the tracks were beginning to disappear. The wind blew almost constantly now. The train moved on. Two days later they were struck by a dust storm. Asa told Catherine to get in the wagon and cover every opening she could find. After helping the Pattersons do the same he returned to her. They huddled down together till the storm blew itself out. Slowly everyone emerged from wherever they had taken refuge. The mother of the dead boy was missing. Her husband said he thought she was in the wagon with the younger children. The children said she was under the wagon with him. No one could find her anywhere.

The train had lost time in the storm, but Dunston allowed an hour for a search party to look for the missing woman. It was to no avail. The grieving husband begged for more time, but the train moved slowly forward. Dunston placed the wagon of the grief stunned husband and his now motherless children in the front where he could keep an eye on them. Quietly, he sent Zeke back to where they had been struck by the dust storm. That evening the Patterson brothers approached Dunston. The Pattersons were leaving the train and turning back. The trip was far harder than either brother had expected. Dusnton tried to change their mind. When Flowers caught up to the train late the next day and said nothing about the missing mother or the departure of the two Patterson wagons.

"Do you think the Pattersons will travel safely?" was Catherine's question. Asa thought they would have an easier time following the trail back than this train was going to have following the trail forward. What he said was "They will need some luck and good weather and bad weather is a few months yet to come."

Dunston assigned Asa to ride with Flowers. The train needed to find graze for the suffering animals. When Asa or Zeke did find grass the little group lost time while the animals were allowed to feed. Flowers was able to scare up a small amount of game, but that still did not take the place of water. Zeke Flowers was a taciturn man who spoke little if ever. On one of his chattier days he told Asa that last year's winter and this year's spring had been one of the driest he had ever seen. Asa thought that might be the man's way of saying he was worried about water.

Asa told Catherine about the conversation. In turn she said, "The women do not like Mr. Flowers. They feel he looks at us in an unseemly manner besides he is dirty," she concluded. Asa wanted to laugh, but Catherine was so serious that he did not.

Instead he replied, "Probably Mr. Flowers does not get to see many white women."

"What other kind of women are there?" she asked.

"Catherine, out here there are Indian women," he answered.

"Indians?" was all she said, but he could tell she was thinking hard on this new revelation.

The days and miles wore on. Asa thought he detected a real rift developing between Dunston and his scout. Dunston sent Asa and Zeke in opposite directions so Asa never had the opportunity to listen if the scout had any thing to say. Flowers did find water, a little. It was off the trail so again they lost time. Flowers began to leave the train for longer periods of time. "Scouting further out," said Dunston if any one asked.

When Zeke did return, he and Dunston had words and didn't seem to care who heard the argument. Zeke wanted to head north and Dunston insisted on straight west. After one such dust up, Flowers left the train and never came back. Whether by his own will or that he met some awful fate was never known, but it did provide some lively conversation for a while and kept the company's mind off the ever-present problem of water. Asa took the scout's place, but he felt he was a poor replacement. Black Jack seemed more Asa's horse than Will Dunston's. More than once Catherine gave her husband a pleased glance and said, "You sit that horse well, Mr. Bennington."

If lack of water was not a big enough problem, Dunston's changed behavior was. Asa was still riding Black Jack all the time, and Dunston was driving his own wagon that is when he was able. He was sometimes drunk. It was happening more and more often. And, he was a mean drunk. All the women and most of the men tried to stay away from him. When he either fell into the back of the wagon, which he often did or slumped over on the seat one of the men would drive for him. Will Dunston, drunk or sober, was all they had in the way of experience. Asa and the other men took to running the small train, which was not very hard . . . follow the tracks and look for water.

Everyone was gloomy and worried. Asa marveled at Catherine. She seemed to be a ray of sunshine in the small, worried world of the twelve wagons. She helped with the children. When one of the pregnant women lost her baby, Catherine was there to help her recover. Asa could only wonder at how hard that must have been for her and that hurt Asa. Most of all she tried to make things as good and as comfortable as she could for him. One evening when the fires were burned low and an occasional snore said that most people were asleep Asa asked Catherine, "Are you sorry we came on this venture?"

She was slow to answer but eventually said, "I thought you deserved a better farm and I still do." He knew she hadn't really answered his question, but he did appreciate the answer she offered. Asa wondered just how he had been so lucky to have ever found her. Ohio, their apple orchard and the cabin near Glenview seemed a lifetime away.

The next five days were bad . . . no water at all. Asa was riding wider and wider circles around the train searching for any stream or small hidden sink. Now atop a small wind swept hill he watched the train crawl slowly along. It was moving too slowly he knew. He saw Dunston's wagon drift out of line. He supposed the man was drunk again. Some one else saw it too, tied their mount to the wandering wagon and drove it back into its proper place.

Asa let his thoughts drift. There was no use turning around. They knew what lay behind them. For weeks now Asa had a watched a blue smudge on the horizon turn into mountains. He figured correctly, they were approaching the Rocky Mountains. The blue smudge was a surprise at first, because it appeared almost on his left. At some time, the train had veered a little to the north he reasoned, but there was no doubt he was looking at mountains, big ones. He knew it was late summer. There would be no crossing the Rocky Mountains, let alone the Sierra Nevada before the snows came but where would they go? Where could they winter over? Not here. No water. No trees. Just the never-ending wind and the endless grass and that was to often thin.

A change in movement of the train brought him out of his deep thoughts. The worn out animals seemed to have picked up the pace. Black Jack began to pick up her pace and toss her head. It was only then that Asa saw the glimmer of water that the animals had already smelled. It was not much but water just the same, hidden from the train by a small rise.

He let the horse have her head. By the time he reached the train with a few of the last slower moving wagons, the early arrivals were at the water's edge. Some people were already in the water happily splashing, pushing the green scum away to fill cups, pots and pans. People were carrying water to those travelers not able to scramble quickly enough from the wagons. Children were splashing each other. The thirstiest simply bent face down in the water to satisfy their thrust. At first to Asa, it was a joyful sight or was it? Something was wrong.

Something was terribly wrong. The oxen were standing with heads down at the water's edge. They refused to drink. What few horses they had, including Asa's Black Jack approached the water then moved slowly away. The water must be bad!

Asa yelled and shouted, "Don't drink! Don't drink! The water is bad. Look at the animals." Most of them paid no attention to him. The thirsty travelers continued to drink not understanding his words, not wanting to hear his words. Where was Catherine?

He found her near their wagon helping to give water to a little girl. Dashing the cup from her hand he yelled, "Did you drink the water? Did you drink the water?" Before she nodded, he knew the answer. There was a green line around her mouth. "You must vomit! The water is poison! Now!" He helped her.

Other people were now aware of the probable danger. Except for the sound of crying children and retching the group was mostly silent. They moved away from the pond already recovering itself with scum. It was only a few hours before the first ones began to sicken. It started with the smallest children. They cried as the cramps in their little guts doubled them over. Next came the uncontrollable dysentery. This was followed by a bloody flux. The first babies were dying as the younger children developed the early symptoms Next the older children followed by the young adults and finally every one that had consumed the water was sick. People trying to help lay out the bodies became sick themselves. Some people curled up on the ground died unattended. Other tried to care for their loved ones but became too sick to even take care of themselves or the loved ones.

Asa and Catherine helped where they could and all the while Asa kept a close eye on his wife. The stench, the sounds of the dying, the sounds of the grieving, it all made them feel they were in a living hell. It was the horror of war all over again. For Asa his own hell was yet to come. What he feared most happened. Catherine doubled over and sank slowly to the ground.

He knelt at her side. He felt her fingers dig into his arm as the pains swept over her. "Oh Asa. It hurts," she managed to say. He hushed her gently. He knew he was probably loosing her. He would not let her die surrounded by this collection of other dead and dying. Picking the thickest comforter from the wagon and as gently as he could he carried Catherine way from the train.

Finding a hillside mostly out of the wind, he laid her down, covered her with the comforter and slipped in behind her so he could cushion her against his chest and hold her close. He tried to keep her warm with his own body. He felt her shiver. She tried to apologize but couldn't quit finish the sentence. He could feel when the pains swept her body, but she no longer had the strength to grip his arm. Slowly with great effort she said, "I should have told you but I wasn't sure. We . . ." the sentence trailed off. Her voice was so soft he was not sure what she said. Catharine was dead.

He did not know how long he sat there. The sun was setting on the day and on his life. In the eastern sky, the first stars were showing. Asa knew he had to bury her.

Going back to the wagon, he retrieved a shovel and pick ax without noticing what was happening around him. Returning to the sheltered hillside, he hacked at the stubborn sod and dug until his muscles and back rebelled. The grave was deeper than need be but he didn't want any animal desecrating her resting place. He gently placed her in the hole making sure the comforter was arranged so no dirt would touch her face. He never knew he was also burying the baby she had tried so hard to tell him about.

He wished he had the rocks from the far away orchard in Ohio. He took no notice when the thin moon sliver faded away. He had no more tears. He didn't see the first long shadows cast by the beginning sunrise. He was still sitting by the grave when he heard a single shot from the direction of the encampment. Some time after the shot, a small frighten boy found him and said, "Mr. Bennington, sir. My Pa says you need to come. Mr. Dunston, he done shot himself." Going back to the wagon train Asa knew he would never see California or have a farm. It did not matter. He did not have that one person to share it with.

Chapter Three

Fort Layton

The survivors buried the dead as best they could. The last to die were buried poorly. The travelers were give out, grieving, despondent, each one wrapped in a personal loss. No one had a notion of what to do next. The train now consisted almost entirely of orphans, widows, and widowers. Mothers responding to the hungry and still thirsty children brought camp life back to a semblance of routine.

The following day, men not caring for confused sad children went through Dunston's wagon. They found cases of whiskey many of them filled with empty bottles. They divided up the liquor. Even if you didn't drink, it was a good disinfectant. There were maps that didn't mean much to anyone. No one objected when Asa asked if he could have them. Firearms and food were divided up among the wagons. The wagons that had drivers were reloaded with condensed people and their belongings. Asa deliberately arranged it so that his wagon was full of supplies and not people. He wanted to be alone. The remaining wagons and their contents were abandoned. The draft animals were harnessed to the wagons that would move out.

The small, woeful train crept westward once more. The very next day the worn travelers stumbled upon water. It was pure and sweet. They drank with thankful caution and begin to feel that there might be a little hope. After several hours with no one falling ill, they began to think beyond the need for water. They would spend the night and try to come to a plan.

They needed to move on but to where? Now most of them were aware of the great mountain range to the west of them. They knew they needed a place to spend the winter. Neither California nor Oregon was a possibility now. They needed water, shelter, firewood and food, and direction. They were lost.

Asa was able to kill an antelope. With unlimited water and meat for dinner spirits rose as much as possible after what they had all been though. Until the natural light died, the men again studied the maps from Dunston's wagon. Asa suspected they were the wrong maps for the area. Giving that up for the evening most everyone sat quietly near the fire. Each person was wrapped in his own thoughts. All was quiet as the sunset faded.

That is when they saw the silhouette of a mounted Indian on a hilltop to the north. The Indian watched them, then wheeled his horse and rode out of sight just as the light faded. A dread fell upon the camp. It seemed wise to set out watches, but no one slept.

In the morning all was quiet. The wagons were circled as tight as possible. It was the first sighting of an Indian, and no one really knew what to do. Everyone watched the skyline. They topped off the water barrels. No on went to search for cow chips or wood. Neither Asa nor any other man left the camp. Not until afternoon did they hear hoof beats heading in their direction.

Several women fell to their knees in prayer. One or two remembered what they had been told about Indians and wondered if they should shoot their children and then themselves. Before they could make that fatal choice the riders came into to view. They were cavalry riders.

The Indian that had filled their hearts with such fear was a scout attached to Fort Layton. He had ridden during the night to report to the commanding officer about finding a small, lost wagon train to the south headed in the wrong direction. A detachment of troopers was dispatched at first light to rescue the pitiful group. Some soldiers were sent to bring up the abandon wagons. Others took over the driving chores. Everyone was issued army rations. Spirits rose just a little for some.

The train had almost missed Fort Layton, and they certainly would have bypassed the bigger Fort Laramie. Fort Layton may have been one of the smallest posts in the west but to the incoming train members, it appeared to be a mighty fortress with its rough log walls and strong gates. Inside there were real buildings with windows and roofs, a small chapel, and an infirmary. Asa saw nothing of this. He put the wagon where he was directed. He took care of the animals including Black Jack. Asa closed his eyes and rested his head against the horse's warm neck. "Mighty fine animal you got there. Interested in selling her?" The speaker saw the expression on Asa's face and walked away not expecting an answer.

In reality, Fort Layton was a small fort and boring to most of the men assigned there. Located in the southeast corner of what would become the state of Wyoming, nothing exciting ever happen so the rescue of the wagon train caused a stir of excitement. The commanding officer, Major Shelby, often felt that the Department of the Army forgot about him. In the East when people talked about Wyoming, it was to debate the truth of the wild tales describing a land of geysers, hot springs, colored mineral pools, located to the north and west of his small fort. The stories were all true plus more, but it would not be until 1872 that the remarkable area would be named Yellow Stone and become the first national park in the United States.

Major Edward Shelby was not concerned about scenic points of interest that may or may not exist. He had much to do. His first order of business was to house the new comers. With the help of the chaplin and the post-doctor, the orphans were dealt with first followed by the widows with children, the widowers with children and finally the single men. This last category included Asa, and he didn't care what they did with him. Asa was already gaining a reputation as another, bitter loner. Because of Asa's obvious ill temper, he was bunked up with the only other man at the fort with a similar disposition. The older man's name was Charlie Lamb.

When Major Shelby told lamb, he was assigning Asa Bennington from the newly arrived wagon train to share Lamb's quarters for the winter it was widely reported that Lamb let out a string of profanity that made even the Shelby blanch. Lamb added he was not about to have some SOB, green horn farmer to stupid not to stay in the east where he belonged bunking in with him. The major prevailed. Lamb's words got back to Asa, and he thought maybe the man was right. Catherine would be alive now if not for his own wish to go west.

Lamb was an experienced scout and hunter, and it fell to him to provide meat for the fort over the winter months. The next thing the major said to lamb was, "You take this Bennington and you teach him everything you know. We have many more to feed now." For once, Lamb was silent. If Bennington could learn from Lamb maybe the fort might have two meat hunters. That was the commander's thinking. Both Asa and Lamb hated the arrangement.

Chapter Four

Winter

Lamb's quarters consisted of a chinked lean-to affair located up against the south sidewall of the fort. It was warm. It was dry. It was small. If the two men were different in age, they were alike in disposition. They wanted no more than to be left alone in their individual bitterness. Each withdrew into himself. Troopers began to lay down wagers as to how long the living arrangement would last. Their money was on Lamb and that Bennington would be dead in a snowdrift some morning with a knife in his ribs. When the two men began leaving the fort together to hunt the wager changed to betting Lamb would return alone. They would all be wrong.

Winter came early. In the first three weeks of their new living arrangements, the two men probably didn't speak ten words. Lamb spent most of his time in the saloon because he could no longer drink in the solitude of his cabin. Lamb did not play cards, and he shut his ears to the talk about the miseries of the wagon train. For his part, Asa spent time with Black Jack. Asa asked for and received permission to ride out with the troopers. He didn't talk much and let the trooper's conversation wash over him, but he did listen.

The old scuttlebutt was that the major would retire in two to three years and most likely the fort would be closed. The second subject was new. The fort had no women until the wagon train arrived. This changed everything. The troopers acknowledged that many of the women were in mourning, but life on the frontier moved fast. Christmas was coming and maybe the major would agree to a dance.

For Asa, the time outside the fort was an escape. He was not aware that Lamb watched him. Lamb was not so much interested in the man as he was the horse. Lamb was impressed with the way Asa handled the horse, and he knew he had seen the horse before but he could not recall just where. He would think on it.

If the winter and spring of the previous year had been dry, Mother Nature made up for it in the winter of 1877 and the following spring. The snow fell early and deep and stayed long, but the inhabitants of the fort ate well. In an effort to get away from each other and the confines of the fort Asa and Charlie hunted often. On their first venture out of the fort Lamb could no longer hold his curiosity.

"That Will Dunston's horse you riding?" Lamb asked. Asa by nature was not a rude man, but they rode a ways before Asa answered.
"Was," he replied.
"Where's Will now?" Lamb continued.
A few more paces . . . "Dead," answered Asa.
"You kill him?" Lamb's voice had a little edge to it.
"No, he shot himself." Asa didn't hesitate to answer that question.
"You see him do it?"
"No"
"Will still having a problem with the bottle?" continued Lamb.
"You could say that." This time there was edge to Asa's voice and Lamb took note of it.
"You hold that against a man?" was Lamb's last question.
Asa turned in the saddle and looked Lamb directly. "If he hadn't been drunk maybe I wouldn't have had to bury my wife." Lamb read the sorrow in Asa's face and was surprised to learn there had been a wife. Asa saw but could not read the look that crossed Lamb's face. They rode in silence till they began to hunt. Lamb was pleased to see Bennington was a better than fair shot.

As the winter deepened, it became hard hunting and willing or not they had to work together. Asa showed himself to be a learner. Begrudgingly Charlie began to teach him, if for nothing more than to make the hunting easier. Charlie was still a man of few words, which reminded Asa of Zeke Flowers. Were all guides just naturally reticent?

Charlie could read sign. Charlie could read the stars. Charlie knew plants and herbs and the habits of animals. Charlie could speak Sioux and had Indian friends. Charlie began to fill the gaps in Asa's survival skills.

In November, the major decided it would be good for moral if the fort celebrated Thanksgiving. This was a relatively new holiday only put into effect by the late President Lincoln a few years earlier. The major asked Lamb and Asa to find and shoot some turkeys for the dinner. At Christmas, there was a dance. Neither Asa nor Lamb attended. Asa listened to the music from outside. Lamb drank himself into a stupor and Asa hauled him back to their cramped quarters. On the next trip out of the stockade with the troopers, Asa heard there had been a little sparking going on at the party between some of the younger soldiers and a couple of the widows. Asa supposed it was hard for a lone woman or one with children on the frontier. If anything came of the sparking he wished them well.

In January, Asa learned about the contents of Lamb's possibles bag and experienced his first whiteout snowstorm. As usual they rode out together. Asa knew that Lamb always carried a good knife and so did he. Lamb also carried a small tomahawk and a kit he called his possibles. They agreed to split up and were to meet later. After about a half hour, the snow began falling. Next the wind picked up. Before he knew what happened, Asa could hardly see his hand in front of his face. The snow swirled in every direction. Even Black Jack was reluctant to step forward. During a slight let up Asa took refuse in a stand of trees and waited, hoping the storm would not last too long. He was getting cold, and he felt hunger pangs and still the snow continued.

Charley Lamb found Asa and thought at least Bennington has sense not to wander around in circles. Pulling back further into the shelter of the trees, Lamb opened his possibles bag. With the flint, the steel and some precious dry tinder he was able to start a fire. Also from the bag he produced jerky, some parched corn and even some dried apples. He took one cup and had tea. He shared with Asa who had decided he would have his own possibles bag by the next hunting trip. Asa knew full well that Lamb could have left him out there to possibly die, and no one would have thought about his death.

The winter was so long in leaving as to cause the doctor to begin recording the stories of the of the wagon train survivors. Asa refused to talk to him. As others told their personal recollections, a picture of Asa and Catherine Bennington emerged. The stories remained in doctor's personal journal. When he died just one year later, the journal came into the possession of his replacement, a by-the-book-man who thought the stories had no place in the fort since they did not relate to post life. The journal was forgotten and gathered dust on a top shelf until the post was closed, and the buildings became part of the small but growing community of Layton. It was the first record of the

Bennington family who in the coming century would have a profound presence in the area and the state of Wyoming.

If Charlie may have saved Asa' life outside the fort, Asa returned the favor inside the fort. When Charlie was not hunting, trapping or scouting he was drunk, falling down drunk, passing out drunk. He was a solitary drinker, allowed no one to become a friend and therefore nobody noticed him missing except Asa. As the night wore on and the temperatures dropped and the snow piled up, Asa would go look for Charlie. Usually finding him unconscious in the snow, Asa would carry him to the lean-to where he treated any wounds that needed tending, put the man to bed and made strong, black coffee.

When Charlie would regain his senses he found he was still dressed in dried, stiffened clothes often caked with mud and even dung depending on just where he had fallen down. He didn't like himself much, and Asa Bennington seemed to be blocking his path to self-destruction.

Following one of these episodes when Charlie came to, he was sick and not from too much drink. He coughed so badly it reminded Asa how his father sounded before he died. Charlie ran a high fever. The doctor looked in on Charlie at Asa's request. Keep him warm. Keep him away from the whiskey or only let him have enough to ease the cough and put cool rag on his forehead was the doctor's advice? He would have someone bring soup over later. Asa knew the first part and was thankful for the soup when it did arrive. That night the fever rose, and Charlie Lamb talked to himself. He spoke up so loudly and so suddenly that Asa who had dozed off, jumped.

"Killed them both. Found the two of them in my bed. A man can tell when his wife is cheating on him. Just never figured it would be him." Charlie lapsed into French, which Asa did not understand. In English he continued, "They were going at it in our house, in our bed. They didn't even know I was in the room till I stuck my knife in his back. I stuck it real slow and twisted it. I wanted him to hurt. She was screaming. I slit her throat. I did that quick. Took the jewelry and the cash and just left, went to Texas." Asa was stunned. He was living with a murderer even if the man thought he had cause. Well, perhaps he did. Not only that but a good portion of Charlie's words were in French.

Charlie was quiet for a while, then he again began too ramble again. This time he spoke about a fine valley, green grass, and cattle ranching. Asa tried to make sense out of all Charlie's English and French finally deciding he was not the only man with a dream that would never came true. The fever broke about

four in the morning. Singing a soft French lullaby to himself Charlie drifted off
into a healing sleep. Asa had much to think amount. Even in Charlie's most
drunken moments he had never uttered one word of French till this night.

Charlie began to regain his strength. Asa had to hunt alone for a time.
He did not enjoy it as much as when the two of them hunted together. At last
spring made the snow retreat some and Charlie was back with Asa. The first
time out Charlie said, "I was pretty sick wasn't I?"

"Yes you surely were," and Asa was telling the truth.

"Did I talk much when I was fevered?" For Asa, this was a difficult
question. He was never one to lie but to tell the man he knew his secret might
be folly.

"You did."

"What about?" was the question Asa did not want to answer.

"Oh . . . about Texas, about cattle, a ranch . . . a big green valley," said
Asa hoping that might settle the matter but it didn't.

"And?"

"You told me how you lost your wife," Asa waited.

He could tell Charlie was turning all this over in his mind.

"You going to tell anybody?"

"No reason to. It was a long time ago, somewhere else. You're probably
a different man now and it is none of my business." Asa watched as Charlie
mulled this over.

Changing the subject completely Charlie asked, "You know anything
about raising cattle?" Asa was pleased with the question, because it did not
deal with the murdered wife.

"No. Had a couple of milk cows over the years." Charlie was quiet for a
long time.

In fact he was quiet for several days, and Asa wondered if he had some
how offended the man. Today, spring was in the air. Early out of the fort,
Charlie showed Asa how to build and set a fish trap. Returning to the stream
about noon, they found three fat trout. The fish had been eaten. The small fire
was almost out. The two men sat protected from the wind and soaking up the
welcome warm sun. Charlie spoke.

"You still plan on going on the California?"

Asa shook his head no. He didn't know when he had given up that idea
but he had.

"When I was sick, you said I talked about a great valley." Asa nodded.

"The valley is not in Texas." Asa had assumed the location was Texas.

Asa turned to look at Charlie, "It is about three days ride north of here. I saw it a few years back. I did stay in Texas for a time, till the wanted posters showed up. I learned a lot about cattle. I feel certain that for the right kind of cattle this valley is perfect . . . year round water and good grass and several good cabin sites.

One man can't do it alone. You want in for half ownership of whatever we can build?" Charlie watched the smile play across Asa's face. It was almost wolfish.

Slowly Asa asked, "You sure you want a partner like me . . . an SOB a green horn farmer to dumb to stay back east where he belongs?" Charlie heard the very words he swore at Major Shelby when he learned Asa was to bunk in his cabin.

"I do" and Charlie held out his hand. The two men shook hands. Both were smiling now.

Chapter Five

Blue Feather

All the troopers who had laid wagers about Bennington and Lamb surviving the winter together were wrong no matter which man they thought might win. Not only had the two developed a strong friendship, to the shock of all, they had partnered-up. Asa was the only man for thousands of miles that knew Charlie's real name was Charles Batiste Lambeaux. In the City of New Orleans, he was still wanted for stabbing death of his wife and her lover even though that was many years ago.

Asa traded his household items for tools and supplies. Charlie traded up for some better guns and ammunition. They hitched up Asa's wagon. They loaded Charlie's gear. Asa took Catherine's trunk with the quilts under which hide the photograph Catherine had so dearly wanted taken before they left St. Louis. However, before repacking the photo, he removed it from the cheap frame and carefully tore his own image from the picture. Now only Catherine's face was hidden beneath her neatly stitched quilts.

There was a lot of talk and some envy about the two men leaving the fort permanently. The post-commander knew it would be hard to find replacement hunters, but he wished them well. In his own heart, the doctor wished he was going with them too and was glad he had recorded the stories in his completed journal.

Charlie said the valley of his dreams was about three days ride. They were glad to put the fort behind them and they were in no hurry. Asa drove the wagon and Charlie rode. They traded off. Charlie drove and Asa rode Black Jack. Asa liked it best when Charlie rode the horse because when Charlie found something he wanted to show Asa, plants, tracks, bird droppings, bird feathers, hair in the bark of a tree, Charlie had Asa stop the wagon. They went over the items together.

Neither man talked much about the past. They both were looking forward to the future. Charlie talked so much about the land that Asa thought he could almost see it. Charlie also talked about the Indian band he hoped to find. The chief was a man named Spotted Dog, a sub-chief and a wise and fair leader. "It would be in our best interest to earn Spotted Dog's blessing, so to speak, before we march in and start building cabins and putting up fences. If there is going to be any problem it might be with some of the young braves. All through the various tribes, the younger bucks are not to happy with the white settlers, the rail roads, the army and the gold seekers." Over all Charlie felt the Indians would probably be friendly. At least, they were the last time he saw them. Charlie mentioned that the Railroad Act of 1861 had given a lot of Indian land to the railroads and probably even the Sioux in Wyoming knew about that. Charlie said all this over and over again.

He also tried to educate Asa on the culture of these people. One thing that puzzled Asa was Charlie's warning, "Don't think you can dally with the women unless you are asked." Asa thought he wouldn't anyway even if he was asked.

The second afternoon they found a pleasant stream with a grove of cottonwoods and lots of downed wood for a fire. They decided to make camp for the night. Tomorrow by noon, Charlie assured Asa they would see the area where Charlie thought the southern boundary of their proposed ranch should be.

As usual Charlie looked over the possible campsite and the sand along the steam bed. This time he had Asa stop the wagon before even reaching the camp spot. He motioned Asa over to look at the hoof prints along the stream. Five horses. Asa could now read that much. The horses were unshod. Probably Indian ponies but that did not mean the riders were Indian. Four heavy riders and one other either pack horse or one with a light rider was Charlie's opinion. Charlie told Asa to keep the animals out of sight and quiet and no fire. He disappeared up stream. Asa did as Charlie asked. Charlie was gone a long time, but there were no unusual sounds, no gunshots. After a while Asa could smell campfire smoke. Whoever was out there must be planning on spending the night. When Charlie did return it was from the other direction.

"I found their camp, down stream," Charlie said. "Four Cheyenne bucks with a Sioux captive. A woman. It took me a while, but I know who she is now. Her name is Blue Feather. She is the daughter of Chief Spotted Dog." Asa was beginning to wonder what all this had to do with them. Charlie answered Asa's thought when he announced. "We have to rescue Blue Feather. Don't you see? If we return her unharmed, her daddy is going to be mighty pleased.

Even the young bucks won't say anything about our taking over the valley."
Half his statement was delivered in French, but Asa was getting used to
Charlie's mixed languages. French or English, he didn't think he was going
to like what Charlie said next. "Here's my plan. Their ponies are a little way
from the camp. I figure we can sneak down to them. Run them off. We kill
the first, hopefully maybe two braves that come down to investigate. Then we
kill the other two. Blue Feather will know where her people are camped. She
will take us there."

Asa thought is sounded to simple. The only men he had ever killed were
during the war, and they were trying to kill him. Well, he guessed the Indians
would be trying to do that to him too. Besides he couldn't think of a better
idea.

The plan might have worked except Charlie made one mistake. He and
Asa came in down wind toward the ponies. Once the ponies picked up the
scent of the white men, they made so much noise that one brave was already
there when Asa and Charlie reached the spot. Without breaking stride, Charlie
burst into the clearing and shot the brave dead. He then ran straight toward
the camp. Asa had no choice but to follow his friend and partner. Asa shot the
second brave. By then it was close quarters and hand-to-hand. After a year in
the fort, Asa discovered he was out of shape.

The brave on top of him was young and fit and inching Asa nearer to the
fire pit. The fight had scattered hot coals all over the ground. The Indian did
not appear to have a weapon, it was just muscle against muscle and Asa was
losing. He could feel the heat of some coals near the right side of his face.
The Indian muscled Asa's face nearer the embers. The Indian shoved and
Asa screamed. The pain was more than he could ever have imagined. Besides
the pain now burning along the right side of his face he began to feel heat on
that eye. "No!" He would not be blinded. Asa heaved with all his remaining
strength. From somewhere, the Indian found a knife. As he fell off Asa, he
sliced Asa's arm. That was all Asa would remember for a long time.

It was mid-summer before Asa's thought process began to function. The
arm wound did not penetrate muscle but shaved off a long patch of skin. He
would learn he had bled a lot. It had healed well and with work his arm would
be fully functional. The right side of his face was badly burned. He drifted in
and out of consciousness.

Now he and Charlie sat outside the teepee that had become Asa's home.
Even in the summer sun wrapped in a heavy robe Asa shivered. He was very

thin. He was on the mend, however. He knew that. He could not get enough to eat and Blue Feather kept a steady supply of food coming his way. Charlie sat in silence waiting for Asa to begin asking questions about the time since the fight with the Cheyenne.

"I don't remember much," is how Asa started. "That big bastard had my face in the fire. After that I only have snatches of memory . . . you and Blue Feather, painted faces, smoke, a lot of smoke, sounds like chanting and pain, so much pain." Charlie filled in all the blanks.

"You managed to throw the brave off. That gave me a clear shot. I killed him but not before he burned the side of your face and cut you arm. Blue Feather recognized me as a friend. We stripped the Cheyenne of anything of value. We rounded up the ponies. She was happy to help me take you to the wagon, and she did lead us to her father's camp.

Right now we are in pretty good standing with the entire tribe. As for the smoke and the painted faces, the medicine men have been treating you, removing all the bad spirits. I think they are relieved to see you up and about. Chief Spotted Dog would be none to happy if you stayed in the happy hunting ground so to speak."

This was a great deal of information for Asa to digest, but he did have one question. "You the one that's been taking care of me all this time?"

"No sir. You have Blue Feather to thank for that. She wouldn't let any of the other women even come near you. By the way you gave her father those Cheyenne ponies." Asa was to tired to notice the gleeful look on Charlie's face. Charley did have one concern about Asa. Eventually Asa would have to see his own face. Charlie was not sure how his friend would take it.

That happened a month later. Asa was now able to ride away of the encampment for short periods. He even did a little hunting with Charlie and with some of the braves. Today it was just he and Charlie. They dismounted at a small beaver pond to get a drink. The water was clear and still and Charlie knew what was about to happen.

Asa leaned down toward the water and for the first time saw the puckered red scar that covered the right side of his face from his hairline to his jaw. Asa made no noise, just sat back suddenly and carefully and slowly felt the scar with his fingers tips. No one in the camp even gave him a second look. He was unprepared for the sight of his own damaged face. Charlie said, "You're not going to be to welcome in polite society, lease ways not white society."

Asa looked at himself again. His smile was crooked on that side, because the scar tissue was tight. A little bit of that end of his eyebrow was gone. He remembered everything about the fight, especially the heat from the burning coals as the Indian drug him nearer and nearer the fire. He remembered the pain. He remembered he did not want to be blind. He was not. He had the use of both eyes. He would concentrate on that. He was quiet for several days. Blue Feather asked Charlie what had happened. Charlie told her.

Asa recovered both physically and emotionally. Charlie didn't worry now and was not surprised when Asa asked when they might be moving on. "Well," replied Charlie. "We have a bit of a problem. It is so close to winter I don't think we can build a cabin and set in supplies before the snow . . ." Asa could understand the logic, but Charlie was not done.

"Blue Feather has decided she wants you for her husband. In fact she has said that very thing to Chief Spotted dog. He likes the idea." Asa's mouth dropped open pulling at the scar tissue. "Seems Miss Blue Feather was married before. Had a husband for a whole winter. In the spring, he rode off on a raid and got himself killed. Didn't leave her with a baby. Miss Blue Feather believes you can do a better job."

"Why the hell would she think a thing like that?" Asa exploded.

Charlie had a slight grin on his face. "Maybe she likes what she saw."

Asa looked blank. "Asa, think about it. Blue Feather has taken care of you for over two months." Asa was still blank. "She probably knows more about your body than you do." Asa was still confused. "Oh hell, Asa, She likes your balls and your pecker." Asa understood, but he didn't have to like it.

He knew that Charlie had warmed many a squaw's blanket since they arrived. "You randy old bastard! You marry her. You know more how these people think than I do. You would make her a better husband." During this outburst Charlie was slowly shaking his head no.

"Why not?"

"These people know me. They know I don't make babies. Besides Blue Feather wants a baby with sky eyes."

"Sky eyes?"

"Oh Asa think about what color your eyes are," was all Charlie had to say. Asa's eyes were blue. Charlie watched Asa's shoulders slump.

"I suppose if I were to turn down this er . . . proposal it would be looked upon as bad manners?"

Charlie was not smiling now. "You got that right. You don't marry her you can kiss the ranch, our welcome and maybe even your pecker good-bye."

Asa thought about it for several days. He hadn't planned to ever marry again. Even if he wanted to, no white woman would want anyone with a face like his. To marry an Indian? That went against a lot of Christian preaching. Blue Feather had cared for him with out condition. Wasn't that a rather Christian act? In the end Asa knew he was beaten so he asked Charlie what was the next step. "Have to find a fine wedding present." was Charlie's answer.

"For Blue Feather?" Asa was thinking about bolts of cloth, or good pots and pans.

"No. You have to find a good gift for Spotted Dog. A gift worthy of a chief's daughter," explained Charlie.

"Like what?"

"Horses are always good." Asa knew perfectly well there were no horses any where in the area. Reading Asa's mind Charlie went on, "We will have to come up with something." Before they left camp everyone knew that Asa was going in search of a proper wedding gift, and it was considered good. They didn't need to find horses. They shot a bear . . . a big bear. Meat, skin, claws, and teeth, it was a perfect gift. Chief Spotted Dog was very pleased. He announced the wedding day.

The ceremony was short and simple. Asa didn't understand many of the words but knew he was married. He was still uncomfortable about the situation, but he tried to look pleased. Charlie looked down right smug. Ever since he partnered up with Asa, he began to realize Asa was the kind of man that ought to be married. That was neither bad nor good it just was. Once he was that kind. After Charlie saw the burn on Asa's face, he knew no white woman were ever look past that scar to see Asa's good qualities.

Charlie also noticed how Blue Feather cared for his friend. Blue Feather hadn't given the injured man much thought till, according to Charlie, she learned Asa was mainly responsible for her rescue. Around many an evening campfire when Charlie recounted the skirmish with the Cheyenne that is how he told the story. That was also why when he gave the Cheyenne ponies to Chief Spotted Dog he told the chief the gift was from Asa. From time to time, he would comment to Blue Feather about Asa, always saying things that should please a young Indian woman. Blue Feather began to look at the injured white man in a different light.

Chapter Six

Sleeping Robe Trouble

Charlie was not the only one thinking about the young couple. The mother of Blue Feather had been dead for several years. Her aunt, Snake Woman, sister to Spotted Dog, had taken place of a mother for her niece. She also watched the young woman care for the white man with the blue eyes. She thought many of the same thoughts as Charlie did. Snake Woman was wise. Had she been born a man she just might have been chief instead of her brother. Spotted Dog listened to his sister. Snake Woman began to drop little hints and make subtle comments to the point that Spotted Dog thought it was own idea that Asa should marry his daughter. By the time Blue Feather came to ask her father's permission he had already made up his mind, but he made her wait five days before he told her yes. As far as Charlie, Snake Woman, Spotted Dog, and Blue Feather were concerned things could not have been better.

Not so for Asa. Maybe he was married, but he did not have to welcome his bride into his nighttime robes and he didn't. Blue Feather was devastated. After several months of not being a real wife, she consulted with Snake Woman and even Charlie. Charlie was worried. Blue Feather talked to her friends who talked to their husbands and brothers and before long the men of the village knew the white man was not a real man. The gossip and ribald jokes came to the ears of Spotted Dog. He was unhappy and summoned Charlie, who knew what was coming.

After observing the proper manners of eating, talking of horses and hunting and a good smoke. Chief Spotted Dog said, "Tell your young friend, the husband of my daughter, I want to be a grandfather!" Those were not his exact words but that is how Charlie said it when he told Asa of his required visit with the chief.

One of the reasons Asa had held back his desires because he was worried. In eight years of marriage to Catherine, she had conceived only twice. Apparently in a whole winter of marriage, Blue Feather had not conceived even once. Asa was afraid the odds of making a baby might not be in their favor. However, Asa knew when he was defeated and welcomed Blue Feather into his bed that night. By noon the next day there were no more jokes about Asa and his husbandly duties. Six weeks later several squaws reported seeing Blue Feather with the sickness that comes in the mornings. She was happy. Spotted Dog was happy, Charlie was relieved and Asa was amazed. To add to that, real married life was as good as he remembered.

The baby was due in the late summer. Charlie and Asa reasoned they could go their valley, build the cabin and be ready for the next winter. When Asa suggested he should be present for the birth of the baby, Charlie said, "When it comes to birthing most squaws don't want the men folk around." In his broken Sioux, Asa talked it over with Blue Feather and she didn't seem to mind his going. Besides having his baby, she would prepare things for their new home. Asa asked Blue Feather one favor, "If our child is a girl I want you to pick her name." Blue Feather nodded. "If we have a boy I want him to be named Charlie." Blue Feather nodded. She understood.

As soon as Asa saw the valley for the first time, he comprehended why Charlie had been excited. In the first few days, they explored the land from corner to corner. Roughly the area they wanted was a long rectangle. A year round creek meandered from the northeast corner down to the south west corner. Bordered by willow and young cottonwoods it offered several good building sites. The northern border was an east west running range of small mountains and foothills. They reminded Asa of teepees and that's what he and Charlie called them. Years later a mapmaker's clerk would misread the name and record the mountains as the Peetees. The name stuck. In the north west corner were several box canyons full of strange sandstone formations. Despite the fact, it seemed to be mostly snakes, pricker bushes, rock, and sand the area fascinated Asa. Only later would they discover that two of the canyons contained deep pools with big trout. Asa and Charlie decided where the boundaries should be. They marked the corners with stone cairns, and Charlie made it quite clear to Asa that at some point they would have to learn the legal requirements to make sure the land would always be theirs.

They decided on where to build the cabin. Of course the little one room structure with cots for two men had now become a bigger dwelling with a common room and two bedrooms, the bigger of which was for Asa and his little family. Neither man could see building two cabins. Using slate they found on the property Asa built a stack stone fireplace. Charlie was impressed. Once the cabin was finished, they stood back and admired the structure. "I wish we had thought about windows," said Asa.

"Yeah. It is a little dark in there," agreed Charlie. Summer went fast but in some respects not fast enough.

Asa worried about Blue Feather. Would she lose this baby as Catherine had? On the white man's calendar his life with Catherine was not very long ago. Yet, his life had changed so much that he felt he was someone else now.

The partners worked well together. They talked about how to acquire cattle. Asa still had the money saved for the farm in California. He was pleasantly surprised at how much cash Charlie had. Asa assumed that every month Charlie had probably spent most of his army pay back at the post-saloon. Asa was also pleased to hear that Charlie was planning on purchasing cattle. Some times Asa thought Charlie had a little trickery in his mental makeup. Asa had no desire to start this venture with stolen cattle.

Charlie explained that the great cattle drives from Texas to Kansas had begun back in 1861. It was his hope they might only have to go as far as Kansas to purchase the start of their herd. They would not be able to bring back a lot of cattle with only the two of them to make the drive. They were not in a position to hire an extra hand, at least not yet.

Nights now had the bite of autumn. They were nearing the time when they could return to Spotted Dog's camp. This particular night they were tired, sore, and weary. Asa was missing his wife. Charley was also missing Asa's wife. Charley thought it would be nice to have a woman to cook a real meal. Neither man was much of a cook. Asa was thinking different thoughts. The talk turned to what to name the ranch. A real ranch had to have a name and a brand.

Asa suggested, "We can call it the Lamb-Bennington Ranch." He could tell Charlie was please and surprised when Charlie turned down his suggestion.

"We don't want some sheep word on a cattle ranch sign," said Charlie. "I think we should call it the 'Double B' for Bennington and Batiste." Asa vaguely remembered that Charlie's middle name was Batiste and maybe this all has something to do with the old wanted posters. Charlie went on, "My mother's name was Batiste." That was good enough for Asa. Charlie had a stick and was drawing a design in the dirt. "I think our brand should look like this. See? It's two "Bs" back to back. The Double B." Asa did see and he liked what he saw. It was decided.

The high country trees were all golden when Asa and Charlie retuned to the Indian encampment. Young boys had spotted them coming and run to the camp to spread the news. People were outside their teepees to welcome back the two white men. From a distance, Asa could see Blue Feather. She had a bundle in her arms. He rode up to where she was standing but before he could dismount she handed the baby up to him and said in her best English, "Char-lee." Asa had a son . . . a round, chubby cheeked, healthy baby boy who stared up at his father with sky eyes. Asa let out such a whoop that Little Charlie let out an amazing wail. Blue Feather had never been so happy but thought her husband had much to learn about being a father.

That fall turned to early winter everything was good. Asa was beginning to feel a deep affection for his wife. She was a very good mother. She did everything to make the cabin a home although Asa suspected she did not quite like the cabin as well as a tepee. She cooked for both Asa and Charlie. She was a quiet woman and Asa appreciated that. Blue Feather loved little Charlie and his father. She considered herself lucky. Her husband did not beat her, and he was slowly learning her language. Baby Charlie was leaning both English and Sioux with no problem. Big Charlie or Uncle Charlie as Blue Feather now called him was fairly content. If he only had a woman of his own. Baby Charlie was a delight to all of them.

It amused Charlie when Asa said, "I think we should celebrate Christmas."

"Hell," said Charlie, "We don't even know when Christmas is."

"We'll pick a date," was Asa's solution to the problem. "Besides Little Charlie needs to know about these things." Upon returning to the Cabin Asa tried to explain Christmas to Blue Feather. His Sioux was not good enough and finally it fell to Charlie to help Blue Feather understand Christmas was a day of celebration because their one God had given a gift of his son to the world. Privately, the idea of a one deity seemed very silly to Blue Feather. Everyone knew that it took many gods to keep the world in balance. If Chrees-moss, as she pronounced it, made her husband happy she would celebrate the day.

Charlie also explained the part about giving gifts to those people who were important to you. Asa had not thought about giving presents. Looking at his wife, he knew she was thinking over the idea of giving and receiving and what gift items might be acceptable. He decided he better start thinking along those lines, also. Because they each wanted to make some sort of gifts for each other and, especially Little Charlie, the date they finally selected was actually in late January.

At six months Little Charlie enjoyed his first Christmas day if for no other reason than he sensed his family was happy. He liked the carved whistle from his Uncle Charlie. Blue Feather had made fur hats for both men and a little one for Baby Charlie. Asa had one gift, and it was for all of them. It puzzled Blue Feather, but she could see that Uncle Charlie was very pleased. The gift was a wooden plank on which Asa had carved white man's symbols. Asa explained the symbols were the name of their ranch, their land. It was called the Double B.

Chapter Seven

Going to Kansas

Following their Christmas, they waited till willows along the stream began to show their buds, and they all knew that spring was finally on the way. The big question was how could Asa and Charlie travel to Kansas and purchase cattle? Asa did not want to leave Blue Feather and the baby alone. In fact neither Charlie nor Asa felt safe in leaving the property. True they had not seen another soul since leaving the Indian encampment back in the fall, but you never knew who might show up in the spring. A few trappers were still trying to search for beaver, and then there were always the miners searching for gold. The answer to their dilemma came in the form of a messenger from Chief Spotted dog. With the spring thaw, he was moving the camp. He wanted to see his grandson. He was relocating the camp to just north of the cabin. Charlie and Asa were more or less congratulating themselves on this fortunate turn of events when Blue Feather said, "This will be very good for Little Charlie. He will be surprised to discover he is not the only child in the world. He will have to learn to get along, and he will not be the biggest frog in the pond." Not for the first time Asa thought he had married a wise woman.

Spring came and so did Blue Feather's people. There was feasting. Little Charlie was in shock at the number of people, some his own size and the many dogs. Little Charlie had never seen a dog. He liked to play with the new animals, and he would learn to enjoy eating them also. To start with he was afraid of Spotted Dog. Fortunately, the old man thought it funny and was patient with the child.

Asa and Charlie packed their gear and their money and rode out in late May. If they found no cattle in Kansas, they might have to make the long trip to Texas. They did not know when they would be back and that depressed Asa.

They rode southeast for many days and saw no one. They had no reason to go in the direction of Fort Layton. Had they done so they would have been surprised to see the fort was in the process of being abandoned, leaving behind a small community that people were calling Layton. Asa and Charlie angled across the corner of what would become Colorado and finally entered Kansas. Traveling along a wagon track almost good enough to be called a road they saw a few sparse farms. The only other person they, saw told them they were headed in the direction of the town of Hayes. The man saw Asa's face and didn't want to talk long. Only then did it occur to Asa and Charlie that Asa might have to stay in the background while Charlie conducted any business matters. From time to time, they saw faint black smoke along the distant horizon. The rule of thumb was that white or gray smoke was usually a grass or timber fire. Black smoke probably indicated a structure fire. The black smoke bothered both men.

It was a pleasant night except the skeeters were keeping them awake which is the reason both Asa and Charlie heard the faint gunshots . . . rifle shots in Charlie's opinion. They listened for a while but all was quiet. "You smell smoke?" queried Asa.

"I believe I do." They stayed alert for a while. Nothing more happened, but they slept light. The next morning they found the source of the smoke and the gunshots. They had not ridden to far when they crested a small rise and saw the smoldering ruins of a house and barn. They reined up and studied what they saw. At first they detected no movement, but there was one person down there. It appeared to be a woman.

Arriving in the yard that person was a woman hiding two small, frightened children in her skirts. A dead man was on the ground. The woman hefted a shotgun, aimed at Charlie and Asa without saying a word and pulled the trigger. The blast knocked her off her feet and went over the tops of the Asa and Charlie's heads. They quickly dismounted. There was no rush to disarm the woman. She had fainted into a heap on top of her children. All three were crying. When she could talk and had decided she had nothing to fear from them she told them what happened last evening.

She spoke with a deep Southern accent, "We came here two years ago. That's my husband." She indicated the body on the ground." We had nothing left after the war. He wanted to start over so we came here. It took almost every thing we had to buy this place. He wanted to raise beeves." Asa was not familiar with the term "beeves" but Charlie was. She went on, "Some people here are still fighting the war. They told us to get out, that we were not wanted here, that we should go back to the South where we belonged. Course we couldn't . . . no place to go back to. They came last night." She waved her hand to indicate the burned out buildings. "I have absolutely nothing now." She began to cry again and that started the children into sobbing along with her. Asa fetched water from the well and handed it to her averting his face.

"We need to bury you husband, ma'am. If you might tell us where."

She did and they set to work digging the grave. Quietly Charlie said, "Look out there," and nodded over his shoulder. Asa did and he saw a few goats. Further out he saw cattle. They were thin but cattle nevertheless. "Suppose she would sell?" Asa suggested.
"All we can do is ask."
When Charlie made the offer he spoke with just a trace of Southern drawl.

"You from the south?" the woman asked.
"Was once," was all Charlie said. She seemed satisfied. Seemed like very one had come from somewhere else. The matter of price was the next question. Neither the woman, nor Charlie nor Asa knew the going price for cattle. She told them what he husband paid for them a year ago. Charlie offered her US$300 over that. She said on one condition. Asa was holding his breath.
"I have no food. I have no way to get to Hayes, which is a full day's ride from here. I can't shoot the damn gun." The children's eyes widen at their mother's use of profanity. "I have a cart" she waved at one of the few items that were not a pile of burned rubble. "And I have no horse. You have two horses, and you need a bill of sale. If you will take me to Hayes, I will write you out a bill of sale at the bank. You can have the cart and the goats."

It was a deal. Asa would stay at the burned out house just incase the nighttime raiders came back. The raiders did not retune but when Charlie did he still had the cart and he had two surprises. In the back of the cart in carefully packed in straw were real glass windows for the cabin, and Charlie also had vegetable seeds, peas, beans squash, and corn. Next year he said they would have a real garden. They had cattle and windows. They felt rich, and they felt civilized. Asa didn't ask the cost of the windows. He didn't care.
Returning home took much longer for two reasons. The cart with the glass windows didn't go just everywhere and the cattle were thin because they were hungry. Charlie and Asa let them eat their way to their new home on the Double B. As a result, they were in much-better shape than when they left Kansas. The year was 1870 and Asa declared he would carve that date on the ranch board.

Much had changed when they arrived. Little Charlie was walking. He threw himself into Asa's out stretched arms. Spotted Dog thought the goats were a gift for him and ordered all but two of them roasted to welcome back his son-in-law.

There was feasting and music and drumming. Asa felt he was truly home. Charlie immediately took up the nights with a favorite squaw and Asa and Blue Feather had the cabin to themselves for the first time in their married life. It was nice, very nice. In the following days, Spotted dog told them that there had been new white men in the valley. They had not stayed long but they had seen the green grass and the water. "First thing in the spring we have to lay legal claim to all this" warned Charlie and Asa agreed. Till the snow covered the ground, Asa and Charlie worked at putting in pole fencing and watching for strangers.

With so many people around they missed Christmas. In the spring, they counted their cattle. They had the same number as they bought up the previous year. Only some of the original had died, and some had given birth. It was a good start. They now had five goats. Blue Feather was pregnant. She said the baby would come in late summer. Asa had no worry about this baby arriving safely. Asa tried to teach Blue Feather about planting a garden. Basically her people were nomadic. Planting seeds in the ground seemed to be another white man oddity, but she worked at it. She did like the results.

In early summer, they were still building fences and Asa remarked to Charlie, "We are cutting down an awful lot of trees."

Charlie said he had been thinking the same thing. He had a suggestion. "You know up where the creek makes that little dog leg turn?" Asa nodded. "Remember the dead fall up there?" Asa nodded again.
"I'm thinking we could take one of the horses and maybe snake a few of the better trees out and use them for the fence." Seemed like a good idea to Asa.

A few days later they took horses, ropes, and their hatchets. They told Blue Feather where they would be. She sent food with them, because they would be gone all day. Reaching the dead fall they stopped loosely tied up the mounts and studied the tangle of trunks and limbs. "The wood is better than I remembered," said Asa.
"There's more than I remember. Maybe we should have asked Spotted Dog for help," added Charlie.
They settled on a plan. With the help of the horses, they had pulled several good stout trunks away from the dead fall. Charlie was pointing out one tree near the top he thought would make a good straight post for Asa's ranch sign. Asa thought they should pull out a few more small ones before going for that particular tree.

"Oh hell, Asa. I'm going up there" and before Asa could object Charlie began to climb the jumble of old timber. Asa thought for an old man Charlie was really agile. Asa was paying out the rope, and Charlie was moving so fast that when Asa came to the end of the rope there was only enough left if Asa moved to the bottom of the timbers and he did.

Maybe because he was so close to the base of the pile is why he heard the sounds of cracking wood. Charlie did not. The whole mass began to move. A tree, not dead but still a little green and under tension was released. It hit Asa in the back propelling him into the moving tangle. Asa knew two things. He was pinned, and Charlie was screaming. Just as suddenly as the fall had begun moving it stopped. All was quiet. There was no sound, not from the dead trees and not from Charlie. Out of the corner of his eye, Asa could just barley see a portion of Charlie's body. Charlie had to be dead. Asa could not feel his own legs either. He could hear Black Jack cropping grass near by. He thought maybe he heard a moan from Charlie's direction, but there was no response to his calls. Asa knew he was going to black out. It would be a long time before Blue Feather would have enough worry to go to her father to ask for someone to come look for them.

It was sooner than he thought. Black Jack went home. Finding her husband's riderless horse in front of the cabin door, Blue Feather grabbed the baby, mounted the horse and went for help.

The braves gently freed Asa. He was in great pain. He curled up on the ground. Blue Feather handed off little Charlie to another woman. She tried tending her husband, but she did not know what to do. Freeing Charlie was another matter. His body was badly broken, but he was not dead. He begged to be freed. He knew he was dying, and he wanted to talk to Asa. Asa could not go to Charlie. Charlie had to be moved to where Asa lay. The braves were cautious about the dead fall. Asa and Charlie were their friends, and this was a bitter experience. It took a long time before they could put Charlie on the ground next to Asa who saw that Charlie was dying. Blood oozed from Charlie's mouth and nose. He spoke earnestly but with great difficulty, "You must register our land. It is all yours. Take care of it, partner." He was barely able to reach out his hand to Asa. They shook hands till Charlie's hand dropped from Asa's grip. They buried Charlie on a wide knoll over looking the cabin. Asa was still in too much pain to dig, and he was stooped over. The pain would go away, but he would never stand completely straight again.

Blue Feather's wild ride to seek help had not harmed her baby. She blossomed into her pregnancy. That and Little Charlie was what kept Asa sane as he recovered from the accident and from the loss of his best friend and only partner. Asa told Blue Feather that he didn't hurt. She knew from the sounds he made when he turned over in his sleep that he had not told her the truth. He was recovering and leaning to do all that he wanted to do from a stooped over stance.

Chapter Eight

Small Leaf

She was sure she was not far from her delivery date. Because it was hot they often sat along the creek in the afternoon, Asa and Blue Feather with their feet in the cooling water and naked baby Charlie having a fine time. Asa look at his son and marveled. The baby belly was gone and he was taller. Asa wonder what he was going to look like as a man. Asa himself was not all that tall, but he was stocky and muscular. People were surprised that he could move fast when necessary.

Asa's thoughts were interrupted when little Charlie said, "When will Uncle Charlie come back?" Asa had been dreading that question, but Blue Feather was ready with an answer. "Your Uncle Charlie is on a long journey. It is a very long journey. He won't be coming back."

"Not ever? I won't see him ever?" Little Charlie's eyes were very big.

"You will not see him till you make the same journey."

"I will make a journey, too?"

"We all make that journey some time," replied his mother.

"Is it a hard journey?"

Blue Feather thought for a moment, "If you are as good a man as your Uncle Charlie, it is not a hard journey."

"I will be as good as Uncle declared Little Charlie."

Asa said, "Of course you will. That is why you have his name."

Little Charlie was amazed. This was exciting news, something he had never thought about. He was named for Charlie, his Uncle Charlie. Uncle Charlie was big and knew everything. From that day forward, he refused to be called

"Little or Baby Charlie" anymore, which was just as well since the new baby was due shortly.

Blue Feather knew her time was near. She was prepared. She had picked a birthing place. She knew full well she could have this baby by herself. She did think having Snake Woman with her would have been nice, but the band was to far away.

Charlie apparently satisfied with the serious talk had gone back to playing with pretty stones from the creek bed. "Look Papa," he said and held up a dull yellow stone. Asa knew what it was before Charlie handed it to him. It was a gold nugget. Asa and Uncle Charlie had already found several scattered along this same creek. They had always planned on looking for the source but just never got around to doing it and now Big Charlie was gone.

Looking over the nugget as if he had never seen one before, said, "Not bad. If you find any more, save them for me." Little Charlie was already looking. As Asa and Uncle Charlie had agreed, they would not tell either Blue Feather or Charlie what the stone was. If they didn't know they would not have to lie if anyone ever asked. The last thing Asa wanted was goldseekers swarming all over his land. If Asa had known the meaning of the word ironic, he would have understood it described his life. He left Ohio to go to California to be a farmer not for the gold. Now he was a fledgling cattle rancher in the Territory of Wyoming, and he had in his medicine pouch some decent-sized gold nuggets.

In the middle of the night, Blue Feather felt the first cramp. She decided the baby would come tomorrow. In the morning, she fed her husband and her son. Asa left to go repair a fence. She set Charlie on a robe and encouraged him to play. She felt the moisture between her legs and the first real labor pain. She picked up her birthing bundle, told Charlie to keep playing and went to her secret place to have her baby. The birth went well. She cut the cord and took care of the after birth. She cleaned the baby and then herself. She offered the correct prayers and welcomed her daughter into the world. Asa was some ways away when he heard what he thought was a strange bird. The second time he heard it he knew it was not bird it was the cry of a new born. He dropped his hammer and ran as fast as his bent body would allow toward the cabin.

She was already there. Just as when Asa came to her after the birth of Charlie she held out the small bundle. "Her name is Small Leaf" is all Blue Feather said. Charlie saw the look between his mother and father. Often he did not understand his parents. Some how things had changed. His mother looked different. The bundle in his father's arms was crying. His father unwrapped the bundle and examined the red, crying baby. She was all Indian, dusky skin, brown eyes, and black hair. There was no hint of Asa. Asa wondered if he was seeing what Blue Feather looked like as a baby.

Asa went in the cabin and opened Catherine's chest from Ohio. Pulling out the first baby quilt he came to he returned to Blue Feather. Together they wrapped Small Leaf in the yellow and white Irish Chain. Blue Feather knew the chest-contained things from Asa's first wife. It didn't bother her. She had had a first husband. The blanket was the most beautiful thing she had ever seen. Asa explained. "The blanket has a name. It is called Irish Chain," said Asa pleased he remembered. Blue Feather practiced saying the name.

In Charlie's mind, a puppy would be more welcome. His whole world came crashing down when Blue Feather set the baby to nursing. That part of his mother's body had always belonged to him. He did not like this baby sister. Things did even out. Blue Feather could again hold Charlie on her lap, at least when Small Leaf was not there. Asa tried to pay more attention to his son, which helped Charlie, adjust.

The small family settled in to a new routine. Blue Feather watched Asa climb the hill and sit by Uncle Charlie's grave. "What is Papa doing?" asked Charlie.
"I believe he is talking to your Uncle Charlie," replied Blue Feather.
"People can do this thing?" asked Charlie.
She smiled at her son, "Some people can."

Asa was really thinking about Charlie's last words. Asa knew he needed to do whatever was required to make the ranch legally his. He would have to go to Fort Layton. He assumed he would have to sign his name. He had not written a word of English since the long ago wagon train left St. Louis. Oddly he had the maps from Dunston's wagon. Those maps had not helped the wagon train but per Charlie showed clearly the Double B valley. Charlie had marked the map telling Asa over and over again this will be all we need to record our deed. Asa made a decision. A soon as Small Leaf was able to travel he would take the whole family to Fort Layton. After all young Charlie had no idea how many white men would be in his widening world.

That time came when Small Leaf was about two months old. Blue Feather knew from Asa's preparations this was a very important trip to his Fort Layton. Out of Asa's old trunk, he pulled a pair of blue military pants. They were too small. She thought he must have been thin a long time ago. He was not fat. He was a mature man and well muscled from hard physical work. He ended having to wear his buckskin pants and from the trunk, a homespun shirt. He had always been clean-shaven, especially since the scar made any beard impossible. His long hair was tied in a strip of leather.

Blue Feather selected her best deerskin dress and the yellow and white quilt for Small Leaf. For Charlie, it was a different problem. In the summer, he mostly wore next to nothing. Now Blue Feather discovered he had grown out of all his winter clothes. She would just have to make something do for the trip.

It was a three days ride to Fort Layton. They camped along the way. The morning came when Asa could first see Fort Layton, or where Fort Layton should have been. Asa saw the fort walls were gone. He saw a main street with houses and stores from the looks of it. He pulled the cart to a stop and stared hard at the new collection of buildings. Blue Feather watched his reactions, but remained quiet. Well. He thought, he owed Charlie Lamb. He clicked the horse forward.

It was a real town, small but real. He saw a general store, a church, which he thought might be the old fort chapel. He saw a bank, and a few doors down a big sign that said, "Land." He went there first. Inside the clerk was eating his lunch. "If I want to lay title to my land is this where I go?" inquired Asa. The clerk looked up and paused with the spoon midair. He had never seen such a scar. He did not know this man. He forgot about his lunch. "Yes, I can do that for you," he said trying not to look Asa in the eye.

After the legal process was complete, the clerk could hardly wait to be rid of the man with the scar. Asa thought it was because of his face. In reality, the clerk could hardly wait to run to the bank and tell bank president, Rupert P. Spindler about this stranger that just filed on the biggest parcel of land ever recorded in the area. The strange man with the scared face called it the "Bennington Ranch," a cattle ranch. Nobody even knew of the man or that the Bennington Ranch existed, at least not until today.

Rupert P. Spindler sat back in his big, leather, office chair and watched the comings and goings on Main Street from his office window. He had just taken his lunch at the Lady Layton, a combination saloon and eating establishment. It was the only one in town just like his bank was the only one in town. His tellers had a standing order that he was not to be disturbed until possibly 2:00 p.m. Unless, it was for important banking business.

Now, looking out his window and almost asleep he saw a cart he did not recognize nor did he know the couple in the cart. As the only banker in town, he made it his business to know about everyone. These people were strangers. He watched. The woman was Indian. She carried an infant. A small boy, perhaps age three or four, sat between the woman and the driver. It was the man that Spindler studied. Clean-shaven with a hat pulled down to hide the right side of his face. Even from his chair Spindler could see why the man wanted to hide the scar. Long hair, not all that unusual, buckskin trousers and a homespun shirt made Spindler think "squaw man." He wondered why any man would take up with a woman not of his own race.

The couple appeared to be heading toward the bank. The bank employees knew that Spindler did not tolerate any riff raff or ner-do-wells in his bank. Spindler had just dozed off when there was a knock on his office door. At his response, the door opened and his head teller ushered the "Squaw Man" into the office. The clerk stammered, "Mr. Spindler this is . . ."

"Bennington. My name is Asa Bennington," Asa finished the teller's introduction.

The teller went on, "Mr. Bennington wants to open an account, sir." Spindler was wondering why the teller had not simply taken care of the request when Asa opened his hand a placed two gold nuggets on the blotter pad in front of Spindler. The banker quickly regained his professional manner.

Offering his hand to Asa, he invited him to sit down. The teller returned to the room with the scales for weighing gold. As he placed the scales on the desk, Spindler said, "I presume you want to deposit the value of these nuggets?"

"Only part of it. I need some spending money," answered Asa. Asa was holding his breath. He had no idea what the nuggets might be worth. As Spindler fiddled with the scales, he said to Asa, "Get these from your claim?"

Asa had anticipated this question, "No. Had them for a long time. Found them down Colorado way."

"Maybe. Maybe not," thought the banker.

The weight of the nuggets even impressed Rupert Spindler. Asa worked hard at remaining calm when Spindler announced the value. He told the banker the amount he wanted to deposit. Spindler was in for a second surprise. The account was to be in the names of Asa James Bennington and Charlie Lamb Bennington. Asa explained, "Charlie Lamb Bennington is my young son. He is named for my late partner and this is for our ranch, the Bennington Cattle Ranch." Spindler was just as surprised as the recording clerk at the land office. No one even knew a ranch somewhere north and west of Layton existed. The banker would also be impressed when he learned how large the ranch was.

Chapter Nine

White Man's Welcome

The whole time he and Asa conducted their business Spindler was taking quick glances out of his office window. He was unhappy when he saw several young boys, his own son included, throw dirt clods and small stones at the Indian woman and her children who he was quite sure belonged to Asa Bennington. Next, several of the good women of Layton came by. Seeing the Indian baby wrapped in a quilt of such fine quality offended these ladies so they glared at Blue Feather. One of them even hissed. Lastly a man walked by and spat at the cart muttering something under his breath. Blue Feather did not know the English word. She would ask her husband.

Blue Feather did not know what she had done. As far as she knew she had broken no customs. She had dressed in her best. Yet these whites were so different from Asa and Uncle Charlie. She tried not to cry. She wanted to go home. Why didn't her husband come out of the building so they could leave?

Spindler had one more question for Asa. "Are you interested in acquiring any new stock?"

"Might be," answered Asa.

"You should talk to Ian McDermott. He had a ranch south of here. Mrs. McDermott became ill and has returned east. He is selling out. He has the meanest bull this side of hell. Can't find anyone to take it off his hands."

Asa was interested. "Where might I find Mr. McDermott?"

"He was having lunch at the Lady Layton, just down the street. You can't miss him. He will be the only man in there with red hair. Oh, . . . and you might leave your rig and family here. There are often rowdies in the saloon."

78

Asa caught his meaning but failed to see Blue Feather's distress when he told her he was going to walk down the street to talk to a man about a bull. As soon as Asa was out of hearing, Spindler told one of his men to go outside and make sure nobody bothers that Indian woman and her children. Asa Bennington might just be his best depositor.

In the Lady Layton diner, Asa spotted McDermott. He was a big man with the mop of red hair and matching beard all streaked with gray. The man was just finishing a plate of steak and beans when Asa approached the table and said, "Mr. McDermott."

"Aye," answered McDermott wondering who the hell is this man. McDermott did not recognize the stranger with the scar or bent posture. He was not hiring. In fact, he was just about to let go the last of his hands. He relaxed when Asa said, "My name is Asa Bennington. I have a ranch about three days ride from here. Mr. Spindler at the bank says you have some stock, a bull, you might be wanting to sell."

"Sit down young man. Have some lunch," McDermott invited. Others at the near by dining tables and in the saloon watched.

"Sorry, my family is outside but thank you," replied Asa. They quickly came to an agreement about McDermott's remaining cows and the mean red bull. They shook on the deal, and McDermott walked outside with Asa to accept his money. Asa handed McDermott the agreed upon amount, and they shook hands again. "I'll give you directions to my ranch. You send your hands down and pick up the cows and the damn bull any time in the next ten days."

"I don't have any hands replied," Asa.

"You don't have any hands, no ranglers?" queried McDermott.

"No sir," Asa answered. "Just me and my wife."

That got McDermott's curiosity up. "I'll bring the stock up myself . . . about five days time. I'd like to see your spread." The deal was set, and Asa was very pleased. So was McDermott and so was Rupert Spindler, who watched from his office window as the two ranchers shook hands.

Blue Feather breathed a sigh of relief when Asa jumped into the cart and finally headed them toward the outskirts of town. Her relief was short lived, because Asa had one more stop. Nothing happened to Blue Feather while Asa left her, and the children in front of the mercantile. No one came by to throw dirt or to spit at her. Inside Asa purchased a bolt of blue, cotton cloth, peppermint sticks, coffee, sugar, one tin of peaches, salt, a lamp and lamp oil, nails and a new hammer, and several newspapers even if they were old.

Blue Feather was again relieved when Asa exited the store with his arms full of mysterious packages. A passing man said something as he walked by, but Asa paid no attention. Asa was too pleased with the day's events, and he had much to think about. He thought Charlie Lamb would have been satisfied. The mercantile owner was most certainly pleased. By the end of suppertime, everyone in Layton knew about the new cattle rancher with the scared face, stooped posture, an Indian family, and the gold nuggets.

Asa knew that the news of the gold nuggets would spread fast so he watched behind him as he left town. No one seemed to be following him. However, he was pleased when Blue Feather suggested they move away from town as far a possible before finding the night's camping place. Her reason was not the same as his.

Small Leaf was fussy for a while because she has sensed her mother's earlier distress. Now the baby was quiet and happily nursing. Charlie was curled up in Asa's lap. Everyone was sucking on a peppermint stick. Blue Feather liked it. Charlie complained it bit his tongue but kept on licking till he said to Asa "Papa. Why did they throw dirt at Mama?"

"What?" said Asa looking over Charlie's head at Blue Feather. She told him what happened. The boys throwing dirt and stones, the women with their hateful looks and the spitting man mumbling a single word and he walked by.

"What did the word sound like?" questioned Asa.

Carefully as she could, Blue Feather repeated what she thought she heard the man say, "Breed. It sounded like he said breed."

When Asa heard what she said, he understood what the man outside the mercantile had said to him . . . "Squaw Man." He felt sad and saw the confusion on Blue Feather's face. He smiled at her and said, "Some people are just plain ignorant." He hoped she felt better. He had much more to think about.

Two days later and their first night home Asa presented his final gifts. Blue Feather touched the blue cloth. She thought it one of the finest things she had ever seen. She said it was sky eyes color. Asa opened the tinned peaches. It was a huge treat for all of them. She was not sure about the coffee. She knew about salt. Sugar was perfection.

She noticed he had not purchased anything for himself. "I have everything I need," was his answer. In truth he was thinking about a pair of real boots. Boots seemed like a large frivolity, and he had passed them up. It seemed odd to him that years ago walking home from Virginia to Ohio, boots had been one of his major concerns. Now he could do without them. However, he still wanted a pair . . . someday.

Chapter Ten

Big Red and the Rocking Horse

Good for his word, one of McDermott's riders appeared five days later announcing that McDermott was about three hours away. Asa let Blue Feather and Charlie know that white men were coming and that it was fine. He could tell they were not so sure. When McDermott arrived, Blue Feather stayed in the shadow of the cabin door and Charlie hid behind her peeking out at the collection of white men, cows, and a huge red bull all standing outside his home.

McDermott was not riding a horse but driving a wagon. Asa invited him down and discovered he could not invite the man into the cabin, because the cabin roof was to low so they stood next to the fence and watched the cowboys move the cows into Asa's pasture. The bull had a ring in its nose on a long lead rope. He didn't look too mean, but then you never knew when it came to a bull. The cowboy stubbed the rope off to a post and moved away.

With his arms folded across his chest, Asa slowly walked around the bull. The bull did nothing more than look back at Asa. At times Asa ignored the animal. Finally, Asa took the rope off the post, led the bull into the pasture and took off the lead rope. "Damn!" said McDermott after Asa closed the gate and joined him to lean on the fence. "Never seen anything quite like that." He looked at the cattle in Asa's little herd. He was impressed. He had expected to see scrub cattle.

He studied Asa for a moment the asked, "You know what breed of cattle you have there?"

"No. Guess I don't," said Asa.

"Son, you have Herefords. They look like good ones, too." This was a touchy question but McDermott asked it any way. "How did you . . . acquire your start up stock?"

Asa gave a big laugh. "Me and my late partner bought them complete with a bill of sale, and Asa repeated the story of the burned out, newly widowed woman he and Charlie found when they thought they were on their way to Kansas City."

"How did you lose your partner?" continued McDermott.

"We were snaking logs out of a dead fall. It shifted on us. Killed Charlie, but not right away." Asa was looking into the distance.

McDermott followed Asa's gaze and said, "You have a mighty fine piece of land here. So let me tell you what I have learned about the cattle business so far." He talked for more than two hours. The Northern Pacific Rail Road was already in Cheyenne, which was much bigger than Layton due to the railroad and the army camp, which operated as the main supply post for many of the frontier forts. Big money people from both the east and as far away as Europe, were looking at the whole area for vast cattle ranches. These men were telling their investors that Hereford was the perfect breed. These same businessmen were not looking to build up family ranches. In fact they would frown on such people as the Benningtons and the McDermotts. McDermott ending by saying, "You are going to need some ranch hands, a place for them to bunk, a cook and some cow ponies to start with. If my bull does what he is supposed to do you'll be needing these items sooner rather than later."

Preparing to leave, McDermott was unhitching the team from the wagon. "You keep the wagon. Also I brought you some things. Didn't get the price I wanted for my spread. I'm not leaving the new owners anything," said McDermott. He tipped his hat to Blue Feather and then said to Asa, "I thought your boy might like this." From the wagon, he lifted a painted rocking horse. Still hiding behind his mother, Charlie's eye went wide. McDermott tipped his hat to Blue Feather a second time and with his cowboys rode back toward Layton and the trip east.

To a couple of his trusted hands he said, "You come back this way next spring you might look in on Mr. Bennington. He is going to need help."

One hand suggested, "Kind of a shoe string operation, isn't it?"

"Right now it is; probably not for long" was McDermott's answer. After McDermott left, Asa looked at the items in the wagon: an ax, a maul, two shovels, a hoe, a hand saw, six tin plates, an unopened bottle of whiskey, a length of lace and a flower pot containing a plant Asa thought might be chives. He was amazed.

The tall, loud, white man with hair the color of fire finally left. Charlie even waited a bit to make sure they didn't return before he approached the rocking horse. Next to Spotted Dog's fine headdress it was the most exotic thing he had ever seen. The horse was painted in reds and greens and blues. The mane and tail were lacquered shiny black with touches of gilt. Red leather reins attached to the horse's nostrils in golden rings. Just as he had seen his father walk around the bull, Charlie folded his arms across his chest and began a small circle around his new prize. It was Blue Feather's laughter that caused Asa to look up from the items in the wagon. Charlie was a miniature of his father.

Summer slipped into fall, and Spotted Dog moved his band south saying they would come back in the spring. Riding Black Jack, Asa made one last, quick trip to Layton. Banker Spindle saw Asa ride in on a fine horse, noticed Asa was still wearing moccasins instead of boots and hoped for another deposit of another nugget. He was disappointed. Asa simply wanted to thank him for suggesting he talk to McDermott. "I won't be back till spring," said Asa as he started to leave the bankers office, "So Merry Christmas even if it is early." The banker thought that Asa was not as stooped over as the last time he was in the office.

Christmas was much on Asa's mind. His family was going to do it up right this year. In the mercantile, he selected a cast iron fry pan for Blue Feather, a soft blanket for Small Leaf and for Charlie he settled on two storybooks with drawings. A tin of baking powder, cinnamon sticks, dried apples, flour, needles and thread completed his shopping and used up most of his money. For himself, he purchased a coffee pot and only looked at boots. "Someday," he thought. "Someday."

Winter came and so did Christmas. They even celebrated it on the correct day, because they had a calendar. Blue Feather was pleased with her pan even if it was heavy. Charlie liked his books not knowing they were beginning of his education. Charlie's education had been much on Asa's mind ever since the family's trip to Layton and after everything McDermott told Asa. One day Charlie would inherit the ranch, and he would have to exist in the white man's world. Charlie would have to be smarter than Asa even thought of being . . . but how? Asa could start with sums and reading. He could do that much. They would start in the spring. They would count the geese as they returned even if Charlie was only going on four.

Asa also pondered the idea of having hired hands, a bunkhouse and a cook. He thought about the snug cabin with a roof so low he had not been able to invite in his one and only visitor. The cabin was fine now but what if they had more children? He thought about the houses in Layton and wondered if he could build one like those.

To keep his hands busy during the winter, he carved a wooden marker for Charlie's grave. He did not know his partner's birth date and was not sure how to spell Charlie's last name. Instead he carved the name Batiste and the double B's his partner had envisioned for the ranch brand.

Chapter Eleven

Changes

Spring had chased the snow into the shady places. The morning sun felt warm on Asa's face. He had taught Blue Feather how to make coffee. This morning he soaked up the sun, enjoyed his coffee and watched with interest as four riders were approaching on the ranch rode. There were several routes by which a person could reach the cabin, but this one road Asa thought of as the ranch road because most of it's length was visible from the cabin. He could tell that two of the riders had pack animals.

Inside the cabin he could hear Small Leaf. Whatever motherly thing Blue Feather was doing, Small Leaf didn't like it and was making a fuss. Asa let his wife know strangers were coming. He could make out three white men and an older Mexican man. He thought he should recognize two of the white men but couldn't quite place them. They reined to a stop in front of him. The white men appeared to be brothers and cowboys by the look of their gear but studying the Mexican told Asa nothing.

The middle brother was the first one to speak. "Mr. Bennington, we rode for Mr. McDermott for the last few years till he went back east. He told us you might be needing hands this spring." All three nodded. The Mexican remained quiet.

Asa was sorry to have to turn them men down, but he was running short of ready cash and didn't expect any income till fall and he was holding on to the few gold nuggets he still had. "Did McDermott tell you I don't have a bunk house and that I can't pay till fall and then only if everything goes well?"

"Yes sir, he did." All three nodded. "You see sir, we wintered over near Taos," continued the middle brother. The youngest brother was beginning to grin and the older one punched him in the ribs. "Young Billy here got us into a mite of trouble . . . and well . . . we need to stay low for a while."

"You kill anyone?"

"No sir!"

"You steal anything?"

"No sir!" Asa could guess what kind of trouble young Billy had gotten himself and his brothers into.

"Can you build your own bunk house?" The three nodded yes.

"I don't have a cook"

The three cowboys looked at the Mexican who was now the one ginning broadly. Several of his teeth were missing, and Asa saw he was not a young man.
"I cook, senior. I cook good."

Asa thought, why not. "Any of you have a problem with Indians?" They were a little slow to nod no but they did, so Asa explained. "My wife is Sioux. In the summer, her people either camp on the ranch or at least near by and they visit back and forth. They are peaceable people."

This time it was the older brother speaking, "Your word is good enough for us, Captain." Asa had never been call captain before and he rather liked it. So it was that the Bennington ranch had two top hands, the Smith brothers, Ed, Bob and young Billy, and a Mexican cook named Enzo. Asa knew Smith was not their real name. Billy was not much of a worker and Enzo never told Asa his last name, but it all workout fine. They were respectful of Blue Feather and made Charlie one of the building crew.

A bunkhouse was constructed in short order, and it was pretty decent thought Asa, but bigger than he expected. Ed explained they were preparing for more cowboys. Enzo was a good cook if you liked Mexican food and except for Blue Feather everyone did.

McDermott's bull had done his work and there were many calves this spring, and they hadn't lost many cows over the winter. Maybe this fall, Asa thought, he could sell some stock. Ed agreed. Ed knew more than Asa about beeves and how to market them. Ed said Cheyenne was the place to go to sell. Asa was willing to listen.

Spotted Dog and his band returned. They did not come all the way to the ranch but set up camp a day and a half east. Asa could tell the old chief was aging and wondered how many more summers they would enjoy the visits of Blue Feather's father and Charlie's grandfather.

Early summer a messenger from the camp arrived with a summons for Blue Feather from Snake Woman. Spotted Dog was ill. Blue Feather should come now. Blue Feather would take Small Leaf, but leave Charlie to help his father and the crew. She hugged Asa. "I should be back in a few days. Don't let Charlie eat the sugar. Don't give him coffee. Don't let him climb on the bunk house roof." She finally ran out of instructions and rode off with the messenger toward Spotted Dog's camp.

Ten days passed with no returning Blue Feather and no message. Surely if Spotted Dog had died someone would have come. Asa was uneasy. At last he told Enzo, "I'm going to ride to my wife's family's camp. You keep Charlie here." Enzo could see Asa's worry. Asa threw a few things together and Enzo handed him a small bag of food as he rode out on Black Jack. His first view of the camp told him something was not right. There seemed to be no activity, and there was not much campfire smoke. He studied the scene for a bit longer then rode forward till he saw the first body. Dismounting he approached, recognizing one of the older woman. He rolled her body over and jumped back. Her face was covered with spots, pox spots.

The camp had small pox. Asa covered his mouth and felt sick at heart. He took the horse away from the body. Putting a neckerchief across his face, he made his way slowly back to the camp. Dead friends lay everywhere. He found Blue Feather's body. She must have been holding Small Leaf when she died. Asa was not aware of the agonizing scream he hurled at the sky as he stumbled away from this place of death.

He walked back to his horse and sat on the ground till he could think straight. Asa knew the recommended practice was to burn the village and everything in it. He thought of Spotted Dog's magnificent war bonnet going up in flames. What other treasures were hidden away in other teepees? No one would ever know. He fired the village. The glow that night was seen by many people, but no one knew what they were seeing.

In the morning, Asa ate a little and cleaned himself up in a near by stream. Then and only then it occurred to him that he might be infected. He could not go home or at least not be around Charlie and the men until he was sure he was not sick. He heard horses. The band's small herd of ponies was in a gully not to far away. Asa was reluctant to leave the resting place of his second wife and another daughter. He stared at the remaining smoking ruins and vowed never to love or marry again. He had lost two wives and three daughters. That was enough.

If he didn't return someone would come looking for him and that would not do. He rounded up the ponies and headed toward the ranch. When he could see the bunkhouse roof he stopped and shot into the air three times. It was Ed that rode out slowly to meet him. "Small pox," he yelled. Ed waved that he understood. "I'll stay way till I know if I am sick." Ed waved again. Asa turned away and left it to Ed to gather up the scattered ponies.

For three weeks, Asa camped down wind from the cabin and the bunkhouse at a distance he felt was safe. Every two days Enzo rode out and dropped off items for Asa . . . blankets, a razor, and food. Asa had a lot of time to think. At first it was all about Blue Feather and Small Leaf and even Catherine. Slowly those thoughts were replaced by thoughts of Charlie and Charlie's future. At the end of three weeks, Enzo came with a wagon and said, "You come home now Senior Asa." Asa was ready.

Driving toward the cabin Asa saw Charlie running toward them. Enzo said, "He sleep in your bed. I didn't say no."

"Thank you, Enzo."

Asa climbed off the wagon and met Charlie who flung himself into his father's arms. Asa didn't know a child could hold on so hard. They stepped aside to let Enzo go by with the wagon. A ways down the road Asa sat down in the shade of a pine tree and handed Charlie a hunk of jerky. Charlie cuddled down into Asa's lap. "Papa, are Mama and Small Leaf on their journey?"
Asa remembered how Blue Feather had explained Uncle Charlie's death as a journey.

"Yes, son. They are."

"Do you think they miss us?"

"Just like we miss them." Asa didn't understand the wetness on the back of his neck came from his son's tears. They finished the jerky. Charlie didn't seem to have any more questions. They headed back to the cabin. Asa let Charlie set the pace. Charlie slept with Asa for over a month. For Asa the bed did not seem so empty, but he did wonder how he would get Charlie back into his own bed.

Enzo had the answer. "Your boy, he needs a perro."

"A what?" asked Asa not understanding the Spanish word for dog.

"A puppy" answered Enzo after hunting for the right word. Asa smiled and thought the time was right to go to Layton and talk with Spindler about how and where to sell a few cows. Fall was coming, and he would need to pay the Smith brothers and Enzo. He would also look for a puppy.

The banker saw Asa coming and was ready to shake his hand as soon as Asa entered the office. Spindler noted that Asa looked older. As a matter of good manners Spindler said, "How's that family of yours?"

"My daughter, my wife, and all her people are dead. Small pox." To cut off the Spindler's condolences Asa said, "I need to find my son a puppy."

"Puppies are good for a boy," was Spindler's remark and he rang a small bell on his desk. A clerk quickly appeared at the door. "Mr. Bennington needs a puppy. Go find one and make sure it is a good one." Turning back to Asa, he continued, "Is there anything else I can do for you?" They talked cattle. Spindler it turned out was part owner of the Layton Lady and offered to purchase ten head just to keep the restaurant in steaks. That would pay the owed wages and give Asa money for the coming winter. Asa was pleased he did not have to go to Cheyenne.

The Bennington ranch would have its first cattle drive even if it was only ten cows delivered to the small town of Layton. Asa returned home with a basket containing a small, fuzzy black puppy. The bank clerk assured Asa the puppy was weaned.

Charlie was spell bound. Asa told Charlie they could not all sleep in the same bed because if Asa rolled over on Charlie's new puppy, the poor dog would be squashed. Charlie was content to move back into his own bed with his new best friend. Asa was lonesome. It took Charlie a week to name the dog, and he decided on Spot. When Asa asked why he picked the name when the dog did not have a spot on him Charlie replied, "For Grandfather. Spotted Dog is too long a name for such a little dog."

The small cattle drive was complete and Asa paid off the Ed, Bob, Billy, and Enzo. Except for Billy, the others asked to stay on through the winter. Young Billy was moving on. There had to be an easier way to make a living. Asa was surprised and thankful to have the men stay.

Charlie and Asa could look north and see snow on the tops of the mountains they called the Teepees. Right now father and son sat on the slope above the cabin where Uncle Charlie was buried. Spot sat between them, closer to Asa than Charlie. "Can we make markers for Mama and Small Leaf?" The question from Charlie surprised Asa.

"We did not put their bodies in this ground like we did for Uncle Charlie, but yes we can place markers if you would like."

"If they are on the journey," reasoned Charlie, "they should all have markers." That winter Charlie helped Asa carve the markers. They would place them when the snow melted away.

Chapter Twelve

The Kitchen Stove

In the twenty odd years since Charlie Lamb had first suggested the idea of a cattle ranch to Asa, much had changed. Theodore Roosevelt was the twenty-sixth president of the United States, and there was a good feeling about the direction of the country. Closer to home, Wyoming had achieved statehood. Cheyenne was the state capitol. The railroad had a spur in Layton just for the surrounding cattle ranches. Everything that McDermott had talked about had happened. The big eastern businessmen had brought in big cattle money to Wyoming and Montana. There had been some violence. Some small ranches went under but the Bennington ranch continued through it all. Barbed wire and free grazing could spark an argument. Asa and Charlie still found a gold nugget now and then and still didn't know where the nuggets originated.

The nearest community to the ranch was Silver Bend. Located where the Crystal River made a big bend, it had been settled by miners that came for a small silver strike. The silver petered out, but enough miners stayed to begin a permanent community. The First National Bank of Wyoming had replaced the First Bank of Layton with offices in both Layton and Silver Bend. The Bennington Ranch was a good customer as were the father and the now grown son.

The ranch itself, had a barn, a forge, assorted out buildings, a small orchard, a summer garden, a fair sting of horses, and a real house with two bedrooms. The Double B brand had a reputation for fine Herefords. Asa Bennington and his son Charlie had a reputation for honesty even if they were a little rough around the edges.

Everything was better and bigger than Asa could have ever imagined, but Asa did have concerns about Charlie. Asa was in his midforties and Charlie was eighteen. Asa had taught Charlie everything he knew. Charlie could read well enough and do sums in his head better than Asa. Every time Asa made a trip to the bank, or sold cattle or made any other business arrangement Charlie was there. Charlie was good with a knife, his fists and could shoot almost as well as Asa. Charlie knew his manners more or less. He tipped his hat. He opened the door for the ladies. He helped them in and out of the carriage. He offered his seat. He knew basic table manners.

The two things that concerned Asa were Charlie's temper and his lack of knowledge of women, nice women good enough to be a wife. The temper was a Bennington trait. Charlie was known for his short fuse. To his face nobody called him, a half-breed but everyone remembered his Indian mother.

Asa knew for that reason, most of the young ladies in either Layton or Silver Bend would not be allowed to step out with Charlie. Because of the distance and the never-ending ranch work, Charlie had never attended a church social or a barn dance. When it came to the ladies, Charlie was rough. Asa could look at his son, a healthy young man with normal needs and knew Charlie needed a woman in his life, preferably a good wife.

The solution to finding a wife for Charlie would come from an unexpected direction. Asa and Charlie went to Cheyenne once a year to order big items for the ranch house. This trip they purchased a real kitchen cook stove. Right now it was lying on it's back in their wagon at the livery. Asa wondered how many men it would take to move the damn thing out of the wagon and into the kitchen once they returned home. They enjoyed their trips to the big city. They stayed at nice hotels, and they ate at good restaurants. Tonight was their last meal before going home in the morning. A long time ago Asa had stopped worrying about what people thought about his scar. The father and son didn't drink. Asa never had been able to afford it and Charlie had learned the hard way he couldn't handle liquor for two reasons. It made him very sick and he couldn't control his temper.

Tonight they were just walking off the big, rich dinner and taking in the sights and sounds of the city. It was the sounds of a woman screaming that caught their attention. The noise of a scuffle came from the alley. Both Asa and Charlie were aware that this could be a way to lure them into the alley for the purpose of robbery but they didn't think so. In the shadows, they could see a man attacking a woman.

They never even consulted each other but turned in unison into the alley. Asa pulled the man off the woman, and Charlie hit the attacker hard. There was a huffing sound as the man crumpled to the ground. The man was a middle-aged white man. The woman was a young Mexican girl. She was sobbing and fearful that her rescuers might be just as bad as her attacker.

"Don't hurt me, please," she pleaded.

"No, ma'am. We don't intend to harm you." Asa offered her his hand and turned the bad side of his face away from her. Once on her feet she was a little shaky. Asa saw that she was really not a girl but a young woman, a pretty young woman except for the scratches on her face. Her ample breasts were some what exposed. Asa picked up a shawl from the ground and handed it to her. She covered herself and looked at both Charlie and Asa with deep, brown eyes still wide with fear. Charlie was simply staring at her with his mouth open. "Are you hurt?" asked Asa.

"No, but he will try it again when he wakes up." she replied. "I will go with you."

Asa ignored the last statement and asked, "He, your husband?"

She spat on the ground and said, "Step father."

Before Charlie closed is mouth, he muttered, "Shit!"

"What about your mother?" continued Asa.

She stood a little straighter, looked at Asa hard. "Dead. I spect he killed her, but no one would believe my word over his. I'm just a Mex and after he is finished with me he will expect me to whore for him or he will kill me if he can. I will go with you," she repeated.

Charlie closed his mouth again and repeated "Ah shit," again.

Before Asa could say that was not possible, Charlie offered his arm to her and inquired, "Do you have any belongings?"

"In the wagon out in the street," she replied. The two, young people left Asa standing in the alley with the downed man who was beginning to groan. Asa kicked him. The man was silent once more. Asa had to lean against the wall to catch his breath. This had happened a couple of times before. He supposed he should go see a doctor, but he really didn't know one. He took a deep breath and followed Charlie and the young woman to the street.

By the time Asa reached them she had introduced her herself. Her name was Margarita. Her belongings consisted of a traveling bag and a guitar. They could not take Margarita to their hotel so they checked out. At the livery, they woke up the boy who speculated about the pretty woman with the injured face and her companions while harnessing the horses to the wagon containing a big cooking stove.

Asa handled the reins and Margarita sat between him and Charlie because the stove took up all the room in the back. She played her guitar and sang. Asa thought correctly by the time the wagon arrived at the ranch Charlie would be in love.

By the time they reached the ranch he and Charlie knew Margarita's story. Her real father had run off leaving her mother and three older brothers and little Margarita. After several hard years, the mother had taken up with the white man. The brothers had run away and her mother had turned to drink. The stepfather had turned his attentions toward Margarita. The night in the alley was the first time he had really tried to force himself on her. Asa was glad they had come along when they did but what were they to do with this lovely young woman? He thought about the big stove in the back of the wagon and wondered if she could cook.

Asa always marveled at how fast news could travel. By the time they pulled up outside the house every man except the range riders knew there was a woman in the wagon with them. Several of the more ignorant men thought maybe the woman was for their pleasure. Others knew better but were curious as to the circumstances of the woman's arrival. If any of them thought she might be fair game, they quickly learned better. It was hands off. Young Charlie made sure they got the message.

Sleeping arrangements had to be sorted out. Charlie and his father moved into the big bedroom. Margarita was given the small one. In her entire life, she had never had her own room. This one even had a door that locked. The cook, who had been worried by her arrival, was pleased to learn she could not really cook and he had not lost his job. She could do laundry. She became the ranch laundress.

Many a cowboy was suddenly interested in clean clothes because on a good day when she was busy at the washtubs they could ride over and maybe look down her neck as she bent over to work on the scrub board. A look was worth the try and better than nothing.

Asa watched as Charlie moped around and snapped at people for no reason. "Pa, did you ever go courting?" he asked one day.

"Twice," answered Asa. Charlie had forgotten about his father's first wife. Asa told his son about the courting gifts he took to Catherine's aunt and uncle for a whole year.

"A whole year?" marveled Charlie Asa told him how he and Uncle Charlie went out to look for horses for Chief Spotted Dog and returned with a bear. Asa left out the part about being a reluctant bridegroom.

Charlie was thoughtful. "Pa, how can I court Margarita when she has no family?"

"Charlie, are you sure you want to marry her? Not just bed her?"

His son was thoughtful again. "Well I do think about . . . about the bed part." For some reason, Charlie didn't want to use the crude bunkhouse terms in front of his father. This too was important. "I feel something else for her." Charlie gave a big sigh. Asa vaguely remembered that young love could be painful and confusing.

"Charlie, if I were her father this is what I would want from you if you were courting." Charlie listened. "Trim you hair. Shave at least every other day. Take a bath. Some times you smell like your horse." Charlie looked crestfallen. "Women like clean men in their beds." Charlie brightened up. "You will have the ranch some day so you can provide for her. When it actually comes to Margarita or any other woman of your choice you need to be gentle." Asa heard the long ago words of his father coming out of his own mouth.

"How do we get married? I mean what about the ceremony and all that stuff? Women like those things, I guess."

"If she accepts your offer of marriage you will have to ask her what she wants. You are very right. Women do like those things. It gives them something to tell your children." By the look on Charlie's face Asa suspected he hadn't thought about children. Asa knew children were the natural result of what Charlie was really thinking about.

"You need to ask her to walk out with you. Look at the sunset. Stay out of her knickers." Charlie looked crest fallen again. "That comes when you are married. Give her some flowers. If you are serious about this we will ride into Silver Bend and pick out some nice gifts." It was all much harder than Charlie had ever thought. He did every thing Asa suggested. They went to Silver Bend and purchased small gift items. Charlie began the courtship of Margarita.

Margarita liked Charlie well enough. She knew what Charlie was about and he would make a decent husband, especially for someone like herself. She liked Charlie's father a lot. He was a kind man, but she was worried what he thought. Finding Asa alone on the porch she asked, "Senior Bennington, may I speak to you?"
He nodded yes and motioned her to a chair.

"I believe your son is courting me."

"I believe that is true," agreed Asa.

"How do you feel about that, Senior?" Asa looked puzzled.

"I'm a Mexican. Your grandchildren will be half Mexican."

Now Asa understood. "You know that my wife, Charlie's mother, was a Sioux Indian?"

It was Margarita's turn to nod yes. "Does that bother you?" he asked.
"Es no problemo, Senior."
"Then that is the answer to your own question," Asa answered. She jumped up from her chair, kissed Asa on the cheek, and returned to the kitchen. From the shadows of the barn Charlie watched Margarita and his father on the porch. When she kissed his father, Charlie felt a pang of jealousy. He didn't like the way it felt. He didn't have to worry.

One moonlight night in August Charlie walked Margarita to the edge of the creek. There was music coming from the bunkhouse. He held her hand. "Will you marry me? Will you be my wife?" was all asked.

"Yes" and she kissed him in a manner that caused him to ache in a way he didn't know was possible.

As far as a ceremony, she had been raised a Catholic and she really wanted to be married by a priest. There was a small Catholic Mission in Layton. Asa suggested that they take the wagon with supplies for Charlie and Margarita. He would take his own mount and return home after the ceremony. The newly weds could go up to the lake and camp for a few days. Asa told Charlie to dress in his suit. Asa took Margarita to Silver Bend where she found a simple white dress. When Margarita said she could not pay for the dress Asa told her it was his wedding present to her. Just briefly Margarita wished she were marrying the father and not the son.

On the day of her wedding Margarita unbraided her beautiful, black hair and wore a circlet of wild, white daisies on her head. Asa did not know that margarita meant daisy in Spanish. He thought his new daughter-in-law was beautiful. Charlie thought his wife was beautiful.

The priest spoke in Latin. None of them understood the words. Charlie thought from the look on his bride's face it was good. Asa remembered that when he and Blue Feather were married by Spotted Dog; he didn't understand a word either and look how well that turned out.

By the time the newest Mr. and Mrs. Bennington retuned home, Asa had moved Charlie and Margarita's belonging into the big bedroom and he and his old trunk were comfortably in the little bedroom. He played with the idea that he should let them have the whole house. The old cabin was long gone. He didn't want to bunk in the bunkhouse. He would stay put. Maybe they should make the house bigger.

Chapter Thirteen

Tia Rosa Potts

Watching Margarita be sick every morning made Asa suspect she had conceived on her honeymoon. He didn't remember either Catherine or Blue Feather being this ill with their pregnancies. Charlie came to Asa deep in worry. "I don't know what is the matter. I think we should take her to see Doc Worton. She is so sick especially in the mornings. She is not hungry and she is so cranky," complained Charlie.

"Charlie, don't you two talk?" Asa realized that was probably an unkind remark in Charlie's worried state. "Charlie, your wife is going to have a baby. You are going to be a father." Charlie choked on his coffee.

"Damn!!" In their bedroom late that night Charlie asked, "Are you really going to have a baby?" For the first time that day, she didn't feel sick and she thought it funny that Charlie had just figured it out. She let him caress her beneath her sleeping gown as she said, "Yes, Charlie. We are having a baby. In the spring I think."

"Damn! Maybe we should add on to the house." He continued to move his hand up her leg. "Maybe I should just make you another baby," he purred in her ear.

"I don't think it works that way, but you can try. It will be the last time," she informed him.

"What are you talking about, last time?" he said it so loudly that Asa heard him through the thin bedroom wall.

"It is not good for the baby. This is the last time," she repeated. "Damn," he thought. Married life was not turning out to be exactly what he had expected. Just how many months away was spring?

Asa was right about one thing. Charlie and his wife didn't talk much. They bickered and argued just about everything. Today they were discussing baby names. Margarita insisted the names had to come from the Bible. Well, there were many names for boys, but the only woman's name Charlie could remember was Mary. Margarita refused to even consider Blue Feather for a girl's name. Asa thought that was probably wise. Charlie was hurt. They continued the conversation through dinner and into the evening.

Asa walked down to the bunkhouse to give the young couple some privacy. He would do this a couple of times a week through out Margarita's pregnancy. The crew welcomed him. They always called him Captain or Mr. Bennington. They called Charlie, Charlie.

In November, there was not much snow yet. It was late in coming this year. Asa took his coffee to the porch, because Charlie and Margarita were bickering again. Charlie was angry because dinner was not up to his expectations, and Margarita had told him he could do the cooking from now on out. Asa thought he would cook before he ever ate his son's cooking. The door was not quite shut. From the inside, the voices were becoming louder when Asa heard the sound of a slap followed by Margarita's cry then silence. Charlie slammed out of the house and stood at the other end of the porch away from his father.

Inside Asa found his daughter-in-law on the floor. A bright red patch shown on her cheek, where Charlie had hit her. Asa helped her up and onto the settee. Asa could feel his temper rising. He retuned to the porch not making a sound in his moccasins and not slamming the door. He grabbed a surprised Charlie by the shoulder, turned him around and pinned him against the roof support. "If you ever hurt or hit that woman again, I will kill you!!! Do you understand?" hissed Asa in his sons' face.

Charlie knew he had his own Bennington temper. It had gotten him into trouble more than once, but he had never seen his father lose control like this. Charlie almost wet his pants. "You go back in there. You tell her you're sorry and that it will never happen again! You take care of her. You understand?" Charlie nodded. Charlie returned to the house. He didn't see his father trying to catch his breath. Asa sat in a porch chair till he could breath normally. Maybe he would have to see the doc.

Things were better after that. The snow finally came and so did Christmas. Everyone had gifts for the baby. Margarita seemed happy but very tired. Charlie assumed this was normal, and Asa began to wonder if something was wrong. Many evenings in January her father-in-law went to the bunkhouse to play cards. Margarita knew he went down there just to give her and Charlie some time to themselves.

She and Charlie were in the living room. She was dosing and watching the fames in the fireplace. He was rereading an old newspaper when he heard her gasp. Looking up from his paper, he expected to see something wrong but she was smiling. "Charlie, come sit with me" and she patted the seat next to her. He settled carefully in beside her. She was so big it was hard to get near her. Taking his hand, she placed it on her belly. He felt his baby kick . . . really kick! It finally registered with him that inside his wife's stomach there was a small person.

By the end of March, the snows were beginning to recede and Asa felt was relieved. He wanted to go into Silver Bend to talk to Doc Albrecht about Margarita. She was too big. She hardly ever left her bed. Even with Charlie's ignorance in these matters he was also concerned about his wife and was happy with his father's suggestion.

In the doctor's office, Asa described everything he could think to tell the doctor about Margarita's condition. The doctor listened and watched Asa closely. "You need someone at the ranch to help with this delivery. I have three other women that are about due. I can't come all that way and be gone that long." Asa felt worry creeping into his heart. "I will give you the name and address of a woman, a midwife. She will probably come with you. You will have to pay her." Asa didn't care about paying.

He did care about his grandchild and yes, his daughter-in-law, too. He read the paper handed him by the doctor. The woman's name was Tia Rosa Potts. Asa looked back at the doctor. "It means Aunt Rosa. Mrs. Potts is a widow woman and a damn good mid wife. She speaks Spanish, which just might be a good thing for your Margarita." Asa shook the doctor's hand and was about to leave when the doctor asked, "How are you feeling, Asa?" He thought Asa looked gray in the face. "Fine, just fine," Asa said. He was in a hurry to find this Tia Rosa person and head for the ranch.

He located her. She was a woman tiny in stature and big in attitude. She read the note from the doctor. She would come. She didn't ask but ordered Asa to hitch up her buggy, which she loaded with several bundles, a big black umbrella and an 1873, 32-20 lever action Winchester. The way she handled the rifle made Asa think she knew how to use it. Good gun for a woman he thought.

At the ranch house, she marched up the back porch stairs and walked right into the house with out knocking. Charlie stood up as the strange woman entered followed by his father.

"Where is the mamacita?" Charlie pointed toward the open bedroom door. Tia Rosa stopped in the doorway. Looking at Margarita in the bed, the old woman made the sign of the cross. She shoved Charlie back into the living room and shut the door. The only thing the two men could hear was the sound of rapid Spanish being spoken. They waited.

The door opened. Peeking in Charlie could see his wife propped up on some pillows. She looked all right. In fact she appeared rather pleased. Tia Rosa looked at both Charlie and Asa then fixed Charlie with a serious stare. "Your wife is going to give you two babies. She is carrying twins. And pretty soon I think."

"Damn!" said Charlie as he sat down so quickly he almost missed the chair. He began to grin. Tia Rosa could see the look of concern on the father-in-law's face.

"Mrs. Bennington is a healthy young woman. It will be a difficult birth, but I feel it will go well. I have delivered twins before."

Tia Rosa set Asa and particularly Charlie to cleaning the house, washing bedding and doing the cooking. It needed doing and they needed to be kept busy. She insisted that Margarita do nothing. Charlie grumbled to his father but was quiet in front of Tia Rosa. The tiny woman made him uneasy.

The day was a beautiful early spring day. It was the kind of day that hints of summer. Tia Rosa eased Margarita into a wide chair on the porch so she could enjoy the sun and the fresh air. Tia Rosa told Charlie to open all the windows, to put clean sheets on the bed, to stack towels near the bed and in the kitchen and to draw plenty of water for heating.

At noon Margarita felt her first labor pain. Charlie heard her gasp and saw her grip the arms of her chair. "Find Rosa" was all she said. Together Charlie and Rosa helped Margarita back to bed. There were no more pains for a while. The two women talked as if nothing was going on. Charlie had fetched his father, and now they sat and waited.

Margarita's first scream brought them both out of their chairs. At the bedroom door, Tia Rosa pointed in the general direction of the bunkhouse and said firmly to Charlie, "You go. I will let you know." When Asa followed his son toward the door, Tia Rosa said, "You stay. I will need help."

Margarita's labor lasted well past midnight. Her agony could be heard down at the bunkhouse. It unnerved the men. Charlie felt physically ill. Asa heated water and handed towels to Rosa, doing whatever she asked. He made coffee but didn't drink any. He burned his fingers. Occasionally, he stood on the porch where Charlie could see him and shook his head no.

The sun was just peeking over the Eastern horizon when Asa heard the cry of a newborn. He let out his breath. Rosa came to the door and handed him the wrapped baby. "Healthy boy" was all she said. Margarita was not making as much noise as earlier. Another baby's wail reached Asa ears. He was glad he was sitting down. His knees were weak. When Rosa opened the door, she was covered with a lot of blood. The bundle in her arms was crying lustily which set off the other baby in Asa's lap. "Healthy boy," she said. The grandfather and the mid wife grinned at each other.

The grin disappeared from Rosa's face. Mrs. Bennington is going to be fine but maybe there will be no more children for her. In the bedroom, Margarita was propped against some pillows looking wan, pale and happy. With the babies on either side of her, it was a pretty picture. Asa kissed her gently on the forehead and said, "I'll bring Charlie."

As soon as Charlie saw his father step off the porch, he stared running toward the house. "Everything is fine" was all Asa said as Charlie rushed past him.

Inside, Rosa slowed Charlie down long enough to say, "You have two fine healthy boys. Their names are Peter and Paul." It would be a very long time before it would occur to Charlie that he had nothing to say in the naming of his boys. What he did know was that these boys were the future of the ranch, the Bennington Ranch for the Bennington Brothers, the Double "B"! Peter Asa and Paul Charles were entered into the family Bible later in the next day.

Asa was sitting on the porch looking at the moon but not really seeing it. Tia Rosa Potts sat down in a chair next to his and handed him a glass of whiskey. It seemed appropriate. He sipped his. She tossed hers down neat.

Tia Rosa became part of the family for two months as Margarita began to recover. Charlie and Asa discussed how they might enlarge the house. Asa was sleeping on the porch and he sure didn't want to be there next winter. Spring was cold enough.

In the beginning, the babies were easy to tell apart. They were both bald but Paul, the last to be born, was smaller. After two months, he was the same size as his brother and they were identical in every way. Margarita put a small mark on Paul's ear.

They didn't like to be apart. If one cried, the other did also. If one laughed, the other joined in. No one could quite decide whom the babies looked like. With Rosa's help Margarita healed slowly but nicely. She didn't tell Charlie there could be no more children.

Margarita was sad, not because of her sweet babies and not because of her life with Charlie but because she knew any day now Rosa would announce she must return home to Silver Bend. In Margarita's young life, she had never had a truly loving mother, a sister, or a female friend. Tia Rosa had become all those things. Caring for her boys, her husband and her father-in-law were going to be a big task. She felt she was up to it, but she would surely miss Rosa and she would be lonely.

Charlie, on the other hand was secretly pleased to learn the old woman was leaving. He understood he owed her more than money could pay for the safe births of his sons and for Margarita's recovery but just the same he was happy she was going. Sometimes he felt Rosa encouraged Margarita to stand against him on different issues. When it came to the raising of his boys he wanted no interference. He believed he knew best.

When the departure day arrived, Rosa held each baby. She hugged their mother. "If you come to town, you come visit me," she said. "The door key is under the cactus pot if I am not there." Rosa promised to come visit. Even if the ranch were closer to town Rosa understood none of the Silver Bend ladies would come to see Margarita. The businessmen in town respected the Benningtons and the Bennington money. Too many wives remembered the Indian mother and saw a Mexican wife.

Charlie politely asked Rosa how much he owed her for her stay and didn't protest at the figure she stated. He was glad to get rid of her. He even handed her more than she had asked for. She didn't say thank you instead she said, "Charlie, you get yourself a milking cow. Those boys will need milk."

It irritated him that people called him by his first name and addressed his father as Mr. Bennington.

Asa was loading the last of Rosa's belonging into the buggy. Automatically, he checked her Winchester to make sure it was on safety. It was. Margarita stood on the porch with one babe in her arms the other in a basket at her feet. Margarita knew that Rosa was hoping for a kiss from Asa. He shook her hand instead. Inwardly Rosa sighed. "Guess you can have your bed back now," was all she said.

Driving away she thought she would have gladly shared his bed. After all you couldn't see his scar in the dark, but she figured no woman was ever going to warm his bed again. Charlie was thinking about what Rosa said about the milk cow. Maybe if Margarita was not so busy nursing she might think about their bed as a place for more than just sleeping, more babies or not.

When the boys were six months old Asa knew they looked just like Small Leaf at that age, dusky skin and black hair that stuck out in all directions. They were all Indian with not a hint of Margarita or Charlie to be seen. Charlie was delighted. In his eyes, the sun rose and set with his boys. Margarita and Asa to some degree thought maybe looking so Indian might make things difficult later in life as the boys grew up and moved in the white man's world, which they would surely do as owners of the ranch.

Ranch life was hectic. Builders were enlarging the house. Back to their old ways, Charlie and Margarita argued about everything, the paint colors on the walls, another new and bigger kitchen stove and, especially when Charlie wanted to give the boys each a big horse. Asa silently agreed with Margarita most of the time but stayed out of it and went on round up with the hands when he could.

For the twin's first birthday, Charlie gave them each a derringer. "They are only babies, Charlie, they need to do baby things until they are old enough to do the manly things," Margarita explained over and over again. Charlie didn't see it that way. Just as a matter of family conversation Asa remarked to his son, "Don't make them grow up too fast. You will miss these years."

Charlie had both boys with him on his big horse. He didn't acknowledge his father's statement but turned the horse away and trotted of briskly. Despite the fact that their little heads bouncing in an alarming manner, Asa could hear the twins laughing.

Asa determined early on that the boys were very smart. They seemed to have a language all their own. They quickly learned to play Charlie and Margarita off one another. This didn't work with him and that did not please the twins. Charlie played rough with the boys. As soon as the boys could walk, Charlie taught them to run as fast as they could and jump on him. He would pretend to fall down. Charlie would rough house with them till they were either tired or near tears. When Margarita complained, Charlie insisted, "Peter and Paul are Benningtons. The ranch will belong to them some day. They have to be ready"

"Charlie, they are only two years old," countered his wife. Charlie gave her a big bear hug that hurt and suggested they go for a walk down by the creek where he knew the buttercups were in bloom. Both boys were safely napping. Charlie took a blanket. He was thankful the expansion of the house was almost complete. He wanted the boys out of his bedroom.

When Asa discovered the boys poking sharp sticks at a corralled cow he scolded them. They gave him angry looks but threw down the sticks. It was not the first time Asa had seen a mean streak in the boys. He noticed the dogs stayed out of the boy's reach. For ones so young, it bothered him.

Tactfully Asa said on evening when it was just he and Charlie, "I think the boys are old enough we should begin talking to them about the proper care of the animals on the ranch."

Charlie puffed up and scowled at his father, "You saying I'm not raising my boys right?"

This was not the response Asa expected so he tried another tact. "As you always say, they will inherit the ranch. Probably not to early too start with the simple ideas."
"And I'll do it myself . . . my way when I see fit!" Charlie stomped away. Margarita had heard the whole conversation. Looking at Asa, she shook her head sadly.

Rosa had come on one of her visits. She shook her head when Margarita confessed she was two months pregnant. If Rosa was pleasantly surprised, Margarita was depressed. She remembered every miserable thing about the nine months waiting for the twins and the long painful hours of the birth. Rosa thought that there was something more.

Margarita broke down. "I love my boys. I am happy that Charlie is so proud of them." "I worry . . ." She didn't know the correct words in either Spanish or

English. "I feel they are not quite right." She cried harder on the old woman's shoulder. The baby would come at the end of summer when the twins were a little past their third birthday.

Charlie was pleased. Three or maybe four Bennington Brothers were better than two he reasoned. Some how Asa thought the twins would never share. They were too close to one another. The subject of again enlarging the house was discussed. They had just settled into the house after the last renovation. Another set of twins would make it necessary. That was when Asa decided to build himself a stone cottage on the site of the old cabin. The growing family needed their home to themselves and he needed peace and quiet. Was he getting old? The twins were never quiet. Charlie saw to that.

Chapter Fourteen

The Stone Cottage

There was a stonemason in Silver Bend. Mr. Bettini had a good reputation for his work. Asa could see why when he approached Bettini home. The rockwork on the house and the wall surrounding the house was beautiful. Mr. Bettini answered the door himself. He was about Asa's age, short, squat, well muscled and stooped over from working with heavy rock and stone all his life.

A man from the old country, he offered Asa wine. Asa declined the wine but accepted coffee. Apparently there was no Mrs. Bettini. When manners permitted Asa explained that he was living with his son and his son's growing family and he needed and wanted a space of his own. Asa did not understand why Bettini was laughing when Asa finished outlining his wishes.

Bettini walked to a window, threw back the heavy curtain and pointed to the large house next door. "My daughter, her husband, his mother and all the bambinos. That is why this is my house. I understand your needs completely." Before Asa left the two men were calling each other by their first names. Ed Bettini promised to come in the spring with plans and tools. Asa was to locate river stone and haul in as much as possible before the snows. Asa assured Ed he knew where there was slate for the floor. They would need concrete. Ed would order it and bring it in the spring. Asa had also learned that Ed liked to fish. As they said their good-byes each man thought he just might have a new friend.

"You think my father has gone crazy, bringing all that damn rock onto the place?" said Charlie. Margarita shook her head no. She understood his father's need for quiet even if Charlie didn't. There was none in this house except

107

when the boys slept or she would bring down her old guitar from the top shelf where she kept it well out of the reach of the twins. When she sang, the boys were spell bound. Christmas was not far off, and she wanted to be able to sing Christmas songs. The music only lasted till Charlie felt it was time to wrestle on the living room floor.

Margarita felt she had much to be thankful for this Christmas. This pregnancy was so much different than the first. Not much sickness in the morning, and she was hardly showing which is why she was able to hold the guitar comfortably and the boys when they would allow her. On her last visit in the fall, Tia Rosa promised to come for the birth. Charlie complained about having to pay her. Margarita informed him, "She is coming as a friend." Charlie just grunted but didn't comment.

Christmas that year was most likely the best ever at the ranch. Margarita had learned to cook over the last few years. The holiday dinner was better than ever. Even Charlie was impressed. Margarita was not surprised when Charlie's gifts to the boys were small bows and arrows with sharp points. He was disappointed when the neither twin had the coordination to shoot their new toys. Asa gave them storybooks. They were not interested even in the pictures. They tried to use the books as targets after Margarita refused to let them shoot at household items. When Charlie wasn't looking Grand Papa Asa blunted the arrow tips.

The boys had been a handful their second year throwing temper tantrums only Charlie could stop by walking them up and down the porch or in decent weather taking them to the barn to pet the horses. Margarita was certain she was not going to have another set of twins and maybe one more child would not be too hard. Everyone wanted spring to hurry.

Margarita wanted this baby to come and Grand Papa Asa wanted Ed Bettini to come and start work on the small house. To that end Asa began hauling rock as soon as the mud allowed the wagon to move. It was the ranch foreman that found Asa gasping for breath and holding onto the wagon for support while he worked at unloading rocks. Once Asa could speak he said, "You don't tell anyone what you just saw."

"Yes, sir," the foreman promised. Asa was well liked and respected by the hands, and it was not long till one at a time each hand just happen to have a few free hours to help the captain with his rock project. Charlie thought it was a good idea not, because he ever heard about Asa's breathing problems but because it allowed him more freedom to run the ranch they way he saw it.

One thing Charlie was going to do without consulting his father was to run off some squatters that had built a small house and some pens on the ranch's southern boundary. Charlie had warned them once. One of these nights they just might have a fire.

Ed Bettini arrived just as he said he would with plans, tools, concrete, and a fishing pole. He was gracious to Margarita, looked at her belly and the twins and decided he needed to build as quickly as possible for his new friend. The plan he showed Asa was not much different from his own house. It was a square containing a big room for daytime use, a sleeping alcove and a small area with a door. "Future toilet area," he declared. "Indoor plumbing is here to stay." That made Asa chuckle. Ed also planned a private entrance opening onto an outdoor sitting area. It would face the creek and the mountains. "It would be shaded by an arbor," he explained to Asa.

"A small patio," exclaimed Margarita when she saw the plans. If they ever did have to change the house again she would think about a patio, even maybe a fountain like the ones she remembered from her childhood.

The foundation was built and while the concrete set Asa took Ed up into the Sandies. That is what Asa and Charlie called the sandstone box canyons in the northwest corner of the ranch. They fished for the big trout in the two hidden pools only Asa and Charlie knew about. When Ed mentioned seeing the burned out buildings along the ranch's southern side Asa thought he would have ask Charlie. It was news to him.

Retuning a few days later, Asa saw Tia Rosa's buggy in the yard. Surely the baby hadn't arrived yet. The baby had not come, but it was near enough to her time and Margarita was glad for the companionship and the help. Rosa cautioned, "Second baby always come faster." Charlie felt crowded. Asa and Ed slept on the porch or down at the building site and Rosa was back in Asa's bedroom. Two hands quit because they did not like nesters, but they didn't like burning them out either. He knew the other men were not happy about his late night actions.

As the cottage grew upward, Margarita expanded outward and her irritation with Charlie increased over all. In a fit he announced, "I am taking Peter and Paul camping." He knew it would anger Margarita and she would ask him not to go. He liked the thought of that. After all he thought, all she was doing was having another baby.

Instead she said, "Good" and began telling him all the things he should pack. By the time, he was ready to leave he was well ticked off. He had to take a wagon, because the boys were not big enough to ride by themselves for a long distance. Inspecting the Christmas bows and arrows, he wondered just what the boys had been using the arrows for. The points were very dull.

With Charlie, Peter, and Paul gone, the ranch house was pleasant. Rosa was doing most of the cooking. Often Ed showed up in the kitchen to help with dinner. After supper, the four of them would sit on the porch and Margarita would play her guitar and sing. Ed would join her. They often knew the same songs but not always in the same language. One evening Ed invited Rosa to come look at the progress on the cottage. When Asa started to go with them, Margarita caught his eye and shook her head no. He sat back down. After they were gone Margarita said, "Papa, I do believe your Mr. Bettini has a sweet eye for my Tia Rosa."

"Damn!" said Papa Asa sounding just like Charlie.

Chapter Fifteen

The Second Catherine

The baby came before Charlie returned which was all right with Margarita and Rosa. Margarita was hanging wet wash on the line when Ed saw her slump to the ground. It took both Asa and Ed to carry her into the house and into the bedroom. Rosa took over from there. Neither Ed nor Asa wanted to go back to building. They sat on the porch in comfortable silence. It did not take long. They heard the healthy squall of a new baby. Ed turned to Asa and shook his hand "The little one is here, a perfect baby girl. Mr. Bennington, your daughter wants to see you," announced a smiling Tia Rosa. The minute Asa entered the house Rosa gave Ed a big hug. It seemed right so he hugged her back.

In the bedroom Margarita shared with his son, Asa looked at his daughter-in-law. She was flushed but pretty; not pale and worn like after the birth of the Peter and Paul. The new baby's tiny pink face peeped out at him from the mound of blankets beside her mother. The baby had a full head of black hair, Margarita's beautiful hair he hoped. "Papa Asa, since my husband is not here, I would like you to name this sweet baby girl, please," she added the please because she did not want to sound like she was ordering him to pick a name.

He knew Blue Feather would not do for a name, so without a second thought he said, "Catherine, I would be pleased if you would name her Catherine." Margarita agreed. Asa held up his hand and left the room. When he returned he offered Margarita a beautiful baby quilt. "My Catherine made it. She taught me that quilts have names, but I don't remember the name of this one." was all he said. It was Catherine's Double Nine Patch. Catherine Rose Bennington was already entered into the family Bible and was three days old before her weary, tired and exasperated father came dragging in with her dirty big brothers.

Only Peter and Paul had enjoyed the first Bennington family camping trip. It never occurred to Charlie that he didn't have anything to say about this baby's name either.

Just as before, Rosa stayed a while to help. She was no nonsense with Peter and Paul and they didn't like it. Their pa was much more fun. He didn't make up so many rules. Charlie was a little afraid of his tiny pink black-haired daughter. Girls and women in general were fragile in his opinion. He was pleased she was healthy and happy that his wife was no longer pregnant. Secretly he congratulated himself on not having to change the long-range plans for Peter and Paul and the ranch's future. A girl did not enter into ranch business at all.

Asa thought that Ed seemed to be building at a slower rate until Rosa departed for home. Suddenly the work rate increased, and Asa suspected Ed might have courting on his mind. Ed even declined to go fishing. The charming cottage was finished by early fall. Before Ed left, he produced a bottle of wine, a small bag of salt and apologized for not having any bread, explaining in his country this was the way of welcoming people to their new home. Ed Bettini thought once he was home he might take a little gift of vino and visit the Widow Potts.

As soon as possible Charlie helped Asa move into the new quarters, bed, books, coffee pot, and a rocking chair on the patio. Margarita insisted Asa take his meals with the family. Peter and Paul moved into Asa's old room. As far as Charlie was concerned not much had improved. There was still a baby in the bedroom. He was not quite thirty years old, and some times he felt older than his father. Well, that was not quit true. Asa did look old to Charlie, but he seemed healthy enough for his age. The year was 1894 and Asa was fifty-one. The rumors of an Ohio Anti-saloon League were in the newspapers. The Great Northern Railroad between the Mississippi and the Pacific Coast had been completed the year before. The country was going to need beef.

Catherine Rose was a sweet, quiet baby. She did have her mother's beautiful blue-black hair. People, especially her grand papa Asa, were surprised at her bright blue eyes. Since he only looked in the mirror when he shaved, he didn't see the baby's eyes were his own eyes. Charlie didn't pay any attention. That summer Peter and Paul were five and Catherine had just turned one, the whole family along with the newly married Ed Bettini and Tia Rosa Potts Bettini went camping. It was a wonderful week. Grand Papa Asa was happy for his friend and content with his own life. Little Catherine was his joy. In her little world, Grand Papa Asa was the center followed by her mother and her father. The noisy brothers didn't count.

Charlie more or less ignored his daughter and took Peter and Paul everywhere with him. He reluctantly agreed they would have to attend school when the time came if only because they would inherit the ranch some day. Just once Margarita had taken them shopping with her. They had been so disruptive she never took them again. If they went to town, it was with their pa or Papa Asa.

Asa preferred Catherine to the boys and she turned to her grand papa and her mother in the almost absence of her father. It seemed a good life for everyone. When the twins turned six, Charlie bought them each a horse. This time he selected smaller sized horses, and the boys began to ride. Margarita didn't complain. In fact she commented to her husband, "The boys look good on those horses."

"Of course, they would look good. They were Benningtons weren't they?" Asa watched. The boys would not be good riders he thought. For whatever reason, these horses and most other ranch animals were not at ease around the boys. Well, they were wild and noisy but they were boys as Charlie was quick to remind everyone.

1896 was a big year. Everyone was talking about the Klondike Gold Rush and Margarita found she was pregnant again. "I don't want another baby," she told Rosa. "Baby Catherine is a sweet baby, but the truth is the twins are hellions. Unless Charlie changes his thinking they will only get worse." Rosa believed Margarita spoke the truth.

This baby would come in the late winter. Most likely, Rosa would not be able to reach the ranch because of the winter roads. Margarita was not worried and now a days she was to busy to feel really lonely. With little Catherine to keep her company, it was not quite as bad as the first years.

Her father-in-law was a great help. On hot days he often took Catherine down to his patio where it was shaded and cool. Catherine liked to be read to. She sat quietly in his lap. Even after the book slid to the floor and Asa' head sagged on his chest she sat quietly for some time. Margarita was alarmed when she saw Catherine toddling toward the big house, alone. Asa James Bennington, Grand Papa Bennington, was dead. They buried him next to Charlie Lamb and next to the Markers for Blue Feather and Small Leaf.

Losing his father changed Charlie for a while. He sought Margarita's company just because he needed her comfort. His attitude toward Peter and Paul confused the boys. He had turned into a father instead of a playmate. The boys discussed it as much as six year olds could. "I want the other pa back," whined Paul.

"I think Grand Papa made all this happen. He shouldn't have gone away," was Peter's explanation and Paul agreed. "Baby sister cries too much," added Paul.

They were right. Catherine could not understand why her papa was no longer in her little life. When the weather permitted, Charlie or Margarita would walk her down to the empty, cold cottage hoping she would understand there was no longer a Papa. She sobbed for long periods of time and clung to Margarita while she did. If Catherine was not clinging to her mother she was following her from room to room, never letting her out of her sight. It was turning into a long, sad winter. The new baby, spring and warm weather couldn't come soon enough for all of them.

Chapter Sixteen

Harlan

This pregnancy didn't seem that much different than when she was carrying Catherine. Therefore, Margarita knew she had only a month to go. She was putting clean linen on her bed. Catherine was trying to help. She had just picked up Catherine when a pain ripped through her belly. She eased her daughter onto the floor and fell beside the frightened three year old. "Charlie! Charlie!" She called. He and his boys were in the barn and couldn't hear her.

Catherine backed into the corner of the room as tight as she could and watched. Margarita knew the baby was coming. It was to soon. She pulled up her skirts and petticoat. She managed to remove her undergarments just as a flush of blood and water issued from her body. Margarita pulled the fresh bedding onto the floor beside her. There was no getting onto the bed.

The baby came . . . a small, red, wrinkled boy. The cord was a problem. She chewed it apart just as she had heard about other mothers having to do. Her face was smeared with blood. She smacked the baby on his small behind. No sound. She smacked him again this time harder. He cried. It was a pathetic cry, but it lasted. He breathed. She covered herself in her skirts and wrapped the baby in a bed blanket as best she could. The last thing she saw before she fainted was her horrified little daughter crouched in the corner.

It was time for lunch. Charlie was retuning to his old self. The boys were relieved. Pa the playmate had returned. They had a wonderful snowball fight all the way from the barn to the house.

Knocking the snow off each other, Charlie and his sons entered the kitchen expecting to be greeted with warmth and the aroma of stew and corn bread or biscuits and beans. The kitchen was cold. The fire was out. The room was empty. Going through the house he stopped so suddenly in the door to his bedroom that the twins bumped into him. They thought it was just another game and shoved back as hard as they could. He thumped them both on their heads and said, "Stop!" His action startled them. They did stop and at the same time they saw their mother on the floor in a pool of blood and something that looked like another baby almost.

Charlie moved into the room. The twins followed him. Picking up the baby, Charlie was alarmed at his color. The little thing was breathing. Placing the baby on the bed, he turned his attention to Margarita. She was conscious but not really aware of her surroundings. He carefully moved her onto the bed and covered her. In all their married years, he had never used terms of endearment . . . no honey . . . no dear . . . no sweetness so when he said, "Darlin" for the first time, she thought she heard him say "Harlan." If he wanted to name this baby Harlan, that was fine with her.

Charlie heard what he thought sounded like a kitten. It was not the new baby. He turned just in time to see Catherine launch herself out of her corner in his direction. He caught her. She wrapped her little legs around his middle. She buried her face in his neck. She held tight with her arms. She made no sound, but he could feel tears inside his shirt collar. He tried to put her on the bed, but she held on tighter.

Turing away from the bed and moving toward the door she relaxed a little and he was able to pry her away from his body. To the twin's surprise, Charlie placed their little sister firmly between them and ordered, "Take care of your little sister." Over her head, the boys exchanged looks. They each took one of her hands, gently guided her into the living room where they helped her onto the settee. They sat beside her and waited.

Charlie cleaned up Margarita a best he could then began cleaning the floor beside the bed. She smiled weakly at him. He started a fire in the fireplace. Peter, Catherine, and Paul were shocked when he shoved the folded up bedroom rug onto the blaze. It smelled bad but gave off heat. They were cold. He made dinner. He checked on his wife. The baby was nursing but still seemed gray in color. When Charlie finally sat with the children, he told them they had a new baby brother. "His name is Harlan. He is not well."

"And Mama?" asked Paul.

"I think she will be fine." Charlie was not entirely sure. He felt bad about every ill thought he ever had about Tia Rosa. The children did not want to go to bed. To give them something to think about, he made a special effort to write the new baby's name in the family Bible. He told them they were witnesses and that made them important. Charlie only entered the name Harlan. He did not give the baby a middle name because he didn't expect the baby to live through the night. Harlan Bennington did live but never did receive a middle name.

Bedtime was difficult. Charlie didn't know what to do. The new baby's cradle was not ready. Catherine still clung to him whenever possible. He resorted to calling bedtime a game . . . an indoor camping trip. The twins drug their bedding in from their room. Charlie brought Catherine's blankets in from her little bed. He arranged all the bedding including some blankets and a pillow for himself on the floor by the fireplace. They settled in. The children were asleep in minutes. The floor was so damn hard he couldn't sleep. He could hear the sounds of life from the bedroom. In the morning, Margarita was lucid and the baby was an almost normal color but so small.

In the spring, Ed and Rosa Bettini arrived at the ranch driving a wagon containing a heavy load. In the back were four beautifully, carved granite head stones. On Charlie Lamb's, Ed had done a beautiful rendition of the Double B underneath which was carved Charlie's death date. On the head stone for Blue Feather he had carved a feather design and on Small Leaf's he had chosen leaves along with the death dates. Asa's stone was the most elaborate. It read: "Asa James Bennington, Husband, Father, and Friend, 1896." Charlie was suddenly deeply sorry he had never taken time to learn more about his father. His grief surprised him.

Rosa was pleased with Margarita's health after she heard the story of Harlan's birth. He was still small but seem normal in every other respect. It was Catherine Rose that worried her. The little girl seemed to not want to have anything to do with Margarita. Catherine even shied away from Rosa. Margarita told Rosa, "Catherine saw every thing, the whole birth." The two worried women watched Catherine.

Ed was trying to make Charlie understand how a second story could be added to the house. Catherine stood so close to her father he could not make a move without being fearful he might step on her. Charlie wanted Harlan out of the bedroom and he didn't think it was proper to have Catherine sleeping in with the boys, at least not much longer. In other ways, the boys were beginning to present problems.

Chapter Seventeen

Ezra Slater

Last year Charlie had insisted the twins start school. The boys hadn't liked the idea in the least bit to start with. Because it was such a long ride to town, one of the hands had to take the boys in, wait all day and bring them home. It was considered easy duty till Peter informed his father the responsible hand was spending the day in the saloon. Peter embellished the story quit a bit. Charlie didn't bother to check but fired the man on the spot. This was not the first time the boys had gotten one of the hired help into trouble. Paul related to Peter, "Pa cussed him out real good. Told him to pack his damn gear and be the hell off the ranch before dinner."

"Never liked the ass, anyway." This was a game they like to play with each other. They hung around the bunkhouse as much as they could. They savored every word of profanity they heard but they only used it on each other. They didn't know the meaning of some of the words, but they liked the reaction from the rough, hearty men when the words were used. Words about woman and making babies were especially good.

Their ability to swear was one of many things that got them into trouble at school. The two boys were only eight, but they were older in behavior. They were leaders but in all the wrong things. They gave the teacher a terrible time by refusing to answer when called upon saying the teacher had the wrong twin. The other students thought it was quiet funny. If that were not enough, Paul and his brother insisted on wearing their hair long in what they thought made them look more like an Indian.

Despite Margarita's pleas, they insisted on wearing buckskins rather than normal pants and shirts. Charlie as usual didn't back her up on this issue.

118

Each boy liked to carry a knife like his father used which was not the usual small pocketknife carried by some of the older boys. The teacher and several parents complained to the school board. They did not want the Bennington Brothers attending school. Charley was pissed but what did it really matter when his sons missed half the year because of the weather?

All this and more was over heard by Ezra Slater in the general store as Charlie talked to the sheriff about the poor quality of schoolteachers and the ass holes on the school board.

Ezra approached Charlie, "Excuse me sir, might I have a word with you? I might have a solution to the problem I couldn't help but over hear you discussing."

Charlie nodded. The man was a stranger but looked familiar. Charlie decided the man seemed familiar because he looked almost like President Abraham Lincoln because of his stovepipe hat. Charlie never paid any attention to men's fashions, but he did know that men didn't wear that kind of hat anymore.

"Ezra Slater, sir, at your service. I am a schoolteacher, recently from Mason, Missouri." I had to come west for my health and had hoped to find a teaching position in this fine country of yours." Except for the part about being a schoolteacher, the whole thing was a lie. He had fled a small Nebraska town when he was caught diddling one of the young girls he was supposed to be teaching. Well, he had been teaching her, hadn't he?"

The only reason Slater made good his escape was because the angry father spooked his own horse and was thrown, breaking his leg. Slater needed a place to lay low for the winter and a ranch that was more or less snowed in seemed perfect. "Perhaps for room and board and a small remuneration at the end of the school year I might offer my services as a tutor. I, of course, would be happy to teach any other children you might have." Ezra waited.

"What the hell was a remuneration?" thought Charlie. The offer of a tutor was the answer to his dilemma about Peter and Paul's education. Catherine was a girl and to little any way. The matter was settled.

When Charlie introduced the twins to Mr. Slater. He was pleased at how they conducted themselves. Mr. Slater offered his hand to each of them and in turn they shook the offered hand just as Charlie had taught them to do. Each one knew exactly what his brother was thinking about the new tutor, "Bastard."

Mr. Slater smiled politely and thought, "Little bastards."

Charlie directed the boys to start moving items out of the cottage so that Mr. Slater could move in and start setting up his class space. "Sure Pa," they answered in unison. They had no intention in helping. They were going to their secret place in the barn and talk over the new tutor. As they walked away they heard Slater say to their father, "Mr. Bennington in the interest of leaning, I do not believe in sparing the child and spoiling the student. I do often find it necessary, especially with young boys to rap knuckles upon occasion."

"Mr. Slater, I want my boys to learn. Do whatever you feel will result in that. They are the future of the Bennington Ranch." Both Peter and Paul heard the conversation as Mr. Slater had intended. For the first time, the brothers thought how much they disliked the ranch and what they saw as their future on the ranch.

Safely in the barn and out of anyone hearing them, or so they thought, they used ever profane word they knew to describe Mr. Slater. They felt a whole lot better. However, they were not a lone. One cowboy, sent to fetch something, hid from the Bennington brats and listened in amazement. Not because of the profanity but because the boys were perfect mimics. With every swear word, the listening cowboy could tell which cowhand had taught the boys that particular word or phrase. "I tell you it gave me the willies." was what the cowboy said to his boss when he reported what he had heard. "Those brats are spooky," he concluded.

"Better not call them brats. You know how Mr. Bennington sets store by those kids," warned the range boss. They both knew how many men had been given their pay and dismissed because of something the twins said.

Mr. Slater knew he had the brothers figured out and he would always be one-step ahead of them when it came to advising Mr. Bennington about things and those things would always be offered as in the best interest of the boys' future. He wasn't worried. It was going to be a safe and comfortable winter.

Mrs. Bennington was Mexican. Probably she had been pretty at one time. Now she was just another round woman with a baby hanging on her tit. Even if he had any interest in her, he knew from the looks she gave him he didn't have a chance with her. It was the daughter that did interest him. He guessed she was four or maybe five. In another year or maybe two, she would be a sweet plum and ready to pick. Not for him, Oh no. Twice now he had stolen little girls and sold them. This one with her big, blue eyes and her fine, silky black hair would fetch a good price. He knew just where to go to make such a sale. He would bide his time and try to curb his impure thoughts.

Slater was as good as his word. The boys received so many raps on their knuckles as to draw blood. No matter how Peter or Paul or both of them tried to cast Slater in a bad light, Slater always seemed to be ahead of them when it came to talking to their father. The twins and Slater were sneaky, clever, and slippery about having their way. It was just that Slater had years of experience on the boys. The boys were learning school lessons in spite of themselves.

Catherine made it easy for Slater to watch her. She wanted to do everything her big brothers did so she asked to go to school with them. "Oh, Charlie, what's the harm in it? At least I know where she is," was Margarita's opinion. He grumbled but didn't object. Charlie was thinking about summer. The boys were going to have to start doing more around the ranch. They would be almost ten. He didn't think about Harlan except he wished Margarita would stop nursing him.

She knew she probably should but she felt he was her last child. She would miss that part of motherhood. Harlan was a quiet, almost serious child with light blue eyes and brown hair just like his father's. "Does Charlie realize that Harlan is the only one of his children that looks like him?" asked Rosa one summer afternoon. She was amused when Margarita replied, "Hell no. He doesn't even know the Harlan exists now that the child has his own room."

"What about Catherine?"

"She won't let him ignore her because she won't leave him or the boys alone."

"No," said Rosa; "I mean how is it with you and her?"

Tears welled up in Margarita's eyes, "She barely tolerates me and she says mean things. I honestly think she waits till Charlie can't hear her and she is so young to feel. I don't know what she feels." Rosa had no wise answer.

Summer was here, but Charlie was thinking ahead about schooling for the boys next year. He asked Slater if he would stay on for at least one more school year. The man was delighted and suggested he teach the boys a few classes during the summer just to get a jump on next year. From Slater's perspective, the ranch had been the perfect place to winter, to hide and to plan. One more year wouldn't hurt. When Paul and Peter hear the news they rode out and shot a couple of rabbits just to see the animals suffer. "Do you think we could shoot him too?" asked Peter.

"Naw. He doesn't trust us" Paul had thought it over just as his brother had.

Charlie told the boys they would be going up to the summer range with the herd. They were to do any and everything the range boss told them. "No back talk. No sluffing off their work onto one of the cowhands. No slipping away to swim in the lake. "I hate the ranch," Paul spit out later.

"I don't really want to be like Pa, either. Not all my life. Look how old he is. He don't have no fun," added Peter. They used poor grammar when Slater was not around. "How we going to get out of this shitty mess?"

"Don't know. We'll have to think of something." They were not able to come up with an idea and left for the summer range a week later.

Charlie was going to ride into Silver Bend, and he invited Slater to ride along. Slater didn't particularly like Charlie's company, but he needed to stay on his employer's good side so he said yes and did his best to be pleasant. In town, they went their separate ways agreeing to meet later.

When the sheriff called out to Charlie in the general store, Charlie did not know that Slater, from the next isle over, was listening to everything the sheriff had to say. "Charlie, I have something you need to see." The sheriff sounded concerned. Slater could hear paper being unfolded. "Is that the man living out on your ranch, teaching your kids?" Charlie was a big man with fast fists and a short fuse temper.

Maybe the sheriff's paper didn't deal with him, but Slater decided he didn't want to have to defend himself. Ironic he thought. He procured his job as tutor by eavesdropping right here in this same store and he was about to lose that very job after eavesdropping again.

Slater moved quietly to the front door of the store where he heard Charlie suck in his breathe. "That son of a bitchen bastard. I'll kill him!" Slater was sure the sheriff was showing Charlie a wanted poster or something similar. Whatever it was, Slater knew he needed to leave the store and town quickly. Outside he took his horse and Charlie's. Going down the first alley he came to he tied off Charlie's horse, went through the saddlebags and rode away. It would slow them down, but he wouldn't be wanted as a horse thief. Six weeks later, bug bit, saddle sore, and sun burned the twins came home to learn the tutor was gone. Maybe their summer was not so bad after all.

Chapter Eighteen

Milk

Catherine hated Thursdays. It was sewing day. Patiently, Margarita was trying to teach her needlework, embroidery. Mother and daughter sat beside each other. Now that Margarita could afford beautiful dresses she wore one as often as she could and expected Catherine to do the same. Margarita preferred the dresses with much lace and satin or velvet ribbons. The dresses and the required petticoats were hot and scratchy. Catherine hated the dresses as much as she hated the sewing lessons on Thursday. She admitted to herself that she enjoyed the Friday music lessons, but she would never let her mother know that.

Margarita was explaining again to Catherine how every young lady needed to know fine needlework. The linen piece that Catherine held in her hands was called a sampler. Beside assorted flowers and leaves, it contained the alphabet. "Stitching those cross stitch letters will help you learn your alphabet," insisted Margarita. Thanks to the now absent tutor, Catherine knew her letters but she was not about to tell her mother. Catherine stuck her finger with the needle. Another drop if blood stained the linen fabric.

"Holy shit!" she exclaimed. Margarita's mouth dropped open.

"Young lady you do not use langue like that. Do you understand?"

"Peter and Paul do all the time. Why can't I?"

"Catherine Rose you are a young lady and you will act like a young lady."

Catherine jumped up spilling the contents of the swing basket and dumping her embroidery hoop and thread on the floor.

"I won't be a young lady. I want to be like my big brothers. I hate sewing. I hate it. I hate it!" She stomped out of the room. Margarita heard the bedroom door slam and knew Catherine was pulling off the beautiful gown. She would dress in some old trousers belonging to Peter or maybe Paul. She would saddle up her little pony and disappear till dinnertime. Catherine hated sewing and cooking and table manners unless they were a means to an end. She loved the ranch as much as she loved her father. Why couldn't he see that in her? If he did, everything would be so much better.

Margarita rested her head against the hard back of the chair and closed her eyes and wondered what she was to do with this girl that wanted to be a boy. It was only last week while cleaning Catherine's room she found the baby quilt from Grandpa Asa's first wife. The quilt was neatly folded but on the floor at the back of the closet. With Asa's passing, his old trunk had been moved about and finally had ended up in Harlan's room. Margarita had never looked in it till she went to replace the quilt from Catherine's room.

Margarita examined the contents, two pewter candlesticks, one place setting of china decorated in small blue flowers and a bed-sized quilt stitched in red flowers and green leaves. Underneath it all was a torn photo. Margarita looked at the grainy picture and guessed she was looking at the first Catherine Bennington. Margarita thought about her own Catherine. She would talk to Charlie again tonight. At least he would have to tell the boys not to teach Catherine improper words.

The house was quiet. It was late and still hot. All the windows were open to catch any breeze. Charlie slept in his shorts only. Margarita wore a light shift. He could see her nipples underneath the thin fabric. He thought about just slipping in between her legs when Margarita said, "You will have to talk to Paul and Peter." He lost his urge. It seemed to him that someone was always telling him he ought to talk to his boys. Margarita related the whole sewing session episode. Charlie agreed. He would talk to Peter and Paul again.

Margarita, satisfied she could say no more, turned on her side trying to catch any cool air from the window and fell asleep. There would be no sleep for Charlie. He thought about Catherine Rose. As his wife thought earlier in the day now Charlie thought, "What to do with the girl?"

It was a month ago he found her in the stall with his big horse named Chestnut. The boys, as they so often did, had disappeared from the fence building Charlie sent them to complete. The first place Charlie searched was the barn. That's when he found Catherine asleep in the hay almost beneath the hooves of his big stallion. The horse seemed at ease. Catherine opened her eyes and smiled at her father. "Hi! Papa."

"Catherine, what are you doing in there?"

"I came down to play with Chessy. I guess I took a nap." She stood up. The horse never moved. She caressed his big shoulder and stroked his soft muzzle. Easing out of the stall, she said, "I love Chessy. Papa I want a horse, a real horse, just like Chessy!" Her birthday was coming up, and he had already arranged to buy a sweet little mare. He was pleased with his plans for her horse but not pleased that his big, fine horse was being called Chessy. Taking her hand they walked out of the barn together. Catherine was so happy she could hardly contain herself. Charlie would have been shocked to learn that twice Catherine had ridden Chessy with a little help from her big brothers.

Charlie thought he felt a little cool breeze. Maybe the bedroom would cool off some. Thinking back to the day in the barn, Charlie decided that perhaps Catherine had "the Gift" as people called it. Every animal on the place responded to her. He knew his pa had a way with animals. He didn't and the twins certainly didn't. "Why a girl?" he wondered. He finally fell asleep, thinking about Catherine's up and coming birthday party and the fine little mare. He might even have Margarita put some ribbons on the halter.

Next morning he did talk to the twins. They did not tell a fib when they promised not to teach their little sister any more swear words. They had already taught her every word they knew. When their pa asked them did they know that Catherine was going in the barn and "Playing with Chessy," as she put it. They both shook their heads no and looked Charlie right in the eye. Sometimes, Charlie suspected the twin's version of the truth was not the real truth.

The birthday party was planned for Sunday. Ed and Rosa Bettini were invited. The family would sit in the shade of the new arbor on the new stone patio. Margarita has baked big sugar cookies to go with the cold lemonade. Much to Catherine's disgust her mother insisted on a new birthday dress . . . pink taffeta with ruffles and lace that tickled. Despite what her mother kept saying she didn't feel like a lady or a big girl. She felt stupid, especially when Margarita finished her hair with pink ribbons. "Oh well," she thought. "Her papa was going to give her a horse. She knew just which horse she would select when he asked her to pick one from the ranch ramuda. All this frou frou stuff was worth it."

The boys couldn't eat enough cookies. The adults enjoyed the cool lemonade. Catherine thought they would never get to the presents. She fidgeted and picked at the lace around her sleeves. Aunt Rosa and Uncle Ed, as they were now called, gave her nice leather gloves, a littlie fussy but they would work for riding. That pleased her. Paul and Peter gave her a rabbit skin muff they had probably made themselves. It didn't smell very nice. From Baby Harlan there was soap that smelled like violets or so the box said. It smelled okay she thought, knowing full well her mother had selected it. It was time. Only one gift remained. Her father was smiling down at her. He pointed to the side of the patio. She saw one of the ranch hands holding a small brown horse bedecked in pink ribbons. She looked at her father. His grin was even bigger than before.

"Noooooo!" she wailed. Later the ranch hand would report to the other men, "He never seen a girl pitch such a fit." Catherine threw her cookie on the ground.

"I want Milk, I want Milk," she cried. She was stomping her little feet. She tried to pull the ribbons from her hair, but they were braded in too tightly. She was crying. She was crushing the cookies into the slate floor. The adults looked at one another. Why would a child ask for milk when she had just consumed several cookies and a large glass of lemonade? Charlie glared at Margarita. Margarita shrugged her shoulders. Harlan began to cry. Charlie frowned at the normally quiet boy. Catherine continued to sob.

"Pa, Pa," the twins were trying to get Charlie's attention.
"What!" he snapped.
"Milk is the name she gave that big white mare, the one down in the ramuda. She likes that white horse because he is big like Chessy. Pa, that's the horse she wants! Not some dumb little horsy," Peter added under his breath. The twins knew she would outride them in a year or so. She would now if she just wasn't a still-growing-up girl.

Charlie picked up his dishevled, red in the face daughter and with Ed and the twins walked down to where the horse of choice was penned. Later when they all came back all he said to Margarita was "Damn, that girl can ride!" The birthday girl was smiling from ear to ear. Her beautiful pink party dress was torn and spattered with mud. The ribbons were gone from her hair.

After tucking in Harlan, Margarita put the ruined dress in her father-in-law's trunk. It seemed to her the trunk contained items from events that didn't happen or went wrong. Over the years yet to come, the young Bennington daughter with the long black hair riding the big white horse she named Milk would become a common sight in and around Silver Bend. Town women commented, "What could you expect?"

With summer still in full force, Catherine asked to go everywhere the boys went. Since most of the time her father said no, Margarita wondered where her daughter disappeared to. If Catherine wasn't riding all over the ranch, she was talking the older hands into teaching her to rope. She could throw a decent loop when she really tried. They refused to help her learn to bulldog. She wanted to shoot a gun. They definitely said no to that request.

Long ago Margarita accepted the fact she had lost her sons, not that she didn't love them. She felt Catherine was going the same way. Harlan was almost three and the light of her life. She located all the storybooks from the other children and showed them to Harlan. "Book," she said several times.

"Book," said Harlan right back to her. He had refused to talk for such a long time she and Charlie just assumed he was not normal due to his early birth and he would never talk. Charlie would be pleased to learn his youngest was not mute. She hugged Harlan so tight he complained.

She spent the rest of the afternoon repeating, "Hi, Papa." He did it well. That evening, after the twins and Catherine had disappeared as usual, Margarita asked Charlie, "Lay aside your newspaper. Harlan has something to say." That remark did make Charlie put down the paper. The youngster had not ever uttered a word. "Say hi, papa," instructed Margarita.

Harlan knew who Papa was. Harlan's blue eyes focused directly on his father. Very clearly he said, "Hi, Papa."

Charlie laughed loudly and crowed, "Hells bells!"

Harlan repeated what he had just heard. "Hells bells."

"Well, I'll be damned." Margarita placed a finger gently on Harlan's lips. Harlan would talk nonstop after that. He remember everything anyone said and often managed to bring it up at inopportune times.

"Can't say anything around little brother," commented Peter to Paul.
"Yeah, guess we shouldn't have told him it was okay to piss in Mama's flower bed."

Chapter Nineteen

Schooling

As far as Charlie was concerned, Catherine didn't need to go to school. She should be learning to cook and keep house, maybe even some healing. Yes, it was good she could ride a horse and drive a wagon, take care of chickens, help with the garden when they could get her to do it, but there was no need for book learning. She needed to know how to be a wife. Charlie and Margarita had had the same conversation several times. Catherine was already two years behind some of the other youngsters her age so Margarita tried again.

"Charlie, what if she doesn't marry? You want her living at home cause she can't make her way in the world?" Margarita's argument won the day and Catherine was allowed to attend school until, as usual, the snows set in. This year the snows were light. Charlie had managed to acquire twenty acres on the south end of the ranch, which meant they could ride on Bennington land from the ranch house to a ways just outside of town. This allowed Catherine to attend more school time than Peter and Paul ever had.

How Charlie managed to buy up those twenty acres and just why the owners decided to sell was often a matter of speculation for the gossips in town. No one thought it wise to ask. Charlie felt safe in letting Catherine ride alone to and from school and she only missed attending when the snow was really deep. At the end of the school year, comments from Catherine's teacher were all good. The teacher's only suggestion was that his daughter needed to attend full time if he expected her to go on to higher education. "Higher education, my ass," was Charlie's comment.

With no school for the summer, Catherine asked to be allowed to work on the ranch more. "I want to learn to do everything you do Papa," she would plead. She rode much better than either Peter or Paul, she followed directions and she wanted to know everything. Charlie was very reluctant. She was a girl and beginning to show signs of turning into a young woman. She didn't belong in with a bunch of men. She nagged so much that Charlie relented at least for some ranch work.

Charlie even agreed to teach her to shoot. "Well," he thought. "This is schooling of a sort. Besides all the ranchers in the valley were having trouble with rustlers this year. It wouldn't hurt if she could use a gun, a rifle. Besides she knew the ranch as well as anyone. He wouldn't want her to surprise some no-good while they tried to make off with a few head of Bennington cattle."

For the boys, a different kind of schooling came during this summer when they saw their first naked female. Sure they had seen pictures but seeing one for real would be something else. It took away the excitement of the whole thing, because the woman was a young-not-yet-a-woman girl, their own sister. The brothers and their sister had the day to themselves. "I'll race you to the lake," was all Catherine had to say and the three were off. The lake was a few hours away at a normal trot, but Catherine and her brothers reached it in half that time. Margarita saw them ride away in a cloud of dust. She went back to trying to teach Harlan to count. He was probably the brightest of all four children. As usual Charlie didn't notice.

Peter and Paul were right behind Catherine when they arrived at the favorite swimming spot. She dropped Milk's reins and dismounted. Right in front of her brothers she shucked off all her duds. There was no modesty in her. She looked up and smiled, faced her brothers full on, waved them toward the water and splashed in. For probably the first time in their young adult life, the twins were without words. Finally Peter said, "Damn," sounding just like their father.

"Damn, is right and we can't tell Pa."

"We are going to have to tell her she can't be doing that. Not in front of us. Not in front of anybody." They thought about the whole turn of events as Catherine swam gracefully in the cooling water. It wasn't often she could pull one over on her brothers, but she had this time. It had been hard but worth it.

"You know, she was kinda cute," mused Paul.

"Shut your mouth," Peter said. "You know why the wranglers like to ride behind Catherine?"

"Yeah, I guess I do now. She has a nice little butt and tight pants," offered Paul.

"She's just a little girl."

"Not for long, brother. Not for long. From now on out we ride behind her." Catherine wondered what her brothers were talking about. The wranglers would find out soon enough.

For Charlie, the summer's good news came in the mail. A fat packet containing a large number of bills and a letter stating one Ezra Slater had been found guilty of horse theft and hanged two months ago in Dead Horse, New Mexico. Among Slater's few personal possessions was the enclosed money in an envelope with the Bennington Ranch name written on it. Charlie recognized the money as the bank deposit Slater had stolen from his saddlebag the day Slater high-tailed it out of town. "Hope he rots in hell," was Charlie's comment to the sheriff.

Margarita worked with Harlan every day, spelling, arithmetic, grammar, and table manners anything she could think of. She wished she knew more so she could teach him more. He seemed to absorb it all. He should have started school last year. Charlie had said no. Harlan was too little. Harlan loved the small brown mare that Catherine loudly refused on her birthday. He didn't much like to ride out of the yard, which was fine with Margarita. The old cook's helper taught him about the stars and how to determine directions. Margarita knew Harlan had to go to school, but how?

The answer turned out to be Catherine. When the school year started, Charlie said she could attend but only till the snow made it difficult. He wasn't having his daughter lost in the snow and then having to send out good cowhands to track her down. He certainly was not sending Harlan this year at all either. That he said was his final word.

The sad thing about this summer was Ed Bettini died after a short illness. Tia Rosa was now the Widow Bettini. She was well loved by the Bettini family but chose to remain in his stone house where Grand Papa Asa had first met him. The entire Bennington family drove to Silver Bend for the funeral. Even the twins wore decent funeral clothes. Margarita just wished they would cut their hair. They looked like Indians in white man's clothing. Riding their high stepping horses didn't help the image any either.

Charlie looked at his wife and daughter in the long, black dresses and big hats. They looked proper for the occasion. Margarita was no longer the slender young girl she used to be. Having children did that to a woman he guessed. She was very limited about when and how often they could have sex. She wanted no more children. Charlie still had normal desires. He looked at his daughter. Catherine was slim and loosing her child's body. Somehow Charlie had never thought about her becoming a woman, but the beginning signs were there. She could give him trouble or interested young men could give him trouble. "This was the wrong time to be think such thoughts," he decided. They were on their way to a funeral of a good friend.

The funeral was somber and as often happened when he was at a religious gathering he did not understand what was being said. Margarita was able to guide the family in the proper responses. It didn't pass Charlie's notice that while in town too much attention was given his family.

Following the service Ed's daughter had everyone over for a proper meal. The daughter's family was big and noisy even under the circumstances. Peter and Paul fascinated Ed's older granddaughters. More than once Charlie scowled at the twins. He also stopped them from pouring themselves glasses of wine. Catherine, he saw, felt awkward. She was uncomfortable with manners, but was trying her best. He knew the father was glad when they took their leave. Both Charlie and Margarita felt Rosa's sadness. "Will we feel that way when only one of us is left?" she asked Charlie. He didn't want to think about it.

Later Margarita would say to Charlie. "It seems wrong that Ed has only a wooden marker and he made such beautiful stone markers for our family."

Charlie agreed. "I will try and find a stonemason, if Tia Rosa will permit." Summer was slipping into fall before he did find such a man. Tia Rosa was so pleased she cried on Charlie's shoulder but only do so by standing on her very tiptoes. She seemed so very lonesome despite her loving family next door. The head stone would be done and placed before Christmas.

He was almost asleep when Margarita rolled over, propped up her head on her hand and said, "Charlie." When she said Charlie that way he bet he was not going to like what she was about to say. He was correct.

"Rosa said she would take both Catherine and Harlan for the winter. They would be right there in town and could go to school full time."

"No!"

"If Catherine does not learn how to behave around young men, if she does not go to dances, and dinners and such no one will even court her let alone ask her to marry . . . at least not any one you would approve of. They might of course, if they thought they could get part of the ranch," she added for good measure. Charlie knew when he was beaten because he had been thinking some of these very thoughts himself, especially the part about the ranch.

"Oh hell, send Harlan too. It might be good for Tia Rosa."

Catherine had mixed emotions about the whole thing. Her mother didn't. "Just think! You will be able to attend dances and socials. You will meet new young people your own age. It will be good for you." If her mother said that one more time Catherine thought she would scream. She would miss her horse and her freedom to ride and she supposed she would miss her older brothers. However, if she felt it ought be her, not Peter and Paul, who should help her pa run the ranch. She wanted to learn as much as she could about everything. For that reason alone, she would suffer the dresses, the manners and yes, the silly young people her mother set such store by.

Harlan was so excited he could not breath. The day following Charlie's decision, as Peter and Paul approached the yard, they could see Harlan jumping up and down. Harlan was yelling something, but they were to far away to hear. It didn't look like anything serious so they didn't hurry. "Now, what's up with the twerp?"

"Can't say. He looks happy." They considered their small brother a little strange, "Harmless but odd" was the way one of them had described Harlan.

"I'm going to school! I'm going to school!"

"Yep. He is definitely odd," they agreed when they were near enough to understand his words.

Chapter Twenty

Christmas

The day came. The wagon was loaded with travel trunks even though they were only going to Silver Bend till Christmas. Margarita had insisted they come home for Christmas and invited Tia Rosa if she wanted to come. The twins said their good-byes in the yard. Charlie had to call Catherine twice before she finally said good-bye to Milk. He told Harlan "Sit still!" Margarita went with them just for the ride. The day was what people called Indian summer. Now going home. It was just she and Charlie in the wagon. It was almost too warm to be pleasant, but she didn't mind. "Did you see all the changes in town?" she asked.

"Seems like very time I go in, there is something new."

"Did you see the photographic shop?" He suspected where this was leading.

"The photographer is a Mrs. Arleta Goodfellow. I understand she is a widow and that she does fine photographs." Charlie left out the part about her flyaway red hair and ample breasts that seemed barely constrained in the bodice of her dresses. He had only heard talk. He, himself, had not seen the woman.

"Do you think next spring we could have a family photograph taken? The children are growing up so fast." He thought Margarita sounded sad. Maybe she would change her mind about another baby. He could only hope. He really missed that part of their life.

There was not much cattle theft that year and the snows were light to start with. The boys were not always home. Charlie didn't know where they were.

Dinner table conversation was intermittent. He and Margarita didn't have that much to talk about when it was just the two of then. He missed Catherine. She at least could talk about the ranch, some. When the boys were at dinner, the conversation picked up a little. They showed more interest in fast horses and faster guns and lately they talked about automobiles. That in Charlie's opinion was just ignorant. He wondered about their good sense. He knew the first automobiles had been around since the 1880's, but everyone knew that automobiles would never replace a fine horse.

Charlie resolved to give the twins more responsibility in the coming year. He knew they would never go back to school. He would have to teach them himself as much as he could. Charlie was thinking that tonight the conversation had gone well. When he remarked, he wanted two additional branding irons. Peter said, "The weather looks reasonable for tomorrow. We could ride into Silver Bend and order them for you."

Paul added, "We can look in on Catherine and Harlan, too." Charlie could see that pleased his wife. The blacksmith knew the brand. He had made all the irons for the "Double B." Charlie's credit was good. Charlie would never know that in the minds of many town folk, "Double B" stood for Bennington Brats or Bennington Bastards depending on the nature of your run-in with the Bennington boys. At the dinner table, the next night they assured their mother that Catherine and Harlan were dong well and they and Tia Rosa were looking forward to Christmas. The irons would be ready in two weeks.

Christmas was only a few days away, and Charlie wouldn't let anyone else drive the wagon into town in the drifting snow. He brought Harlan, Catherine, and Tia Rosa and many gifts home for Christmas. As soon as Catherine could escape the house, she ran for the stable, threw a saddle on Milk, and rode off in a flurry of snow. It was a pretty picture Charlie thought . . . the white snow, the white horse and a young girl in a red coat with long black hair streaming out behind her as she raced away and out of his sight. He hoped she didn't break her neck.

Harlan had grown a foot. Margarita was sure. "What have you been feeding my boy?"

"Good Italian food," both women laughed. Catherine and Harlan and I have a surprise for you."

"What?"

"You will see tomorrow. You must clear an area in the living room tomorrow morning. Then you will see."

"Charlie, do you know what kind of surprise Rosa is planning?" Margarita asked her almost asleep husband.

After all these years, he should be used to her pillow talk questions. "No. I don't. However, whatever it is, the twins know about it. They are all planning on going out tomorrow morning . . . even Harlan."

The next morning all four children rode out together. They requested a lunch. They took extra rope and a handsaw. Margarita thought it was the first time all the brothers and their sister had ever ridden anywhere together, willingly. As usual Catherine was in the lead and Harlan brought up the rear. Charlie watched them depart and wondered, "What the hell was going on?" Tia Rosa carefully placed some twine tied boxes next to the cleared space in the living room.

In the early afternoon when children returned, Harlan was proudly in front. With the extra rope, he was pulling a downed pine tree. He jumped off his horse, ran up the porch steps. He didn't notice he threw open the door so hard it banged. "We are having a Christmas tree!!" He yelled as loudly as he could. Charlie was wise enough not to laugh.

The bigger boys trundled the tree down to the barn. Somewhere they found lumber pieces and nailed a stand on the cut bottom of the trunk. In the living room, the tree stood crooked but nobody cared. Rosa began to open the mysterious boxes. She presented round glass "ornaments" as she called them, golden garland, fancy birds made with real feathers and to Charlie's horror real, store bought candles. He could not believe they actually planned to place burning candles on a pine tree in the house. "That's what you do with a Christmas tree," stated Catherine as if her father was a dunce. From the light on their faces, he understood it was six against one and he was the one. Later he would bring in a bucket of water just incase. Before the evening was over, fancy wrapped parcels began to appear under the tree. The biggest one was for him from the twins.

Margarita outdid herself in food and treats. It was Christmas Eve. The candles on their first ever Christmas tree had been carefully extinguished. He and Margarita were not yet in bed. "I feel bad. I didn't think about the tree or consider gifts. I don't have any to give," he said as he watched her brush her hair in preparation for bed.

"Yes. You do. Look under the bed." Under his side of the bed were gifts for everyone from him.

"Well, Damn!" All his life he seemed to say that about one thing or another.

He took his gifts out to the tree and placed them in the back of all the rest.

He didn't really want to go to bed quite yet. He poured himself a small whiskey. Charlie was not one to be sentimental but tonight he stood on the porch and looked into the night sky at the pinpoint stars. He thought about his life. The ranch and the ones belonging to his neighbors were doing well. Margarita was a perfect wife, especially for him he had decided. The twins were healthy. Hopefully they would grow out of their wildness and take their expected place as owners of the ranch. It had a great future and with the right management would do even better. As for Catherine? Well, that was another matter. Five months of town living had only polished the outside. He knew that when he saw her riding with her brothers. Harlan was the surprise. Taller, still quiet and serious, but he often had relevant comments to add to the table conversation. Often Peter, Paul, and Catherine looked at their baby brother as if he belonged to another family. The teachers said he was the best and brightest student they had ever taught. Even now when Harlan did speak up, it was as if he was an adult. Suddenly Charlie missed his father. "Merry Christmas, Pa, wherever you are."

The family opened gifts the next morning. Now the only gift left was the big long box to him from the twins. They had impish grins on both their faces. Everyone was curious so Charlie suspected the gift was going to be a surprise to all of them. He removed the string and the paper. He was looking at a gun case. He undid the clasps, opened the lid and stared in complete amazement. For once he didn't even say damn. Paul and Peter grinned at each other. Charlie knew full well what he was looking at, an 1874 .45-70 Sharps Rifle. It had a beautiful walnut-checkered stock and German silver cap accents. Charlie knew it was considered one of the finest firearms ever manufactured. Before he could say thank you, Harlan said, "You can shoot it in the celebration competition!" The twins nodded in agreement.

"What celebration? What competition?"

Even Catherine knew. "For Independence Day. Silver Bend is going to have its first annual Independence Day celebration. There is a committee. They are making plans now," she explained.

Harlan went on, "There is going to be pie eating and horseshoes and shooting contests and fire works and roast beef and even a roast pig . . . just everything," he concluded. "July 4" he added just incase no one remembered the date of Independence Day.

"Yeah Pa, a shooting contest," repeated the twins.

"Horse racing" put in Catherine but said it so quietly that only Margarita heard her.

Charlie hefted the rifle and said, "I just might do that."

Later in the day, it was just Margarita and Rosa. "I have something new to show you," announced Rosa. From her sewing basket, she pulled fabric blocks of small stitched squares. "I am learning to quilt. It is a great way to make use of scrap cloth. It makes a warm cover. Some woman even buy new fabric rather than use remnants."

"I have quilts," exclaimed Margarita.

"You do?"
"Come look." Margarita took Rosa into Harlan's room, opened Asa's old trunk and brought out the baby quilts and the bed quilt with the red flowers.

"They were stitched by Papa Asa's first wife, the first Catherine. Charlie says quilt patterns have names, but he doesn't know the names of these."

Rosa said, "You should have this big one on your bed. It is beautiful."

"I don't think so." Papa Asa never removed these from the trunk accept for the one he gave Catherine. I only discovered them when I returned Catherine's quilt to the trunk.

"You should learn to quilt. I could teach you as much as I know," suggested Rosa.

"When school is over for the summer come home with Catherine and Harlan. You can teach me then."

"I expect to come into town before school is over. We are going to have a family photograph taken. I will send money with you so that Catherine and Harlan have proper clothing. Especially Harlan, he is finally growing."

"Having your picture taken by the lady photographer in town?" inquired Rosa.

"Yes, Charlie says he has heard she has a reputation." Rosa was aware of the rumors concerning Arleta Goodfellow's reputation, but the talk was not about the photographs.

Since it was all idle gossip, Rosa said nothing more on the subject but added. "Mrs. Goodfellow has a China lady."

"What is a China lady?"

"A woman from China. I understand that she is some kind of servant."

Out in the barn, Charlie was also noticing Harlan's growth. Peter and Paul were rubbing down their horses. Charlie did not approve of the way the twins rode their mounts, but he had to admit in all other ways they took good care of the animals. "Papa, could I have a new horse? One a little bigger but not like Milk or Chessy or theirs." Harlan waved his hand in the general direction of Paul and Peter. "I want a safe horse."

"Well," thought Charlie, "That is an improvement. Do you have one in mind?" Charlie was not about to select a horse after the fit Catherine threw at her birthday party.

"No sir. You decide."

From the other side of the stall, one of the twins said, "Find a good Indian pony, Pa."

"Paul says I should find you an Indian pony."

Harlan patiently corrected his father, "That was Peter and an Indian pony would be fine. Harlan was the only one that could tell the twins apart."

Chapter Twenty-one

Arleta Goodfellow

The day for Catherine, Harlan and Rosa's return to Silver Bend dawned cold and gray. Charlie told Margarita she could not go and she was relieved. He sent Paul and Peter to check on the cattle and possible wind blown drifts. He would be coming home alone which was fine. He wanted to think. Before leaving town, he planned to talk to the photographer lady. He would make the necessary plans for a family picture. It would be a surprise for Margarita.

Inside the photography business, Charlie looked around. The room offered chairs for waiting he guessed. Black and white photos hung on the walls. He recognized the mayor and the banker and their families and many brides and grooms. Wedding pictures must be a new craze. He was surprised to see an oriental woman, Chinese possibly, behind the counter. She smiled politely. Before she could say anything Arleta Goodfellow came from behind a curtain. She dismissed the China woman, extended her hand to Charlie "Mr. Bennington, please come in. How may I be of service?" He took her hand and not knowing quite what to do with it shook it but not to hard.

"I want to have my family's picture taken." There was something to be said for her abundant red hair, her tiny waist and yes her breasts did seem strain at the dress fabric.

She pulled back the curtain and motioned him to follow her. "Come into my office, please. I need to talk to you so I might know what kind of photo you are interested in." The so-called office seemed more like a parlor to Charlie. Big soft chairs and little tea tables were complimented by interesting oriental wall hangings and thick carpets. Vases with dried flowers and soft pillows made the room very comfortable. She showed him to the biggest chair. He thought he could a smell a light fragrance. Was it her or perhaps incense?

"Tea?" He didn't want tea, but thought he should be polite. She clapped her hands. The china lady appeared. "Soo Wah, we'll take tea. Mr. Bennington will have his stronger than mine, please." The China lady left without saying a word. "Now Charles, I may call you Charles?"

"My name is Charlie, just Charlie."

"Oh posh! A man of your position should be addressed as Charles.

I will call you Charles. Now tell me about your family and the type of photo you desire." The tea arrived. The first polite sip told him what she meant when she told the China woman about his tea being stronger. It was laced with some kind of alcohol and a lot of sugar. He found himself talking about the proposed photo, his family, the ranch, and finally himself. As she listened at tentatively, she pulled out a small silver box, removed a thin black cigarette and lit it. He was fascinated. She inhaled deeply which made the fabric even tighter across the swell of her breasts. Delicately she blew the smoke toward the ceiling. It drifted down, filling the room and making Charlie a little queasy. He wanted fresh air. "Spring. I would like the photo taken in the spring. I will bring my wife and my oldest sons. The other two children are in town till school lets out." Arleta rose gracefully to her feet and showed him the way out. He thought when she moved he could hear a tinny bell. Once outside he gulped at the cool air. She watched from the door. She knew a lot of things about Charlie Bennington. She planned on learning more. She watched Charlie, and the China woman watched both of them.

On the ride home, he had planned to do some thinking. The twin's Christmas gift of the fine gun bothered him. H didn't pay them or give them any money at all. So? How were they able to have such a fine gun in their possession? He would ask around before he confronted Peter and Paul if it came to that. His thoughts drifted off to Arleta Goodfellow . . . interesting woman.

Another thing he wanted to think about was Harlan, such a different child from the other three. Perhaps he had placed his dreams on the wrong child. Maybe Harlan was the future of the ranch. He probably would never be a good rider. He never once asked to have a gun or a knife although he carried the small knife given to him by his brothers. Asking for a bigger horse was a new step for the boy.

The boy was smart, seemed to remember everything he ever heard or read. He made reasonable deductions based on the information at hand. Once he even built a new and better corner brace on the fence. Harlan was a deep thinker. His Christmas gift to Charlie had been thoughtful and even clever . . . copies of old newspapers. From the time, he and Catherine moved in with Rosa, Harlan must have collected every newspaper he could find. Old editions to be sure, but so much news that Charlie had missed. The were many copies of the Layton Gazette, one Kansas City Star, two Denver Posts, and several Cheyenne papers. Mostly the collection was made up of the Silver Bend Banner, the small, local weekly paper. It amused Charlie to see that Harlan had circled all the articles relating to the Independence Day Celebration. It would be a good family outing. It was good for Margarita to go into town. Rosa's family made her feel welcome. Thinking about Margarita made him think about the family photograph and that made him think about Arleta Goodfellow, interesting woman.

Spring was coming. Calves were dropping. At this rate, the herds were going to increase nicely. Right now Charlie and his lead wrangler were looking at the brown and white Indian pony Charlie had purchased for Harlan. It would be here when school was out in a few weeks, a surprise for Harlan.

"Seems like a good pick for your son," commented Bo Winston. He had been on the ranch for several years. So Charlie thought he could bring up a subject that had been on his mind since Christmas, the fancy rifle. After thinking about it for all these months Charlie thought the gun was either stolen (Lord, he hoped not) or the boys had won it in some sort of contest.

"Do Peter and his brother ever come down and play poker with the hands?"

Bo Wilson hated the question. It was one he didn't really want to answer.

"Not anymore," Bo said carefully.

"What do you mean not anymore?"

"When your boys were little, before I came, I guess the cowboys taught them to play a little poker. Just for the fun of it, mind you. They did okay for kids. After that Mr. Slater, that teacher, was here them boys got better and started playing real good. They kept on getting better and better, especially Mr. Paul. Our hands won't play with them anymore." Bo was so nervous he was picking splinters out of the wooden pasture fence. Nothing more was said while Charlie thought this news over.

"Any big games going on in the area or maybe Silver Bend?"

Bo was kicking at dirt clods with the toe of is boot. "Sir, you asking me about that beautiful Sharps rifle?"

"Yeah, Bo. I speck I am."

Bo sighed. "Last fall, a big game down in Layton. Some city dude came up from Cheyenne. Paul won the gun off him. The dude swore to kill him, but had second thoughts when he saw both your boys."

"Bo, do my boys cheat?"

No sir. Nobody thinks that. They are just damn good at cards. Just to damn good, especially Mr. Paul. Ever since that night, some big name card players have been asking around about the Indian kid that won the Sharps.
"Thanks for telling me, Bo."

"You going to shoot that gun in the July 4 contest?"

"Probably not." was Charlie's reply. Bo was disappointed because he believed his boss could win with that gun. He also thought his boss had made a wise decision.

Spring flowers were appearing in the wake of the retreating snow. Margarita was talking about the return of Catherine and Harlan and hoping Rosa would come and stay for a while. Over the winter, she had busied herself cooking. It showed around her now ample waistline. She was showing some strands of gray in her hair as well. Well, so was he but he had managed to keep his weight down. That might have something to do with hiking through snow drifts to rescue cows bunched up against the fences or pulling the mama and baby calves out of the swollen, muddy streams. Many days he didn't get lunch and was to tired to eat much dinner. He didn't mind.

Dinner was a silent affair with little or no conversation except when Margarita jabbered about the children. In bed at night, she turned away from him. She snored. He almost missed the old days when she would keep him awake with pillow talk questions. In another week or so he would ride into Silver Bend and talk to Arleta about an appointment for the photograph. Charlie had already told Paul and Peter they would be properly dressed and presentable for the picture-taking day whatever the date might be.

While he was shaving for the trip to town, he reminded Margarita, he planned to stop and visit Rosa first. He would go make the photo appointment, and then he planned on stopping by the bank and the sheriff's office just to see if anything was going on in the community. Lastly, he would pick up anything she might need before retuning home. He was standing in his bare feet and only his pants on when she looked at him and said, "Charlie Bennington, you are still a handsome man." He was pleased.

At Rosa's, she made fresh coffee and invited him to visit, which he did. Dutifully she told him everything she thought he might want to know about Catherine and Harlan. Both were doing well at their studies. Of course Harlan was way ahead of his sister and everyone else for that matter. Harlan was excited to be coming home, because he thought Charlie might have selected a horse for him. Several young men had come to pay their respects to Catherine. Rosa said, "She wasn't particularly interested but she was polite. I think they won't come back. Your daughter talks too much about ranching. She knows more than most." Charlie frowned. Rosa continued. "The other thing you should know is that she wants to ride in the Independence Day horse race."

Charlie's frown deepened. "They are letting women ride? Doesn't matter. My answer will be no."

By the time, he reached the photo studio he was not a happy man. The silent China woman nodded to him and motioned him into the office parlor where Arleta was arranging flowers in a bowl. "Charles," she smiled, "I am so glad you returned. Soo Wah, lemonade for Mr. Bennington," she ordered. He hoped it would not be hard lemonade. She moved gracefully about the room and yes he did hear the tinkle of a tiny bell somewhere on her person. She sipped her lemonade and asked if he was ready to make an appointment for the family to come in for the photo. Her eyes were an unusual green he noticed. She placed her glass on one of the small tables, leaning over in such away as he could see much cleavage in her lacy open neckline. He tried to look away.

"Excuse me. I will fetch my appointment book" she returned to the room and sat down beside him near enough he could smell her fragrance and easily look down her neck. He didn't look away. It was hard to concentrate on the dates she offered. "Yes, the second Tuesday of June would be fine," he stammered. He was extremely glad when she shut the book and left his side. Returning from the other room, she handed him a fancy card on which was written his name and the agreed upon date. He rose to take his leave, which he needed to do quickly. She was making him very uncomfortable, and he did not want to embarrass himself of her.

"Please, if you could stay a moment. I have a favor to ask. It is personal." He sat down and covered his swelling crotch with his hat. She sat opposite him and leaned forward just a little. He tried to concentrate on her green eyes. She was twisting a small hankie in her long fingers.

"When the late Mr. Goodfellow passed away it was unexpected. He left me with very little." Some of her red hair had escaped its ribbons and curled around her face. He noticed the interesting hollows in her cheeks. "I have been fortunate to find business opportunities in this community, but the taking of family portraits does not always cover my needs, you see." Charlie did not see. "I have been able to augment my income by taking pictures of the beautiful places surrounding Silver Bend. Individuals as well as the newspapers in the east pay well for pictures of your western country. I understand that you know the area very well. I was hoping I might prevail upon you to perhaps show me some particularly beautiful places to photograph."

Charlie was thinking no but he was nodding yes. She spoke softly. "They pay particularly well for pictures of wild, secluded places. Places that stimulate the imagination." Imagination was not the only thing being stimulated. She stood up. "My next appointment is here. If you agree, perhaps after the July 4 celebration? I am looking forward to meeting your family." She was gone.

Charlie felt as if he were escaping. The sheriff's office was a relief. It smelled of sweat, cigars, and the slop jar. It was just a little chilly. "Anything new since I last saw you?" inquired Charlie.

"No, not really. Just everyone is getting excited about the July 4 Celebration. You bringing the family in?"

"I thought I would. Margarita gets lonely out there with no women folk."

The sheriff knew how the town women looked down on Bennington's wife. He had met Margarita once or twice and she seemed just as nice as she could be. "Going to enter any of the contests?"

"Hadn't considered it. Probably, no." Charlie wondered if this was an indirect question about the rifle or the boys, but the sheriff changed the subject.

"Any trouble with any of your horses?"

"No. Why?"

"A couple of the other ranchers have lost some. Said the animals had trouble breathing. Sounded just like a kid with the croup, up and died a few hours later."

"Damn. That's bad. Think we'll ever get a vet in this town?"

"Don't know but B. J. Smith is riding down to Layton today to talk to the vet there. B. J. lost three horses including his favorite."

The bank was a little different. It was warm and smelled like leather and cigars. As with the sheriff, the banker talked about July 4. He asked if the Double B would donate a beef. Charlie had expected the request and said, "Yes."

"Any truth in the rumor your daughter is going to ride in the horse race?"

"No truth, No truth at all."

"To bad. She rides better than a lot of the cowboys around here."

Charlie was in a bad mood when he left the bank. He picked up everything Margarita had on her list and headed home. His thoughts drifted back to Arleta and her request. Well if showing her some pretty spots helped her out what was the harm? He kept thinking of the words she had used; "wild," "secluded," and "passion." He thought he knew just the place.

Turning into the ranch road, he saw a rider coming toward him at a gallop. It was Bo Wilson. Skidding to a stop he said, "You better come quick."
"Miss Catherine's horse is sick."

It was exactly as the sheriff described. Milk sounded as if she had the croup. She stood with her head hung low. Standing next to the big white horse, Charlie could feel the heat radiating off her. "Get her out of the stall if we can. We'll put her in the big pen away from any other animals. Make sure she has water."

"Doubt she'll drink, Mr. Bennington. She don't look good."

Bo was right. The horse died a few hours later. A lot of the cowboys took it hard. Milk was a fine horse, and they all knew she was Miss Catherine's favorite. A favorite mount was something very special for the likes of Miss Catherine.

Charlie and the other men were still standing around the dead animal when the twins arrived.

"Damn!"

"Holy shit!"

"What happened?" they said in unison. Charlie related everything he knew including the conversation with the sheriff.

"What are you going to do, Pa? You can't just drag this carcass off and leave it to the varmints like usual." It was Peter who asked the question that every man present was turning over in his own mind.

"We're going to bury the body." Heads turned in Charlie's direction.

"For two reasons. We don't know what killed the horse. We don't want any other animals to come down sick and we are doing it for Catherine. The men silently nodded their heads in agreement. It took four hours. The horse was big and the ground was still frozen a few inches down. Charlie had the twins clean every thing out of Milk's stall and burn it. They didn't complain. Before the men dispersed Charlie said, "Not a word about this unless it happens again. I don't want my daughter to learn about this from some town gossip. I'll tell her myself when she comes home from school.

He felt beat. Entering the kitchen, Margarita put her arms around him. She had seen everything from the kitchen window. He could tell she had been crying. He felt like crying himself.

Photo day came to quickly. He reminded Margarita and the boys they were not to say s word about the dead horse. Not to Rosa and especially not to Harlan, who couldn't always keep his mouth shut.

The boys and Charlie wore their funeral suites. He thought his sons looked good. It pleased him that he could see a little bit of Blue Feather in their faces. He was thankful they had pulled their hair back and were not wearing headbands. He might ask Arleta to take a photo of just him, Peter and Paul. Well, maybe Harlan also. Margarita was wearing a gray dress with too much trim. It was a little tight and seemed to accent her gray hair. The four of them were quiet as they rode into town.

The thoughts of the dead horse were bad enough but now Charlie began to wonder about how Arleta would present herself to his family. Harlan was so excited that Catherine did not notice her family was quiet. Catherine was a delightful surprise. She was beautiful. Her pale blue dress was trimmed with dark blue ribbons, which were also in her hair. The blue of her dress and ribbons reflected in her blue eyes. Charlie felt a little better for looking at his family.

He felt even better when Arleta welcomed all of them into the real studio and not the cozy parlor. She was wearing no makeup nor jewelry. Instead she was dressed in what she called her work apron, a large covering that hid all the charms she had displayed to Charlie. Her normal mass of red curls was contained in a black net at the back of her neck. She made Margarita feel welcome. She fussed over Catherine. She knew about the reputation of older boys and was nothing but professional whole time. She did not call him Charles.

The sitting took to long as far as he was concerned, but he did ask about a photo of he and his boys. "I would be delighted," she said. "And I do have time to do that for you right now." She gave him a smile he hoped no on else saw. Turning to Margarita she asked, "Mrs. Bennington, would you care for tea? Soo Wah can prepare it quite quickly." The China woman appeared at the sound of her name. Maybe it was because the tea had to be prepared or maybe it was because Margarita was not sure about the China woman. Whatever the reason, Charlie was relieved when Margarita declined the invitation. She and Catherine would go shopping while the second photo was taken.

Peter and Paul left as soon as they could escape once the picture was taken. Harlan ran after his mother and sister. "Your photos will be ready to pick up next week," Arleta said with just a slight purr. "I hope you haven't forgotten my little request." She was removing the work apron. Somehow several of her bodice buttons were undone. Her neck was a soft cream color. She re-buttoned them very slowly never moving her green eyes from Charlie's frank stare. Charlie, and Margarita managed lunch with Rosa and Catherine and Harlan. "Do I have a horse yet, Papa?" Harlan must have asked the question a dozen times.

To hush him up Charlie finally said, "Yes. You have a horse. You will have to wait till you come home and I am not saying another thing on the subject of horses!" Margarita deftly turned the conversation to the date when school would end . . . three weeks. The conversation moved around him. It was time to take their leave.

"Are they paid for?" she asked.

Riding home he was absorbed in his own thoughts. He was thinking about Arleta's neck when Margarita said. "Our photos will be ready next week?" The question made him jump.

"Yes."

"Well, you can send Peter or Paul. That way you don't have to make another ride into town till we come back for Catherine and Harlan," she decided. He nodded knowing full well he was not sending either of the twins.

The following week the twins were gone for several days. When they did return one of them had a black eye, and the other had cuts on his hand. They avoided their mother and volunteered to go out with the wranglers for a few days. That made it easy for Charlie to tell Margarita he was going back to town for the finished photos. "A quick trip," he said. He would not even stop at Rosa's. He would hurry back with the pictures for her to see.

At Arleta's he had to wait his turn as she finished with a customer, a young couple with a baby. They seemed to take forever deciding on a frame. From time to time, Arleta looked over their heads and smiled a smile that made Charlie silently cuss the couple's slowness. After they departed she invited him back to her parlor. He sat in his chair (he thought of it as his chair) and she across from him. She leaned forward a little bit and was close enough to rest her hand on his leg, just a little to the inside. "Charles, have you had time to think about my little request?"

He had promised himself he would say no. Instead he said, "I believe I know the perfect spot." They agreed on the Wednesday following the Independence Day Celebration. He gave her directions. She would bring a light lunch in case as she said the spot was so delicious she took a lot of photos.

"Shit! Shit! Shit!" Was what he said all the way out of town. When Margarita saw the two photos she almost cried. She had not expected them to be framed so beautifully.
"Please hang them so they are the wall when everyone comes home." Charlie felt like hell.

The night before he was to go after Catherine and Harlan it was unusually warm. Margarita had set the table in the cool of the patio. He could tell she was happy and sad. The twins were missing again, but Peter had promised they would be home when Catherine returned and learned about Milk. They weren't home yet, and the whole thing lay heavily on both parents. Charlie said thoughtfully, "I think if you were here in the house when we return, I could send Harlan directly in to you. I will take Catherine to where we buried the poor thing, tell her right there, get it over with." She agreed. "Is Tia coming back with us?"

"No. Not till July 4," I think.

That was the plan. Telling Catherine about her horse went as Charlie hoped it would. As soon as his father told Harlan to go into the house and see his mother, both Harlan and Catherine knew something was amiss. He thought it would be about his new horse. To learn that Milk was dead and even buried in the corner of the south pasture was a shock for both children.

Together mother and son watched the distant figures of the father and daughter out in that pasture. Charlie was gesturing with his hands. They saw Catherine lean into him and knew she was crying. It seemed a very long time before she climbed down out of the buggy and Charlie returned alone to the barn. Harlan met him there. Together they unharnessed the buggy and put the horse in its stall. Harlan never asked about his new horse.

Peter and Paul came home before nightfall. Catherine remained by the grave all night. Her big brothers sat with her. She returned to the house in the morning only to stay in her room except for a few trips to the privy.

Charlie showed Harlan his horse. Harlan had trouble containing his happiness. "Its okay son, you can be happy if you want. Your sister will be eventually." "Harlan thought a moment, I will name this horse Happy because that is what I want our family to be." Charlie got all choked up when he told Margarita about the horse's name. She sniffled.

Catherine slowly came around, but she was withdrawn and did not want to attend the July 4 doings in town. "Leave her be," said Margarita and Charlie agreed. Down at the bunkhouse he asked which men were planning on attending the festivities. Most hands went up.

"I have a favor. Miss Catherine wants to remain at home. I need someone to stay and keep an eye on her. From a distance." Several hands went up. He was hoping to see two particular men volunteer and they did. They were the oldest men in his employ. Jokingly they said they were to old to go sparking the fillies in town . . . be glad to stay on the ranch. Everyone laughed. Peter and Paul also declined to go into town. That made Charlie wonder what kind of trouble they had been in.

The day was going to be hot. He and Margarita rode in the wagon in order to bring Rosa and her baggage back with them. Harlan rode Happy. He was riding surprisingly well thought Charlie. Considering everything, it was turning into a pleasant day. Rosa's family welcomed Margarita. Charlie and Harlan visited the various competitions. They watched the shooting contests and Charlie knew he could have won the prize easily. People had horses for sale.

"You going to find another horse for Catherine?" asked Harlan as they walked around the picket line.

"If she wants, I will." He was already looking at a big gray gelding. He asked the owner for his name and address just in case. At noon they retuned to the women and everybody in town moved to the meadow where the pig and the Bennington beef had been roasting. The amount of covered dishes was amazing. Harlan was already feeling ill because Charlie let him eat all the different kinds of pie he wanted. Margarita frowned at him but not too much. She was having a good time. Charlie was glad they had come and glad Tia Rosa was coming home with them.

From a distance, he saw Arleta several times. She was taking pictures of the activities for the Silver Bend Banner. Only once did she approach him and Harlan. Addressing Harlan she said, "Master Bennington." That made Harlan giggle. "Mr. Bennington," she said looking at Charlie. "Perhaps we'll see you again in the near future."

"She want us to have more pictures?" Harlan asked after she left them.

"Something like that," answered Charlie.

Going home, Happy was tied to the rear of the wagon. Harlan was asleep in the back with the luggage. Rosa and Margarita talked about the fine celebration. Charlie thought about four days from now and his . . . what? What the hell did you call the time you were planning to spend screwing another woman? He sure as hell was not going to take pictures, and he was pretty sure she wasn't either. He was being honest, he thought.

The day came quickly. The twins rode out early. Catherine was somewhere, and Harlan was busy with a new book. Rosa was giving Margarita another quilting lesson. No one missed him when he rode away from the house. He wore his work clothes, Levis, a work shirt, clean to be sure and he had shaved well he thought. It was warm. His shirt was open and his sleeves were rolled up. She was waiting for him in her buggy. He noted assorted cameras and equipment as well as a picnic basket and a blanket. He led her off the road.

She watched him ride. She thought his forearms were sexy, muscled and not much hair. She didn't like hairy men. She wanted to see the rest of his body. She hoped he was not one of these men who didn't want to take off their underwear. She wanted to feel the whole man. She would insist, she decided. He was thinking the same thoughts. He wondered why on such a warm day she wore a jacket. When she did take it off he understood. She was only wearing a chemise underneath. Her nipples were already hard. He could see them against the sheer fabric.

They tied off the horses. No words were exchanged. He pulled off his clothes as fast as he could. She undid her skirts. He heard the tinkle of a little bell again. It was a tiny silver bell on the garter holding up her black stocking. As he pulled her down onto the blanket, he laughed. The sight of the silver bell, so near to where he wanted to enter and holding up a schoolteacher stocking seemed funny. It didn't occur to him that he was inexperienced, but the sounds coming from Arleta's throat and the movements of her hands were driving him faster than he wanted to go. She raked his back with her long fingernails and arched her back.

He heard the shot before he heard the whistle of the bullet over their heads. She didn't know what she heard. She kept stoking him. He did know.

A second bullet ricocheted off the rocks above them. This time she was aware someone was shooting at them. Even before the third shot they were rolling away from each other and scrambling for their clothes. His rifle was over on the horse and his pistol was under the tangle of the clothes he hastily removed only a few moments ago. No more shots. They listened. Nothing. Charlie could hear hoof beats fade away. All Charlie could think about was that the departing shooter was his daughter. Suddenly he felt sick at heart. Worse, he felt dirty. Arleta saw the expression on his face. When he said, "Move your ass the hell out of here," she did.

He thought about the whole incident riding home. Charlie knew that who ever had been doing the shooting could have hit them easy. The shooter had chosen not to. He forgot about Arleta raking his back with her fingernails. Getting ready for bed, Margarita asked him about the marks. "Low branch." Was all he said. Now he was a liar. Over all, he the thought the summer had been lousy. He wanted the winter to come.

He didn't go to town for several weeks. Someone else did and brought Margarita a copy of the Silver Bend Banner. The front-page photo of July 4 activities was Harlan with his face smeared with berry pie. The relating article made it clear that the national holiday would be celebrated again next year . . . bigger and better. Catherine reread the part about the new and improved horse race. She needed a horse. She would ask her pa. It was time.

Chapter Twenty-two

Silver Cloud

"I think I am ready to find a horse," Catherine announced at the breakfast table. Even Tia Rosa smiled.

"I have one you might want to consider," answered Charlie slowly.

"You haven't already bought it have you?"

"No, daughter. I have not." They all remembered the fit she threw at her birthday party. Everyone laughed. "I can make arrangements for you to see it if you wish. It is a big gelding. Harlan and I saw during the fourth of July."

"He is big," put in Harlan, who of course, remembered the exact horse.

A week later they went to look at the horse. By themselves, Catherine turned to her father. "I'm not going back to Tia Rosa's for the school year. I'll ride in until the snows make it difficult."

"Why not?"

"I think it is to hard on her with both of us there and Harlan needs education more than I do. She is getting old. Harlan makes her laugh and I don't." She paused. "Her grandson, the older one with the squeaky voice," she paused again. "He tries to put his hands on me. He wants to do things only married folk should do." Charlie caught his breath. Was this her way of telling him she knew about Arleta or was she just talking to him as his daughter. Looking at her face he decided it was the latter. He saw a young girl on the verge of womanhood. He felt old.

The owner of the horse for consideration was surprised. The horse was for the daughter, not big Charlie Bennington himself. The gray gelding was a big horse. The owner watched as Catherine walked around the animal. She felt and touched and looked at every spot on the horse just as he had seen sharp, horse buyers do. He was startled when she swung herself up, bare back on the horse. She looked down at her father. "I like him, Pa." She galloped away leaving her father and the now former owner in a cloud of dust. She was smiling. She felt sure she and Silver Cloud would get along just fine. The gelding was perfect. Charlie didn't have enough money in his wallet. The ex-owner knew Charlie Bennington was good for it.

"Damn, Pa! You got her a really big horse! was Peter's opinion. Paul nodded."
"Told you so," chirped Harlan. His voice was beginning to change.

Away from their father and particularly Harlan, Peter remarked to his brother "You know what Little Sister is going to do with the big gelding?"

"I sure as hell do. She's going to enter next year's race."
"Pa won't let her"
"She won't tell him."
"Want to put money on her?"
"Yeah."

Summer wound down and it was time for Charlie to take Harlan and Rosa back to town. Charlie was sorry that Rosa was leaving. All summer his wife and Rosa had sat in the shade of the arbor. Rosa was teaching Margarita to quilt. Margarita seemed to be enjoying her newfound craft and the company. Seeing the wagon ready to leave, both Margarita and Catherine gave Rosa big hugs and watched as the wagon move slowly down the ranch road. He settled Rosa and Harlan into her little house. As usual, he would pay a visit to the sheriff and his banker before heading home.

In town, the first thing he noticed was Arleta Goodfellow's photo studio was empty. Inside the sheriff's office, the sheriff was speaking to Charlie but looking though a stack of new wanted posters on his desk. "Long time no see. How are thing's at the ranch?" Before Charlie could answer, the sheriff rambled on. "Heard that daughter of yours has a new horse."

"Shit." Charlie wondered, "Was there no private business in this town?"

"Guess you heard about the picture-taking lady. Seems that woman had a thing for Leroy Arnold. Clovis Arnold caught them two buck naked in the barn. She took a buggy whip to both of them. Ol'Leroy was on top. Clovis got him good with the whip. He ain't sitting down too well and still living in the barn from what I hear. You know what they call that red headed picture woman, don't you?" Charlie shook his head. "Mrs. Goodbody. Seems she had more going on than photography. She left in the middle of the night. Ain't that a corker?" The sheriff looked up. Charlie wasn't smiling. Watching Charlie walk down the street toward the bank the sheriff thought. "That man is too serious. Maybe that's why he has one of the best spreads around."

At the bank, Charlie was able to stop the banker before he heard the Leroy Arnold story repeated. The banker moved on to a related matter. "Mrs. Goodfellow left the China lady here."

"What's she going to do?" asked Charlie. "She can't speak English."

"Oh, she speaks just fine. Has some education I guess. She thinks she wants to open a laundry. She came in here and asked me to lend her the money."

"A laundry in Silver Bend? Hell, we don't even have a vet."

"Well, we are not about to have a laundry either. I'm not lending money to a woman and a Chink to boot." After Charlie said good-bye, the banker decided his Chink remark was stupid in front of Charlie. The Bennington Ranch was one of his bank's best customers, and he better remember Charlie Bennington's mother was full-blooded Indian and his wife was Mexican.

Catherine kept her word and rode into school every day. Notes coming home from school indicated she was doing acceptable work, but the teachers would like her to participate in activities more . . . like her brother, young Harlan. She seemed too preoccupied with things not related to school. Charlie wondered what things.

One early November morning Charlie asked Catherine if he could ride into town with her. He had some shopping to do. He did have Charismas gifts to buy but he was at a loss as what to give Margarita. He told his daughter that.
"Pa," she brought Silver Cloud to a compete halt. "Tell me something. Did you and Mama ever really get married?"

"For certain we did; that little Catholic Church in Layton. Why?"

"Mama doesn't have a wedding ring."

"No, I guess we didn't have any money. Your grandpa had to buy her the dress she wore."

"Don't you think it is about time you gave her a ring? Pa, women like those things."

"You think it would make a good Christmas present?"
Catherine laughed. "It would be a perfect Christmas gift." She clucked at Silver Cloud and left her father thinking about the possibilities.

Now sitting with Rosa he had just repeated the whole conversation. "I don't know where to buy a ring . . . Layton maybe. Probably, all the way to Cheyenne? Rosa, I don't know about these things."

Rosa patted his knee. "Stay right there." Charlie could hear her in the next room. Sounded like she was opening and shutting dresser drawers. She returned and handed him a well, worn, velvet ring box. He opened the fancy box and saw gold wedding band.

"Yours? From Ed?" Charlie asked.

"No, no. From Mr. Potts. You forget. I had two husbands. It was too big from the start." She wiggled her tiny hand in his direction. "He never had it sized and I never did wear it. Been in the box all these years. I'd be pleased if you wanted to have it for Margarita and don't think about paying me." He accepted the gift and left with instructions from her to buy a big fancy, store bought Christmas card to replace the worn box. "Pick one with a strong envelope so the ring don't punch through," Rosa added.

He was very pleased with the outcome of the day. The ring and the card were safely tucked inside his shirt. He would stop, as he always did, at the sheriff's office and the bank and then head home. He would not even tell Catherine about the ring. The sheriff was out. On the way to the bank, Charlie stopped and stared at what was the old photo shop. It was a Chinese Laundry, the "SooWah Laundry" according to the sign across the front. Once inside he said to the banker he said, "I thought we were not going to have a Chinese laundry in town."

"Well, I didn't lend her the money. Your good friend Rosa Potts Bettini did."

"Rosa?"

"Yes, and I sure am sorry I didn't. The China lady is making money hand or fist. Didn't think there would be that much call for doing laundry. Even the hotel is sending over their dirty linen. Fortunately, Miss Wah does not hold a grudge. She has opened an account with us." The banker was shaking his head. Charlie hid his smile. "Oh, by the way, we'll be getting a vet come spring."

"Do we know his name?" asked Charlie with interest.

"His name is Mat Caldwell"

"Isn't that the vet down in Layton?"

"The Layton vet is Sirus Caldwell. This is his son."

"Bout time is all I can say."

It seemed to Charlie that Christmas would never arrive. As was now, the custom the family did put up a Christmas tree. Rosa didn't come this year. Charlie was barely able to bring Harlan home because of the weather. Christmas morning all the gifts had been opened. He could tell that Margarita was trying hard not to notice she had no gift from him. Catherine kept giving him sour looks.

"I have one more present," he announced and handed the envelope to Margarita. "Catherine told me it is about time." Margarita opened the lumpy envelope, and the ring dropped onto her lap. She was completely silent. She picked up the ring holding it in the palm of her hand. She looked at Charlie with watery eyes.

"Put it on, Mama," said Harlan and Catherine at the same time. Slowly she eased it onto the proper finger. It fit perfectly. Catherine gave her father a big grin.

Later, Catherine said, "How did you come by a ring? Especially a perfect fit?"

"My secret," was all he said. He might tell her some day but not before he told her mother.

In the spring, Bo Wilson broke his leg and probably wouldn't be riding for several months. Not as many calves as last year, but just as many seemed to get into trouble and needed to be rescued. Catherine said she was not going back to school. "Because of the work I did over the winter, I'm ahead" was her reasoning. Charlie was tired of arguing about schooling so he let it slide. The twins seemed to be more help or at least he thought that till the weather really cleared.

At the same time, Catherine was gone each day on Silver Cloud. Often when she rode in the horse was lathered or winded. She cooled him out and rubbed him down and fell into bed exhausted.

"Do you know where she rides?" asked Margarita. Charlie was not happy that he didn't have an answer to her question.

Chapter Twenty-three

Susan Washington

He most certainly wished he knew that answer when she didn't arrive home for dinner as normal. She had ridden out in the morning, not talking to anyone as usual. She carried a light lunch per Margarita who she didn't think Catherine had a coat or a jacket. It was early summer so it was warm but she was always home for dinner.

After it was dark, Charlie walked down to the bunkhouse. None of the men had noticed anything different about this morning or Miss Catherine's departure. They were used to seeing her ride out early. Charlie and the twins sat on the porch for a while. Margarita came out every now and then. At bedtime, they left a lantern lit on the kitchen table. Margarita left a covered dinner dish.

Three different times Charlie got up to check Catherine's bedroom. In the hallway, he ran into the twins doing the same thing. "We'll go out at first light. Be ready to go." was all their father said.

In the morning, they took a wagon with a few supplies and their own mounts. Margarita stood in the back door; her night wrapper pulled around her tightly and watched her sons and her husband go out to begin searching for her missing daughter.

"Do you know where she likes to ride?" Charlie eventually asked.

"Not for sure. We know she likes to swim the horse in the lake."

"Why would she be doing that?" demanded Charlie. Peter and Paul knew they were getting into something they would rather not discuss with their father.

"She was strengthening Silver Cloud," said Paul.

"Why?"

It was Peter that answered. "We think she is planning to enter the July 4 cross-country horse race." Paul nodded. Charlie remembered the sheriff's question.

"You sister hasn't asked me."

"Pa, if that is what she is planning, she probably is not going to ask cause she knows you will say no."

"You can bet your sweet ass I'll say know!" Not much was said after that.

"How was she going to pay the entry fee?"

Peter said, "Borrow it from Harlan."

"Harlan has money?" Charlie wanted to know.

"Yes, sir . . . not a lot."

"Where did you little brother get money?"

"Harlan has been working at the new vet's place ever since it opened."

"Doing what and why?"

"Harlan thinks he wants to be a vet when he grows up, and he is saving his money because he wants to buy you that fancy hat you look at every time you go in the general store. Harlan pays attention to everything you do." This gave Charlie quit a bit to think about. The three rode in silence.

If they had been talking they wouldn't have heard the horse. It was Peter that held up his hand to stop the wagon. It was the sound of a horse, a horse in distress. It was coming from a grove of aspen trees down and to their left.

They came upon Silver Cloud first. The beautiful gelding was so badly mauled each of them knew it would have to be put down. No doubt a bear.

"I'll do it," volunteered Peter. The sound of the shot echoed around in the trees followed by silence.

"Catherine . . . Catherine, where are you?" Both boys could hear the tremor in Charlie's voice. No answer. Following the blood trail left by the wounded horse, they watched for movement, either Catherine or the bear, which might be wounded. They all saw Catherine at that same time. She looked as if she were peacefully, asleep except for the odd angle of her neck. The bear had not touched her but she was dead just the same. "Leave me," Charlie commanded. Paul and Peter went back to the wagon and waited. They each pretended not to see the other swipe at tears.

"He is going to have to tell Mama."

"Harlan and Tia Rosa, too."

Charlie emerged from the trees carrying Catherine's body. He placed it gently in the wagon and covered it with one of the blankets. His eyes were red but dry now.

"Go get my horse. We will take Catherine home."

Margarita was watching for them, as were the ranch hands. Seeing Charlie driving the wagon and no Silver Cloud or Catherine, they all knew it was bad.

Margarita was out the door. Charlie was faster and off the wagon seat before she could reach the wagon. He crushed her to him and talked softly in her ear. Margarita collapsed in his arms.

Tia Rosa took the news somewhat better and came to the ranch to help with Margarita who had retreated into shock. Harlan would hardly let Peter, Paul or his father out of sight. Some one went into town for a coffin and that was how Silver Bend learned of the death of Catherine Rose Bennington.

It fell to Rosa to prepare the body for burial. She selected a pretty dress from Catherine's closet. But Margarita stopped her. Speaking for the first time since Charlie told her the news, the grieving mother said, "Leave her dressed the way she is. She is wearing what pleased her most." Margarita wouldn't speak again for a very long time.

The funeral was brief attended by Rosa's family and a few Silver Bend businessmen and their quiet wives. A silent Margarita barely made it through the service supported by Peter and Paul. Only because of Rosa and her family was there refreshments to serve following the service. Finally the day was over. Just Rosa and Charlie were in the kitchen. "I'll take care of the headstone if you will let me," said Rosa.

"Seems like we order too many of the damn things," she nodded in agreement and continued. "I am to old Charlie. I can't stay and take care of you, your boys and Margarita till she recovers from this. It may take some time for her." It was his turn to nod. "I have a woman I can recommend."

"Who?"

"Susan Washington. You know her as Soo Wah, but her real name is Susan, Susan Washington."

"The China woman?"

"First she is a Christian and only half Chinese. Grew up in a missionary school where her not so missionary father pretended she was not his but kept her mother on the side. She knows some nursing. She was with that Mrs. Goodfellow only because her father owed the late Mr. Goodfellow some kind of debt, which Mrs. Goodfellow claims, is still not paid. If that Goodfellow bitch files a charge against Susan, no one will listen because she is Chinese."

That statement took Charlie back to the first time he saw Margarita in that long ago alley when she said to his father, "I go with you. Nobody will believe me because I am Mexican."

"Damn! Damn! Damn! What about her laundry business?"

"She and I were planning to sell it. That rascal banker is most interested in buying it. It will turn a handsome price for both Susan and myself when I get finished dealing with him." That gave Charlie a small smile. Rosa continued. "At first Susan was planning to move on. Now she believes this is the one place that Arleta Goodfellow will not come back to." "That would be nice for everyone," thought Charlie to himself.

Susan Washington moved to the Double Ranch without much excitement. Everyone knew that Margarita Bennington was not getting over the death of her daughter. The twins and Harlan were concerned about their totally silent mother. They did not know how to deal with it and to start with they were angry about the China woman being at the house.

As their mother drifted into a silent world all her own they came to respect Susan Washington because of the care she gave Margarita. At first Susan lived in the little stone cottage by the creek. When Margarita showed no signs of improvement Charlie asked Susan to move into the house. He took Catherine's room. Susan and Margarita shared the big bedroom. At least Charlie now got sleep when the bad dreams kept Margarita awake. Harlan didn't finish school that year, and he gave up the idea of becoming a veterinarian. They did not attend the Independence Day Celebration. There was no Christmas celebration.

A year had passed and still Margarita drifted in and out of reality. Charlie, Margarita, and Susan sat under the arbor. Charlie tried to spend as much time every day with his silent wife. Susan always kept Margarita clean and dressed her every morning. Susan cooked for the family, which was usually just Charlie and Harlan. The twins were around less and less.

"Susan, do you think she will ever come back?" was Charlie's question.

"Grief is a terrible thing, Mr. Bennington but I have seen worse and people do sometimes recover. I know it is not my place to ask, but what are you going to do about young Harlan?"

"Harlan? What's wrong with Harlan?"

"He lost his sister. To all effects he has lost his mother and you are still wrapped up in your own grief. He wants to think he is like his brothers but he is not. He needs a whole father and a house that is not so sad. Mrs. Bennington might respond if you and your boy brought some joy into the place."

"Well, Soo Wah" as he sometimes called her just to see her bristle, "How did you get to be so smart?" Next morning Charlie talked to his headman. He was taking his son up into the Sandies and fishing for a few days. If there was a big problem, the foreman knew where to find him.

Susan was pleased as she watched the father and son ride away the next morning complete with enough pack animals and gear for four days if the fishing was good.

Charlie gave Harlan a side ways glance. The boy was not really a boy anymore. Yet at fourteen, he was still a kid in so many ways. Harlan was serious and quiet. "You bring your fishing pole?"

Harlan looked down cast. "No sir. I forgot it."

"No matter. I brought two." Harlan offered a small smile.
"Pa"
"Yes"
"Can we talk about Catherine?"
"If you like."
Harlan was silent. Taking a deep breath he said, "Why didn't Catherine like Mama?" Off and on over the years, as Catherine's hostility toward her mother bubbled to the surface, Margarita and Charlie had discussed what to say if Harlan ever asked this question. Just keep it simple and Harlan was to never know the truth. He must never think that his birth was the cause of his sister's attitude toward their mother.

"We don't know, son. Sometimes it just happens in families. Your mama wanted your sister to be a girl. Grow up to be a lady someday. You sister wanted to ride and be apart of the workings of the ranch." To change the subject, Charlie went on. "You saw the way she was with animals. All animals but especially horses?" Harlan nodded. "I think she had the Bennington gift." Harlan was very interested. Charlie went on to explain that Grandpa Asa had the gift, which more than likely came from his father before him.
"Do I have the gift?" inquired Harlan.

"I don't think so." He could see Harlan was disappointed "I don't. Your brothers most definitely don't. Your sister did. Maybe some day you will have a son who does." This was a whole new line of thinking for Harlan. The boy was quiet. Charlie let him be. Besides Charlie also had a new thought. He had just told Harlan that Catherine always wanted to be a part of the working of the ranch and just because she was a girl he had never noticed. "Damn."
"Which pool? Papa."
"Which ever one you think is lucky. We have to catch our dinner."
Charlie caught the first fish. Fortunately, it was big enough for both their dinners because when Harlan got a bite he became so excited he fell in the water.

Charlie knew there would be no more caught fish for the rest of the day. He stripped down completely and joined Harlan in the water. Harlan was shocked. Naked men and boys were nothing new, but seeing his father happily splashing around in the water was something different. He was happy also. So was his father for the first time in many months.

Harlan asked endless questions over the next few days. It was as if a dam had been opened. Charlie told him about his grandfather coming across the prairie, about how he partnered up with Charlie Lamb; about Blue Feather and Chief Spotted Dog. Harlan asked if he could practice his Sioux, all three of the boys were fairly good at the language of their grandmother. Charlie continued his family history, but left out the part about the gold nuggets. He knew where to find them now. Even told Harlan about the rocking horse.

"Is that the one up in the barn?"

"Well, if is in the barn we should bring it in the house. You might want it for that son of yours someday." Harlan's grin was wide.

"Pa, I think I want to go back to school."
"I think you should."
"You do?"
"If you are going to help me run this ranch you need education."
Harlan looked so serious Charlie had to hide his laugh.
"You always say Peter and Paul will run the ranch. You been saying that as long as I remember."
Charlie surprised himself when he asked Harlan, "Do you honestly think your brothers want to have any thing to do with running the ranch?"
"No sir."
"Well you better return to school this fall."
"Can I stay with Tia Rosa?"
"You're big enough. You can ride back and forth except for the worst days."
Harlan's chest puffed out a little. "I want to work for Doc Caldwell"
"Who is Doc Caldwell?"

"The new vet in town." Charlie suddenly felt deflated.
"Thought you didn't want to be a vet anymore."
"No sir, I don't but if I'm going to help you run the Double B then I want to know everything, just everything." It was Charlie's turn to puff out his chest.
On the ride home Harlan became quiet. "Pa, when we get home do we have to be sad again?"
"No. I think we should be as happy as we can be. I think we should tell your mama everything we did these last few days. Tell her about the fish we

caught, the eagles we saw, the coyotes we heard. Tell her you fell in. Share everything we did with her."

"She won't talk."

"No, I expect she won't but she will listen. It might give her something pleasant to think about. Something very pleasant."

Drawing near the ranch Charlie could see a rider coming out to meet them. This usually meant bad news. It was the foreman.

"Before you reach the house, thought you should know your boys are gone."

"Gone?"

"Yes sir. Rode away last night. Took two pack animals and lots of gear. Said to tell you as soon as they get some money they will send it to you for everything they took. Said they left a note in their room."

All the note said was "Give the ranch to Harlan." His own feeling startled Charlie. It was relief. The two boys had been a problem for a long time. Maybe it was for the best since right now Margarita wouldn't notice. A lot of sons didn't stay on the home place. He guessed he'd seen it coming but again he hadn't noticed it either. "Damn."

After cleaning up and dinner was done, Harlan and Charlie told Margarita everything they had done on the fishing trip. Harlan was a little to graphic about his father stripping down and diving into the water. Charlie knew that Susan was listening from the kitchen. "Was Margarita absorbing any of this?" Charlie wondered.

Later that night, father and son were sitting on the back steps, Harlan asked that very question.

"I don't know," replied Charlie. "But it did make me feel good to tell her about our adventures."

"Me too." Harlan paused. Harlan was tapping his foot up and down which he did when he was about to ask something important. "Pa, you going to marry Susan?" Charlie was startled by the question. Susan who was inside and just passing by the kitchen door stopped to listen.

"Of course not son. I'm married to your mother."

"Yeah, but lots of husbands have . . . another sort of wife don't they?" Apparently, Harlan did not know the word for mistress.

"Not the Benningtons, son. Not the Benningtons."

Susan walked quietly away, but she was smiling. "You came real close Charlie Bennington. Real close. If I had not put a couple of shots across your bare, randy ass while you were out in the weeds tying to hump that hussy, Arleta Goodfellow, you might not be sitting here with your fine son." Charlie would never know.

Chapter Twenty-four

Spilled Coffee

Harlan did go back to school. He stayed with Tia Rosa, and he went back to work for Mat Caldwell. Caldwell was the one to see Harlan get into his first fight. Caldwell could not hear the other kid's remark about Harlan's mother being crazy so the vet didn't know why Harlan jumped on the bigger boy. Harlan was smaller but so scrappy that the other kid decided it was not worth the effort and walked away.

Caldwell watched Harlan come into the barn and go to the cabinet in which the liniment was kept. The boy never said a word. Just tended his cuts and went to work mucking out dirty stalls. At home he smelled like dung and Susan noticing his cuts and bruises, thought how hard it must be to be a veterinarian. Matt Caldwell would tell Charlie Bennington about the fight if he every got to meet the man. Caldwell thought Harlan handled the thing well even if he did start it.

The cattle were all down from the high country. The ones to be sold were gone already. There was always some sort of work to be done so Charlie was not in the house when Margarita said to Susan, "I didn't like you at first." They were in the kitchen. Susan was washing dishes and tried not to show excitement when Margarita made that statement.

"Why?"

"Because, you look different." Susan remained quiet. "Then I remembered how people have treated me, and I decided I didn't want to be like them."

"Some people have not treated me well either. That is true," ventured Susan.

"Tell me about yourself." Susan forgot the dishes. She poured coffee for both of them and told Margarita her life story.

"Don't you ever want to get married?" queried Margarita.

"I would like to have a fine husband like yours, children, and a real home of our own. I do think I should have a Chinese man if I could find one."

Margarita was sipping her now cold coffee and looking out the window. "I want to visit my daughter's grave."

"Mrs. Bennington, you should ask your husband to walk you up there." Under the table Susan had her fingers crossed.

"Perhaps I will." Susan said nothing to Charlie about Margarita speaking. Time would tell. Margarita said nothing for several days.

"At Sunday breakfast just as Charlie blew on the hot coffee in his saucer," Margarita said, "I want to go visit Catherine's grave." He dropped the cup and saucer spilling the coffee into his lap. He jumped up trying to keep the hot liquid from reaching his privates.
"When?"

"As soon as you change your pants." Neither Charlie nor Susan saw the smallest smile on Margarita's face. The sun was warm, but the wind was chilly on the cemetery hill. Margarita looked at the fine head stone, Catherine Rose Bennington 1894-1909. She fingered the carved flowers. "Who provided the head stone?"

"Rosa."

"I thought so. These flowers are roses, I think. Tell me about Peter and Paul." He put his arm around her and walking back down the hill he told her all he knew which was not very much. "And Harlan?" she asked.

"He's great. Just great." She could hear the pride in her husband's voice. Normal life in the house did not resume right away. Margarita began to take over some of the household chores. Some days were better than others. She asked Charlie to put a chair in the graveyard. She walked up and sat from time to time. Harlan did not come home for Thanksgiving. Prior to the holiday, he told Charlie that he was worried about Tia Rosa. Harlan thought she was not feeling well, but she was talking about coming for Christmas.

Prior to their Christmas arrival and at Margarita's suggestion, she and Charlie moved back into their own room. Susan moved upstairs so Rosa could have the remaining downstairs bedroom. Charlie had no intentions of doing anything more than cuddling his wife. It was Margarita that invited his lovemaking.

Harlan had been right to be worried about Tia Rosa. The old woman was very frail. "I would not have missed this Christmas for anything," she said several times. She stayed only a week. She was tired and Charlie, Margarita, and Susan were also worried. Before Charlie was to return Rosa to Silver Bend, Margarita took Susan aside. "I think your work here is finished. Would you consider going back to Silver Bend and caring for Rosa?"

"I would like that very much. I will go and pack." Susan Washington left the Double B just as quietly as she had arrived only with tearful hugs at departure time. Charlie could not remember the last time he, and Margarita were totally alone . . . maybe just before the twins arrived? He wasn't sure, but he liked it.

Spring brought unusual rain just about the time the new calves began to drop. Charlie didn't have time to go into town. Harlan brought the letter. The return address was Creyville, TX. The writer was the Creyville sheriff. As a father himself, he thought Mr. Bennington should know that both Peter and Paul Bennington were dead. Charlie expected it to be a gunfight or something of that nature. It was not. The two boys had been quietly eating dinner when a drunk outside in the street cut loose with a big bore gun. He shot several people before he was stopped. Only Peter and Paul had been fatally shot. They had been properly buried with the proper words said over them. Their gear and horses went to pay for the coffins. Charlie waited two days before he decided to tell Margarita. She handled it better than Harlan. "I thought they would come back. I really did." He was trying hard not to cry. Later Margarita would ask Charlie if he wanted to put up two more gravestones over empty graves. He thought not. Maybe they would visit to Creyville, TX some time.

It was not a good spring. Besides the letter concerning Paul and Peter, Tia Rosa died. Harlan came home in the middle of the week to bring the news. The funeral would be in two days. Margarita said they would go. The roads were better now, and they took a buggy. It was the first time the citizens of Silver Bend saw that Margarita Bennington was no longer ill. Again Charlie did not understand the service. Rosa would be buried along side of Ed in the Silver Bend Cemetery. Rosa's family despite the sorrow made everyone feel welcome. Charlie saw that Susan Washington was now a part of the extended family. Margarita wanted to visit so Charlie strolled down to the vet's. It was time he met Matt Caldwell. Besides, Charlie was concerned. The ranch hands were finding too many dead cattle. The animals were dead with no obvious reason.

Caldwell recognized Charlie Bennington right away. He was Harlan's father and of that there was no doubt. They shook hands. "I speck your here about the dying cattle," was how Matt opened the conversation.

"Am I the only one?"

"No. From what I hear, it is all over the area."

"Do you know what it is?"

"No, not yet.
I have friends back east that know more than I do. I telegraphed them a few days ago. I am waiting for an answer. If possible I would bury or burn the carcasses if you can."

Charlie changed the subject. "My son is doing a good job for you?"

"I have several youngsters working for me. Harlan is one of the best. To bad, he doesn't want to be a vet."
"Do you know what changed his mind?"
"When the kids first come they all want to be vets. After they have to lie in shit and cow crap in a cold wet stall because the calf is turned wrong and the owner didn't call me soon enough and they have to put their arm up inside the mother and turn the little calf and maybe it works or maybe it doesn't most kids decide this line of work is not for them and they leave."
"Has Harlan done that?"
"Yes. Twice. Both times he was successful. First time he went outside and vomited. He didn't like doing it but he did."

"He never said."
"Charlie," the two men were on a first name basis. "I don't think Harlan would say anything. He goes off and thinks about how he could have done a better job. I don't mean to speak out of turn, but Harlan ought to go on to school. I mean higher education. Times are changing. I believe that ranches like yours will have to change with the times."

On the return to the ranch, Charlie was quiet. Margarita remarked that Susan was intending to leave Silver Bend.

"Where does she plan on going?"

"San Francisco."

"Why San Francisco?"

"She wants to find a China man. She wants a family and a real home of her own."

"I wished I had said good-bye and wished her well. Maybe we should have given her some money," he added.

"She has money, Charlie. She has the money from the laundry and Rosa left her some."

Charlie was again quiet and Margarita thought it was because of the funeral. That was part of it, but Charlie was thinking about every thing Matt Caldwell had said about more schooling for Harlan and changing times.

Spring came and the cattle stopped dying. Matt Caldwell thought he knew what killed them. He thought it had to do with the buffalo that still roamed the area, but he was not sure enough to say. He did know that it could happen again. Part of the changing times he mentioned to Charlie Bennington and any other ranchers that would listen included new methods about caring for cattle.

A week or so later Harlan was riding along side his father and knew Charlie was irritated about the Hathaway's. Several of their cows had been found to far inside the Bennington pastures. The Hathaway spread was a poorly run twenty-seven, acre ranch on the northeast corner of the Double B. The way the property lines ran the Hathaway spread jutted into the Bennington property making it to easy, as Charlie suspected, for the Hathaway cattle to graze on his land. He also believed that more than one Bennington cow became part of Hathaway's herd.

On the official county maps, there was no argument about the property lines. How it happened, nobody knew. Everybody said it looked like an old clerking error. Probably happened when the mountain range everyone called the Teepees show up on the maps as the Peetees. Nobody believed that old Asa Bennington would have drawn up the property lines in that manner. It didn't really matter. Just as the mountains would forever be called the Peetees, the lines were official and the Hathaways were here to stay.

Charlie was saying to Harlan, "Twice I have offered old man Hathaway a decent price." Harlan had heard the story many times and knew what his pa said was true. When the Hathaway ranch had almost gone under the years cattle prices plunged his pa had offered a fair price, especially considering the times.

"I'll rot in hell before I ever sell any Hathaway land to any Bennington, ever!" is what the old man had yelled at Charlie. The two neighbors had not spoken a word to each other since.

"Why don't they like us?" Harlan wanted to know.

"I wish I knew. Some people are just hard cases. Don't have to have a reason. I expect some folk don't like us for the simple reason that our ranch is doing well, very well."

Charlie went on, "Before you were born, we had nesters on the south property line. There was a fire. They moved on. That's why our fence line borders the whole length of road down there now." "Solved the problem."
Harlan had heard storied about the burned out nesters.

"Well, those were the old days. Pa, you can't do things like that anymore."

"It worked! Why not?"

Harlan could tell Charlie was more than a little irritated now, but he plunged on. "Times have changed. Just think! That Mr. Ford is making automobiles. People say there are two Model Ts driving around Cheyenne already. We have the telegraph now. There are trains coming to Cheyenne. There is even talk of a spur to Layton. You can't do things like you and Grandpa did twenty years ago."

Harlan decided he better stop talking. He was thinking about the letter he had yet to show his father. The letter was from several of his schoolteachers. He only had one year to go. They wanted him to go to college. They wanted to help send him to college, and Harlan wasn't sure how his pa would take the offer of help.

Charlie was thoroughly pissed now, and he knew it. "So Mr., you think you have all the answers. You think you understand all about changes and your old man don't. You think you know everything?"

"No sir. I don't know every thing. I do know times are changing and if we don't change with them they are going to run right over the ranch and us."
"And that is why I am going to college . . . with or with out your help!"

Harlan spurred his horse harder than he needed and galloped away from Charlie before his pa could see the tears. In his seventeen years, Harlan had never talked back to his pa and it hurt even if he did feel sure he was right.

"Son of a bitch!" Charlie muttered to himself. "Son of a bitch." His anger drained away as he watched Harlan disappear into the distance. "The kid had spunk." "He believed in something and he had stood up for what he believed," reasoned Charlie. "Was there a possibility Harlan was right?" Even Matt Caldwell talked about the new times coming. Matt was educated. He would talk to Matt Caldwell again.

At dinner, Margarita wondered what has happened between her husband and her son. There was a barrier between them. That had never happen before.

Later when Margarita was getting ready for bed, Charlie noticed Harlan down by the barn, leaning on the fence.

Charlie joined him there. "I think we should look into college. I thought I might talk to Matt. He is college educated." Harlan nodded. Charlie held out his hand. What he really wanted to do was hug his youngest. That is just what Harlan did to him.

Back in the bedroom Margarita asked, "What is wrong between you and Harlan?"

"Not a thing. Not one damn thing." Charlie was smiling.

Before the end of the school year, Charlie did talk to Matt Caldwell. Now he was trying to explain the whole college idea to Margarita.

"What do you mean, Chicago?" she exclaimed. "It is to far way. Why can't he go to Layton or even Cheyenne?"

"Matt and all Harlan's teachers all say the same thing. He should go to school back east, preferably Chicago. Matt even says Chicago is going to be the center of the beef industry."

"But," her lower lip was trembling, "He will be gone for four years."

"Yes, but it is best for his major," said Charlie. He was having a hard time explaining it to his wife when he didn't understand it as much as he wished.

"Who is this major? Harlan is not going in the army."

"In education, a major is the main subject of your studies. Harlan will study how to raise beef."

"Why does he need that? You already taught him about beef?" The discussion was not going well.

"Margarita, Harlan wants to go."

She sniffled, "Will he come home for Christmas?"

"No."

"Will he come home for the summers?"

"Maybe."

"Are you sure he will come home when his major is done?"

"I believe he will," answered Charlie. He knew full well that children did things they were not supposed to do and often did things that were not expected, but he was fairly sure that Harlan would return home and take his rightful place as owner of the Double B. "Besides," said Charlie hoping to make her feel better, "We have him at home one more year." Margarita sniffed again.

Chapter Twenty-five

The Letter Years

For his parents, the year went too fast. For Harlan, it couldn't go fast enough. Many people helped him prepare his entry application. His teachers assured him his grades were good enough. Charlie commented to Matt, "I suspect if it comes to a choice between my boy and some eastern politician's son, Harlan will be turned away despite the good grades." Matt knew that was always possible.

Christmas was nice, but different with no Susan and no Rosa. They waited for the letter from the university. Spring was the usual calving time. No more sickness in the cattle herds was seen. The cattle were driven up to the summer pastures.

The letter arrived when Harlan was gone. Charlie waited. The three of them opened the letter together. Margarita really didn't want her son to go away but she didn't want to see his dreams dashed either. She watched him read and knew by the expression on his face he was going to college.

Harlan was torn between spending the summer in the high country and staying with his parents. He knew he would miss it all. They attended the July 4 festivities. Harlan was surprised at how many people came up to him and wished him well. Charlie was shocked at the cost of college. Sure he could afford it, but it was a lot more than a very good horse, several good horses in fact, which is what he said to Matt. A sign of the changing times he guessed. Harlan could hardly wait. He was going to ride a train . . . all the way from Cheyenne to Chicago. In answer to Margarita's repeated question, yes he would write at least once a month.

He was gone. Charlie suspected that Margarita cried when he was out of the house. She was busying herself with her quilting. Without Susan or Rosa and now Harlan, he suspected she was lonely, again. As soon as he thought, they might have a letter he went into town. Nothing came from Harlan. He was more disappointed than he expected. Matt Caldwell told Charlie the freshman students didn't have much time. They were kept busy. For young men like Harlan, the whole big city and college experience was going to be a shock. Plus, kids like Harlan were usually very home sick.

When the first letter did arrive it was everything Matt described. Margarita didn't read well and didn't write, so it fell to Charlie to read the letters and write the answers. Charlie read everything to her. He writes he was so home sick he thought about giving it all up and coming home. Says he even looked into the cost of a return ticket. He has made friends. Right now his best friend is from Colorado. He is taking a lot of classes. Chicago is very big.

Charlie wrote back that the round up went well. The rancher north of the Double B was having trouble with the Hathaways. Everyone in the valley had done very well this year. Several of the ranchers were getting together and having sort of the End-of-Roundup celebration. They were not inviting the Hathaways.

From Harlan: The city has electric lights. People put up special ones and it makes Christmas look very festive. The church choirs are very big. The Christmas music is very serious. His friend from Colorado drank too much at New Years and was sick. "Harlan says the Colorado friend is flunking and will probably fail and leave at the end of the semester," read Charlie.

"Students can fail?" questioned Margarita.

From Charlie: Too much snow this year. Several ranches are going to lose cattle, because they can't get feed to them. If it weren't for the fences the cows could keep drifting with the storms. There is a Model T in Layton now. Belongs to the banker.

From Harlan: My grades are good. I think my teachers like me. Several are interested about my being able to speak Sioux. I wish you were here so we could practice. When I come home this summer we must use the language often. I have met one student that doesn't like me because my grandmother was an Indian. His uncle was with General Custer at the Little Big Horn.

"Why shouldn't his teachers like Harlan?" remarked Margarita.

From Charlie: Lots of calves this year. I plan on hiring more hands. Someone set the schoolhouse afire. Burned right down to the ground. The sheriff is going to retire. They have asked me to run for the office. I turned them down. I have enough to do running the ranch. While I was in town last, a young lady named Madge said to tell you hello. She is looking forward to seeing you when you return this summer.

"Who is this Madge?" asked Margarita when Charlie read his letter to Harlan.

"I don't know."

From Harlan: I have attended a real stage play. It was magic. Don't encourage Madge. In three of my subjects, I am the top of my class. How is my horse? There are stables here, but it is not our kind of riding. To many people ride English. You should see the trolley cars.

"What is a trolley car?" inquired Margarita.

From Harlan: We will be having tests soon. I plan on studying very hard even though my grades are good. I have my ticket home already. I will arrive in Cheyenne on the June 17. Please be there. Can we all go to the July 4 celebration?

Charlie and Margarita were at the train station. The team didn't like the train or the automobiles on the street. Charlie had a hard time keeping them under control. Harlan was taller than Margarita when she embraced him. Harlan and Charlie shook hands. Charlie didn't dare let go of the reins of the spooked animals. Loading his luggage, Harlan said, "Let's go home" and he meant it.

Finally at the ranch, Harlan took his luggage into his room. The first thing he did was to put on old clothes, and they were too short. With Charlie, he walked out to the bunkhouse, shook hands with all the men he was familiar with and introduced himself to the new ones. Charlie was proud. At the dinner table, Harlan had just given himself a third helping of chile verde. "Don't they feed you?" Margarita asked.

"Yes, but it is not as good as your cooking." Margarita beamed. Charlie noted that Harlan was taller and had filled out some. He decided Harlan would be a nice looking man not realizing that Harlan looked exactly like him.

Margarita was thinking the same thing a few days later at the Independence Day festivities. She watched her son and her husband walk toward her. Charlie was a little taller and beefier. Same light brown hair although Charlie had some gray now. Same light blue eyes. Their stride was the same. When they talked with their hands they used the same motions. Some times their laugh sounded the same. "You have a nice looking son, Mrs. Bennington." Margarita did not know the woman but they exchanged pleasantries and the woman moved on. That happened three times during the day.

Charlie introduced Harlan to Tom Logan, the new sheriff. Charlie commented," Logan was a good choice for the job. He knows the law. He and the judge get along well. Seems like law and order have come to Silver Bend, at least most of the time." He said this as he and Harlan walked over to visit with Matt Caldwell who had a lady on his arm.

Going home Margarita related how ladies she didn't know stopped to talk to her. Charlie explained, "I suspect they have daughters and Harlan looks like a good catch." Harlan was embarrassed.

"The pretty lady with Matt? Is she going to be Mrs. Caldwell?" Harlan changed the subject with the question.

"Wouldn't be surprised."

Two days later over dinner Margarita asked Harlan, "Do they have young ladies at your college?"

"Yes, they do. Some are very smart and interested in their studies. Others are attending school just to find a husband." Suddenly Charlie was listening.

"Do you walk out with any of the young ladies?"

"It's not like here. You don't walk out. You might ask a girl to dinner at a nice restaurant or take her to a park on a Sunday if the weather permits, or maybe an evening at the theater if you could afford it but no I don't take any girls anywhere."

"Why not. You are a nice young man," was his mother's response.

Harlan sighed. "I am considered a rube. They think my cowboy boots and hat are funny." Charlie was frowning.

"What is a rube?" Margarita wanted to know.

Harlan looked at his father for help but saw none was coming. "People consider me a rube, because I have not learned all my big city manners yet."

"You have always been polite," persisted his mother.

"When you go to a proper restaurant, the table is set with a nice white table cloth, napkins to match and crystal candle holders are on the table just to make it pleasant not because they need the light. There can be as many as three forks, and three spoons all for different foods. When you know big city manners, you know which fork goes with which food, and two different glasses, one for wine and one for water and your coffee cup has a saucer, which is used only to hold the cup. You never pour your coffee into the saucer to cool. And another little glass for an after dinner drink. The menus can be written in French. If you are not careful you could end up ordering snails in butter and garlic."

Margarita did not believe the part about the snails. "Do you know all those things?"

"I'm learning."

"Is it part of you schooling?"

"No, but it is part of getting along."

Later when Charlie and Harlan were alone, Charlie said, "Do people really think your boots and hat are funny?"

"Some people do. When it comes to big city or small town, they both have some people that are plain ignorant." Summer vacation was almost over. Harlan asked if they could go trout fishing up in the Sandies, for a few days. Then, he was gone back to school.

Fall roundup came and went and no letter from Harlan. Margarita fussed. When the letter did arrive. It was short.

Letter from Harlan: "I have a part time job," read Charlie. "I am working in a motor car garage. I am learning how an engine works. I am also learning to drive. I do believe that motorcars and such are here to stay. Pa, you should think about buying one for the ranch. We could have "Double B' painted on the doors."

Letter To Harlan: The round up went well. Neighbors came together for a second End-of-Roundup celebration again this year. There is talk about making this an annual event for the local ranchers. There is a new general store moving into town, and there are plans for a hospital in Layton. Matt Caldwell did marry the young lady you met last summer. Charlie avoided all mention of motorcars.

From Harlan: I mailed you a Christmas box. My grades are holding up. I broke two fingers on my left hand, but I have learned to ice-skate. I have discovered the library. I have never seen so many books.

Harlan's box arrived a week before Christmas. For Charlie there was a book of pictures taken during the War Between the States. The photographer was named Mathew Brady. Per Harlan's note, the photographer was being recognized as one of the best for pictures taken of the war. Perhaps some of these scenes were what Grandpa Asa saw during his two years in the Union Army. Margarita's gift was also a book, one containing quilt patterns. A lady at the library told him what to buy when he mentioned his mother did quilting. She could also recommend a shop that sold acceptable cotton fabric.

Not till March did they hear from Harlan again. Because of the weather, they received two letters at one time. Harlan had mastered his city manners and taken a young lady to dinner. He had enjoyed it enough to ask her out again which was followed by an invitation to have dinner with her parents. The evening was nice, but Harlan felt the father asked too many questions about the ranch, its future and its worth. "Smart young man," thought Charlie. The second letter said nothing about that young lady. Harlan wanted to know what people were saying about the war in Europe. He had done well on his semester tests. He was already thinking about summer. "He said no more about a young lady?" asked Margarita. Charlie reread the letter.

"No."

To Harlan: The biggest news is that old man Hathaway shot himself. No chance to buy the land. The oldest son, Stub, is going to run the ranch. I think Stub was in school about the time you were. We had lots of calves this year, but I wish the grass was a little better. Your mother is waiting for summer.

It was a short letter, because Charlie wasn't going to tell Harlan everything Tom Logan related to him about old man Hathaway's death.

It was a normal day in town for Charlie till Logan flagged him down and invited him to sit. "Guess you heard about old man Hathaway?" Charlie hadn't at that point. The way Stub Hathaway is telling it, the old man was ranting and raving some. No warning. Put the pistol up to his head and pulled the trigger. Stub is taking over the running of the ranch but you know he is about as smart as a post. I suspect he also takes after his dad when it comes to the bottle."

"What was he upset about?" Charlie wanted to know.

"You."

"Me?" said Charlie. I haven't seen or talked to any of the Hathaways for over two years.

"Stub says the old man said you were plotting against him. Said you were after his land. Says you caused his dad's death."

"Sure I wanted that land. Tried to buy, it twice when they were having a bad patch. He turned me down both times.

"Everyone in town knows that," concluded Logan "except for maybe Stub. He says he's going to kill you. I can't arrest him for talk." Charlie's mouth dropped open. Nobody had ever threatened to kill him with or with out reason. "What I'm telling you is keep a sharp eye. If he so much as looks in your direction the wrong way, you let me know." Charlie left all that out of his letter to Harlan, and he didn't tell Margarita either. He scanned the street when he was in town. He avoided alleyways. He watched the skyline when he was out on the range. He was never without his rifle or his pistol, but he didn't look any different than a lot of men in the area. Nothing happened.

His second summer and Harlan returned home. "But Pa," he said as they started for the ranch. "People ought to be concerned about the war in Europe. What about the sinking of the Lusitania?"

"Well I guess Europe and the Atlantic Ocean are a long way off for most folk out here. Do you think we should be concerned?"

"There are people back east that say we will enter the war eventually," answered Harlan. Charlie thought about that answer. Did it mean young men like Harlan would go far away to fight a war not everyone understood? The world was getting too small. He was not going to let such thoughts spoil Harlan's summer at home.

Charlie and Margarita now had a small circle of friends. They were all invited to the Double B to a party to welcome Harlan back for the summer.

Quickly June turned into July. Everyone in the area it seemed, arrived in town for July 4. A number of young ladies approached Harlan and a number of mothers and fathers looked him over as well. "What they are doing, is sizing up the ranch," Charlie grumbled to his wife at bedtime.

The summer was going by to fast, and Harlan wanted to do everything. He wanted to go fishing. He wanted to camp at the lake. "We can take Mama. A wagon will make it up there. If you had a motorcar she could really be comfortable." Charlie loaded the wagon and ignored the remark about the motorcar. Margarita took more food than necessary but Harlan and Charlie ate better than they ever did going by themselves. "We should do this more often" Charlie remarked to Harlan. Charlie, however, was thinking about a motorcar but kept his thoughts to himself. Margarita had a wonderful time and thanked both Charlie and Harlan.

Several days later and just a few days from when Harlan had to return east, the father and son were riding in the northeast pasture looking at the grass. "As I wrote you, it is sparse," said Charlie.

"The experts are talking about planting special pasture grasses," said Harlan and as he turned to explain Charlie's hand flew to his forehead, which showed blood, and he watched his father fall from his horse. Then Harlan heard the shot. He dove to the ground.

"Pa?"

"Shut up! Listen." They both heard what sounded like laughter and then receding hoof beats.

"Pa?"

"Yeah. I'm hit. Son of a bitch!" Charlie was right and he was bleeding freely. "I think its not, bad just a scalp wound. Damn, they do bleed." Looking at is father sitting on ground and holding his head, Harlan didn't like what he saw. After helping Charlie clean up, it was just as Charlie had said, a scalp wound that bled a lot. Harlan was relieved but not happy that it had come so close to being a fatal headshot.

"Who . . . ?" Charlie cut Harlan off and related the story about Stub Hathaway and his drunken boasts.

"What are we going to do?" asked Harlan.

"What I am not going to do is tell your mother."

"Well, you are going to have to think of something." A bandage now covered the wound and Charlie's cowboy hat covered the bandage as long as he wore it over to one side. It hurt like hell.

"You sure as hell can't go to bed with your hat on. Mama might notice"
Harlan was trying to be serious but not doing a very good job of hiding a smile. It did seem funny and both of them laughed.

"I will tell her I did something stupid and I don't want to talk about it. I have said that before, many times," Charlie confessed. "She won't ask many questions." Harlan grinned at his father.

Charlie was right. Margarita didn't ask any more questions of Charlie but tried to pry information out of Harlan. Harlan just shrugged his shoulders. The afternoon of the following day, Margarita looked out the window and commented, there is a rider coming down the ranch road. Doesn't seem to be in a hurry."

Looking over her shoulder, Charlie identified the rider as Sheriff Logan. He and Harlan went out to meet the sheriff. "Heat up the coffee. Maybe he can visit a while."
"Tom, Can you stay for coffee?"

"No Charlie. I was just out this way and I thought I might stop by and see how you were feeling?" Harlan and Charlie exchanged looks, which did not go unnoticed by the sheriff.

"I feel find. Why shouldn't I?"

"I hear Stub Hathaway rode into to town late yesterday afternoon, all liquored up and bragging that he shot you. Saw you fall off your horse."

"Well, that lying son of a bitch. I've never fallen off my horse in my entire life!" Charlie was fit to be tied. He seemed angrier about the falling off the horse comment than he did about the bullet crease in his scalp. Harlan and Logan were laughing. Logan stopped laughing when Charlie pulled off his hat to show him the bandaged wound.

"Hathaway do that?"

"Probably. Didn't see the shooter. Just heard laughter."

Logan was frowning. "I can arrest him but it will be your word again his. He is known for being a loud mouth, a braggart and a drunk. Charges won't hold up in the end."

"I know that. I can take care of the problem myself." Now Charlie was serious. Logan was shaking his head.

"You can't be taking matters into your own hands, Charlie."

Before the brewing argument could erupt Harlan said, "I have an idea." The older men let Harlan talk. "If you are willing sheriff, you could just mention in town that you happened to drop by this way just as we were coming home from several days of fishing up in the Sandies. That way it will sound as if Stub was running off at the mouth."

"As usual," muttered Charlie.

Harlan continued, "If Hathaway does think he shot someone he will have to start wondering who and maybe they might come looking for him." The sheriff did like the idea and was relived when Charlie agreed.

The following day was hot enough that Sheriff Logan and his deputy were fine with the office door being open. Logan waited till a certain passer-by, town gossip and drinking buddy of Hathaway's was just even with the door and then he remarked loudly to the deputy. "Stopped by the Bennington place yesterday. Charlie and his son were just back from three days fishing up in the Sandies. Biggest damn trout I ever saw." The ease-dropper couldn't move from the door fast enough. The deputy noticed the sheriff's smile.

"What you smiling about, Tom?"

"Just big damn trout. That's all." Later that night when Stub Hathaway heard the tale he was not happy. He was so sure the man he shot was Charlie Bennington. Saw him fall from his horse. Well, maybe he dove off at the sound of the shot, but damn he shot someone. If the fallen man was not Bennington, then who the hell had he shot? As Harlan suggested Stub was worried.

Margarita was sad that Harlan's summer vacation was over. Today they would take the buggy and go to the new train station in Layton and send Harlan off for his third year of college. Looking back it seemed the first two years had passed quickly. Harlan was twenty-three. That he had two more years of schooling before he come return to the ranch for good might as well be twelve years from his mother's perspective. She hugged him and tried not to cry. The train moved slowly out of the station in a cloud of steam. She waved knowing full well he couldn't see her.

Back at the buggy, she saw luggage still in the rear seat. Look! Harlan didn't take some of his belonging, she pointed out to Charlie.

"That's our luggage," Charlie smiled.

"Ours?"

"Mrs. Bennington, we are spending the night in town at the Hotel Layton. I have reserved one of their best rooms. We are going to have a fine dinner tonight. Tomorrow after a great dining room breakfast I thought you might like to go shopping. Maybe purchase a new bonnet? Then we will take a slow ride back home."

"Oh, Charlie. I'm not dressed properly."

"You were dressed well enough to say good-bye to your son?"

"Yes."

"Then you are dressed well enough for dinner with your husband." Passersby saw her tears and thought how hard it is when you have to say good-bye to someone.

Charlie knew as soon as he saw the bathtub at the hotel Margarita would want to know if they could have one at the house. "Well? Why the hell not?"

Letter from Harlan: I visited the stockyards this week. I have never seen so many cattle. The operation of the yards is something I would never have imagined. I'm proud we raise cattle and some of my classmates now have a different opinion of us "cowboys" from the western states. Mama, the lady from the library says I should ask you about Indigo. She says for quilting ladies, it is a very popular fabric . . . dark blue in color I believe. If you would like me to send you some, she said she would show me where I might purchase Indigo as well as notions. She had to tell me that the word "notions" means pins, needles, thread, and things like that. Let me know what you might want. It will have to be your Christmas present.

To Harlan: Round up went well. Again this year we had an End-of-Roundup Dinner, but it was cold. Still, more people attended. Someone suggested we should have it prior to roundup for better weather. The few farmers that raised alfalfa are going to expand next year. I'm pleased to have growers right here in the valley. Matt Caldwell and his wife had a baby. The banker is going to retire. Have not met his replacement. I talked to him about his Ford Motor card. He likes it but is unhappy because his wife wants to drive it. Thinks that is unseemly. Your mother said to tell you the baby was a girl and Indigo or anything pretty would please her. Needles are at the top of her list, I believe.

From Harlan: More snow this year. I am pleased with my grades, but it does seem very easy for me. Mr. Penrose says I should change my major to business. He says ranching is going to be big business. He has offered to take me to the stock exchange. He says that is part of big business also. Lillian is taking me to the shop to purchase items for Mama. Margarita asked three questions. Who is Lillian? Who is Mr. Penrose? What is a stock exchange? Charlie didn't have the answer to any of those questions.

To Harlan: We are having a lot of snow also. Your mother wants to know who Lillian is and Mr. Penrose also. I talked to the new bank president, Jeb Pearson. He explained the stock exchange to me. Are you sure you want to change you major? I guess you were right. We can't just raise cattle without knowing more about what's going on in the rest of the country. What are people saying about the war in Europe now? It has become a subject for talk here.

December was a big snow winter. It was the first winter for mail delivery to the mailbox at the end of the ranch road and because of the snow they opened their gifts from Harlan in January. For Margarita, Harlan had sent a box of all sorts of quilting items some of which she had no idea of their use. Charlie studied his silver shaving mug and decided he liked the scented shaving soap. But having the Double B brand engraved on the mug was very fancy and one of those thoughtful things only Harlan would think of. Perhaps he needed to talk to Harlan about an increase in his allowance.

From Harlan: I have changed my major and business is much more difficult than animal husbandry. Maybe it is because it is so new to me, but I am having to study more. Mrs. Penrose invited me to tea. I think I handled it rather badly. Lillian said not to worry. The letter was short. Before Margarita could ask who were Mr. and Mrs. Penrose and this Lillian person, Charlie held up his hands and said, "I don't know." He wished he did.

Just as Charlie didn't tell Harlan all the news, Harlan was not telling his parents all his news either. When he wrote about Lillian, the lady at the library, he omitted the part that Lillian was his own age and in the same year of school as he. Because they did not take the same classes or move in the same circles, he did not know anything about her till they met at the library. She over heard him asking about books on quilting and since she did some quilting, having learned it from her grandmother, she answered all his questions.

They ran into each other often at the library and formed a friendship independent of the college activities. He was doing a lot more studying as he had written. That was true, but he was studying in the library just so he could possibly meet Lillian.

He had asked her out on several occasions. She had accepted. She introduced him to her father, Cecil Penrose who thought Harlan Bennington was a cut above some of Lillian's silly young friends. Manners dictated that Lillian's mother invite him to tea. Not only had Harlan not written about any of this, when he did at last write about Lillian Penrose he would omit the fact that Cecil Penrose was Judge Cecil Penrose and that Lillian's mother was a Tarker of the Boston Tarkers before she married Lillian's father.

Now Lillian and Harlan stood in the vestibule of the gracious Penrose home.
"I bungled it very badly," moaned Harlan. "I can tell your mother disapproves of me already."

"Oh, Harlan. Don't worry. Mother is often somewhat stuffy. Besides Daddy likes you," Lillian patted his hand. Harlan found he rather liked it.

At the same time in the parlor Trudy Penrose fixed an unsmiling eye on her husband and said, "What on earth does your daughter see in that young man? He was absolutely awful this afternoon. I suspect he has never been invited to tea in his life."

Sometimes Cecil thought, his wife could be pompous and this was one of those times. "Trudy, I would venture to guess that if we were in his element we might be a little fumbled fingered also." Trudy made her usual huffing sound but said nothing more.

Letter from Harlan: Margarita could hardly wait. "Hurry. Maybe he will tell us when he will be home." Charlie opened the letter and scanned it quickly. Silently he reread part of it. "It says here he is not coming home this summer. He is going to work at the stock exchange."

Margarita's face fell. "Not coming home?"

"He is going to visit the stock exchange in New York with Mr. Penrose."
Charlie slowly read on. Mr. Penrose is the father of this Lillian he has
mentioned. She is a student at his college. He met her at the library. Charlie
read on to himself.

"Charlie! What? Tell me what."

"He thinks he wants to court her. He has not talked to her about this. He
is only telling us incase he needs money for a ring . . . perhaps in the fall."

"Our Harlan? A girl? Oh, Charlie." Margarita burst into tears. Charlie
put his arms around her.

"We knew it would happen some day."

"But he is so far away. We don't know anything about her. What if she
doesn't like the ranch?"

Charlie was way ahead of her. "What if Harlan didn't come home at all?
What about the future of the ranch, the Double B? What about the war in
Europe? Would Harlan feel he should be a part of it? Did he want his son to
be happy? Yes! Where did Harlan's happiness lie?" He wished he had the
answers.

Letter from Charlie: We are disappointed you are not coming home for
the summer. Charlie didn't know what to write after that. He decided on a
neutral ground and talked about Harlan's education . . . yes the change in
his major was correct. If Harlan thought working this summer at the stock
exchange would benefit the ranch then it was a positive step in his education
and that was good. Charlie thought a long time before he ended the letter. In
conclusion he said, "If you think this young lady is the woman to support you
and to share your life here on the ranch, then you should court her. Yes, we
have some money for a ring if that is how it comes about." Margarita listened
to what he wrote and burst into tears again.

Even after he posted the letter he needed some time to consider just exactly
what thoughts he was expressing. It was the first time he thought about or
even realized Margarita's support over the years. The support of good women
was . . . ? "Well damn. It was mighty important." Why hadn't he and Harlan
ever talked about marriage and the responsibilities that came with it? Asa

had Blue Feather. Before that he had the wife named Catherine who believed in his dream and so they came west. Charlie had Margarita in all their good times and bad. Would this Lillian be there for Harlan as the first Bennington wives been there for their men and the shared dreams?

In Chicago, it was a warm Sunday afternoon in June. Lillian and Harlan were strolling in the park, as were many other young couples. He decided he did not like Chicago in the summer. He did not like humidity. If he were home he could be at the lake as naked as he wanted to be and feeling the cool breeze blowing down from the Peetees. He had not yet received an answer from his parents acknowledging the fact he was not coming home or his thoughts about Miss Lillian Penrose.

At the moment his white, starched shirt was making him itch. If there were a breeze blowing off Lake Superior it was not reaching the park.

"You are very quiet today," said Lillian.

"I'm sorry. It is that I have not heard from my parents. I'm not sure they will understand my not coming home for the summer."

"Are you sorry you decided to stay and work the summer here?"

"No. I couldn't do both and I am here to learn as much as I can. The rest of this summer and finally my last year . . . then I will be home for good."

"Would you ever consider living in the east?"

"No. I could learn to fit in but I will never belong here." His answer pleased her and when she related that conversation to her father, Cecil Penrose concluded Harlan's answer was "sound."

Cecil glanced at his grown up little girl, "Daughter, are you having more than thoughts of friendship about this young man?"

"Perhaps."

"Your mother will not be pleased."

Lillian sighed. "I know. I think she is inviting her second cousin's son, Martin Verduft, to her Fourth of July party for that reason."

"In that case you better invite your young man. Verduft is self-centered spoiled, shallow man with no future unless he marries up despite his family connections."

"I shall invite Harlan. And, thank you Daddy."

"Mother is hosting a Fourth of July party. I want you to come."

"I would bet a kiss your mother doesn't want me at her party," grumbled Harlan. "She doesn't like me and we both know that is the truth."

"Harlan!" They had been around each other long enough for him to know when she said his name that way he was going to be put in his place and he could forget a kiss. He hadn't had even one yet. "You are not arm and arm in the park with my mother. You did not just ask my mother for a kiss, which I might consider after the party if you attend. Besides I am asking you to the party as my special guest. If my invitation is not good enough well maybe you had better take me home right now." Several people stared at them.

"Tell me what to wear" was all Harlan said.

Sitting on the patio and feeling the cool Rocky Mountain evening descend upon them, Charlie said, "You do want to go to the July 4 Celebration?" Margarita was slow to answer. He knew she was thinking it would not be the same without Harlan.

"Yes. It wouldn't seem right not to go. I think we should. You have never shot that rifle the twins gave you. Could you enter one of the shooting contests with it?"

"I would have to practice some but I will think on it." He liked her idea. In fact he liked the ideas so much that by the time they went in he had already decided to enter a match with the Sharps rifle. He would keep his thoughts to himself till he tried shooting the gun.

A week later he took the rifle down from the wall and thoroughly cleaned and checked it. He set up a target behind the barn and began shooting. It would take some practice, but it was a sweet weapon. One of the cowhands watched. "Mr. Bennington, you going to compete with that gun on the fourth?"

"Thinking about it." That night in the bunkhouse every man was counting out his money to bet on the boss man.

It seemed appropriate that July 4 was hot both in Chicago and in Silver Bend. Lillian could not decide on a dress. The only damper on the day was that she had met Martin. Not only was he everything her father said, but also he was an ass. "Ass" was not a word she ever said out loud but it perfectly fit Martin Verduft, second cousin or not. What her mother saw in him was a mystery. Lillian decided on the white dress with blue ribbons. She would add a red ribbon for the holiday. She could at least look cool even if she didn't feel that way. She had suggested to Harlan what to wear although she suspected no matter how well dressed he appeared her mother would find fault.

On that same morning Harlan had lain in bed thinking those very thoughts. He would, as Lillian suggested, bring Mrs. Penrose a bouquet of flowers. He was also going to wear his cowboy boots. The boots would remind him of July 4 at home. The boots were black. His trousers were black. If Mrs. Penrose didn't like the boots more than likely, it didn't make any difference.

For the reminder of the day till party time, he read about New York City and about the stock exchange. In two weeks, he would accompany Mr. Penrose to New York. They would go to Wall Street, and he would visit the New York Stock Exchange. While Mr. Penrose took care of some personal business, Harlan planned to see all the city sites he could. He felt a little guilty. He should have found a job for the summer. He needed more spending money, especially since he purchased a gold pocket watch and chain for his father. It would have to be for Christmas.

On the day of Mrs. Penrose's party, lack of funds was the reason he rode the trolley and then walked the distance to the Penrose home. On their street, many of the houses flew the American flag. Several homes also had red, white, and blue bunting hanging from upstairs windows. He liked the idea of a flag. The ranch should have a flag. He might consider that for another Christmas present.

From the number of cars parked along the curb he guessed that there were other parties going on in the neighborhood. Now in front of the Penrose home he was admiring a new touring car "Beautiful piece of mechanical engineering," said a gray-headed man standing off to one side.

"Indeed it is."

"Are you Harlan Bennington?" The man's glance lingered on Harlan's boots.

"Yes. I am."

"Perhaps after dinner, I might have a minute of your time. My name is Henry English. I am a friend of Cecil's" Changing the subject he looked at the flowers in Harlan's hand. "Are those for Trudy or Lillian?"

"Mrs. Penrose," answered Harlan never daring to call Lillian's mother Trudy.

"Well, don't worry about Trudy. She acts like a dragon. She is mostly huff and steam and not much fire." The man tipped his hat, put out his cigar and walked up the stairs and entered the Penrose home.

"Well," was all Harlan could think of. He looked at his small bouquet of daisies which all he was able to afford at the moment. Since meeting Lillian, the allowance didn't seem to go far enough. He smiled as he looked at the flowers. In Spanish the blossoms were called margaritas, his mother's name. By golly! He had margaritas and his boots. It was going to be a good evening.

Inside the house, Trudy had out done herself in patriotic decorations. She politely accepted his flowers and didn't notice his boots. Lillian had told Harlan that both she and her father added names to the guest list so he recognized some of Lillian's friends and some of the older gentleman in the room. To start with there would be drinks and conversation. The buffet would start at 7:00 p.m. Everyone would have to look for their place cards at the small tables scattered around the dining room and the veranda. Desserts and coffee or after dinner drinks would be served at about the time the first fire works were expected to began.

Lillian greeted him warmly but as daughter of the host and hostess she quickly moved on to new guests. Just before the dinner bell she and a tall beanpole, young man approached Harlan. "Martin, I'd like you to meet a good friend of mine, Mr. Bennington from Wyoming." Martin did notice Harlan's boots and with what amounted to a smirk, slightly tipped his head. "My cousin, Martin Verduft," said Lillian and only so Harlan could see rolled her eyes toward the ceiling.

"Mr. Verduft." Harlan didn't have to shake his hand because the dinner bell sounded.

Harlan was not surprised to find he was seated at a back table with a returned missionary couple and their daughter. The man spoke nonstop about his good work in the islands, which required Harlan to have to only nod and smile at the proper times. Amazing the man managed to empty his plate and talk all at the same time. Harlan offered to fetch dessert. "Let me help you." It was the only thing the daughter, whose name he had already forgotten, had spoken all during dinner." He pulled back her chair and together they went to dessert table. "I apologize for my father. He is a bore. You don't have to stay at the table. I shall say you were called away." Picking up three plates of chocolate cake she added, "Thank you for being polite." She was gone.

People were moving toward the veranda and the lawn with their desserts or coffees. Harlan selected a piece of peach pie and found a quiet corner. He was content to be by himself when Henry English approached. "May I join you?"

"Please. Be seated." was all Harlan could think to say.

"I understand you speak the Sioux language?"

"Some, I am not as good as my father."

"I am a curator at the Museum of Natural History. The museum has been given a number of donated items such as war bonnets, etc. To be perfectly honest none of our staff knows what we are looking at. We really don't even know the origin of any of these gifts. Would you be able to stop by my office and perhaps look at these items?" Mr. English was very serious and Harlan was sorry to turn his down. Besides Harlan had just seen Martin Verduft walking Lillian down the path to the gazebo by the boat dock.

"My grandmother died of small pox long before I was born. My grandfather was not able to keep anything of hers so I don't think I can help you. I am sorry." Harlan could see the man was very disappointed and hoped he would take his leave quickly.

"Was that peach pie you had there?"

"Yes sir. It was very good. There might be a piece left if you hurry." Henry English thanked Harlan for his time and ambled toward in the direction of the desserts but decided on a brandy instead.

The flower lined path leading toward the boat dock and the gazebo wandered into some trees and the sounds of the party were replaced with water lapping at the beach and the pilings of the dock. When the path forked Harlan stopped and listened. To his right he heard Lillian say, "Martin, I am not going to ask you again. I want to return to the party, now." Harlan wished he had moccasins instead of boots. The gravel under is boots was making to much noise. Hopefully the water and wave noise was louder. The gazebo came into sight. Lillian was just inside the structure and Verduft was blocking the only way out. Harlan could not hear what Verduft was saying but from the expression on Lillian's face she was distressed.

Harlan didn't hit him. Instead he spun Verduft around and taking a handful of shirt collar and the patriotic bow tie, he said softly but clearly into Verduft's startled face, "Go back to the party now, alone!" Harlan's grasp on the collar was cutting off Martin's air. Martin nodded as best he could. He was a little wobbly as he made his way back to the festivities. "Are you all right?" inquired Harlan.

"I am now, she answered. With out a thought he wrapped his arms around her, pulled her tight against him and kissed her full on the lips."

"Marry me!"

"Yes. I thought you would never ask." The second kiss left both of them as wobbly as Martin Verduft but for a different reason. Trudy Penrose was busy bidding Martin good-bye who was apologizing for the sudden headache that was causing him to leave early. She did not see Lillian and Harlan rejoin the party, but Cecil Penrose did. Nobody saw his smile because of the cloud of cigar smoke around his head. The first fireworks lit up the sky.

In Layton, Wyoming it was still too light for the display of fireworks. Just the same Charlie and Margarita were on their way home. They could not talk much because of the noise from the three turkeys in crates lashed to the back of the buggy." That is why they call it a turkey shoot," he explained over the noise. He would shut the stupid things in the barn for tonight. He and Margarita would have a drink on the patio. They each missed Harlan, but all in all it had been a nice day.

Now on the patio, Charlie had his shirt and shoes off and was enjoying a sip of good whiskey something he still only did on rare occasions. Margarita had a smaller drink and was wiggling her bare toes in the evening breeze. "You did very well with that gun, today," she said.

"It is a very good rifle," he replied modestly.

"And you are a very good shooter. You quit competing after you started winning didn't you?"

"Yes."

"Why?"

"Expect I could have beat them all. But the day is supposed to be a good time for everyone. By the time I had won the fourth turkey some of the men were not even bothering to enter. It seemed the right thing to do." The fact that he thought he was having trouble seeing out of his left eye was something he would keep to himself for the time being.

"Is that why you gave the other turkey to that little boy?" The child Margarita was talking about was a small boy with no shoes and some very poor clothes. The skinny kid had attached himself to Charlie asking if he could be of any help during the competition. He would do anything he said. Charlie didn't need any help, but the youngster was so earnest that Charlie said he could hold his cowboy hat. When Charlie decided to quit, he gave the last turkey to the boy saying he could not afford to pay him for holding his hat and besides he probably brought him luck. The grinning child was barely able to move the crated turkey. A few smiling bystanders gave the boy a helping hand as he disappeared into the crowd. "Do you know who he belonged to?"

"No. Anymore there are people in town I don't know. But I think he looked like there is not much food on the table at his house. You were busy chatting with all the ladies."

Margarita said quietly, "I was trying to learn about daughter-in-laws."

"You didn't say anything about Harlan's possible plans did you?"

"No. I just observed. Seems daughter-in-laws are not much different than daughters. Some are loving and some are not." Charlie suspected she was thinking about Catherine.

Changing the subject. "Did you hear that the sheriff had to tell Stub Hathaway to leave the celebration?

"No. Drunk I suppose." She placed her empty glass on the table.

"Do you think Harlan did anything exciting for July 4?" he wondered out loud.

"I am quite sure your son did not come home with three turkeys," she answered. They both laughed. Going into the house he put his arm around his wife and decided he liked the feel of a woman with substance.

For Harlan, the summer could not go by fast enough. For one thing he and Lillian could still only see each other on Sunday afternoons. After the fall term began they would see each other at the library mid week. He was bored clerking at the stock exchange and was looking forward to the trip with Lillian's father to New York. He was not totally sure why Mr. Penrose had asked him to come along but it was an opportunity.

Letter from Harlan: The July 4 dinner hosted by Lillian's parents was very nice followed by fireworks near the lake. I met an interesting, returned missionary and his family and some of Lillian's out of town family. By the time you read this I should be returning from my trip to New York City with Mr. Penrose. I will be glad to have classes start up again. I have not yet asked Mr. Penrose for Lillian's hand in marriage, but she has led me to believe that she will accept my proposal. I would appreciate any advance on my allowance for the purpose of purchasing an engagement ring.

"What is a returned missionary and what is an engagement ring and how much does one cost?" were Margarita's questions. When she asked about the cost of a ring, she was looking at her own gold band. As best Charlie could, he answered her questions.

Cecil Penrose and Charlie made their trip to New York City. Another big city but with a different flavor all it's own thought Harlan. During the day while Cecil was attending to his business, Harlan took in as many of the sights as possible and read, as may newspapers as possible. He thought it was not good that people were calling the war in Europe "World War I." Putting a number on it made it seem as if there could be a second war.

His favorite place was Central Park although it made him lonely to see young couples. He missed Lillian. The couples pushing baby buggies made Harlan think that he and Lillian would some day have children of their own, or at least he hoped so.

Evenings were spent at dinner with a few of Mr. Penrose's business acquaintances some of which were accompanied by young ladies that were most definitely neither daughter nor wife. The conversation was often dull, and he made every effort to avoid the flirtatious looks from some of the woman. Two things occupied Harlan's thoughts. He did not know how he would afford it but he felt he should offer to pay for part of this trip and he wanted to ask Lillian's father permission to marry her. Lillian's exact words were, "If you ask father while you are in New York then we can become engaged in September. We will have an engagement party and that gives mother a little less than a year to begin planning a June wedding for right after graduation. And we will have a honeymoon of course. Maybe Niagara Falls." Harlan thought but didn't say out loud "And then home to Wyoming."

Harlan was glad when he and Lillian's father were back on the train heading for Chicago. He decided the time was right for asking his big questions. "Sir."

Cecil Penrose interrupted, "For the love of Mike. Call me Cecil."

"I er . . . I would like to contribute for part of the cost of this trip."

"Hell son. Consider it a pre-wedding present. You are going to ask for my daughter's hand in marriage are you not?" Harlan choked and it was not only from Cecil's ever-present cigar smoke.

"Yes sir, I was. I am. I mean yes."

"I am assuming you and Lillian have talked about this. What are your plans?"

"Engagement in September. Graduate in June followed by the wedding, the honeymoon and then return to Wyoming. Lillian says that will give Mrs. Penrose time to plan the wedding."

"Time enough to bankrupt me you mean," laughed Cecil. Turing serious he said, "Living out west can't be easy. My daughter is not necessarily spoiled, but she has been raised with as many amenities as I could afford. Do you think Lillian will adapt?"

This was something Harlan had given some thought to or had avoided giving enough thought. The Penrose home had a full time housekeeper and cook, a laundress and someone to come clip the lawn and trim the hedges. His mother did it all except for the lawn and the hedges and that was only because the ranch house had no yard to speak of.

"We have talked about that. I believe she will do well and my parents will be there to support her in every way." Harlan tried to sound confident.

"You have my blessings my boy. However, Trudy is going to put you through all sorts of hoops with all her wedding preparations. Do me a favor. Humor her. You are taking our only daughter a long ways away when this is all done." Cecil Penrose looked just a little sad and his cigar had gone out.

Harlan congratulated himself. This had all come about easier than he expected, now to hear from his own parents.

Over the years as questions had come up for which Charlie had no answers, he went to town to ask and learn. Matt Caldwell and his wife had become good friends and now Charlie sat in the Caldwell kitchen with them both and asked about engagement and wedding rings. Anne Caldwell had all the answers as far a manners and traditions but not really knowing anything about Harlan's intended didn't help with the decision of how much money to give Harlan.

Anne fidgeted around and finally said, "Charlie, would you consider picking out the rings yourself?"

"Lord, no," he blurted out then said, "Why?"

"Do you know that pawn shop down at the end of Main Street?" He did. "In the window is a wedding set, a beautifully mounted engagement ring and the matching wedding bands? It is quite beautiful, and I believe very old. Perhaps Harlan's lady might appreciate something antique rather than fashionably new and similar to what some of her friends might receive." Charlie went straight home and told Margarita.

"Can we go look at it tomorrow?" was Margarita's suggestion.

Classes were well under way when Charlie at last heard from his parents. The answer came in a small parcel. In side a black velvet box was the ring set. The note said love Mama and Pa. "Holy shit," said Harlan so loudly that his roommate feared the house might be on fire. Lillian was overwhelmed and cried to the point Harlan thought he had done something wrong. As far as Trudy Penrose was concerned she had certainly underestimated the boy from out west.

She began composing the guest list for the engagement party. There should be a special Christmas party since it would be the last one for Lillian at home. A wedding shower was a must; maybe more than one. Trudy would talk to her best friends. A June wedding . . . how perfect. Yes, a honeymoon at Niagara Falls. Perhaps she and Cecil could go too. "No!" Cecil put his foot down to that. There was one thing Trudy did not want to do and that was talk to Lillian about wifely duties, a subject she found very distasteful. Well, she could put that off till May.

Letter from Harlan: The ring set is so much more than I could have ever imagined. That is what everyone, especially Lillian and her mother think. I don't know how I can ever thank you. I suspect there is a story about how you acquired it. Perhaps some day you will tell me (us).

"Cold day in hell," laughed Charlie.

"Hush. Keep reading," admonished his wife.

The Penrose's hosted an engagement announcement party. It was very nice (as usual). The guests included friends of Lillian's and her parents.
"Doesn't Harlan have friends?" asked Margarita.

"I suppose his friends are Lillian's friends," suggested Charlie.
Mrs. Penrose is now planning a lavish Christmas party. I suspect she believes we do not know how to celebrate Christmas in Wyoming. Wait until I take Lillian out to cut our own tree, bring it home so Dad and I can stand it up in the living room and Mama can bring out all our favorite ornaments. My grades are good despite all the extra activities. I am already wishing we were home and it was next summer.

"When did Harlan start calling you dad?" asked Margarita.

Sometimes Margarita's question amused Charlie. "I don't know. Perhaps that is a word engaged young men use now a days. Next Christmas he will be a married man and there will be four of us for Christmas." The thought pleased Charlie, but Margarita was deep in thought.

"Should we give her a Christmas gift?"

Letter to Harlan: Yes there is a story about the wedding rings, but I don't know that we will tell, maybe someday. The important thing is that it made everyone happy. Your mama wants to know if we should send Lillian a Christmas gift? If so, what would you suggest? We are glad to hear you are holding up your grades.

The End-of-Roundup party (people are calling it the EOR party) will be moved to late September next year. Since it has become so big it has to be held outside. This year we froze out butts off. It is hoped that moving the date will give us a better chance for good weather. You and Lillian should be here for next year. Perhaps the Double B will host it in your honor. Charlie had that idea only as he was ending his letter. To Margarita he said, "Lillian and

Harlan will be here for the next EOR celebration. I think we should host it. The idea both excited and depressed her."

"Oh dear," was all she said.

Letter from Harlan: I am having my own problem in what kind of Christmas gift to give to my intended. I asked Lillian to measure her foot. I think she might find a pair of moccasins very comfortable if you would like to send her a pair for your Christmas gift. I do believe she would be pleased.

I have a favor to ask. I am supposed to give Lillian a wedding present or so her mother has told me. I would like to give her a horse, have it there at the ranch when we come home. She rides fairly well but uses an English saddle. I am hoping you might locate her a good horse. Harlan had included the measurement of Lillian's foot.

"Charlie, Lillian's foot is bigger than mine," remarked Margarita who was a small woman with small feet. "Harlan has never said what Lillian looks like. Do you suppose she is ugly?"

"Harlan is a deep thinker. He may not have noticed what she looks like," Charlie doubted that but said it anyway because he also wondered what did Lillian Penrose looked like. He was also thinking about two horses with new, matching, western saddles for his son and new daughter-in-law.

Their Christmas gifts passed in the mail. Charlie had never owned anything as fine as the gold pocket watch. He didn't know the back was unadorned because Harlan could not afford engraving back in the summer when it was purchased in New Your City. Winter snowstorms blew down from Canada and covered the upper midwest to the Rocky Mountains in a deep blanket of snow that stayed till April.

That didn't slow down Mrs. Penrose and her parties. New Years Day afternoon Lillian rose from her chair by the fire and said to Harlan, "Let's go for a walk." Both Cecil and Trudy were sound asleep in the overly warm room. The New Years Eve party had lasted well into the wee small hours, too long was Harlan's opinion.

Outside in the cool, crisp air she held his arm so closely he could feel the swell of her breast through his coat sleeve. It gave him other thoughts, which he admitted to himself he had been thinking about as the wedding date approached. "I never thought I would say this, but I am tired of parties," she commented.

"Me too." He wondered what a whole handful of breast might feel like.

"Soon, I think Mother is going to ask you about your plans for your bachelor party."

"No . . . not having one."

You must. It is expected." He could hear surprise in Lillian's voice.

"No. You don't suppose we could elope? Just be done with it all."

It was her turn to say "no."

Semester exams were done with. He was a little disappointed in his grades, and he was dismayed to discover he was getting pudgy . . . too much rich food and too many parties and to much sitting. He would always be a solidly built man just like his father but he didn't like the way he was heading and there were still four months of pre-wedding preparation. Graduation was June 12. The wedding date was June 24. A two-week honeymoon was to be followed by several weeks of preparation for Lillian to move to Layton and the ranch. He wondered about the several weeks of preparation time before they could board the train and head west.

It was Easter dinner and Trudy Penrose set her teacup down, patted Harlan's hand and said, "Lillian tells me you have not planned your bachelor party."
Harlan patted her hand back.

"I have not planned it because I am not having a bachelor party and that is my final word on it." Trudy Penrose made that little huffing sound she did when Cecil told her no and removed her hand. Cecil Penrose was concentrating on spearing a potato and Lillian was laughing behind her napkin.

Later in the library, Cecil said to Harlan, "Do you have something against bachelor parties?"

"In a way." Harlan had never told the story to anyone before. "In my first year here, I was invited to two parties. The guests seemed a little silly. For some, it simply was an excuse to over drink. In all honesty I hadn't decided about drinking for myself. It seems the Benningtons have a family trait of a short fuse temper. I don't believe I have it, but I have seen it in my father. Liquor doesn't help matters any, if the temper does surface. The second year there was another party and I did drink too much. The conversation had turned to the wedding night and some how that gave someone the idea we could all visit a whore, er . . . house of prostitution."

"I know what they are," commented Cecil.

"We loaded into someone's car and drove to the outskirts of town. By the time we had reached our destination I was sick. I was going to throw up so I walked across the street and proceeded to be sick. By then the rest of the party guests had entered the establishment. I sat there on the grass thinking the whole idea was not good at all. That's when I heard the sirens and eventually the flashing red lights and the paddy wagons came into sight. I moved further back in the bushes and watched. It was a raid. We weren't as far out of town as we thought. The very profane madam, her loud angry ladies and my friends were all carted away and there I sat in the middle of nowhere all by myself."

"Is that when you decided to forego bachelor parties?"

"No. It was when I sobered up enough to discover I was sitting in a pile of dog crap." Cecil laughed so hard Trudy and Lillian heard him up stairs where they were again fitting Lillian into her wedding gown.

Letter Home: Graduation is fast approaching. Truthfully, I am glad it is here. I certainly don't regret my time at school and had I not come east I would not have met Lillian, but I will be very glad to come home to stay.

Margarita smiled and sniffled at the same time. As you can probably guess the wedding will be a fancy affair. I wish you could be here but in some ways I just want it to be over. I know Lillian is starting to feel the same way. After we return from our honeymoon, I will telegraph our arrival date. Do you think telephone service will ever reach Layton? PS thank you for the surprise wedding present. I think I know what it is. I can hardly wait.

Lillian had just been honored at her third and final wedding shower. She was showing Harlan the huge collection of beautiful gift items. "What are you going to do with them?" he asked.

"Why, we take them to Wyoming. We are going to have our own home. I will set up house keeping . . . for just the two of us."

"Hm . . ." was all he said.

On the same subject, Margarita said to Charlie, "Perhaps we should give Harlan and Lillian the stone cottage down by the stream."

"Why?"

"Did you really want your father around when we were first married?"

Some times, like now, her husband's grin was stupid. "No. I guess I didn't."

"Well, we will clean out the cottage tomorrow and replace what needs to be done away with."

Harlan was beginning to think about their wedding night a lot. Having grown up on a ranch and worked with a veterinarian, he knew where babies of all kinds came from. However, he didn't think that knowing that answered all his questions about how to proceed when the time came for him to be a husband. He thought about asking Cecil but decided against it, thinking that Lillian probably knew less than he did.

Lillian knew quite a bit more than he would have expected. First she had listened to her mother's Wifely Duties" speech. "In the bedroom, things happened that were unpleasant but necessary if you wished to have children and keep your husband at home." That was all Trudy Penrose had to say on the subject.

Lillian went to two of her married friends who appeared to be the happiest and asked about the wifely duties. It was a very interesting afternoon and sounded nothing like her mother's "duties." In fact, it didn't sound like duty at all.

For her daughter's wedding night, Trudy had selected a very expensive nightgown, robe, and slippers. The floor length gown buttoned up to just beneath Lillian's chin. She thanked her mother, but secretly hoped her friends were correct and she would not have to sleep in the damn thing.

The day of the wedding dawned hot and sticky. Other than that everything went, as it should. Lillian was the most beautiful woman Harlan had ever seen. He could hear Trudy Penrose and many other women sniffling through the whole ceremony.

In Layton, Wyoming Margarita sniffled over breakfast. Charlie said, "Pack a picnic lunch. Let's go up to the lake for the day. I want to tell you about the motorcar I plan to buy. Can have it here in time to pick up the Harlan and his bride." Margarita didn't know whether to laugh or cry.

While Charlie and Margarita sat in the shade by the quiet lake, Harlan and Lillian were feted at a lavish supper followed by dancing and finally farewell toasts. In their room, alone at last Harlan kissed her the way he had wanted to kiss her earlier in the day. They threw themselves down on the bed thankful to at last be man and wife with no more Trudy Penrose parties. The following morning Lillian watched him shave, and he decided he knew more about being a husband than he had thought. Her thoughts exactly.

They enjoyed Niagara Falls. Mostly they enjoyed their quiet times together. Harlan noticed when Lillian entered the room or sat to dine, the level of attention and service improved. Lillian Penrose Bennington was going to be a shock to Layton. The reverse might also be true. At this very moment, she was about to shock Harlan. It was their last honeymoon night before retuning to the Penrose house and making the arrangements for the trip west.

Her hand had slowly moved up the inside of his leg. Now she was gently fondling him in a way she had discovered produced a very nice reaction in him. "What are these called?" she asked.

"Damn," he thought she was asking a serious question. He placed his hand over hers and moved it a little deeper into his crotch, "I believe you mother would call these the family jewels." She had heard the expression, but this was not what she had envisioned.

"There are other words?"

"Yes."

"Such as?"

"A doctor might call them testicules . . ."

"And?"

Cajones . . . balls . . . nuts." She giggled at the term nuts.

"Wife, this is serious." He rolled over on top of her.

Back at her parent's home, Cecil told them he had made all their travel arrangements including the extra train car to carry the wedding presents and all Lillian's personal belongings and her many hope chest items. Harlan wired his parents of their arrival date and said bring an extra wagon. "Why does he want an extra wagon?" questioned Margarita.

Charlie just smiled. "I will bring an extra wagon and our new car."

Train travel for Lillian was nothing new, but traveling in a westerly direction was and she was fascinated by the changing landscape. The trip went well enough, but they were both glad to settle into their hotel room in Cheyenne for one night before they caught the train to Layton the following morning. Harlan watched as she fussed over her clothes for in the morning. He realized she was nervous about the next day and meeting his parents. "Harlan' tell me again every thing about your family." He sat on the sofa where he could look out the window and pretend he could see the mountains instead of the neighboring buildings. He invited her sit with him.

"The ranch was started by Grandfather Asa Bennington and his partner Charlie Lamb. Dad does not know much about Lamb except he is named after him. Grandfather Asa came west after the War Between the States. He grew apples some place in Ohio and had a wife named Catherine who died on the trip along with most of the people on the wagon train not far from here. The survivors were rescued by troopers from old Fort Layton, which is now the town of Layton where we are going tomorrow. At the fort, Asa met Charlie Lamb and they partnered up and left the fort the following year. Some how they got into a fight with some Cheyennes and rescued Blue Feather, my grandmother. In the fight, Asa was badly hurt resulting in a terrible burn on his face. I guess Blue Feather took care of him and they ended up getting married. A sister, named Small Leaf, and dad completed the family. Charlie Lamb was killed in some kind of wood cutting accident, which also left my grandpa bent over for a few years. The ranch was doing well despite some mistakes and with a lot of luck.

Dad doesn't know if he was eighteen or nineteen, but he and Grandpa went to Cheyenne to pick up a stove and came home with my mother. Their first children were the twins. Dad says they looked just like Blue Feather. They were wild and honestly I am guessing, but I think Dad spoiled them from the start. They were never interested in the ranch. Dad said that almost broke his heart. Next came my sister Catherine. She was just different. She didn't like our mother or me either, I guess. She could ride better than any of us. She had the Bennington gift when it came to animals and especially horses. I was the last child. The twins just rode away one night. A year later Dad received a letter. My brothers had been killed by accident some place down in Texas. By then Mama had almost retreated into herself after my sister died from a broken neck because a bear spooked her horse. I guess I was Dad's last hope for running the ranch, but that was always my dream. He wasn't exactly happy about my going to school especially in the east. That's more or less the family history," he concluded.

She knew there were more details. Lillian had heard most of these stories over the last two years yet every time she asked Harlan to tell her the stories again, he changed or added to the telling somewhat. "You have all this written down don't you?"

"No. Why would we do that?" he asked.

"Oh Harlan, recording the family stories is so important. Our children and our grandchildren are going to want to know everything."

He had a sly grin on his face. "Are you going to write down that your first house in Wyoming has only a pump in the kitchen sink and no indoor plumbing, yet?"

"Is that the truth?" He had not ever mentioned that before today.

"You will discover all that tomorrow, Mrs. Bennington." She didn't know what to say. She went back to trying to straighten the fancy feather on the hat she planned to wear tomorrow.

He continued. "You should understand that my father is a self-taught man. He knows how to read and write only because Grandpa taught him using a few children's books, the bible and newspapers. Pa is one of the most honest men I have ever known. He has common sense. If he does not understand some things, he asks questions till he learns everything he can. Then he forms an opinion or makes a decision. Once he does that he usually sees everything in black or white. There is not much gray in the way he looks at the world. He is rough around the edges but he means well and, well, he may take a little getting used to." Harlan sighed but finished up by talking about his mother. "I don't think she ever had any schooling. She can write her name if she has to. She had probably her own rough edges when they got married. I think her growing up years were sad. She has always been there for dad and the family. She is a sweet woman. Being married to a half-breed, that's what people used to call my dad, and being a Mexican, she was shunned by many of the town's people in the beginning. That has improved some but I think it still bothers her." This last part about his parents was all new to Lillian.

"In the morning I want you to find the hotel manager and have him bring me a small bouquet of flowers. I want them for your mother," was all she said.

The next morning Harlan approached the manager and told him Mrs. Bennington wanted a bouquet of flowers. By that time, the manager thought for sure that the young Mr. and very elegant Mrs. Bennington were a part of the Benningtons that owned the Double B ranch north of Layton. He would find flowers somewhere. He almost ran home.

His wife was in shock to see her husband stomping through her flower garden and cutting off late summer roses with his pocketknife. In the house he shoved the blossoms into her hand and said, "Make these into a nice bouquet. They are for a special hotel guest." Harlan and Lillian were just finishing their last cup of coffee when the out of breath manager placed the lace wrapped, beribboned roses near Lillian's plate. Lillian thanked him graciously.

Chapter Twenty-six

Lillian Penrose Bennington

The train pulled into the Layton station midafternoon. Charlie and Margarita stood next to their new shiny, black Ford automobile. The wagon and its driver were off to the side. The train came to a stop. The conductor emerged and placed the step stool for the disembarking passengers. Charlie could tell Margarita was holding her breath. The first passenger to step off the train was a man.

Next came a woman and Charlie knew without a doubt he was looking at his daughter-in-law. She was nothing he could have imagined. She was half a head taller than Harlan. From her perfect little, big city shoes to the jaunty feather on her hat she was . . . was what?? Charlie could not think of the word. "Elegant and classy" were words that finally tumbled into his mind. Then he felt a wave of sadness. In his opinion, she would not last six months out here.

Margarita sucked in her breath. "Is that her?" she whispered.

"I hope so cause she is hanging onto Harlan's arm and they are headed this way." Lillian knew who they were.

"Papa Charlie." She kissed him lightly on the cheek. "Mother Bennington." She kissed Margarita and handed her the roses with a little curtsy. Harlan was smiling broadly and Charlie's eyes were wide. Lillian was a beauty with pale blond hair in the latest fashion, he suspected. She had the most startling gray eyes he had ever seen. Gray and soft as the breast of a dove was how he thought of them. By the time they arrived home the next day he believed he detected a hint of steel in those gray eyes. Maybe she might last longer than he first believed.

"I've taken rooms at the hotel. We will drive to the ranch in the morning" Charlie announced. The ladies were helped into the rear seat of the new car and Charlie took his place behind the wheel. They had not driven two blocks before Harlan decided he would do the driving tomorrow. His father was a terrible driver. Harlan planned on explaining gear ratio to his father before he ruined the transmission.

At dinner Charlie could not help but notice that Lillian attracted much attention from other guests and the staff. She seemed to notice none of it. Silver Bend might be in for a shock. Lillian Penrose Bennington may just have brought a little culture and refinement with her. What was interesting was she didn't know it. The four of them had a pleasant dinner, agreed what time to meet for breakfast and said good night. Lillian gave Margarita a small kiss good night.

In their room before Charlie had his shirt off, Margarita burst into tears, "She is so beautiful. She is such a lady. It will be to hard for her here. We will lose Harlan." He gently shushed his wife and kept those same thoughts to himself.

"How much luggage do you have?" asked Charlie the next morning as he and Harlan made their way to the station to transfer the luggage to the wagon.

"Everything in that baggage car," pointed Harlan.

"Everything? The whole car?"

"Yes. Lillian plans to set up proper in her new home. The other items will be shipped when she requests them." Harlan knew this was a shock to his father who was watching crates, barrels, and bundles loaded into his wagon.

"Other items? What other items?

"She felt she might have to wait on the piano."

"Piano!! Hell son your mother gussied up the cottage. None of this is going to fit in there." Harlan was trying not to laugh at his father's dismay.

"Well, Dad, I suspect you better think of something by this afternoon."

Later as they drove down the ranch road toward the house, Harlan was glad he could not see the look of dismay on Lillian's face. In Lillian's opinion you could not really call the dwelling a house or at least not what she was used to. As Margarita showed her around the small stone cottage that was to be her new home, Lillian hid her disappointment as she watched Margarita fuss over everything trying to make her feel welcome and comfortable.

"I put this on your bed," explained Margarita. Lillian forgot about the rough accommodations as she gazed on a beautiful white quilt appliquéd with red flowers. "Harlan's grandfather's first wife, Catherine, made it. I know that quilt patterns have names but I don't know the name of this one."

Lillian smiled at her mother-in-law and said, "It is called Ohio Rose. If the flowers were done in yellow the name would be Texas Rose."

Margarita served dinner on the patio. She had forgotten just how crowded her little kitchen could be with four adults. Lillian was pleasantly pleased with the cool evening temperature. Charlie noted the thunderheads piling up over the mountains. "I believe it is going to rain tonight. Better go check the barn before we turn in."

That was two hours ago and now lightening flashes were followed by thunder that seen to roll right over them. Standing in the open patio door of the little cottage Harlan inhaled the sent of rain on the wind. He didn't enjoy it as much as he expected because he felt he and Lillian were about to have their first fight. He had tried to give her a little "let's go to bed" kiss and she had turned away from him. She even went around the corner out of sight to undress for bed.

Standing with his back to her, he knew she was now in the bed, sitting with her knees drawn up under her chin and the covers pulled up even higher. Her voice was very even. The lone candle fluttered in the draft casting moving shadows on the rock walls.

Without turning he said, "This is where I grew up. This is where all my memories are both good and bad. This is my home. I guess I didn't think how it would look to you. No. That is not true. When I did think about how rough it is here, I put it out of my mind." His shoulders sagged. "I was afraid you wouldn't come or maybe not even marry me."

"Harlan." She had to repeat his name. "Harlan." He turned around slowly not sure what to expect from her. She had folded open the covers on his side of the bed and she was patting the lumpy mattress. "Come make me a baby." He shut the door just as the rain began to spatter on the slate floor.

In the main house, Charlie was pretending to be asleep. He knew Margarita was wideawake with her head propped up on her elbow looking at him. It was just like when the children were growing up. They were going to have a little talk. He opened his eyes. "You know that Harlan and Lillian can't spend the winter in the cottage?"

"Well all that household stuff she brought with her can't stay in my barn either," was his comment. "What do you want me to do, build them a house?" He knew as soon as he said it, it was a mistake.

"Yes. They need a house of their own."

"Damn! You didn't want a house when we were first married."

"Charlie, when we were first married, you loved me. Your father treated me with respect. For the first time in my life I felt safe. I would have lived in a tree if you asked. Every woman wants her own home." She added.

"Why can't they just move in upstairs?" he asked hopefully not wanting to think about building a house especially the kind he thought Lillian might want.

"Charlie." She had that you-are-going-to-lose this argument tone in her voice. "Lillian seems like a very genteel woman. But what if she is one of these that screams and yells when she and Harlan have a spat? Do you want to have to hear that?" She rushed on before he could comment. "And when the babies start coming. Do you want to hear a crying, sick baby all night? Do you want to hear them walking back and forth because the baby is cutting teeth? Do you . . ."

He hushed her. "All right. All right. I'll talk to Harlan about building a house next spring."

"You talk to Lillian, too. This winter all of you can make up the plans." Charlie climbed out of bed and shut the window. The rain had started. When he returned Margarita was already breathing deeply and he was wideawake. Yep, just like when the children were little.

Harlan and Charlie turned all their attention to preparation for the EOR celebration. Beside the annual fall get-together it would be Lillian's introduction to all the friends and neighbors. Lillian could tell her mother-in-law was nervous by the prospect of a house full of guests. She thought of her own mother who would march through the preparations like a commanding general. She decided to give Margarita all the help she could.

"Tell me everything I should know about this EOR party," she asked. Margarita filled her in. The annual gathering had started several years ago but always after the fall round up. Now it was held before round up so it could be outside because so many people attended. "Who attends?" she asked.

"It started out with just a few of the ranchers and their families. Now it includes any of the ranchers in the valley plus the local farmers and a lot of the town businesses that help support the ranches. I guess you could call it a community affair. The host ranch provides the beef. The women bring covered dishes and the men bring a bottle of something. Then there are just friends of the hosting ranch," Margarita concluded.

"Are everyone friends?" inquired Lillian.

Margarita was slow to answer. "No, but mostly everyone is polite."

"Will you point out who the real friends are?"

"Yes, I'd be glad to."

"Will you help me decide what to wear?" Margarita had not even given a thought as to what clothes to wear and she was the hostess.

"Yes, and maybe you would help me also." The two Mrs. Bennington smiled at each other.

The EOR party was in full swing. "Were there this many people last year?" inquired Harlan.

"No," answered his father. "Some are here out of curiosity and some are here to take a gander at your new Mrs. Bennington."

"Well, our ladies do look fine." Charlie nodded in agreement.

Lillian liked Sheriff Logan and his wife. She could see why the Caldwell's were such good friends and she determined which ladies had been unkind to Margarita.

Day had turned into evening some people were getting ready to leave so it was a surprise to see a late wagon coming down the road toward the gathering. "Who is that?" Charlie was squinting down the road.

"Stub Hathaway with a woman," said Harlan.

The conversation died down a little bit as guests watched the approaching wagon. Charlie, Margarita, Harlan, and Lillian were all standing near the drive and Stub pulled the wagon to a stop in front of them.

Looking down from the wagon seat, Stub pushed his worn cowboy hat back on his head and smiled at Lillian. "Jest wanted to say howdy to the new neighbor and introduce my new wife to all of you." He looked over the crowd, which was quieted by the surprise announcement. "This here is Spoon, Spoonetta Hathaway, Mrs. Stub Hathaway."

He elbowed her in the ribs. Slowly she climbed down off the wagon seat and approached Lillian. Her clothes were ill fitting and clean but faded from too many washing. She was shaking slightly as she handed Lillian a small bouquet of wild flowers, mostly Brown Eyed Susans. "Welcome to your new home, Miz Bennington," she managed to stammer. Lillian took the flowers but held the young woman's hand in her own. Leaning forward, Lillian gently kissed her on the cheek.

"Thank you for your thoughtfulness," she whispered.

Stub was not happy about the way things were turning out. Once the new Mrs. Hathaway was back on the wagon seat, he frowned down at Harlan.

"Guess you better know I already got my woman knocked-up. So you aren't never going to get your hands on Hathaway land." The gasp from the surrounding women was lost in the sound of retreating wagon.

"What is he talking about?" asked Lillian. Harlan put his arm around her.

"I'll tell you tonight." His voice had an edge to it she had never heard. She could feel he was shaking. Was this the Bennington temper Lillian had heard about? She was correct and the feeling sweeping over him surprised Harlan. Hardly in his life had he ever experienced such anger. Harlan looked at his father and knew Charlie was feeling the same way. Having been married to Charlie all these years, Margarita knew it also and gently entwined her arm in Charlie's hoping no one noticed Charlie's fists clenching and unclenching.

Father and son looked at each other and understood what the other was feeling. Each willed the other to keep control. In the end, they both realized the wagon was to far down the ranch road to do anything about Stub Hathaway but they would have liked to wipe the sneer off Hathaway's face. Margarita stopped holding her breath.

The guests' conversation returned to more pleasant things. By the time everyone left, Lillian had the woman in town excited about a quilting circle. Several of them even thought it was their own idea. The Valley Quilters would begin meeting every month at various homes, weather, husbands, and children permitting.

Before blowing out the lantern Harlan told Lillian all about the Hathaway family. He left out the part concerning the scar on Charlie's temple. "That girl can't be more than sixteen or seventeen," sighed Lillian sadly "and she is pregnant."

Two weeks later Lillian and Margarita were alone on the ranch except for a few hands. Harlan, Charlie, and most of the cowboys were gone to bring the cattle down from the summer pasture. After that, the cattle would be driven to Layton loaded onto the train and everyone could settle down. It was a quiet time for the two women. Out in the barn Lillian worked her way through her belongings and showed Margarita some of the items she brought from Chicago for her new home. Margarita carefully fingered the crystal water goblets and the fine linen tablecloth. "For Sunday dinners or maybe even Christmas dinner," said Lillian. Together they examined each other's various quilting items.

Without Harlan in her bed, Lillian was cold in the mornings. She concluded he had been getting up in the middle of the night or before she awoke to put wood on the fire so the cottage would be warm. She dreaded the thought of spending all winter in the tiny cottage.

As soon as Margarita said, "You and Harlan are going to have to move into the house for winter," Lillian felt even more depressed. Margarita continued, "There are two bedrooms upstairs. Perhaps they would work for you. Let's go look." The stairs were narrow and dark and Lillian was not very encouraged when she saw the two rooms. She was taken by surprise when Margarita said, "I think they could take out this wall or part of it." She was looking at the wall between the two rooms. "That way you could have a little sitting area and still some privacy in the bedroom. You know that in the winter these are the warmest rooms in the house. With rugs on the floor and some nice curtains the new bedroom and sitting room combination would do very nicely."

"You want me to do what?" growled Charlie when Margarita told him of the change in the upstairs bedrooms. Harlan more or less said the same thing to Lillian but not with so much reservation because he was tired of the cottage also. By the first snowfall Harlan and Lillian were living up stairs in the main house. In her household items, now moved back into the stone cottage, Lillian unpacked two tapestries and hung them on the walls for both warmth and color. Christmas Day Lillian and Margarita made the men leave the kitchen. They set the table with one of Lillian's white tablecloths, the crystal goblets, a small centerpiece of fresh pine, and four china plates. Harlan smiled broadly when he saw what they had done. Charley was a little more reserved about he whole thing mainly because at dinner he planned to tell Harlan and Lillian he would build them a house come spring. Charlie knew that once he said it, he was committed. Once said, Margarita smiled and Lillian gave him a proper kiss.

The February snowfall was not much and March's was even less. There was hardly any spring rain. It seemed to warm. Now, after riding a circuit around the northern pastures, Harlan commented, "Everything is too dry, to soon."

"I agree." Charlie was thinking something over. "I want to start branding next week and move the herd into the high country as soon as the branding is over."

"You think the snow will be gone?"

"Maybe. Maybe not but we are not going to have much grass down here."

"Gives us more time to start on the house. I guess that will please Lillian and Mama."

It took two weeks before the herd was ready to move out. Again Lillian and Margarita found themselves alone. On the second Wednesday of the month, Lillian drove them into Silver Bend for a day of quilting. The Valley Quilting group was a big success. Too many ranch wives led lonely lives. The monthly meetings provided friendship, comfort and produced warm quilts for winter nights. Today Lillian had gotten the women talking about the history of not only the area but of their individual families. Driving home she said to Margarita, "Did you hear all the stories? Nothing, and I mean nothing is written down."

"Too many of us can't write" was Margarita's reply. Lillian thought about that statement all the way home. The only gossip was that Spoonetta Hathaway had been seen boarding the train. She was not pregnant, and she did not have a baby with her.

As ranch wives, the two women knew when the men should return. The house was clean. They did extra cooking. They could tell by the smoke from the cookhouse chimney that the one cook left behind was doing the same thing in preparation for the returning cowboys.

Midafternoon they spied the dust of the riders. Only Harlan was in the lead. Margarita could not see Charlie anywhere. The group was moving slowly at the speed of the wagon behind Harlan. A rider detached himself from the group and at a faster pace rode toward the house.

Reining up in front of the worried woman the man blurted out "Gopher hole. Broke leg. Had to shoot him." He saw Margarita go white and realized what she thought. "Sorry, Miz Benningtons. Mr. Bennington he done got a broke leg too. It was the horse we done shot." The cowboy quickly rode away before he could make things any worse.

Charlie was in the back of the wagon, his pants cut from ankle to thigh to accommodate the crude splint. He was dirty, unshaven, and drunk.

"Only way we could ease the pain," explained Harlan at his mother's frown.
"I already sent a rider to fetch Doc Smith." Harlan didn't look much better than Charlie except he was sober. In fact, the whole bunch looked wore out.

Margarita turned down the bed and the men moved Charlie into the house as carefully as they could. Even with the liquor he groaned and cursed loudly. "Who splinted the leg?" she asked.

"Cooky did after he set it. Dad howled something fearsome. Cussed him out too. Mama he is not going to be a good patient. We better clean him up before he sobers up," lamented Harlan. Harlan was correct. As Charlie sobered up and the pain set in he kept the whole house awake all night except for Harlan who fell asleep in his clothes.

Doc Smith arrived in the morning. Looking at the leg, he said he couldn't do any better. Charlie yelled at the doctor and the doctor yelled right back. "Six weeks, Charlie. You see these here crutches you can try them in six weeks. In the mean time, you stay down and quiet. I mean it!!" In the kitchen, the doctor wiped the sweat from his brow. From his bag he took a small brown bottle. "Margarita, this is laudanum. You give Charlie a dose in the morning, maybe one in the afternoon and one before bedtime. No more than that and no whiskey."

Harlan walked the doctor to his buggy. "Harlan, you look after your mother. Your father is going to be one bastard of a patient. He will wear her thin."

The doctor was right. By the end of four weeks, Margarita had big circles under her eyes. She lost weight. She had moved out of the bedroom in hopes of getting a little sleep. That gave Charlie one more thing to complain about. He wanted coffee. When she brought it to him, it was not hot enough. His pillows were never right. The room was too hot or too cold. He expected her to sit with him as he ate every meal she carried to the room. He needed the slop jar. The ranch was running quit smoothly, but he constantly questioned or challenged every thing Harlan did. The laudanum had run out. Everyone was wearing thin.

Harlan, Lillian, and Margarita were at breakfast when Charlie roared from the bedroom that he wanted coffee. As Margarita started to get up from the table Lillian stopped her. "I'll take care of him," was all she said. She marched right into Charlie's bedroom without knocking. The first thing he noticed was that she did not bring the coffee pot. The second thing he noticed were her eyes. Those beautiful dove gray eyes he thought were so soft and gentle were now cold, gray steel. He thought they might shoot sparks, which would set fire to his bedding.

It was the thought about bed coverings that made him realize he was rather exposed. He pulled the rumpled covers over his body. Her voice was very quiet and so controlled he had no trouble hearing it. "Charlie Bennington! Do you see those things over in the corner?" she was pointing to the crutches. "You want coffee, or water or your bedding fixed or whatever, you use those crutches and do it yourself. In the mean time, shut the hell up!"

Lillian spun around and slammed the door so hard the glass pane vibrated in the window frame. The following evening Charlie appeared for dinner. He was clean, he had shaved, and he was quiet. Lillian may have won the war, but there would be no new house building this year, which may have been one more reason she was upset.

By fall Charlie was hobbling round with a cane but mounting a horse was not yet possible. He admitted and was even proud about how Harlan handled things. Charlie tried riding in the wagon, but that also hurt. Only Harlan and Lillian attended the EOR that year. Charlie stayed home when it was time to bring down the herd for winter. Charlie felt old and cranky. Cattle sales were not good.

Everyone hoped that the New Year, 1920 would be better. Women were granted the right to vote and prohibition became the law of the land. Radio stations were appearing all over the country. Those owning a radio could hear jazz, the new music for the new age. Depending on your point of view, this New Year was either bad or good. One thing Lillian knew was there would be no house this year either because of cattle prices last year.

Before school ended, she approached several members of the Silver Bend School Board. She was always very tactful when she was about to suggest an idea. "I would like to ask if perhaps some of your teachers would want to under take a special project? Having become acquainted with so many people in and about Silver Bend it seems to me that the valley itself and those good people, have family histories that need to be written down and recorded for posterity." Except for the one elderly man who was already fallen asleep, the all male school board nodded sternly.

"Am I correct that the name of this community came about because of a small silver strike? They nodded again. "I venture to guess some of our own children don't even know that." They frowned. "And what about the families that were attached to old Fort Layton and stayed after the fort was closed? We even have a few fort buildings still standing. Gentlemen, I do believe you have important pieces of your own state history right here in our midst. I can assure you, it will slip away if you do nothing to preserve it."

By the beginning of the next school year, the Silver Bend Banner announced the formation of the Layton and Silver Bend Historical Society. The two communities were starting a full out project to preserve the local history. The beginning effort would be introduced as part of the English classes. Students would be asked to document and record their own family histories thus contributing to their penmanship and spelling skills.

More than one father cussed out that meddling Lillian Bennington. These families had come to the area to forget or escape some private part of family history. Mostly these grumblings were quiet. Overall it was seen as good for the community.

Lillian was probably the most pleased for personal reasons. In her search for the history of old Fort Layton, she stumbled across the journal written by the post-doctor. It was the journal made up of the stories of the survivors of the wagon train, which carried Asa James Bennington west. She worked very hard on her project mainly to avoid thinking about the thing that she and Harlan could not ignore. They were going on their fourth year of marriage, and they had no children. It was not for lack of trying.

After thinking about it for some time, she decided to ask him. "Harlan." The tone of her voice caused him to look up from his book. "I want to go to Cheyenne. I want to see a doctor there. I do not want to tell your parents."

He looked confused and concerned. She went on. "We should have had several children by now. I want to find out if there is something wrong with me." Putting down his book, he invited her to sit with him. He put his arm around her.

"If that is what you want. Tell me when," was all he said.

"I am going to take Lillian to Cheyenne for a week or so, to celebrate our fourth anniversary" was how Harlan gave Charlie the news about the up coming trip.

Later that night, Charlie gave the news to Margarita and said, "Maybe we should go too."
"Oh, Charlie, don't be a dodo."

"What?"

"It's more than for their anniversary."

"It is?"

"Lillian is going to see a doctor."

"Lillian is ill?" He was alarmed.

Margarita sounded a little exasperated. "No, not ill like Doc Smith. I suspect she's going to see a special doctor to try and find out why there are no babies."

"Damn." He lay awake a long time.

Harlan and Lillian took the car. Kissing her mother-in-law, Lillian said, "I will bring you a gift." Automobile was the only way to travel now, except as Charlie was fond of saying motorcars would never replace a good cow pony. Lillian and Harlan both felt a sense of freedom as the ranch disappeared behind them. It was good to get away even if some of the reason was serious.

Cheyenne nightlife was a shock. They took in several good dinner clubs, attended a play and toured the new state history museum. After visiting the museum Lillian mused, "Maybe we could get the good city fathers to restore some of the remaining Fort Layton buildings and turn them into a museum." Harlan just smiled. They watched in fascination at the young people dancing to jazz music. "Are you sure prohibition is in effect?" she asked one night back in their hotel room.

Lillian had her long hair cut into the latest short style. She purchased several new dresses, pairs of shoes, and selected a rose-scented soap for Margarita. Harlan didn't mind the expense. She seemed happier than she had been in a long time. But when the morning of the doctor appointment arrived, she had dark smudges beneath her eyes.

The doctor was a man just a little older than Harlan. Harlan did not know what he expected, maybe some gray, headed, old duffer. The man was professional and pleasant. The office was clean and neat. The rest of the staff was all women, which made Harlan feel somewhat better. The appointment seem to last overly long. When Lillian finally emerged from the office, Harlan tried to read the expression on her face. He could not.

They took a lunch to the park. Sipping her lemonade she remarked, "I don't think this doctor knows anymore than Doc. Smith. I am a healthy young woman and should have no problem bearing children." There was just a little bitterness in her voice. She didn't tell him the examination was painful and embarrassing or that the doctor had ended the conversation by telling her that the problem might be with her husband.

After lunch they walked along the shop fronts when Lillian suddenly stopped. "Look." As near as he could tell the window was full of junk, old junk. "No. These are antiques." she corrected him. "Over there, in the corner." She was inside shop door and back out with a wrapped parcel before he knew it.

"What did you buy?"

"A hand puppet. Didn't you see it? We had puppets when I was growing up, Grandmother Penrose taught us how to make them."

Later, over dinner he asked, "Go home tomorrow?"

"Yes. I'm ready."

"Even if home is a room and a half upstairs?"

"As long as it is with you," she smiled.

The next day as they crested the rise where you could first see the ranch buildings, Harlan pulled over to the side of the road. He shut off the engine. "I know we both want children. If it doesn't happen, then it doesn't happen but I still want to grow old with you." She slipped her hand in his but didn't look at him.

"Me too," she sniffled.

At home Margarita was thrilled with the soap and a little shocked at Lillian's short hair. The usual routine settled in quite quickly as dictated by the seasons and the ranch. The EOR party came, followed by fall roundup. Cattle sales were somewhat better than last year. Thanksgiving was followed by Christmas and lots of snow. "Next year the grass would not be dry" was Charlie's observation. He was irritated because they were stuck in the house because of the weather.

Lillian brought out the hand puppet she had purchased in Cheyenne. It was not often that something brought back a happy childhood memory for Margarita, but the puppet did. "When I was little," she said. "We had puppets come to the village. But the puppets were different. They had strings and the family would make the puppets dance and sing on a little stage they set up on one to their wagons. The puppets told stories. Some were funny and some frightened us. We were very little I think."

"Those were string puppets. These are hand puppets." Lillian put her fingers in the arm and headspaces and made the puppet bow to Margarita.
"Mamacita." Lillian's Spanish was good after five years on the ranch.
I know how to make these," continued Lillian. "The grandmother that taught me to quilt used to make these . . . one for each member of the family."

"Can we do that? I mean one for every member of this family?

The puppets kept the women busy till snowmelt. Margarita thought that Grandpa Asa might have looked like Charlie just as Harlan looked like his father. The difference in those puppets was their clothing. Blue Feather's puppet had a small Blue Jay feather in her black yarn hair. Small Leaf was not really a puppet, but a baby wrapped in a small swatch of rabbit fur. When Margarita contributed two old shirts worn by the twins and the torn birthday party dress belonging to Catherine, Lillian was touched. "Are you sure you want to cutup their clothing?"

"Yes. It is time. I will use the remainder of the clothing in a quilt someday," was Margarita's feeling on the matter. They could listen to the radio and stitch away the snow bound hours. Charlie and Harlan reread old newspapers and books and occasionally went down to the bunkhouse to play cards. There was no use in going over the house plans again. They all knew the plans by heart. Harlan and Charlie hated winter.

When the snow released all the friends and neighbors first from their homes and finally from the ranches, the first meeting of the Valley Quilters was treated to a display of Bennington family member puppets. By the end of summer, there were puppets in almost every Layton County home and more than a few showed up at the county fair that year. Lillian was quietly pleased. Harlan said to Charlie. "My wife sure is a humdinger."

"Humdinger?" queried Charlie.

"Yes dad. It is a new expression nowadays. It means good, a real pistol."

With the good weather the mail delivery was consistent and just because it was spring Lillian walked all the way out to the road and the mailbox after she saw the mailman stop. As she returned to the house Margarita saw she had one letter open and she was crying. Hurrying out to meet her, Margarita embraced her daughter-in-law and learned that both Trudy and Cecil Penrose were dead.

Later Lillian sat beside Harlan as he read the letter. From her Uncle Richard, the letter briefly described the fatal car accident. The parents had a will and in accordance to the contents, Trudy and Cecil were already interred in the cemetery they requested. The will also indicated that all their property was to go to Lillian. Uncle Richard strongly suggested that Lillian return to Chicago as the property included the house, all the contents, two cars, a substantial bank account, and some railroad stocks.

There was no question about Lillian's going home. The travel arrangements were made and the proper telegram sent. Harlan stood on the platform and looked down the empty track long after the train was out of sight. The drive home was lonesome. He wished he had his horse. He would have taken the long way riding through the south pastures. Despite the winter snow everything seemed dry again. He thought Charlie would suggest they drive the herd up to summer pasture early just like he did two years ago. It had worked for them then. It was probably a good idea this year. "Damn the weather."

Harlan guessed right about Charlie's wanting to move the cattle. Because there were an unusual number of new calves, the branding and castration took longer than in past years. Completed at last, the ranch was almost empty of livestock and men and Margarita was alone. She missed her husband. She missed her son. She missed Lillian the most. She thought about a larger vegetable garden. She wished they had some fruit trees. She listened to the radio. Warren G. Harding was president. Washington, DC, Chicago and the high, summer pastures all seemed very far away.

As much as she disliked driving, she took herself to quilting. She offered her house for the next meeting knowing they would all sit outside because the house was so dinky. None of the quilters objected. The men did return and she breathed a sigh of relief. No broken legs or arms or bad cuts. Not even one lost calf. The year was starting out very well.

Harlan had expected a letter from Lillian. There was none. "You should start building the house," stated Margarita. "It would be a special surprise for Lillian when she comes back."

"Guess we could start figuring the amount of the lumber," said Charlie. He felt guilty about Lillian's wedding items still being in the original boxes and crates and still stored in the stone cottage.

Life settled in to summertime. There was plenty of work for Harlan and his father so Margarita found herself alone except for mealtime and evenings. One morning, walking past the clothesline where Margarita was hanging out wash, Harlan looked at his mother. "You seem sad."

"I miss your wife," she mumbled with clothespins in her mouth.

"Mamacita, you are not the only one who misses my wife." Glancing at her son Margarita's tummy did a flip-flop. On his face, she saw the same wolfish grin she used to see on Charlie's face twenty-five or was it thirty years ago. She turned away so that her son couldn't see her smile.

Chapter Twenty-seven

Taking the House Home

The train trip east was faster than her trip west five years ago. She observed the woman and their new-fashioned clothes. She watched the mothers and children. She thought to herself how these mothers did or didn't care for the children as she thought they should. While in Chicago, she would consult another doctor she decided. Harlan did not need to know unless there was good news.

At the station, she saw her Uncle Richard through the train car window. Standing with him was another man. She thought she should know him but she couldn't quite place him. "You remember your cousin Martin Verduft" introduced Uncle Roger. Unfortunately Lillian did.

Uncle Roger and Aunt Marie had a very nice home and went to great lengths to make her feel comfortable. There were the visits to the cemetery, and to the solicitor's office. There were dinner parties, small in keeping with the circumstances, and an occasional tea as there had been this afternoon.

Except for Martin all the other guests had departed. Lillian felt all to often Martin seemed to be present at every opportunity and always at her elbow, Now with Aunt Marie off to fetch another tea tray Lillian and Martin were alone in the parlor. She decided she had never liked him when they were growing up and she liked him even less now. He was, she thought, oily.

He crossed the room and came to stand by her side. He pretended to look out the window at the garden.

He had always wanted her. When she left Chicago with that idiot cowboy husband, she was a young lady. Now she was a mature woman and he wanted her more than he thought possible. Her newly inherited wealth didn't hurt either. "Lillian, don't go back to Wyoming. Stay here . . . for me. I can make arrangements for us." She stepped away from him. He turned toward her and placed his hand on her arm. Her skin crawled. "Lillian I can give you babies better than that lout you made the mistake of marrying."

She slapped him so hard her hand hurt. "You bitch!." He moved across the room and was gone. Lillian had gathered her wits by the time Aunt Marie retuned to apologize for the slowness of the tea tray.

"Martin left?" she asked.
"No Aunt Marie. I asked him to leave." Lillian explained adding "I would be grateful if you did not ask him here again while I am visiting."

Aunt Marie left the parlor to cancel tea all the while thinking that Lillian was a smart young woman. Lillian missed her husband. She wished Harlan and even Papa Charlie were here to deal with the likes of Martin. Tomorrow she would walk through the house that had been her home for so many years. She would decide what to sell, what to give away, and what to take to the ranch and she would put the house up for sale. She would also make an appointment with the recommended doctor.

Harlan returned from the mailbox. No letter from Lillian. At the train station, she had promised to write. Both parents saw his disappointment.
Unusual for their evenings, it was humid. Margarita served dinner on the patio. After dinner when it was dark, Harlan and Charlie stood on the back steps and watched the sky to the east. Lightening flashed but so far away they heard no thunder. "Even if we could have some rain now, it would help" commented Harlan before going up stairs to his empty bed.

In the morning, it was still sticky. He threw his arm across Lillian's empty place still forgetting she was gone. He woke up suddenly. Did he smell smoke? Downstairs he met Charlie only half dressed. Together they stood on the same back steps as last night and looked east again. Yes, out east there was smoke. They watched in silence for some time. Each knew it was creeping their way. "Wild fire" muttered Charlie while studying the treetops trying to judge the wind direction. Generally, white smoke meant grass fire. Black smoke meant a dwelling or structure. This was white, "We better get dressed." Margarita had been standing at the screen door behind them watching and listening.

Once dressed with coffee cups in hand, the three of them studied the smoke and the wind. It was worse. The ranch foreman came up. "What do you think Mr. Bennington?"

Charlie and Harlan issued orders. Open all the gates in the south pastures. Round up as much live stock as possible and put them in that pasture. Load the truck and the car with anything Mrs. Bennington wants. Hitch up the two wagons and load all the tack from the barn and every thing from the bunkhouse. Have every man pack his personal belongings. Use a wagon if necessary.

The last thing Charlie said to Margarita was "Take with us only the things we can't replace. Once the car is loaded you drive to the Caldwell's. We will meet you there. Margarita first found Grandpa Asa's chest. It contained all the old quilts. She added the precious, family photos, and Lillian puppets. She located Charlie's old rocking horse. Upstairs in Harlan and Lillian's bedroom, she tore the tapestries from the walls and filled them with everything of Lillian's . . . dresses, jewelry, partly finished quilt tops and her books about the valley history. Charlie added the strong box with all the children's birth certificates and all the legal documents pertaining to the ranch and lastly the rifles, pistols, and ammunition. It was time to leave. She could not see either her husband or her son when she started the car for Silver Bend at the strong request of the grim faced cowboy who helped her load the car.

Charlie, Harlan, and all the ranch hands watched the advancing smoke. They all paid attention to the constantly shifting winds. "It may go a little north," someone said. When they could see the first far away glow of the low wind driven flames Charlie ordered, Let's leave. Come back tomorrow . . . if you can."

Harlan and Charlie were the last to leave. Pulling up their mounts on the hillcrest they turned to look homeward. The fire was advancing, but its direction was as erratic as the wind.

"Look," said Harlan pointing northeast . . . black smoke. "Could be the Hathaway place or the Jenson's north of them," ventured Charlie. The wind slammed into them. Their horses were nervous. The smoke and dust billowed up. In all directions. They could no longer see the Double B.

Lillian and her aunt met the lawyer at the house. They began to walk through each room trying to decide what to do with the furniture, the artwork and all the personal items. At one point, Lillian sat down on her parent's bed. Looking out the window to the wide lawn and flower garden below she said, "You know Aunt Marie. I love this house."

"Lillian, you are a wealthy woman. Take the idea of this house with you. Have plans drawn up. Surely in Wyoming they can build this house. Go home and in your heart and on paper take your childhood house with you."

"What a wonderful idea!" It was also a solution to the still unbuilt house problem at the ranch. She could actually hire a building crew. That way Charlie and Harlan would not have to take time away from the never-ending ranch work. "I will. Have Uncle Richard recommend some one who can make house plans."

She was pleased by the house idea but dreading the doctor. He was older than the Cheyenne doctor and asked many more questions about family history. The physical examination was just as she remembered it. In the end, the diagnosis was no different. She was a healthy woman that should have no problem bearing children. This doctor added that much was to be learned about the reproductive process, which made Lillian feel like maybe she was another cow that hadn't been bred properly. Like the doctor in Cheyenne, he said the fault did not always lay with the wife. Perhaps she and her husband should consider adoption. Tonight she would write Harlan about the house and the plans and everything she was bringing home. She did think of the ranch as home. She saw no reason to mention the doctor visit. She would think about adoption . . . maybe.

Chapter Twenty-eight

Burned Out . . . Almost

Next morning many town folk decided to drive or ride out to see the damage from the previous day's wild fire. Harlan and Charlie let themselves onto Bennington land in one of the southern pastures to avoid the traffic on the road. They also wanted to avoid conversation till they could access the damage. The bunkhouse and the nearby out buildings were untouched. So were the barn and the cottage. The ranch house was severally damaged. That much they could tell from a distance. Up close the damage was just plain odd. The whole upstairs and most of the downstairs were gone. Only Charlie and Margarita's bedroom and the kitchen remained. "Well, damn!" both Harlan and Charlie said at the same time.

A couple of cowhands had arrived and others were filtering in. "The Hathaway place burned clear to the ground," one of them reported. "Guess Stub holed up in one of those rock dynamite bunkers his old man built years ago."

"I wouldn't wish this on anyone," stated Harlan. Everyone nodded in agreement. They all turned at the sound of the car. Margarita was home. The cowboys dispersed. It was going to be sad. Getting out of the car she stared at what was left of her home and burst into tears. Charlie tried to console her by saying it didn't really matter. They could and would rebuild. That set her to crying harder. "You don't understand. You don't understand," she sobbed. "I didn't remember to pick up the house plans, Lillian's house plans. They all burned up." She was gulping for air and crying harder.

"Mama, it does not matter. We will make new and better plans for a nicer and bigger house," Harlan assured his mother.

228

She looked at him hopefully. "You can do that?"

"Yes, but not before Lillian returns so she can be part of the planning."
Margarita had stopped crying. She was smiling a little, and she had even given herself a case of the hiccups. Charlie didn't know why but he had a sinking feeling about the new and bigger house. I will write Lillian tonight" thought Harlan. Their letters crossed in the mail.

Charlie and Harlan again moved Lillian's household items back into the barn so Charlie and Margarita could live in the cottage. For the time being, Harlan bunked in with the wranglers. He couldn't believe he used to think that was a treat when he was growing up. He was thankful that would only last until Lillian's return. What arrangement to make then?

Chapter Twenty-nine

Coming Home

"The house burned down," said Lillian out loud as she read Harlan's letter.

"What did you say?" asked her aunt.

"A wild fire burned down our house and completely destroyed one of the neighboring ranches. I must go home."

"You need to deal with the architect before you leave."

"As soon as he can meet me, I will tell him what I want drawn up"
She wrote Harlan a short letter that ended with "I am coming home."

The architect was in for a surprise. "You say you want to build this exact house somewhere else?"
"Yes I do."

"You have a piece of property in mind?"

"Yes. It is in Wyoming."

"Wyoming?

She was becoming a little irritated with him. "Yes, in Wyoming; that big state south of Montana, west of Nebraska, and north of Colorado. I want the plans and a complete list of the lumber, the windows, the tile for the baths and anything else you can think of."

"Madam, if I may, I have a few suggestions for some modern improvements."

"Fine. Let's begin." It took several hours. "When can you have the plans ready?"

"It will take six weeks," I believe.

"I want them inside of four." She gave him the mailing address of the ranch." She left him no room for debate.

At the solicitor's office, the final item was to have the railroad stock transferred into her name and Harlan's. At the bank, she had a draft drawn up for deposit to go into a new account in the Silver Bend bank. The new account would be in both their names, and it would build her house.

Harlan read several parts of his letter to Margarita and Charlie. "She is bringing everything with her or having it shipped later." Charlie groaned.
"She has new house plans for a house just like the one left to her by her parents." Harlan remembered the house.
"What was this house like?" asked his mother.

Harlan watched his father's face. "It is a huge two story with a wrap around porch and quarters for the live in staff." Charlie's face crumpled.

"Pa, this part of the letter is for both of us. She says the house is her project and we don't have to do a thing."

"What does she mean?" was Margarita's next question.

"Hell if we know" sighed Charlie. Looking at Harlan, Charlie said, "Once you called your wife a hum . . ."

"Humdinger," finished Harlan.

"You can say that again," was Charlie's final comment.

Lillian wired her arrival date. The telegram again said, "Coming home." Harlan was comforted by the fact she used the word home. He admitted only to himself that he had been worried about the comforts of the big city keeping her from coming back at all.

She emerged from the Pullman car. She was more beautiful than he remembered. Once the luggage was dispatched she said, "I want to go to the bank." She showed Harlan the bank draft. He missed a shift, something he seldom did. Oran Sheldon, the bank manager, had the same reaction.

When the banking account business was completed she said, "We will need a safe deposit box, also. I have some railroad stock coming." Oran Sheldon took her hand, beaming brightly. Looking him right in the eye she said, "I am rebuilding the burned house at the Double B. You can expect some activity in this new account. Do you have the name of a good builder?"

"What railroad stock?" Harlan asked once they were back in the car.

"Oh, something Daddy had. Some D&RG and some railroad in California named Southern Pacific I believe is the name."

"Damn, Lillian," was all he could manage.

As they neared the ranch she asked, "Where are we sleeping?"

"We are, if you can believe it, back in the cottage."
"Where are your parents?"

"Dad has rigged a canvass over what is left of their bedroom. Most of his burned timbers are gone and Mama is cooking in the make shift kitchen. We eat on what is left of the patio."
"What happens in winter?" she asked.

"You better build this house of yours pretty damn fast is all I can say."

Chapter Thirty

The House

Lillian had interviewed three different builders and dismissed all of them after they argued with her about the plans and the changes she wanted to make. Now she stood on what was left of the back steps and watched as a truck drove slowly down the ranch road toward her. It would be Ace Archer, the fourth and she hoped, final builder.

Ace Archer surveyed as much of the ranch as he could. He saw what was left of the house. This was probably one of those spreads where the barn was better and bigger than the original house. Right now it looked as if someone was living in what was left of the house. A very attractive woman was waiting for him.

"Good morning. I am Looking for L. Bennington."

"I am Lillian Bennington and I hope you are going to build my house." He noticed she had a roll of house plans house plans under her arm. Without saying another word, she spread her plans out on the hood of his truck. She remained quiet allowing him to study the drawings. It was not the biggest house he had ever built but it was close.

"I can do this," he said and didn't try to argue about anything.

"Before you decide, I will show you the changes I have in mind." She pointed to the area marked as living quarters for a housekeeper or such. "I want an outside entrance with a nice veranda. This needs to be larger here and here. I want this to be a private, comfortable apartment inside the house for my in-laws." Ace Archer thought it a little odd, but certainly doable.

"That is not a problem," Mrs. Bennington.

"I want the house right here," she indicated the ruins of the original house. "I would like the kitchen to face east." He nodded. "When can you start?"

"Ten days if you can have the work site cleared."

"I want to be in by the time the snow flies."

He shook his head. "That is not possible."

She repeated, "I want to be in by winter." He studied the plans again.

"It will be close, but I can have the house up and completed on the outside, maybe even the apartment and one bedroom rough finished but the remainder of interior will have to be done next spring."

"That will do nicely," she smiled sweetly.

He hoped for a late winter. He did a double take at the check she handed him. He would go straight to the bank and find out if this check was really good. At the bank, Oran Sheldon smiled broadly. Lillian Bennington's checks were very, very good.

Ten days later everyone in Silver Bend knew that she was building a house, a big house. This was obvious by the number of trucks and the amount of building materials and men heading toward the Double B. No one in town minded. The construction brought in lots of business. By the end of August Harlan had to put up a no trespassing sign just to keep the curious away. It did not matter. As the second story took shape people could park on the road. It became a favorite Sunday afternoon outing and pissed off Charlie something fierce. People even brought picnic lunches.

Harlan and Charlie were sleeping in the bunkhouse and Margarita and Lillian were sharing the cottage. Charlie was in an ill temper to start with. As the house took shape, his attitude turned to one of amazement. It was still going to be a long summer. Harlan and Lillian snuck off to the lake and went skinny-dipping after which they took a blanket into the willows and made love. It was nice but not as nice as having your wife in your bed was Harlan's opinion. Besides, by September the water was too cold.

Someone asked Harlan if the Double B could host the EOR party. He politely declined. He knew perfectly well everyone within fifty miles wanted to see the house that Lillian Bennington was building.

Harlan liked Ace Archer. The two men were looking at the growing structure when Harlan asked, "Are you going to be able to meet my wife's dead line?"

"I honestly don't know. It all depends on the weather. Are you any judge of when the first snow fall will happen?"

"I would guess you have between three and six weeks."

Ace turned to Harlan and said, "If I can have four weeks I will be happy."

"If you can have it done before the snow, I will be happy," they both laughed.

The snow clouds came but didn't drop any snow. Four weeks later, the outside was complete except for gingerbread and other trim. The apartment for the senior Benningtons was finished. The upstairs master bedroom was done enough to allow Lillian and Harlan a comfortable and private winter. The kitchen was not completed, but Lillian and Margarita could cook. Compared to the old kitchen, they thought this one was wonderful, completed or not. Archer said he would be back in the spring. The first snowflake fell as he drove away.

Because the downstairs wall were nothing but bare studs, the place echoed. Harlan and Charlie brought in an old plank table and put in the area that would become the dining room. For Thanksgiving and Christmas, Lillian used the linen tablecloth, the crystal, and some of her fine wedding china.

Washing the dishes after Christmas dinner, Margarita gave herself the giggles by saying, "Maybe some day someone will invent a machine that washes dishes. Then we can be asleep in front of the fire in our easy chairs pretending we are listening to the radio." Lillian smiled.

Ace Archer returned just as he said he would and resumed work. Harlan and Charlie took the herd up to the summer pasture, which was just as well since workmen were all over the house. Lillian and Margarita were now back living in the cottage. "Mrs. Bennington I plan to be finished by the end of August," stated Ace.

She hesitated then said, I would prefer that you not finish till the end of September." She hadn't consulted Harlan on her thoughts.

"I can do that if you like," said the surprised builder. He would never understand women he thought.

Harlan didn't understand either. "You asked him not to finish until the end of September? Why?"

"If the house is complete by August every one will expect us to host the EOR party just so they can come and look at the house. I don't want that. This is our home, now. In good time we will invite friends over. By next year maybe we will decide to host. By then the house will no longer be new and people will come because the party is a valley tradition not because they want to snoop around." Harlan didn't see any point in arguing besides she made sense.

He was worried what she would do with her time now that the house was complete. He didn't need to worry. With the arrival of spring she began having the stored items from her parents home shipped to the ranch. First came the cherry dining room table and matching china cabinet. Once the cabinet was in place, Lillian and Margarita began to unpack the wedding presents and hope chest items that have been moved between the barn and the cottage so many times over the last eight years. Beautiful furniture began to fill up the house and both the barn and the cottage grew empty. Charlie was happy to have his barn back once and for all and a little afraid of the fancy sofa and some of the spindly chairs. Lillian didn't tell anyone how she now thought some of the furniture was a little out of date.

In August, two of the smaller ranches offered to cohost the EOR party at the park in town. It had been a good year for the whole community. Charlie, Margarita, Lillian, and Harlan drove into town together along with most of the other valley residents. They were pleasantly pleased to see a number of people show up wearing old-fashioned dress. "It seems appropriate," remarked Lillian.

Chapter Thirty-one

A Passing

No one expected Margarita to die first but she did. That morning in October, Charlie quietly left the bed to use the private bathroom he had come to appreciate so much if only because he didn't have to put his pants or a robe to go down the hall to use the one and only bath in the house. Their room was chilly, and he crawled back into bed expecting to snuggle up to his always-warm wife. As soon as he touched her, he understood that she was gone. It was his loud agonizing "Noooooooo!" that brought Harlan and Lillian downstairs. They found Charlie still in his underwear cradling Margarita in his arms and rocking her lifeless body as he would a child.

The coroner said it was natural causes. Harlan stayed by his father's side for several days. Because she remembered that Margarita had grown up a Catholic, Lillian made arrangements with the Catholic Church in town for a proper mass. The service was well attended, old hostilities long forgotten. Two days later, in a private ceremony attended by a few close friends and many of the ranch hands, Margarita was laid to rest next to her daughter, Catherine. That evening Charlie told Harlan, "I want us to pick out the head stone together." Harlan thought Lillian's feelings might be hurt at not being included.

"No, I don't mind at all. Go when you think he is ready, besides I am tired."

Charlie was listless through the holidays. In the spring the headstone arrived. As soon as the ground thawed, it was put in place. Charlie had not known the year of Margarita's birth. The stone read, "Margarita Bennington, died October 27, 1926. Lillian was pretty sure the carved flowers were

---

supposed to be daisies but asked her husband, "What is the carved thing at the bottom?"

He heaved a deep sigh and told her, "It is a stove"

"A what?"

"A stove." He told me he and Grandpa went to Cheyenne to buy a kitchen stove. It was on that trip that they found her. He said the stove was in the back of the wagon so she had to sit between them. All the way home, she played a guitar and sang and that is when he fell in love with her. If it hadn't been for needing a stove he would never have found her."

"What was I to say?"

"Not one thing. You did right."

Charlie went up with the herd and remained most of the summer in the high, pasture camp. No one asked them to host the EOR for that year and that was fine. Except for when they had occasionally left the ranch over the years it was the first time in all their married life they had been in a house by themselves. It was very nice.

On the first year anniversary of Margarita's death Lillian saw her father-in-law take an old chair up to the graveside and sit. "Papa Charlie seems to have aged so much in just this last year," commented Lillian.

"He is fifty-six or fifty-seven," replied Harlan.

"You don't know for sure?"

"Just last night I looked in the family Bible, but I am not completely sure that grandma and grandpa even knew what year it was when my father was born. Besides, Blue Feather's people did exactly use the white man's calendar."

Chapter Thirty-two

A Proper Fence

"I would like to do something about the grave yard," Lillian mused as she watched Charlie sitting by Margarita' grave.

"Like what?" Harlan thought his wife might have another project in mind.

"A nice fence, a wrought iron fence like the town cemeteries have. Maybe even benches for sitting. You could put in a road in the back so the men wouldn't have to carry the coffin all the way up the slope." She was thinking out loud now.

"Call Ace Archer and see if he can recommend a good iron man."

"I' ll do that very thing, this morning."

After Lillian described what she wanted Archer said he did have a man he would recommend. "His name is Zeb Butaine. He is a Creole, speaks better French than he does English. His three boys help him. He is slow."

"Slow? Ask Lillian not understanding if Archer meant intelligence or work speed."

"The man is an artist when it comes to ironwork. He simply does not work fast." was Archer's explanation. Lillian asked for Butain's number.

Just as he promised, Zeb Butain was at Lillian's front door precisely at 10:00 a.m. Zeb had examined the house as he drove up. Ace Archer was correct. The house was a fine residence. He understood that the lady of the house wanted a nice fence around the family graves. Zeb hoped Mrs. Bennington would be open to something on an equal with the house.

Lillian put on a coat and together she and Zeb Butain walked up the slope to the seven graves. Lillian watched him, as he looked over the area in question. He was well dressed, but even a good coat could not hide his well-built upper body and she saw that his hands were large and callused. Clearly he did his own work. "This is a fine setting," he said as he looked east where he thought he was probably looking all the way to Nebraska. To the north rolling pasture land butted up against the mountains. To the west, he caught a glint off Crystal River. Down below were the house and the beginning of an attractive front yard.

Zeb studied the head stones. "Charles Batiest?" He read the name on the stone for old Charlie Lamb. "French, perhaps?"

"He was one of the founders of the ranch. We don't really now much about him or his family. We believe that Batiste was his mother's name," explained Lillian.

Zeb studied the carving on all the stones. "My suggestion for your family cemetery would be this," and Zeb began motioning with his arms and hands. "A fine fence on the east, north, and west sides. On the north side looking down at the house, I propose a double gate under an arch. For the time being leave the south open, especially if you say Mr. Bennington is going to put in an access road, which I think is a wise idea." Lillian nodded. He continued "If we are done here, I have paper and pen in my car and I could make you a sketch of the idea, if you like."

The October wind had a bite to it, so they returned to the house. While she made them coffee, he sat at the kitchen table and drew on his artist pad. "Looking at all the headstone I believe I recognized carvings of feathers, leaves, roses and daises. Am I correct? He asked.

"Yes. Those carvings were significant to the family members buried there."

"And the double back to back B's?"

"The ranch brand." Lillian was curious. He pushed his tablet across the table for her consideration. She was more than satisfied.
"With your permission I would, as you can see, like to incorporate the headstone art into my iron work."

"I like that idea very much."

Zeb had noticed Papa Charlie's old chair near the newest grave. "I would suggest you have some seating up there also. Along the fence I could include a bench under an arbor . . . privacy for the mourner and a little protection from the elements if you like."

"How soon could you have it completed? At this question Zeb Butain looked uncomfortable.

"How I envision this will take some time to construct. I could have it ready to put in place next May," he waited hoping she would not give up on him because it would not happen in the next few weeks. He wanted this assignment. It was going to be a work of art.

"May is fine, Mr. Butain. Take your time."

"What the hell did you order?' complained Charlie, "That it won't be done till next spring?" Harlan was quietly glad to see his father animated about something.

"Hush, Papa" was all Lillian said.

The holidays were somewhat better that year. "Dad is never going to be his old self," was Harlan's conclusion.

"Maybe something will come along this next year and he will perk up." Harlan looked at his wife, who was already in bed and almost asleep. She seemed tired lately. Maybe with spring she might perk up also.

One mid-January a Chinook blew in and turned every thing warm. Lillian took advantage of the warmth to open the windows and air out the house a little. "I'm going into town for a haircut," stated Harlan. "Want to come along?"
"No. I think I will stay home with Papa."
"Well, I'll see if he wants to stay home." But Charlie had taken advantage of the fine weather and was up in his old chair sitting beside Margarita's grave so Harlan went into town alone, which for some reason ticked him off.

Lillian could hardly wait for Harlan to leave. Once she was sure, he was gone she trudged up the slope to the collection of graves with her own chair. Sitting next to Charlie she said, "Papa." She had to say it twice before the old man paid attention. "Papa, you are going to be a grandfather."

He was quiet for so long she was just about to repeat her statement when he said, "You are going to have a baby?"
"Yes. We are going to have a baby in June."

"Does Harlan know?"

"I plan to tell him tonight."

"You told me first?" Charlie was completely surprised.

"Yes. I told you first because if this baby is a boy I want your permission to name him Asa James.

"What if Harlan wants to pick the name?"

"He can pick a girl's name and besides he won't object to Asa James Bennington."

"No, don't suppose he will. If the baby is a girl tell him, the middle name should be Feather."

Lillian thought not but said, "We'll let him decide."

"Damn!" said Charlie. For the first time since Margarita's death there was a sparkle in Charlie's eyes. "Damn!"

Harlan was still grumpy when he came home. He had driven all the way into town only to discover it was Monday and the barbershop was closed. He didn't see why his father, and his wife had to be so cheerful. Dinner was very pleasant, and he thought he noticed something different in his father.

Upstairs getting ready for bed Harlan asked, "Did you and Dad have a little talk or something while I was gone?"

"As a matter of fact we did." Lillian didn't say anymore.

"Well, what?"

This was the moment she had dreamed of for so many years, so she said it very slowly and watched Harlan's expression. "I told your dad he is going to be a grandfather."

Harlan's blue eyes became very big. He had been looking at her in the dresser mirror. Now he turned and faced her. "You are pregnant?"

"Yes, very pregnant." She smoothed her nightgown over her rounded belly she had been hiding under aprons and sweaters.

"Damn!"

"That's exactly what your father said."

"You told him first?" Harlan sounded a little hurt.

"I was hoping it might give him something happy to think about and I wanted to ask him permission to name the baby Asa James if I have a boy."

"Asa James," repeated Harlan. "I like that idea."

"Charlie said you could pick a girls name, but he wants the middle name to be Feather."

"We'll have to think about that." He became serious. "Are you all right? Have you seen the doctor? When is the baby due?" Are you sure?"

"Yes. Yes. June. I'm very sure."

"Damn! One more question. What did we do right this time?

"I don't know but please figure it out. I want another baby after this one."

Lillian announced her pregnancy to the Valley Quilters at the next meeting. Several members had already figured it out.

Zeb Butain arrived in May with the cemetery fence. It was a work of art. A double gate under a graceful arch opened into the cemetery. The gate latches were back-to-back double B's. The fence top border was a pattern of running roses and leaves that wound from the fence in the back completely to the front ending on the top of the entrance arch. Entwined in the arch roses was the date 1868. Two arbor covered seats were decorated differently, one with daises and one with feathers. Some how it all worked together.

It took Zeb and his sons a week to put the fence and gate in place to his satisfaction. Lillian was very pregnant. Looking at her round body Zeb thought to himself. She could prop the checkbook on her belly to write me the check. Lillian suspected that Charlie liked the cemetery fence even if his statement was, "At least Butain didn't include the kitchen stove."

Lillian's water broke a little after four in the morning. She woke Harlan who jumped out of bed and whacked his toe on the rocking chair, because he forgot to turn on the bedside light. Her bag was ready. They woke Charlie and said the baby was coming. Charlie watched the tail lights recede down the ranch road. He was thinking just how lucky Harlan was to be able to be present at the birth of his child. Charlie had four children and hadn't been present for any of the births.

Several times Lillian warned Harlan to slow down. Only after she said the bumps hurt did he reduce the speed of the car. At the hospital, Harlan was directed to the waiting room and Lillian was whisked away. Harlan called Matt Caldwell. This was Matt Caldwell Jr. The senior Caldwell was Charlie's good friend and Matt Jr. and Harlan were friends. "I'll come and sit with you. The first baby can take some time." Harlan was grateful because the baby did not arrive till early afternoon. During the long wait, he wished he had taken up cigarettes or maybe even a pipe. As it was, the room was so smoke filled because of the other fathers-to-be that Harlan and Matt sat outside. At last a nurse called for Mr. Bennington. "Your wife and the baby are fine. You have a baby boy; they will be ready to see you in about a half hour."

"Congratulation, Dad." Matt shook Harlan's hand. "Go see your wife."

Chapter Thirty-three

The Bennington Brothers

Little Asa was the darling of the maternity ward. At eight pounds, five ounces, and twenty-three inches long he was a nice healthy baby. It was his mop of silky jet-black hair that caught everybody's attention. Lillian was playing with that hair when Harlan was allowed in to see her. "The nurses say it will all fall out."

"I hope not. Margarita and or Blue Feather will be very disappointed."

Harlan searched his wife's face and saw nothing but happiness. "Are you okay?"

"We both are fine."

"When can you go home?"

"Day after tomorrow. Don't you want to hold him? Harlan was ever so careful."

"What color are his eyes?"

"The nurses tell me we won't see his true eye color for a few months." Harlan gave Asa back to Lillian and dropped down into the only chair in the room.

"You look tired," she said.

"I am. We just had a baby." They both laughed.

She turned serious. "Did you have lunch?"

"No. I didn't want to leave"

"Harlan, at home in the refrigerator there is everything you need to make a salad. On your way back to the ranch stop at the market and buy steaks for you and Grandpa Charlie. In the barn refrigerator you will find a case of beer. Take it down to the bunkhouse for the hands. In the back of the kitchen refrigerator, I hid a bottle of champagne. You and papa have a little celebration. You did call him didn't you?"

"Forgot," mumbled Harlan.

"Go home, husband. I have to teach your son to nurse." He kissed her softly and left to find a pay phone.

At the end of six weeks, Harlan was more comfortable holding the baby, but it was Grandpa Charlie that wanted to hold him all the time. One evening Charlie looked up from Asa's little face and said, "This is the first Bennington child I ever had a say in naming.

Lillian said, "You never named any of your children?"

"Nope. I was away when the twins arrived. Tia Rosa was here for the birthing. When I got home the boys were here and your mama had named them Peter and Paul. Nice Bible names is what Rosa said to me. Same thing for your sister." Charlie looked at Harlan, "And you came early. Found both you and your mama on the floor. When I picked her up to put her on the bed she said Harlan. I just figured she already named you like she did the first three. Still don't know where she thought up that name."

A favorite evening topic of conversation was what the three adults expected of the newest member of the family. Charlie said Asa would learn to ride, to rope, to bulldog, to hunt and to fish. He had to know ranch work from the bottom up; after all he was the future of the ranch. Charlie ignored the memory of Peter and Paul not wanting to be connected to the ranch.

Harlan thought Asa should know how to pay the bills, prepare a successful ranch budget; figure out equipment needs and feed purchases and how to rebuild an engine so the equipment would last longer. Lillian said. "He will go to school. And we will not spoil him just because we can afford to." They completely agreed. Christmas morning they all had a big laugh. There were enough presents under the tree for three children. Asa laughed too and looked at the world through his mother's soft, dove gray eyes.

In March, Charlie said quietly to Harlan, "I want you to go into town with me. I want to see Doctor Marks. You don't say anything to Lillian either."

Alarmed Harlan asked "Why?" Charlie wouldn't say more.

In the doctor's office, Charlie described his chest pains and shortness of breath that came at times. Sometimes a weakness in his left arm, also. Dr. Marks was a young man with all the latest knowledge. He asked a lot of question and examined Charlie thoroughly.

"Well?" said Charlie and fixed the young doctor with a hard look.

The doctor looked first at Harlan and then back at Charlie. "You have a heart problem, Mr. Bennington.

"And"

"Your heart is just worn out. There is nothing I can do for you. You can take good care of yourself. Rest when you are tired. I can give you some tablets to ease the pain when it happens."

"In other words, young man, I dying."

"Dad!" exclaimed Harlan.

The doctor was uncomfortable. Looking at both Benningtons he went on. I recommend you stop driving. I believe you have a grandson?" Father and son nodded. "Don't hold the baby unless you are sitting down."
"I could go that quick?"
"It is a possibility. Usually, it will start with your beginning to feel bad enough that I will admit you to the hospital where we can make you more comfortable."

"And I'll come out of the hospital feet first is what you're saying."

"Yes sir." Later that night, Grandpa Charlie went for a walk up to the cemetery, which he had not done, in a long time. Harlan told Lillian everything.

"But he looks so healthy," she said.

Charlie did everything the doctor said. He even said he would not go with the herd up to the summer grazing. Harlan was relieved. He and Lillian watched, and they did detect a slow spiral downward in Papa Charlie.

Harlan was so busy watching his father he did not notice the change in Lillian. Harlan was at work in the office thinking for the hundredth time how glad he was that when Lillian built the house she included an office area.

"I believe we did it again," was what she said to get his attention.

"Did what?" He was really only half listening.

"We are going to have another baby."

"We are?" Some of his worry lines disappeared into a big smile. "Have you already told Grandpa?"

"No, this time I told you first."

"I suppose you have names already?"

"Just for a boy. I want to name him after our fathers . . . Charles Cecil Bennington."

"Papa is just Charlie," explained Harlan.

"I know. The baby's given name should be Charles, but we will always call him Charlie"

"I think we should go tell Grandpa." Grandpa Charlie was very pleased. Lillian Jewel was the named decided on for a girl, Jewel being Lillian's mother's middle name.

Just as the doctor predicted, Charlie did enter the hospital. He died before the baby arrived. Lillian was sitting with him when the time came. Charlie asked her to hold his hand. He looked at her with those same blue eyes she saw in her husband's face. "Lillian, I want to apologize. The first time I saw you step off the train when Harlan brought you home, I thought you would never last out here. I am so glad I was wrong."

They laid Papa Charlie to rest next to Margarita. Charlie's passing was nicely written up in the Silver Bend Banner along with a history of the Double B Ranch.

On November 9, Charles Cecil Bennington was born. It was not an easy birth. Lillian and the baby were fine, but there would be no more children for Harlan and Lillian. They were not terribly disappointed. They had two fine healthy boys.

By the time Asa entered into the Terrible Twos, everyone knew that Little Charlie looked exactly like his father and his grandpa Charlie, same light brown hair, same blue eyes. Big brother Asa was truly excited to have a baby brother.

As the boys developed, they did not look alike. Asa was a skinny kid with the black hair and his mother's dove gray eyes, which sometimes were an angry or cold gray when the Bennington temper erupted. Charlie, like his father and grandfather had a stocky build with light brown hair and smiling blue eyes. The brothers had the same dry humor and the same laugh.

Charlie laughed more often and sooner than his older bother. Charlie hardly ever displayed the family temper. One thing they shared, with out any suggestion from either Harlan or Lillian was their dream of running the Double B together. Lillian thought it a little alarming that two young children could share such a single-minded goal so early in life. Harlan was very pleased.

Chapter Thirty-four

Times Remembered

That was then and this was now. The two brothers were both now in their forties and their parents had been dead for several years. Most of Asa's and Charlie's dreams had come true. They were partners and co-owners of the Double B considered to be one of the best ranches in the state of Wyoming. They were well respected and they were wealthy. That's where their dreams parted company.

Charlie was happily married to Molly, his college sweetheart and they had a grown daughter, Catherine living in Casper. Asa was a widower and living in the little in-law quarters inside the main house. Molly was the best sister-in-law a man could ask for and right now Asa was in deep shit with her.

At the moment, Asa was thinking about the mess he had gotten himself into with Molly but as he looked out over the ranch his mind was wandering off to times gone by. His old saddle creaked comfortably as he leaned forward to enjoy the view. This was one of is favorite spots, hell, one of Charlie's too. From here, you could see the whole north end of the valley and the ranch. In the north east corner was the old Hathaway place. The Bennington Brothers had been trying to buy it for years. Straight north the ranch property ended in the foothills of the small east-west running mountain range called the Petees. At the base of The Petees was Petee Lake and the Sandies took up the northwest corner.

The Sandies were a collection of sandstone, dead end canyons containing strange weathered stone formations. Most people thought of them as dry, cactus, and snake infested places to avoid. Asa and Charlie knew two canyons contained deep, dark pools where big lunker trout would rise to a fat worm. The west side of the ranch stopped at the Crystal River and the old state road. Their south boundary was the road that led to Silver Bend.

Charlie and Asa always thought of the Sandies as being where they had "The" camp out. It could have been bad and it almost was. It had a surprise ending years later. The two boys thought they were invincible. They asked their dad first if they go camping by themselves. Harlan always listened to their plans and usually he would say "It is okay with me if it is okay with your mother."

Lillian was a little harder to convince, but this particular time she said they could go. They were packed and gone inside an hour. Camping gear, fishing gear, treats from Lillian's kitchen just in case the fishing was poor and their two favorite horses.

For years they had been told to stay away from the Sandies, so of course, they snuck up there and explored every nook, and cranny. The boys already knew which fishing hole and camp spot they wanted to try first. It was mid-summer and no school, and they could stay out two nights before someone would be sent to look for them. As soon as they arrived, they got themselves organized. That always came before the fun. "I'll take care of the horses," volunteered Asa "if you start setting up camp."

"Do you want to start fishing?" asked Charlie.

"Probably too early," reasoned Asa. It was hot, not unusual for the Sandies this time of year. They pulled off most of their clothes right down to their underwear. They both agreed that (1), their mother would not approve and (2) no one was going to see them anyway.

"Let's make spears. We can be jungle men," suggested Charlie. Tarzan was a big favorite. For camping and such, they each had a good-sized knife. They made spears, crude spears with fairly sharp points. They had endured, what seem like endless hours, hearing from both their parents and more than one cowboy you don't point sharp things or guns at people. So they threw the spears at cactus and pinecones but never at each other. Asa jumped up on a big rock not far from Charlie and pounding his chest, gave his best Tarzan yell.

It was a very good yell and Charlie caught up in the moment hurled his spear below and to the right of Asa's rock. At that very minute, Asa jumped. The Tarzan yell to turned into an "Oh shit. You hit me." For the rest of his life, Charlie could see the slow motion spear sailing though the air meeting

Asa in midway. The crude spear slid along his big brother's rib cage leaving a thin red line.

To Asa's surprise, he did not land on his feet but plopped down hard on his butt in the sand. He touched his ribs and saw his hand come away with blood. "I'm bleeding, Charlie. I'm bleeding" was all Asa managed to say to Charlie, who was kneeling beside him. Asa opened his mouth to call Charlie stupid but saw the look on Charlie's face and bit back the remark.

Charlie was blubbering. "I didn't mean to do. I really didn't. Asa, I am so sorry. Mom is going to kill me." Only last week Charlie had told himself he was to old to cry, but he was doing a good job of it now. The mention of their mother caused them both to stop and think.

"It's not really a bad cut," said Charlie hopefully. "I'll get the first aid kit."

"Ah damn!" said Asa as Charlie painted him with iodine. They really didn't swear except when it was just the two of them and they thought no one would hear. Their father didn't use bad language. He had lectured them more than once about when and if it might be permissible. Only once had they heard their mother utter a profane word and that was right after she shot the rattlesnake in her rose garden.

It was a story they liked to repeat. Lillian's rose garden was her pride and joy. It was also a constant battle with the deer and rabbits and every other wild critter that like to nibble on the tender dark green leaves. On that particular day, Lillian had come out to pick a few blossoms for her dining room and saw the snake curled up at the base of one of the bushes. Must have really ticked her off they decided later, because she marched straight back into the house. In the office she removed a pistol from the gun cabinet and took one bullet. Back outside she loaded the gun just as Harlan had taught her and blew the snake into little pieces.

The boys, Harlan a couple of hands came running at the sound of the shot. There was their mom, dressed in a white frilly apron holding a smoking gun and snake parts everywhere. Harland's look told the boys not to laugh.

Lillian was a little faint. As he helped her up the front porch steps, both Asa and Charlie heard their mother say, "Damn thing anyway!"

The boys cleaned up the snake remains. "To bad she had to blow it to smithereens."

"Yeah. It would have made a fine hatband. Yes, it was one of their favorite stories."

Once Asa's spear wound was bandaged he said, "Let's throw away the spears and start fishing," Charlie couldn't agree more. Something that amused Harlan and Lillian and impressed the schoolteachers was that often Asa and Charlie understood each other without a word. This was one of those times. Before picking up their fishing poles, the boys looked at each other and together said, "Blood oath." Ever since they read stories about pirates, a blood oath seemed like a very honorable thing.

Asa poked his finger under his rib bandage and as soon as Charlie saw Asa's bloody finger he knew what he had to do. Slowly, he pulled his hunting knife from its scabbard. He cut a shallow but long line on his pointer finger. Putting their fingers together, they solemnly said, "Bennington Blood Oath." Each of them knew the other would never break the oath of silence about the day's events except for the part about the fishing being very good.

Charlie shucked off his underwear and went swimming. Asa regretted not going in but thought he should keep his wound dry. They stayed the whole three days. They had a fine time and were even a little tired of eating fish by the time they returned home. Asa didn't let his mother see his ribs for several months.

The surprise ending to that particular fishing trip happened about eight years later. Asa was home for the summer from his first year in college. He and old Gabe Ruiz were repairing the north water windmill. Gabe was thinking of giving up ranch work and moving to Taos to live with his daughter. This was going to be his last year on the ranch. He was too old to do the climbing and Asa had just come down off the tower. It was a hot day and Asa was shirtless.

He was not a skinny kid anymore. He was lean with muscle. Gabe pointed to the scar on his ribs cage and said, "Lill brother Charlie. He almost got you wit that one." Asa and Charlie had sworn a blood oath to never tell anyone so how did Gabe know? Asa asked him.

"Me, I was wit you. You ninos go campin, your mamsita, she call down the bunkhouse. She say you go look after my boys. We did."

"You mean every time me and Charlie went camping Mom had one of you come with us?"

Gabe nodded yes and added, "We camp out of sight. We watch you with the glass." His hands made circles around his eyes to indicate field glasses. It was the next statement that made Asa laugh. "She pay us in lemon pies."

Even back from collage, Charlie and Asa still shared the same bedroom. That night when Asa related Gabe's story, Charlie didn't quite see the humor. Today the access to the Sandies was only through the Bennington property and the fish only had to fear the two brothers and an occasional ranch guest. Nobody in the area knew the Sandies better than Asa and Charlie Bennington.

As Asa sat on his horse thinking back. He suspected he and Charlie thought this spot was special not only because of the view, but also because above them on the top of the slope were buried all the Benningtons that had helped create the ranch in the first place.

Their mother had been instrumental in the building of the wrought iron fence, which was beautiful but did nothing to keep out the deer. Lillian and Harlan had been laid to rest several years ago. Asa and Charlie expected to be buried here also.

From northeast and the old Hathaway place to southwest, Crystal Creek flowed across the property. The main house sat not to far from a grove of mature cottonwoods in a bend of the creek. Their mother had rebuilt the house after the wild fire destroyed the original house long before they were born. Now the house looked like a step back in time. Inside Molly had redone the kitchen and the baths. Asa occupied the private apartment and could come and go as he wished. Molly cooked, cleaned, and cared for both her husband and his brother. They were family. Charlie's wife used the old stone cottage for a quilt studio. Shit, it was quilts that started the whole brouhaha with Molly.

"Ah, Molly" he thought. She was right he had been an ass but why he just didn't know. Charlie had guests come to the ranch. So did he but they were men and they came for the fishing or the hunting or just R & R. Molly's quilting friend was a woman from California. "Was he still angry or hurt about California? No, that was long over."

This problem with the houseguest had made him irritable as hell. Last night when Sheriff McNabb called to say a drunk driver had again torn out a section of the south pasture fence he and Charlie made plans to repair it this morning.

"I'll meet you down there. I think I'd like to ride" was all Asa said. Charlie would take the truck and the tools, and he was pleased that Asa had decided to ride rather than go with him. Whatever had his brother's back up was beginning to wear on his nerves. Also the situation was a puzzle since Asa usually kept his temper under control. Maybe his brother would sort it out on the back of a horse. Asa had done just that.

He would apologize to Molly for acting like a jerk toward her friend. He would be nice to whatever the lady's name was. Besides Saturday was the EOR. This year the Bennington Ranch was hosting and he was looking forward to the event just as he had ever since he and Charlie were old enough to attend.

He thought back to the first time he and Charlie did not attend. Charlie was about to have his tenth birthday, and he was actively campaigning for a bigger horse like his big brother Asa rode. Charlie hadn't figured out yet that Asa had a gift when it came to animals, especially horses. Charlie would never ride a well as Asa did.

In one of the corals near the house was a big gray mare. The mare was known for her nasty disposition and the owner and neighbor had asked Harlan to stable the horse till the new buyer could pick her up. Charlie saw this as his big chance to prove he was ready for a bigger mount.

He took the saddle blanket and approached the horse as he always did. The horse knew what was coming and wanted no part of it. As Charlie came even with her big hindquarters, she swung them around and pinned Charlie up against the barn. The horse kept pushing. Charlie began to scream.

Asa heard Charlie first and ran for the coral. He saw what was happening. He didn't think about what to do. He just did it. He opened the gate to an adjacent coral. The mare was now wild eyed and pushing harder on Charlie. Charlie was yelling louder which was spooking the horse even more. Asa approached the panicked animal slowly, caressed her nose and spoke softly but firmly. He slipped his hand under her bridle and slowly led her away releasing Charlie who slid to the ground in a heap.

Their parents and several ranch hands had come running at the sound of Charlie's first screams but they hung back seeing Asa in with the big mare. They watched as the skinny twelve year old moved the horse into the other pen. Returning to where Charlie lay, Asa did not see their mother trying to hold back her sobs in her apron.

Someone had cut off Charlie's pants. Experienced hands felt for broken bones. They found none. Charlie was moved to the room the boys shared, put to bed with hot water bottles and given an aspirin. Charley was in pain. Dr. Adams would come first thing in the morning. "I suppose I screwed up my birthday present."

Asa looked at the door to make sure his mother was not about to come in. "That horse was a bitch but I don't think Dad will take that into account. So yeah, most likely you did screw up your birthday present."

The doctor did arrive the next morning and could find no broken bones either. He suggested maybe some deep bruising. After asking a lot of questions, he recommended Lillian keep her son in bed till Sunday.

"No I can't" wailed Charlie "Its EOR." His mother's expression told him he would not be going. Asa heard his parents saying they would stay home also.

"I can take care of Charlie. You two can go," he offered. To his surprise, they agreed. Lillian left them fried chicken, fruit salad and chocolate pudding. Over and over she reminded them of the phone number of where they would be and promised to be home by 10:00 p.m.

Asa carried all the food upstairs. It seemed a treat to eat fried chicken in bed. They spent the evening telling each other how they would run the ranch together when they grew up. They would go to college. They would find the perfect girls. They would marry and raise their families on the ranch. If Charlie hadn't been hurting, it would have been a pretty nice evening.

Charlie's pain would never completely go away and for the rest of his life he would walk with a limp, especially after too many hours in the saddle. He never complained.

The Bennington Brothers thought they were the luckiest boys in the world growing up on the ranch. They learned to ride, to rope, to hunt, to camp and to fish. They swam naked in the stock tank and when older in Petee Lake. As they grew up, they did all the work the ranch hands did but were expected to do it better. They went on round up. They learned to nigh hawk and occasionally they were allowed to spend the night in the bunkhouse. After those nights, their father would have a long talk with them about certain words and jesters that might be used around men sometimes but not in front of their mother or any other lady and they knew he led by example. They never played at cowboys. They believed they were cowboys.

In school, Asa's grades were always above average, but Charlie's were better. One day Charlie told Asa about his secret dream about becoming a real "get paid" basketball player . . . a professional. "How long have you wanted to play basketball?" asked Asa.

"Guess ever since I read about the Harlem Globe Trotters. Can you imagine being paid to playing your favorite sport?" Both boys knew because of his limp that dream was no more. Asa felt guilty. If Charlie were to become a professional basketball player he would not be there to help run the ranch. Asa suddenly felt good about Charlie's slight handicap.

In high school Asa played football. He was a little better than most of his teammates, but his Bennington temper often got him in trouble and the coach was often reluctant to play him. Harlan saw it as a good thing. He and Asa had long talks about controlling that temper. After one particular fight with an older kid named Ludlow, Asa complained to his father, "Ludlow was kicking a dog. I just saw red so I hit him." Harlan knew the Ludlow kid and thought he deserved a good licking but not in the parking lot in front of the whole school and not by Asa.

Charlie couldn't play sports but if Asa was playing then Charlie was there to support the team and his brother whether he played or not. They discovered girls together. Charlie could do that. As they discovered, the opposite sex they were unaware that they were drawing a line about what was shared and what was private. Each was becoming his own man, and they were developing a respect for each other that would last all their lives.

Asa always got into more fights than Charlie. Because he was skinny he was often on the losing end. Harlan took both boys into the barn and taught them a few boxing techniques. More than once up on the summer range with the herd, a cowboy would take the boys aside and teach them some tricks not demonstrated by their father. Asa was still learning to control his temper. "He is doing better," Harlan remarked to Lillian.

"In some ways he is just like your father. Black is black and white is white and there is not much gray in between" was her observation.

"Well. I have something that should keep them occupied all this summer."

"What?"

"A truck. They are both good at mechanics and living out here they will need their own transportation for high school. But they will have to share and buy their own gas. Plus, I don't think it a good idea to give kids this age something brand spanking new."

One Friday afternoon just before summer vacation, Asa and Charlie came home from school and found a junk truck down by the machine shop. Their father said, "If you can make it run you can have it." They were not allowed to start on it till the cattle were taken up to the summer range.

Harlan was correct about all summer. The rebuilding of the truck kept them busy and broke. By September the truck ran almost too well from Harlan's point of view. Lillian worried they would kill themselves or somebody else. They never did any bodywork on the thing. It looked just as ugly as the day it arrived. Privately the boys liked to say, "It runs like a "Striped Assed Ape." They were grown men before they explained to their father why the called the truck "The Ape."

In truth they were both pretty smart drivers. They observed when friends had accidents resulting in either broken bones or lost driving privileges or both. Certainly when they had a date in the truck they drove like their father. Still The Ape was the envy of their friends and a few fathers.

Asa' other favorite sport was rodeo. All through high school, he participated in high school rodeo. Charlie couldn't, but attended every event to support his brother. Asa liked the bronc riding best. Lillian absolutely forbid him to participate in the bull riding competition. Although he was still under age, Charlie would drive The Ape home while Asa slumped in the passenger seat nursing his sore muscles, aching joins and assorted cuts and bruises.

Asa was good enough that Harlan worried his oldest would want to forget college and go on the rodeo circuit. "It is a hard life. Only the best and luckiest work their way slowly into the big money and most riders get busted up at some point in their career," he explained to Lillian more than once.

On night, coming home from a rodeo north of Laramie, Charlie was driving as usual and Asa sat slumped in the passenger seat groaning every time the truck hit a bump. "So you think you want to try going pro?" asked Charlie.

"Well, the buckle bunnies are nice. Did you see that little blond with the tight green pants?"

"Everyone of us saw her."

"I think she kind of liked me," said Asa.

"She liked everybody. When you were in the shoot or on your ride she liked somebody else. When that guy left she liked another somebody else." Charlie could see Asa didn't think much of this revelation. To make Asa feel better he said, "She didn't pay much attention to losers." It didn't make Asa feel any better so he turned serious.

"If I decide to go pro I'll have to be a lot better. I'll have to work harder. I'll have to give up everything else. I'll need my own truck and trailer. Hell, I will be sleeping in the trailer to start with . . . that or really cheap motels." In the end, Asa decided for himself that rodeo life was not for him. He would go to college. Charlie heaved a sigh of relief. They would not have been able to run the ranch together if Asa had decided to rodeo. Lillian and Harlan were also relieved.

Chapter Thirty-five

College

High school graduation was coming for Asa and Charlie could tell his brother was uncomfortable about the approaching parties. Everyone liked Asa and he had several party invitations. Asa also had a problem with girls. Charlie might be two years younger than Asa, but he was already smarter about the opposite sex. Girls flocked to Asa like bees go to honey, and Asa was not even aware of it. Off and on through high school he had had a couple of girl friends. As soon as the girls tried to get to serious, Asa ended the relationship. Now with the year coming to an end too many girls wanted him to take them to the parties. "Too many girl and too many parties?" kidded Charlie.

Asa looked serious. "More than that, I hear that at most of the parties someone is bringing beer. You know what will happen. They will drink too much to fast and end up puking in the bushes. I just don't think that is much of a way to celebrate."

"What would you like to do?"

Asa brightened up a bit. "I would like you and me and Dad to go camping."

"Not Mom?"

"No, just us guys." Charlie was very pleased with the idea. He was part of the surprise to give Asa a car for graduation, something Asa could drive to and from college. If they went camping, then his mom could have the car in the yard when they returned. And that was just exactly how it happened.

Harlan and his boys camped for two nights and three days. The two boys asked to hear stories about Grandpa Charlie and Great Grandpa Asa. Both boys wanted to know about college. The day they came back home Asa was the first to see the car parked at the gate with a big sign "Congratulations, Asa." It was not a new car, but the heaviest sedan Harlan could fine. He wanted Asa to have a safe car to make the trip between the ranch and Cheyenne. Asa didn't have to go back east as his father did, he would be attending the University of Wyoming at Cheyenne.

Asa was totally surprised and pleased until Harlan said, "You know you will need to find a part time job to help pay for your gas and personal expenses."

"Damn. If I'm working a part time job, I can't come home every weekend. I thought I could come home." Asa was dismayed. "I thought we had the money for my college. I thought we, the ranch, were pretty well off," he continued while Charlie listened. Charlie had not known about the part time job requirement so he was also concerned.

"How many times has Dad invited you to sit down and look at the ranch books and budgets?"

"Several."

"Did you ever do it, sit with him like he asked?"

"No."

"Me neither," sighed Charlie. "Maybe we should have." Both Asa and Charlie worried about the ranch finances but Harlan said no more. In truth the ranch was in fine shape and perfectly able to cover all Asa's expenses. It was just that Lillian and Harlan did not want Asa or Charlie, when the time came, to take education for granted.

Harlan thought he might have made a mistake about the part time job. Asa secured a job in a motorcycle shop working on engines and the first weekend he came home for a visit, he roared into the yard on a souped-up Indian Scout. Lillian was horrified. "Next visit," Harlan said, "Drive your car." He smiled at Asa as he said it.

Charlie missed Asa a lot. When Asa did come home, some weekends and most of the holidays it was like old times but not quite. Asa was moving on and Charlie felt he was stuck in high school that would never end. Charlie concentrated on his studies. He was taking no chance that he might not follow Asa to college. Asa missed home like he couldn't believe. A good number of his fellow students were also ranch kids, and they were just as home sick. The first year passed slowly. His grades were okay, but should have been better or so Harlan thought. Asa spent most of his first summer home at the high country cow camp so Charlie did the same. Lillian was sad about not having the boys right under her roof and Harlan was pleased that Asa and Charlie were still dreaming of running the ranch together.

While at home, Asa parked his college car and he and Charlie ran around Silver Bend in The Ape, the whole time Asa was at home. Asa showed Charlie some new things about engines and now you could hear The Ape coming down the county road a mile away from the ranch road. When it was time for Asa to leave Charlie said, "I'll graduate from high school in June. Will you be home so we can go camping, you and me and Dad?"

"We'll do that, for sure."

Harlan and Lillian felt content with their lives. Asa was doing better in his second year. Charlie was going to graduate from high school in the spring and was probably going to have the best grades even attained at Silver Bend High School. Harlan and his two boys would repeat the graduation camping trip in honor of Charlie. Charlie was completely surprised to receive a heavy, older, sedan for graduation just like Asa had received. He figured he would have to drive The Ape. Harlan's comment was "I think we should retire the Ape." Harlan could only guess how many traffic citations The Ape would earn under city driving laws.

Charlie would follow Asa to the University of Wyoming. He could hardly wait. His first year he discovered collegiate wrestling, Charlie had the right build and his limp didn't matter. This time it was Asa that sat on the sidelines and cheered his brother on. During Christmas vacation of Asa's third year both Lillian and Harlan detected restlessness in Asa. Just as a matter of conversation Harlan said to Charlie, "Is school all right for you and your brother this year?

"Yeah, it's great, Dad. Charlie did not look at his father directly.

Asa had mentioned about changing classes, more business and perhaps a little law.

"You think your brother is going to change classes like he said?" continued Harlan.

Charlie looked away. "Asa has a lot on his mind now days."

"You don't suppose he has found a girl," worried Lillian when Harlan told her about the conversation with Charlie. Asa had not found a girl. He quit college.

Chapter Thirty-six

The U.S. Marine Corp Recruit Depot

It was a Saturday night and Lillian and Harlan were watching Perry Como on the television. It was snowing hard all the way down to central Colorado and out onto the Great Plaines, which is why Asa didn't drive home to tell his parents his great news. Instead he called.

Harlan said he would answer the phone and walked out to the kitchen wondering who was stuck in the snow and needed help. "Hello."

"Dad, its Asa." Of course it was Asa. Only his oldest had that deep, soft voice. Even over the phone Harlan could hear that Asa was tapping his foot, a nervous habit he only did when he was about to say some thing he thought was important. "Dad, you know there is a war going on, in Korea?" Of course Harlan knew there was a war. Everyone in the whole world knew. He felt a little knot of worry.

Asa went on, "We think there're going to start drafting" Harlan wondered who "the we" were. The knot of worry grew. "I wanted to pick my own branch of the service. I enlisted. I'm going to be a Marine." Martin didn't know a person could feel pride, dread and worry all at the same time. He wondered about Charlie. That might come later. Right now he was going to have to tell his wife that their oldest was probably going to see combat.

Lillian decided not to go to the bus station in Cheyenne. She said good-bye to Asa at the ranch. She looked out the window at the empty ranch road a long time after the truck disappeared. Charlie skipped classes to be at the bus station to say his good-bye. It was so damn hard. He was almost angry with Asa, especially when he saw the sadness on their father's face after the bus departed.

As Asa often did when he found himself in a group of strangers, he sat back and observed. Most of the young men were his age or even younger. They seemed to be from all walks of life. He was surprised at the party atmosphere. Some of the kids had beer.

In Denver they were off loaded at the train station along with a large number of other recruits. A tough, loud drill sergeant got them into a formation more or less. "Listen up" he yelled. "I am about to read you the oath. Once you take the oath you are in the Marine Corps. You are not, I repeat, you are not a Marine. You are scum. You are lower than scum. Your ass is mine and don't you ever forget it." He read through the oath with Asa and the others responding as necessary.

Asa was only halfway listening. On the platform, he was facing west. He could see the great Rocky Mountains. There had always been mountains in his life. He felt a wave of homesickness already and was glad they were being put on the train.

He liked the train. It was his first ride on a train and now that he thought about it the first time he had been outside of Wyoming. He could hardly wait to see California. As the train steamed south, he enjoyed watching the change of scenery. More beer had come board and the place was loud and rowdy. He moved to a car that was not so noisy and watched the countryside slip by. The seat next to him remained empty till late evening. A kid probably just old enough to enlist took it. Asa recognized hand-me-down clothes when he saw them. "You ever been away from home?" the newcomer asked.

"Just college," Asa answered.

"I never even done that." The boy said no more.

By the time the train reached Los Angle the party atmosphere had worn itself out. Most everyone wanted to take a shower. Asa was fascinated by everything . . . the palm trees, the beaches, and the Pacific Ocean. He immediately fell in love with Southern California. He would write his mother about the profusion of flowers as soon as he had time. From the first train, they were herded into a second train, which delivered them to San Diego. After that they were trucked to boot camp. Whatever the reason there had been no stop for dinner. All eighty of them now stood in a line outside the largest Quonset hut Asa had ever seen. It was ten o'clock at night.

He figured they had been standing there over an hour. Before entering the building, the NCOs as usual with much yelling and swearing, had told the group to stand there until they were given additional orders. Now there was general grumbling up and down the line. The young men were tired, dirty, and hungry with a few hangovers. The NCOs remained inside the hut with the door shut.

"Anyone know what they're doing I there?" No one could even guess.

"Maybe we should look in a window."

"Hell, not me."

"I'll do it" spoke up the big Indian kid standing next to Asa.

"Damn it to hell," he exploded. "They're in there, playing cards. Just sitting around."

"Well, why don't you just go knock on the door" some one suggested.

"That's just what I'm going to do." In response to his knock the door opened. He was greeted by a barrage of swearing and cursing that seem to go on forever. The Indian was a big, strong kid but he was slowly being backed away from the door by a skinny, blond PFC. Once outside the PFC continued his verbal assault on the recruit ending by saying "I just bet you would like to hit me! Go ahead. It is off the record." The Indian kid did. In less than two minutes he was bloodied, beaten and on the ground while the PFC walked away straightening his uniform tie. No one said a word including Asa. They were told to go inside and shower. They were clean but had to put on their travel clothes. There was no dinner. They were assigned bunks.

"You will go by the numbers shouted another NCO just as loud and profane as the others. Asa was already tired of being called a maggot. "By the numbers" continued the NCO, "1. You will stand by you turned down bunk. 2. You will get into your sack. 3. You will be asleep."

From somewhere a small voice asked, "What about pajamas?"

That set the NCO off again. "The Marine Corp didn't give a shit what you sleep in as long as you keep your skivvies on." He began the count again "1."

Every one stood at attention at the foot of their assigned bunk. "2." The recruits scrambled to climb into the bunks with some of the top bunk people trying so hard they fell off the other side. At the count of three, the lights went out.

"Is everyone asleep?" yelled the non-com.

"Yes sir," said a couple of scared recruits. The lights came back on and the whole by-the-number thing started all over again. It took three tries before there was no reply to the question "Are you asleep?"

The following morning was not better. Marched to breakfast, they had twenty minutes to eat. They were given dungarees and a sea bag. Their hair was cut. There was another physical.

It was this particular physical that left Asa both humiliated and very angry. Having played sports in school and spent summer in cow camp Asa was used to seeing naked men. Not every one in the group had played sports and seeing wall-to-wall peckers and balls made a number of recruits uncomfortable. The examination and questions about venereal diseases were something new to most of the men and to some intimidating.

The medics had left and it appeared the whole miserable time was about over. The instructor was slowly walking down the front row where Asa stood at the end. "Well, you bastards, looks like we have a little treat this afternoon." No one felt excited about this statement. "It appears we have an ass hole dancer in our midst. Yes, we do, a real dancer." It was only then that Asa was aware his was rocking back and forth on the balls of his feet. The instructor headed his way. "Step out scum and let's see a little two step of something." Asa did as he was told and did his best at a shuffle step. Once back in line he could not believe how much his privates had shrunk. He was just a little pleased he had held his temper. It had been hard.

Nobody felt much like a hero. It was agreed that none of this looked like what happened in the John Wayne movies. They were marched everywhere and at the end of the day to a large two story Quonset hut located on Guadalcanal Street. There, Asa and seventy-nine other guys would live for the next ten weeks.

Asa thought, "This is going to be hell."

One day melted into another. They never walked. They marched. They learned close order drill. They were given the book of General Orders and told to memorize it. They were told they were no longer civilians. They were scum, lower than scum and a long way from being a Marine. They made up their sack with forty-five degree corners with the top blanket so tight it would bounce a quarter. If it was not perfect and often when it was they were ordered to make it over again anyway. More drill. More class room.

Most recruits settled in and knuckled under. Not everyone could do this as was demonstrated one night just at bedtime. Asa only knew the kid was from somewhere in the midwest. When the kid went bonkers Asa was at the other end of the room but could see the commotion. No warning at all everyone said later. The kid unsheathed his bayonet and went after everyone near him. No one was hurt. The kid was finally subdued. Just when the group started to relax he broke free and threw himself out the second story window. Word got back eventually that he broke his leg in the fall but he was never seen again.

"Tell me again about the Hostess House, asked one of the men.

Asa repeated what he knew. "That Quonset hut down, there with the little lawn and the outside tables is the Hostess House. If you have family that can come visit that is where you meet them but only on Sundays."

"I don't have family even close," complained someone.

"Me neither, but if we are lucky we will get some Poggy Bait."

"What the hell is Poggy Bait?"

"When families come on Sunday, they most often bring home made items. The treats are called Poggy Bait. Generally, the instructors take it away and pass it out to everyone, which means that those of us of us with no family might get a taste of home."

"What do you do on Sundays if you got no family and don't get to go the Hostess House?" was another question.

Asa had a wicked grin on his face when he answered, "You get to fight Fred Trout."

Everyone knew Trout, not only because he was a good boxer, but also because at age thirty he was the oldest man in the squad. He had seen active duty in the army in WWII after which he had joined the USMC Reserve. Now for the Korean action his reserve had been called up. Because of his past experience, he had the squad position of Right Guide. Right Guide was the verbal link between officers and NCOs. On the parade ground, if you could not hear the march commands you watched the Right Guide. Trout did his job well and was liked by officers and enlisted men alike. Asa was now squad leader, a fact that completely surprised him since it seemed he could not do anything right. Right now he was worried about Trout.

Trout had a sickly wife and five kids somewhere in West Texas on a hardscrabble farm. Every letter from home seemed to make Trout more nervous, even jumpy. If Asa, a green squad leader could see it, the DIs ought to notice it too. One day Trout was gone.

The new Right Guide explained to Asa. "Somebody took the time to look into Trout's family's situation. It was bad. Trout was given a hardship discharge and sent home to take care of his family." Asa thought that was a bit of good news.

Two nights later the fire watch found the attempted suicide. The fire watch was a two-man patrol that went around the building every two hours all night long. They checked the outside, the sleeping area, the offices, the latrines, and the showers. That is where they found the recruit hanging by his own belt. He was not dead, but he was another recruit that didn't return.

Asa decided writing letters home was hard. Too much of what went on he didn't want to share with his mother and he couldn't just write his father.

Harlan was reading out loud Asa's latest letter. "He says here, he is a squad leader, but he doesn't know why. He says it seems to him he doesn't do anything right. His squad is often punished for his infractions and he doesn't know what went wrong." Harlan read on, "The squad is moving down the road to Camp Mathews, the Marine Corp, rifle range."

"Lillian said, "Surely he will do well in that. He is a good shot. Maybe they will be happier with him." Harlan had to agree. Harlan was not happy with the war news. The Korean War was not going well.

As Asa had written his parents, he had been made squad leader after which it seemed he couldn't do anything correctly. As a bunkmate observed, "I don't think they like you much, Bennington." Asa thought he might be right.

At Camp Mathew's, the Marine Corps rifle range, he easily qualified as expert. Even that did not keep the officers for finding fault and punishing the whole squad for his failures. A sergeant told the squad if Bennington fell over a footlocker at night there would be no problem. This comment was the same as saying they could beat up on Asa for causing the whole squad so much grief. He never did fall over a footlocker.

At the end of the ten weeks, he and the rest of the men felt pretty much like they were real Marines. He felt a little sad about graduation. No one was there to witness or celebrate with him so he was only half listening as the commandant began to the talk about the award for the class honor man. "Pvt. Asa James Bennington." His name came over the PA system. In the next letter home he said he was embarrassed because he forgot to salute when he walked up to receive the honor. He also wrote he had a short leave which was not long enough to come home so he was going to see as much of Southern California as he could after which he would be reporting to tank school at Corona Del Mar. Charlie wrote back that he thought tank school sounded neat.

Tank school only lasted for two weeks. As the sergeant put it, "The war is going to hell. Live bodies were needed. Gentleman, draw a paper out this helmet, please. If your slip says "T" you are remain here in tank school. If your slip says "K" you are going to report to advanced combat training in Oceanside." Asa drew a "K" and was on his way to Camp Pendleton the next day with only enough time to send a letter home.

"He is going to Korea, isn't he?" said Lillian.

"Yes" was all Harlan said and went to telephone Charlie.

For advanced combat training, they were housed in Tent Camp Two, which was so far out in the boonies, that weekend liberty was never an option. No one had a car. There was nothing to write home about, but he sure did look forward to letters from home. His mother always wrote about what was happening in the community. Harlan would write about the ranch and business. When Charlie added a paragraph, it was about college. Charlie wondered if Asa even cared about college life when he was spending his days in something as serious as combat training. At the end of the twelve weeks, Asa had put on weight. It was all muscle.

Word came down, they were going to ship out. They would sail to Korea aboard the USS Nathan Hayes, a merchant marine ship being used for a troop carrier. The ship was huge and Asa believed the rumor that the ship carried five thousand men. The bunks were four deep and Asa's was the bottom bunk down in the third level. With so many men onboard, the lights burned twenty-four hours a day. With nothing to do the men shot craps and played cards and smoked. Meals were served twice a day, and it took most of the day just standing in line to get your meal.

Asa didn't care about food. He did not know a person could be so sick. His bunk was out of the question. Despite regulations he took his sleeping bag up to the boat deck and wedged himself up against some kind of storage locker. There he stayed. Kindhearted sailors kept him supplied with saltines and water.

None of his training had prepared him for such miserable seasick trip. He didn't care that he sailed up the west coast of the United States and Canada. In the Aleutian Islands, the seas were so rough he could hear the screws turning every time the fantail rose up out of the water.

A short liberty in Japan was welcome. The permitted liberty area was small. Japan was still rebuilding from WWII. GIs were not welcome everywhere. He purchased a few souvenirs and then with a buddy stopped at the Enlisted Men's Club. The EM club was open to every nationality fighting in the Korean Conflict. The men formed their own drinking groups based on country and branch of service. Asa observed this plus the amount of beer being consumed and correctly decided a major brawl was due to break out any time. He was correct. What was left of liberty was cancelled and they sailed to Pusan, Korea. Harlan was correct. His oldest was about to see combat.

In two days, he was assigned to a squad and its company. He was in machine guns. They were trucked and air lifted to an area known as the Pusan Perimeter. The objective was to push back the Chinese coming down from the north and to provide relief for the few survivors coming from the Chosin Reservoir. One of their sergeants said," If I see any of you being easy on the SOB en enemy I will kill you myself."

Everyone thought that harsh till they begin to see the mutilated bodies of the United States and the U. N. soldiers. Many had been shot with their hands tied, their bodies left on the road to rot. Their enemy did not take prisoners. Even with that anger, he felt bad for the civilian population whose country was being torn apart.

Following Pusan came Operation Killer, Operation Ripper and the First Spring Offensive. Like most of the men Asa didn't go anywhere without his M-1 rifle, even in the rest areas. He also carried a .45 pistol, but that was proving to be useless because often no ammunition was available.

Ammunition on a whole was a problem. They were issued ammo left over from WWII. Too many times, it didn't fire or it missed fired injuring or even killing his own men. The North Koreans and the Chinese were having the same problem, but that didn't help. He would write home about his pistol.

It was his mother that was reading that particular letter. "He says he would like you to send him a pistol." She looked across the table at Harlan.

The battle for 749 lasted all day. Once on top of the hill they were given water, K-Rations and told to dig in for a nighttime counter offensive. Only half of Asa's company was alive and unwounded. This was the first time most of them had seen the horrors of white phosphorus, Commonly called W. P., it was a chemical agent that once subjected to air, it burned your uniform, your skin till it was smothered or you died from the burns.

Because the units were in such bad condition, they were relieved and sent back down the hill to the rear. It was on the return trip that Asa was hit. The saying was "you never hear the one that hits you." That was true. Asa felt the bullet penetrate his boot. He hit the ground and covered his head with his arms as bullets kicked up dirt all around his head.

His buddies poured fire down on the retreating sniper. Asa lay still till a familiar voice said "Bennington?" He looked up. "Ah! shit man, we thought you were dead." There was a bullet hole in the toe of his boot. Somehow the bullet missed his toes. Damn, he felt thankful.

Several squads set up camp near each other. "We don't need to dig any fox holes." was heard around the rest area. They did position their machine guns. Asa was ten feet from his gun and had his tent setup. Looking around, he felt uncomfortable despite the fact this was the designated safe area. To one side the South Korean laborers occupied a small hut. At the other side was a stand of eucalypts trees. "It bothers me," he said to the man sitting next to him, "that our own artillery is behind us."

"Ah Bennington. You just got the jitters. Relax." He received a lot of good-natured kidding when he dug a foxhole. Foxhole finished, Asa pulled up a box, looked again at the hole in the toe of his boot and began writing a letter home. The first incoming shell landed to the right. The second shell to the left. He heard the third coming and dove for his hole. The man next to him landed on top of him. Asa could tell by the way the body felt the man was dead.

The hut housing the laborers was completely gone. They all had to be dead. The eucalyptus trees were cut down. His machine gun was nothing but mangled metal. His tent looked as if someone had taken a machine gun to it. Wounded and dying were everywhere.

Asa could not hear a sound. He was deaf. Those that could, grabbed their rifles and headed for whatever safety they could find. A medic seeing Asa's bleeding ears and nose sent him to the MASH unit where the doctor cleaned up Asa and examined his ears. Speaking loudly the doctor said, "You have a concussion. "Your hearing will come back a little at a time. Even though this is a temporary condition you have earned the Purple Heart. I have to fill out this paper work for the medal. The award will go on your record and a letter will be sent home to you family."

"No."

"You don't want your Purple Heart?"

"All that letter says is that I have been injured. It doesn't say that I am okay. I don't want that kind of letter going to my family," stated Asa flatly.

"Well, come back in a few days. I'll recheck your ears. If you change your mind about the medal, I'll forward the paper work then." Next day Asa moved out with his unit. His hearing improved each day.

Once in a while, he wished his hearing was not returning. He hated the nighttime propaganda announcements coming from behind the enemy lines. It happened often when there was a stalemate in the combat. Under the cover of darkness, the enemy would set up speakers. First would come scratchy music meant to remind everyone of home and then the female voice, they named Peking Rose, would ask about their thoughts about home and loved ones. She suggested that their girl friends were out with someone else and that their country had abandoned them to an unnecessary, capitalistic war. For that reason, they should lay down their arms and surrender. It pissed off most of the men, because they understood it was crap and it ruined their sleep.

"He needs me to send him a gun?" Harlan was surprised.

"Yes. Beside his rifle, he says he is carrying a side arm most of the time." Lillian didn't know she had a worried expression on her face. "It is a .45. It is too heavy and too much of the time they can't get ammunition for it." Harlan took care of Asa's request that afternoon. A month later Asa received a .38 Smith and Wesson with one hundred and fifty rounds of ammunition and a shoulder holster.

The war continued. Asa was part of the Second Spring Offensive, Operation Strangle, Operation Detonate, Operation Pile Driver, and the Battle for the Punchbowl and the Assault on hill 749. Nothing had prepared Asa for the hell they encountered in the taking of Hill 749. 749 made all the newspapers at home and all the TV evening news. Harlan, Lillian, and Charlie waited for letters that were to far and few between.

He temper was not always held in check. Coming off the line after a bitter eight-hour fight he and his buddy Ortega were cold, tired, dirty, smelly, and very hungry. Standing in the chow line a clean, new-from-state-side sergeant told them to get to the back of the line and muttered that usually the NCOs had their own mess. The first thing Asa could grasp was his metal mess kit, and he hit the man as hard as he could with it sending the utensils flying in every direction. The fight was on. The chow line simply moved away and let them have at it. Only after Asa began to hit the man with his newly acquired .38 did the other give up and they were separated. Back in line Ortega said only one thing "You know you hit an sergeant?

"Yeah," replied Asa.

Three days later the sergeant appeared in the door of their tent "Are you Bennington?" he asked. Asa nodded and stood up. The man stepped forward. "I've been talking around. I was out of line. I want to apologize." The man offered Asa his hand. Asa gladly shook it. As he started to leave the tent he turned "Did you have to hit me with that damned gun?" Asa just smiled. He never saw the sergeant again.

The war continued for Asa with the battle of Bunker Hill and Outpost Bruce. The winter was so cold he cut up his summer sleeping bag and used it for a poncho. One good thing was the Mickey Mouse boots. They might be heavy, but they sure as hell cut down on frost bit toes and feet.

One evening the lieutenant approached Asa. "Bennington, I have an opening in mortars. Do you want to transfer?" To Asa, it was a stupid question. As machine gunner, he and his men were always on the forward slope facing the North Koreans or the Chinese. The mortars were always positioned on the reverse slope so they could shoot mortars and flares up over the hill in support of their own machine gunners and riflemen.

"Yes, sir." Asa didn't have to think about his answer.

Asa was assigned to a mortar squad and began to learn about firing mortars. It was common at night for the enemy to send in men to probe the machine gun line for weak spots. When that happened, the mortar men were ordered to send up flares but they were often under fire themselves from the enemy's big guns on the opposite hill. Mortars did have one advantage. You got more sleep. Asa settled in. He kept his mouth shut, and his head down and learned as much as he could. It would serve him well.

One particular night the word came that probes were being sent in and the forward positions need flares. The mortar positions themselves were under fire, the sergeant ordered a young, skinny blond kid named Hickerson to go out and fire the flares. Hickerson fell down on the ground and began whimpering that he couldn't do it. "This is worse than Hill 749," he sobbed.

Asa had been on 749 and this was not good but not at all like 749 and he said so.
"Give me the damn flash light. I'll do it."

As Asa exited the bunker, the lieutenant who had been watching the whole thing said, "Be careful." Asa reached the gun, set the charge and sent the flares high into the dark night sky. By the time, he retuned to the bunker they could all hear the faint cheers from the front side of the hill.

Asa forgot the episode till in the rear several months later. When possible, the enlisted men received a beer ration and the officers received a liquor ration. It was not unusual for an enlisted man to be invited into the officer's tent for a drink but until today it had never happened to Asa.

The inviting officer was the lieutenant from the night Asa fired the fares. Asa would always remember the officer poured Canadian Club. Without much fan fare the officer said, "I want to promote you to squad leader. It means you will have to be promoted to acting corporal."

Asa accepted but added, "It won't go down well. I'm the newest in the squad." The officer knew that and was not worried.

Outside the squad tent lieutenant called the men together and announced, "Bennington is your new squad leader."

Immediately the sergeant began to argue. "Hickerson is senior. He should have the promotion." The lieutenant looked once at the sergeant and returned to the officer's tent.

Asa looked at the group. "I didn't want the job. I didn't ask for the job.
I have the job. I'm going to do the job." There was no more grumbling and inside his tent the lieutenant was smiling,

Asa and his men were sent north and the scuttlebutt was they were headed toward Wonsan Harbor a main enemy supply port. Somewhere north of the thirty-eighth parallel the word came down to retreat. "What the hell?" They just got there. The companies behind them had all ready retreated. They were surrounded and they were stranded. There was very little gunfire from the enemy. They could just wait for the Americans to run out of food and water.

It took a while but marine corsairs arrived and began to repeatedly bomb the surrounding enemy. Marine helicopters, each able to carry five men, began to airlift the stranded men. Asa and his mortar squad were the last ones left. Just before Asa climbed in to the waiting helicopter, he threw his remaining W. P. grenade. "Take that you bastards!" he yelled.

The grenade threw up a huge white cloud. Immediately the corsairs changed their tactics and began strafing the hilltop where Asa's helicopter had yet to take off. On the radio, the forward observer was frantically trying to get the corsairs to cease their fire. To the men in the planes, the grenade smoke looked just exactly like the prearranged signal that the hill was clear. Later an angry message came down from the old man, "Who the hell set off a flare?" No one seemed to know.

At home Lillian had been marking off the days on a calendar. "His enlistment is almost up, isn't? It's been such a long time."

"Probably a lot longer for him," suggested Harlan. His father was sure Asa would be asked to re-up.

His enlistment did come to and end and just as Harlan thought, Asa was asked by his sergeant to ship over for another tour of duty. Asa said, "No." The sergeant was disappointed. Asa Bennington was a good man. Asa would be credited with two years active duty and would remain in the reserves for another six years. In the meantime, he just wanted to be a civilian. Beyond that he didn't know what he wanted to do.

He reread the latest letter from home. The ranch is doing well. Harlan had put the ranch into his and Asa and Charlie's names. Asa's parents held the controlling interest. Upon their deaths, each son would receive a half. Harlan, Charlie, and Asa were all receiving a monthly salary. Asa's was going into a bank account to be there when he came home. There was always the latest news from Silver Bend. Charlie wrote he was looking forward to graduation. It was their mother that put in the fact that Charlie would graduate with honors and he had met a girl. "Her name is Molly."

Molly Linton was a farm girl from Kansas where her family grew wheat. Charlie was more or less going with someone else. The evening was going to be a double date with Charlie's friend and his girl. That girl was Molly. By the end of the evening, Charlie wanted to know a whole lot more about Molly from Kansas. She felt the same about him. He was a slow mover and Molly almost gave up on him. Besides she had two more years of college and she was determined to finish. For her to attend college had been a big, often painful, family issue. Her father felt then and still did that college was wasted on girls. All they did was find a husband and quit school, which in his opinion they didn't need anyway. His red headed daughter would prove him wrong.

Asa ended his duty and was assigned a ship home. He would try to think about what he would do with his life once he was stateside. No seasickness this time. He couldn't get enough to eat. He could sleep anywhere. He was incredibly thin. His eyes never missed anything going on around him. He gave some of the other men the creeps. He collapsed in the chow line one day out of homeport.

When he regained consciousness he found himself in a regular, nice clean bed in the El Toro Naval Base hospital. He was in quarantine. The medics were not too sure just what he might be carrying. The eventual diagnosis was fatigue, malnutrition, and parasites, lots of parasites.

He wrote home that he was stateside; leaving out the part about being in the hospital and the fact he would have to attend a two-week debriefing class. In a month, more or less, he would be a free man.

"Do you think we should have a welcome home party?" suggested Lillian.

"Might be nice. Let's wait and see" was Harlan's idea.

Asa didn't mind the hospital. He took more showers than he needed. Hot running water was such a treat. When finally Asa was allowed to have a small piece of steak, he wondered if it was Bennington beef. He looked out his hospital window or sat on the hospital veranda in the California sunshine. He watched the palm trees blow gracefully in the sea breeze and decided he would finish his education.

Sitting at the kitchen table while Lillian dished up some apple pie, Harlan read Asa's latest letter. He took a bite of the pie and said, "He is not coming home." Her fork stopped in mid air.

"Why?" she asked.

"He is going back to college in California, in San Diego. He will send us a new mailing address."

To begin civilian life was a challenge. Asa really wanted to start classes with the spring semester. He needed his transcripts from Wyoming, and he needed a real civilian address. Despite the fact he had money he couldn't buy a truck because he had no address.

The used car dealer solved most of those problems. Asa walked down the street not to far from the base and glanced at the used cars in several lots. In the rear of one he saw an old truck that in some ways reminded him of The Ape. He knew the salesman was watching him from the sales shack. Sure enough as soon as Asa walked back to the pickup, the salesman and probably also the owner followed him. The man was smoking the vilest cigar Asa had ever smelled.

"Back from Korea, son?" Asa assumed that until his hair grew back and he gained some weight he would be asked that question often.

"Yes, sir. I need a pickup truck."

"Well, this here one needs some work. There's a couple up front that might suite you better. We have a nice payment plan if you are interested."

"I'll be paying cash. Do you mind if I listen to the engine and maybe take a look under the hood?"

With the mention of cash and the thought of getting rid of the junker the salesman said, "Here's the key. Take a look." Asa listened, he looked and he tinkered. With in the hour the truck sounded much better and the salesman was impressed. Let's make a deal," said Asa. That was when he found out he needed a permanent address.

"You need a job?" the man asked. This was one of the things Asa planned on. He had the ranch money and he was grateful. However, he did not feel he had earned it, and he was going to try and not spend it; at least not now.

"I'm going back to school but, yes I need a part time job," Asa answered.

"My brother has a motorcycle shop on the other side of town," continued the man. He just lost his mechanic. Job doesn't pay much but does come with a partly furnished apartment.

Lillian read over the latest letter. "It says here, he has a truck. Says it reminds him of The Ape. He has a part time job in a motorcycle shop as a mechanic, and he will start classes in a few weeks. He has an apartment. He included his new address and says he is having a telephone put in."

"At least no one is shooting at him, commented Charlie.

Chapter Thirty-seven

Peggy Connors

Peggy Connors liked to think she collected men. Well that was sort of a miss-statement. They had mostly been boys and young men but not what she now thought of as real men. There had been high school sweet hearts. Okay, one got her in a little trouble, but her father took care of that and now she had birth control pills. There had been a couple of college beaus, just fun and a tumble now and then, nothing really great but at present she was in between guys and she guessed she was on the hunt which was why she was studying the interesting man in the campus book store.

He was standing by a table full of textbooks and talking to a clerk. Peggy walked over and pretended to look at the books. She thought the titles were weird "Land Law and You," "Water Wise Grasses," which she doubted was about marijuana, and "Bovine Diseases and Prevention," "What the hell was a bovine?" she thought.

The man she thought interesting was tall. He seemed dark not really in his coloring but in his attitude. Either he needed a shave or he had a real heavy five o'clock shadow. His clothes were clean but not new. His haircut was poor. Okay. She figured it out, a GI cut growing out. He was probably just back from Korea. He looked undernourished. She pretended to be interested in the book selections and said, "You need these for your class?" He did not look up just nodded yes and kept reading the jacket of the book in his hand.

She picked a book at random and asked him his opinion. This time he stopped reading and looked directly at her for the first time. She had never seen eyes like his, so gray, so soft, so looking right into her soul or maybe just under her panties. A slow, warm feeling spread across her belly. She had to keep talking. To him, she babbled on about something she didn't even remember later. He still had his gaze fixed on her, so she took a chance "You look like you could use a decent meal. You know the waffle house around the corner?" He nodded yes. "Meet me there tomorrow morning, eight o'clock. I'll buy you breakfast" She stood on her tip toes as close to her ear as possible and with a little puff of breath she said in her softest voice said, "By the way, my name is Peggy Connor. See you tomorrow."

He watched her walk away. She was thinking, "He probably won't come. Oh hell! I didn't even ask his name." She looked back. He was standing just as she left him; book still in hand, but a small smile played across his solemn face.

For his part, Asa was hooked. He had never seen anyone like her. A petite girl, she had a sexy as hell body, a pixy face and long blond hair held in place today by a purple headband. She didn't really like hippy clothes, and she only wore it because it looked cool and it accented her violet eyes. "Damn!" Damn!" He said twice as she disappeared out the door. He glanced around to see if anyone noticed he was muttering out loud.

The following morning he was there. He was early. She was late. She selected a booth way in the back and was fascinated as he ate, ham, eggs, hash browns with a side of pancakes. She toyed with her blue berry crepes.

Today he wore better clothes and was clean-shaven. His table manners were fine, but she thought he probably did not know the difference between a seafood fork and a salad fork. The whole time she got him to talk about himself.

He grew up on a ranch in Wyoming. "Wow," she thought. "A real cowboy." Later, she would learn that he did not like to be referred to as a cowboy. She could never remember if his home state was Wyoming, Montana, or Idaho. In her mind, all those western states ran together and that would irk him also. "What kind of name is Asa?" she asked. It was not the first time in his life he had been asked that so he patiently explained.

"It is a family name. The first Asa James Bennington came west after the Civil War."

His parents, Harlan and Lillian were still living on the ranch. He had one younger brother named Charles Cecil also a family name. Asa explained, Charlie, as everyone called his little brother was probably going to marry someone named Molly.

Peggy was correct. He had served in Korea. Now he was finishing up some weird AG major that would allow him to go home to the ranch. He lived in a small apartment over a motorcycle shop. The apartment, which included the use of a washer and dryer, was rent-free because he tuned bikes all day Saturday. She thought that might have to change.

He learned she was the only child of Jerry and Melissa Conners. Her father was in construction. Her mother was an invalid with in home care. Peggy was majoring in English Lit, as she liked to say, and was really only going to school, because it made her parents happy as long as she made a C average and that was even hard.

She was the brightest thing that had ever entered Asa's life. She was sunshine to his dark soul. By the time, he insisted paying for breakfast they had a date to next Tuesday's basket ball game and to a concert the following weekend. The concert was a big success, some new group called the Beach Boys. Peggy refused to ride in his truck. Driving home in her old MG. Asa remarked, "I think that musical group might make it to the top."

Inside of three weeks, they were a couple. Peggy had found her new guy and a new project all in the same. Asa Bennington was a diamond in the rough, and she intended to polish off the rough edges.

Chapter Thirty-eight

Battle of the Sexes

Driving her car Asa realized it needed work. He offered to work on it if she would fix dinner. "You like Mexican food?" she questioned.

"Sure I do." On Sunday, he arrived and was working on her car while she sat along the driveway and watched. Right now he was under the car on a thing he called a dolly. She was looking at his crotch and thinking about sex. She supposed if she touched him there he would bump he head on the underside of the car. He would be mad. She suspected he had a temper, which he was very good at keeping under control.

Life was good, and Asa could not believe the doors that Peggy opened. She introduced him to new places, new people, new food, books, live theater, and music. He liked traditional jazz, he discovered light classical music and especially enjoyed classical guitar. His mother had always had music in the house, but he supposed he hadn't paid any attention. Peggy took him to concerts, art museums and Disneyland.

Either he was really hungry for sex or she was sending a lot of signals. It seemed a long time ago that Asa and Charlie had one of their long discussion about the opposite sex. They were most definitely interested, but they agreed not in just casual sex. Looking back now, he suspected neither he nor Charlie had a clue about the subject. Peggy Connor was going to be a problem. He wanted no commitment, at least not the kind most women wanted.

His grades slipped a little but not bad. He was learning other things. Summer vacation began. She couldn't believe he signed up for summer classes.

She stomped her foot and glared at him. "What do you mean you signed up for summer classes? What about me? I had plans for us. You're just a shit." She was prissy for several days.

He didn't like it when she swore, and he was already pissed off at himself because he had forgotten the date of Charlie's wedding and now he could not attend. He was supposed to be the best man. He was even more irked at himself because he made that information known in a letter instead of calling home. Peggy helped him select a wedding gift, a lace tablecloth with napkins for twelve. Peggy doubted that any ranch had a dining room or a table that would seat twelve. She rather hoped that Charlie and what's-her-name would just drop out of Asa's life.

Charlie and his fiancée, Molly, sat on the back steps of the ranch house. Molly had her dander up, "What do you mean your brother is not coming to the wedding? He is supposed to be your best man?" Charlie handed her the letter.

When she finished reading, Charlie said, "We can ask your brother." Molly saw the hurt in Charlie's eyes so she said nothing more about the brother she had yet to meet. Who ever this Peggy person was she had selected a nice gift and the tablecloth fit Lillian's antique dining room table perfectly. They would use it for the reception along with the Lillian's fine china.

Molly suggested Charlie ask his father to stand up with him. He squeezed her hand and said he would ask. He thought as he often would for the rest of his life, he was a lucky man. Harlan did stand up with Charlie. Molly would be more than a daughter-in-law. She would be the daughter that Harlan and Lillian had always wanted.

On the front porch, Asa's parents were having almost the same conversation. "Not coming to the wedding?" Harlan echoed the statement just made by Lillian.

"No, Asa has classes," she repeated from the letter she was reading.

"But Asa is supposed to be Charlie's best man. Who will Charlie ask?"

Lillian thought her husband was one of the smartest men she had ever met. Time and time again he made decisions about the ranch that were beyond his time, but when it came to matters of the heart he often didn't have a clue.

"Harlan." She made sure he was paying attention. "Asa has a girl." He looked perplexed. "Look how many times the name Peggy appears in his letters."

"Damn" was all her husband said and she agreed. That about summed up her feelings too. She hadn't lost her son in war. She was losing him to a woman. An old nursery rhyme floated into her head. "A daughter is a daughter all of her life. A son is a son till he takes a wife."

Asa couldn't get Peggy to stop giving him gifts, shirts, slacks, jackets, and accessories. When he asked her not to do that any more she pouted and produced a few tears. Since he enjoyed making her happy, he relented but the gifts did slow down. He couldn't even do the same for her. She had everything and appeared to think shopping was a hobby.

When photos of Charlie and Molly's wedding arrived, Asa was pleased to see Peggy taking a real interest in his family. She did look at the pictures. Lillian Bennington was not what she expected. A tall blond woman almost patrician in looks, she was a head taller than her husband. Harlan was a stocky man with light brown hair showing a little early gray and bright blue eyes. Charlie looked just like his father. The only family resemblance Peggy could see in Asa was Lillian's fascinating gray eyes.

In the background, Peggy was quick to note a big table draped in the lace tablecloth she had selected. The table was set with what appeared to be old silver and china and crystal. The new bride was an attractive red headed woman, and she was dressed in an exquisite wedding gown. On the wall behind, the newly weds was a quilt. "Now just how hokey is that?" thought Peggy. The obvious happiness of the family irritated the hell out of her.

Looking at his family made him ask again, "When am I going to meet your parents?"

"You know mother is ill. Daddy's out of town" was her regular answer. Asa thought at home it was just plain bad manners not to meet the parents of the girl you had been dating for nine months. Yes, it had been almost nine months and he was surprised. For the rest of the day she was short with Asa and he wondered why.

Once in a while, Asa took her to the motorcycle races when he worked in the pits as the mechanic for the shop riders. This was a whole new experience for her mainly because she was not the center of attention. She thought he looked good in his required whites, and she could tell the riders respected his ability. So she could be in the pits also, she was expected to wear white and she had purchased hers at a nice boutique not far from her bungalow. She was sure she looked good, but she did not get hit on as much as she expected. She didn't get it that everyone there knew she belonged to Asa. That was not how she looked at their relationship. He belonged to her. She had plans.

Up until her Jr., high years Peggy had dreamed of being a professional dancer. As her father was fond of saying, "Dancing was the only thing she really stuck to." It was not to be. She was too short. She was a good dancer, and she knew and enjoyed all dancing, waltzes, the Charleston, the Latin dances, and even the simple two-step. The first time she danced with Asa she knew he needed lessons.

He said, "No."

As usual she batted her lovely violet eyes and made him feel rotten. She brought up the fact that he was in summer school, which he had done with out consulting her and ruined all her summer plans. Just to see her sunny smile he took the lessons.

He found he liked dancing. He was a natural athlete. Dancing was fun. Just like when Peggy taught him to surf, he learned well, maybe too well. The dance instructors wanted him to enter a contest and represent the studio. Peggy lied. "Oh, I don't think you are really that good. They just can't get anyone else. Besides school is about to start. You won't have time." Asa was a little disappointed, and he suspected he was a good dancer and not the kind he was in boot camp only a few years ago. However, she was right about one thing; it was time to go back to hitting the books. One more year and he was done.

Life was so perfect he could not believe it. Well, it was not totally perfect. They were having more frequent arguments over sex. She wanted it. He didn't. That was not the truth. Of course he thought about Peggy in bed. He knew every male over twelve probably thought about it as soon as they were around her.

As he explained to her during every argument, he did not believe in causal sex. Every time she replied, "It is not casual. We have been together since March." He was not sure what a date had to do with it. They never spoke of the future. As far as he knew, there was no commitment and he believed sex involved a commitment. "That's just plan stupid," she complained. "You are too old fashioned," she added. More than once, he stormed out of the bungalow because he almost lost control. He would either hit her or screw her and neither was how he wanted it to be. The neighbors thought the young couple rather interesting.

On those nights even before he started up the stairs to his apartment, he could hear his phone ringing. She would be sorry and ask him to come back. He could hear her crying. He wouldn't return. He would study. Usually, he stayed away a couple of days.

In fact he gave up studying at her house. He wanted better grades this year. She would not leave him alone. Walking up behind him, she would press her small hard breasts into his back. Her hand would creep under his shirt and start to wander down toward his belt buckle. She would hike up her skirts and straddle his lap and play with the hairs on his chest. Damn she made him ache, so he studied at his apartment. She didn't have anything else to do but study too. Her grades actually went up.

If Peggy and Asa were sometimes at odds, her parents were close and caring. Contrary to what Peggy led Asa to believe her father traveled only when absolutely necessary. Often in the evening, Peggy's father would spend the time in his wife's bedroom just visiting, watching television or listening to music until she became to tired. He would kiss her goodnight and leave so that the full time nurse could prepare her for bed.

This evening they talked about Peggy. Peggy's first quarter report card was on the coffee table between them. Her grades had improved. "Have you ever met this young man?" Melissa Connor asked her husband. He shook his head no and frowned. It bothered him. As near as he could tell they had been dating since spring and this new young man did not have enough manners to come to the house and meet them but then, Peggy in the past, had brought home some losers. He just hoped this wasn't another one.

Melissa watched her husband and knew exactly what to say. "Perhaps she said we should ask Peggy to bring him to our Christmas party?" He caressed his wife's thin hand and agreed.

It was a few weeks later when Peggy said to Asa, "Guess what?" He could never guess with her and besides she didn't really expect an answer. It was her way of making sure he was listening. "Mother and Daddy want me to bring you to their annual Christmas party." While she had Thanksgiving dinner with her parents he had called the ranch. Wyoming had a light dusting of snow. Charlie was going to take Molly on the traditional perfect Christmas tree hunt in a couple of weeks. Asa wished everyone well. He felt very low so the prospect of a holiday party seemed pleasant.

He was eating a plate of turkey and all the trimmings she brought him from her parents. It was good, very good, but not like his mom's. When he heard what she said two things crossed his mind. At last he was going to meet her parents. From the very first, he had repeatedly suggested to Peggy that he should meet her parents. Peggy always offered some reason why it was not a good time to visit. He still felt it had been bad manners on his part.

Secondly, he thought about Christmas. He hadn't had a real Christmas in what seemed like a very long time. He thought of past holidays. He and Charlie and their dad would find the perfect fresh pine. Cut it down. Haul it home and set it up in the living room for their mother to decorate. He could even remember that his father drilled hole in the tree trunk to add branches to make it more perfect. Some of the decorations were keepsakes from Christmases past. Some were construction paper items made by him and Charlie when they were little. The scent of the pine would compete with gingerbread and fudge and fresh yeast rolls, and a big roast turkey. Peggy brought him back to the present when she said, "You will need a tux."

He suspected this would be another one of her requests that he ended up complying with, so just for the hell of it he said, "I can't afford it."

"Silly. It's my Christmas present to you," she laughed. He knew he'd lost besides he didn't really know a thing about her parents or their Christmas party or buying a tux, but he was going to find out. It was hard to get her to go home that night. She kept bouncing on his bed as they talked.

The telephone connection was not good. "Yes," he repeated to his mother, "I am finally going to meet her parents. It is a family and friends gathering. I am wearing a tux." Lillian could hear his laughter even over the poor connection." Before leaving to pick up Peggy, Asa looked at himself in his bedroom mirror and wondered if he looked okay or just like a penguin. Lillian was thinking he would look very good in formal wear.

He drove to Peggy's bungalow where he would leave his truck. He had a house key but as he always did, he knocked first before he entered. She was posing by her Christmas tree. She took his breath away. He now understood the term 'little black dress." Hers was black velvet held up by thin rhinestone straps. He knew immediately that her glittering earrings were real diamonds. Her golden hair was up swept into lovely curls into which she had tucked small sprigs of mistletoe. Only Peggy would think of that. She was gorgeous, and he told her so. Kissing her lightly, he could smell her heavy perfume.

What Asa didn't see was that he took her breath away. He no longer wore the haunted, hungry look. Well, maybe little hungry but it suited him. He had filled out in all the right places. Asa looked good in the formal attire just as his mother thought he would. Plus, Peggy noted, Asa looked at ease.

They would drive her car because, as always, she refused to ride in his "junker" as she continued to call it and besides, as far as Asa was concerned, she was a terrible driver. Peggy missed shifts and ground the gears, which made Asa grind his teeth. He had already tuned the engine once and wondered how long before he would have to replace the transmission. Briefly, he considered giving her a transmission for Christmas but had decided on a fine gold bracelet with links fashioned to look like ocean waves. She was wearing it tonight. He was pleased about his gift, because she seemed to like it.

As they drove toward the ocean side hills he felt very happy, damn happy in fact. He was dressed to the nines, and he liked the way it felt. He was driving a very nice MG that purred like a well-tuned sports car should. Beside him in the passenger seat was a beautiful woman. It was going to be a great evening. He felt a lightness of heart he hadn't enjoyed in a long time.

Peggy gave him directions, and they headed along the coastal hills. A half an hour later he commented on the brightly lit, beautiful hacienda style house on a hillside above them. "That's where we're going" she said and added, "That's my house." The tall mature palms were perfectly up lit along the curving driveway. Christmas lights were scattered through out the yard and luminaries were lined up on top of the rustic rock wall.

She suggested they park in the back and showed him where to turn. The parking only contained a few cars, which he expected belonged to the staff. Also parked off to the side was a bright red Ford pickup with a small flat bed trailer holding a small tractor. The truck and the trailer were painted with the name J. J. Connors Construction. He knew he should recognize that name. Finally, it came to him. J. J. Connors Construction was the biggest freeway builder in Southern California. "Your father is J. J. Connors?"

She smiled sweetly. "Of course and by the way Aunt Maud will be here tonight and she is looking forward to meeting you." He reviewed what he knew about her aunt Maud. The lady was Peggy's father's older sister. She had buried two husbands. Each one, of which left her richer than the last one. Peggy didn't know it but in the future Asa would learn Maud was one of two silent partners in J. J. Connors Construction. From time to time Peggy enjoyed spending the weekends with Aunt Maud. The niece and aunt shared a passion for shopping.

Peggy confessed to Asa that she confided in Aunt Maud things she would never discuss with her parents. It was rumored that Aunt Maud took a young lover now and again. The men never stayed long and Maud had the good sense not to flaunt them in public. Not exactly a black sheep but apparently a real character and it was clear to Asa there was deep affection between the aunt and the niece.

The kitchen was a busy place. Several older Mexican ladies smiled widely at Peggy and wished her Merry Christmas. Asa guessed correctly that they had probably been part of the household since she was a little girl. The dining room contained a table laden with holiday food and a generous bar with two busy bar tenders. Small tables were scattered around. Some guests sat, others stood. The hum of pleasant conversation didn't quite hide the music coming from an open patio where couples were dancing.

The house, he thought was probably decorated for the holidays by a professional. No construction paper ornaments here. Peggy sent him for drinks while she went to find her mother. Peggy ordered champagne. Asa decided on ginger ale. Seemed a wise choice besides she would probably drink a little too much and be tight by the time they went home.

Peggy's mother was indeed an invalid. Beautifully dressed and sitting in a wheel chair with a soft, cashmere wrap over her knees, Asa could see where Peggy's beauty came from. Melissa's was now faded. Asa had the good sense not to tell her how beautiful she looked. He looked down at the wheel chair and remembered a friend of his mother's also dependent on using a chair. The friend always complained loudly about how hard it was to always have to look up at people standing around her. Asa squatted down so he was eye level with Peggy's mother. He took her thin hand in his own. Her hand was cold and without thinking he gently rubbed it and said, "Now I know where Peggy gets her beautiful smile." He was rewarded with a flash of that same smile and it hinted at her former beauty. Across the room, J. J. Connors also observed his wife's smile.

Asa and Peggy worked their way across the room. Hugs, kisses and holiday greetings followed them. Peggy seemed to know everyone, and he was introduced to all of them. Asa didn't notice that many of the women gave him the once over but Peggy did and she was proud. She felt she had done her job well.

Peggy's father shook Asa's hand. It was a firm shake from a solid man who by the looks of his tan apparently spent more time in the field than in his office. "Mr. Connors."

"Call me J. J.," her father replied and then went on "I'm finally glad to meet the man from Montana that our Peggy has talked so much about."

"Wyoming, sir. I'm from Wyoming" and Asa wondered if Peggy would ever remember his home state. Asa was sure that J. J. was about to ask him to come for a little chat when Peggy tapped J. J.'s arm.

"Aunt Maud is here."

Asa followed their gaze. Aunt Maud was a big-boned woman with her gray hair in a short almost masculine haircut. She was wearing a Christmas red gown with enough diamonds to dazzle anyone. She reminded Asa of a big red battle ship, and he was sure she had set her course straight for him. She arrived in a swish of taffeta. Even before Peggy or J. J. could make an introduction she said to Asa, "So you are my sweet Peggy's cowboy from Idaho."

He was tired of the whole cowboy and wrong state thing. Making his best imitation of a bad western drawl he replied, "No ma'am" drawing the word out with a twang, "I am from Wyoming."

Maud raised one eyebrow. "Well son, wherever you're from you better ask this old broad to dance."

Asa drew himself up as tall as possible. He clicked his heals together and bowed. "At your pleasure maaam" and led her onto the dance floor.

She was not much of a dancer and Asa tailored his steps accordingly. He nearly missed a step when her hand slid beneath his coat and she grabbed a hand full of his ass. He never changed expression. He looked hard into her eyes and ever so slowly began to squeeze her other hand till he knew it hurt. "Knock if off Bennington" was all she said.

He didn't ease up but said in a very quiet, controlled voice. "I will if you will." She laughed so loudly that several people looked at them but she did remove her hand.

For a few steps she was quiet. Then she asked "Are you homosexual?"

"No!"

"Well, how come you haven't taken my niece to bed?"

This time, his voice made her shiver, "That, madam is none of your damn business." She liked this young man. To soon for her and not soon enough for Asa the dance came to and end. He escorted her back to where Peggy and her father still stood.

J. J. quickly took over the conversation by asking Maud and Peggy to check on Melissa. Walking across the room, Maud said only so Peggy could hear, "He is a keeper, if you can hold on to him." Taking Asa by the elbow J. J. led them into a lovely library. Asa stared out the big windows thinking he might see the ocean if it were not dark outside. J. J. closed the door. Here comes the your-dating-my-daughter-questions thought Asa. J. J. offered him a drink. Asa declined.

"You don't drink?"

"Sometimes, sir but not tonight. I'm driving your daughter's car."

"You the one that tuned up that car?" Asa nodded. "Have any plans for your future?"

"Finish my major."

"You're an AG major?" that wasn't really correct either but that was what people here seem to understand so he nodded his head yes. J. J. felt he was not getting much information and besides he had other guests so he switched the conversation to sports, finished his whiskey and they retuned to the party.

J. J. Connors thought Asa was so interesting he made a note to have his personal lawyer and a private investigator friend do a little checking up on Asa James Bennington. This was not the usual guy Peggy brought home and he wondered if his sweet Peggy might have bitten off more than she could chew. He hoped not. Despite everything, he loved his daughter deeply.

Asa was right. Peggy drank too much. He managed to untangle himself from her embrace and help her inside the bungalow where he deposited her on her sofa. He was out the door and had it locked behind him before she managed to rise from the sofa. She would probably sleep it off right there.

Driving home he stopped at a liquor store and picked up a six-pack. The clerk thought he was interesting, very well dressed, buying beer and driving a real clunker. Once home he opened the beer, pulled off his tie, loosened his collar and stared out the window. The window faced northeast, and he liked to think he was looking homeward.

Yes, the evening had been fun and most interesting. Peggy's parents were not at all like she had made them sound. Aunt Maud was a tough old bird. From the household staff to Aunt Maud, they all loved Peggy. That was evident.

Not far away, a storefront sign must be flashing off and on pink and purple and the colors reflected in the low fog made him think of Peggy's aluminum Christmas tree with the rotating color wheel. He hadn't thought to put up decorations of his own. As soon as she saw he had none she had gone right out and purchased a huge poinsettia, which was, at the moment, very wilted.

He thought about Christmas at home. He bet his father was looking forward to going with Charlie and Molly to find the perfect tree. His mother would give some kind of sign that only long married people understand, and his father would suddenly remember he had some work to do. The newly weds would go by themselves to hunt for a tree. Before he let himself become too homesick, he remembered where he had spent the last few Christmases. He watered the poinsettia.

Their proposed New Year's Eve celebration started another argument. "The party is going to be at Manny Blue's." I told them we would come." Peggy hadn't consulted Asa because she knew he did not care for Manny. In truth, Asa didn't have much in common with most of Peggy's friends and Manny was definitely on the bottom of Asa's list. Manny Blue was what Asa called a professional student. Plus, Asa didn't trust him and second Asa could spot a drug user right away.

"Oh, Manny is okay. He just likes a little fun. You never like my friends and they like you a lot. Besides New Year's Eve is supposed to be fun. Anyway, I have already accepted the invitation and I told him we would be there." Seeing the scowl on Asa's face Peggy flounced into the bedroom and shut the door just a little too hard.

She always banged the door. In her mind it ended the conversation and she always hoped he would follower her in to the room and into her bed. Instead he turned on the TV and watched a football game. Several times after a really major argument she had done this and he turned on the game so loud he couldn't hear her pretend sobs. At half time, he left. She apologized the next day as she always did. Now with New Years Eve and the stupid party he wondered just when had their relationship started to feel like a contest?

The party turned out to be a mute point. Peggy came down with a head cold and went to her parent's home for a week. As she told him over the phone, "I am going where someone will take care of me." If that was supposed to be a dig it didn't work.

Asa had a fine time. He walked the beaches. He ate clam chowder out of a paper cup from is favorite fish joint. He rode a shop motorcycle up the coast. He read just for the fun of it, not because it was required for a class or because "everybody is reading" it as Peggy liked to say. During their first dinner after she returned to her bungalow she was not pleased to learn he'd had a good time while she was in total misery. He had had a good time without her and that worried her.

January rolled into February and semester finals were coming up very fast. For Valentines Day Peggy's mother had the cook prepare J. J.'s favorite strawberry cheesecake. Peggy's parents sat in Melissa's room enjoying the cake with coffee. She thanked him again for the dozen long-stemmed red roses. Besides being a beautiful flower there was a special meaning for the couple. On that long ago day, years before, when J. J. proposed he could only afford a single blossom. Now he could easily to give her several dozen if he wished. It had been a pleasant evening and J. J. was looking forward to later having a whiskey. Plus both Asa Bennington reports he had requested were now waiting in the library. Right now he would enjoy his wife's company until she began to tire.

Downstairs, at last, J. J. stoked the fire, poured a generous drink, put his feet up and began to read. From the private detective, he learned about daughter's current beau. Asa did grow up on a ranch near a small Wyoming town named Silver Bend. The town had a population of maybe one thousand. Nothing interesting about his growing up years. His parents still lived on the ranch, and he had a younger brother named Charlie recently married to a young lady named Molly. They also lived on the ranch. Half way through Asa's third year at college he, apparently with out consulting his family, enlisted in the USMC. He had served with distinction, earning two battlefield promotions as well as the Purple Heart, which he declined. (No reason given) Following the end of his tour, he declined to reenlist and returned to the stats where he spent two weeks in the hospital followed by debriefing classes.

Once released by the military, he returned to school. His grades were very good and the teachers liked him. He lived in a little apartment, which was rent-free in turn for his working as a part time mechanic at a small motorcycle shop. The shop owner said he was one of the best mechanics he had ever had and was worried a bigger shop would hire him away. Asa drove an older truck. He owed no money and paid his bills on time. He had no debt. He had a respectable bank account because every month he received a check from the ranch. He had no criminal record. The PI concluded the report by stating he was pretty sure Peggy and Asa were not sleeping together.

"Well, none of this information was expected" and J. J. wondered just how much Peggy knew. Indeed, Asa Bennington was not like Peggy's other young men.

The lawyer's report included some of the same information, but the ranch was a surprise. It was a real, working, large ranch earning a fine reputation for quality grass fed beef. Officially known as the Bennington Ranch it had a registered brand of two back facing "B"s. Asa might not be living on the ranch, but he was still a joint-owner along with his father and the brother. When the father passed away, his shares would go to Asa and his brother. The ranch had a very good bottom line. J. J. Connors was impressed, if not a little surprised. Again J. J. wondered how much about this man did his daughter know.

Peggy and Asa celebrated Valentines Day much differently than her parents. She gave him a watch. He gave her a giant, fluffy pink (her favorite color) elephant with satin hearts on the ears. He took her out to dinner. It was a lovely evening. Later he would believe they both had had a little too much wine. He pulled her car into her little garage and pushed the door opener closed. Without saying a word she leaned across to him, slid her hand between his legs and began rubbing his penis.

"Ah, damn" was all he said. She had surprised him, and there was no holding back, not this time. He was tall enough to come over the gearshift after her. He cupped her sweet chin in his hand and leaned into a kiss so filled with pent up desire she felt her knees go weak. She knew this time she had him. He was not going to stop. They couldn't get out of the MG fast enough. They left a trail of clothing from the kitchen to her bed.

He gave her sex as no one else ever had. It frightened her that she wanted it so.

Usually as soon as she was satisfied, she wanted the whole activity to come to an end. It didn't happen with Asa. He was slow and gentle and brought her to a climax long before he reached his. She tried everything she knew. He entered her again. It registered with her that she was not the one in control and for the moment she didn't care.

At last they were both completely satisfied. She was wideawake and thought she just might go have a drink as soon as he went to sleep as most men did. He turned over on his side facing her. Pulling her body gently into the curve of his own, he put his arm over her and dozed off. She wouldn't be getting up any time soon.

Five hours later he woke quickly from a strange noise, plus the room was stifling. The noise turned out to be Peggy's snoring. He looked at the bedroom . . . pink everywhere, pink-flowered wallpaper, pink-ruffled bedspread, pink pillows, and lampshades. Everything pink . . . He decided he didn't like the color pink. They must have left the heat on and slowly it came back just what had happened the night before. "Oh, son of a bitch!"

He got up, covered the snoring Peggy, located his slacks but couldn't find his underwear and left the bedroom, shutting the door behind him. He needed to think. He turned down the heat, found the pot and made coffee. He was surprised at how empty the kitchen cupboards were. She always served wonderful meals.

With strong, black coffee in hand and nothing on his feet so he could feel the cold of the stone patio, he sat outside and watched the sun come up. "Damn," he had done just what he said he didn't want to do. How did this change things or did it? Yes. He had to think.

The sex was terrific but perhaps a little like another contest to start with, he thought. Some of the things she did made him wonder just where she had learned them. Well, he was no virgin and he hadn't expected her to be either but just the same it did bother him.

Did she use birth control? He simply jumped her bones and never thought about protection. Sure, some day he wanted a wife and children but not now. Not this way. Did he love her? No. Was he falling in love with her? Possibly. Did he see her as a wife? Maybe. Did he see her as a mother? Hopefully, but not likely. Did he see her happy on the ranch? No. That answer was always the same.

Should he have been considering the question before now? Yes, but he hadn't. In his opinion, he had crossed a bridge and burned it behind him. There was no going back. He lay his head back and felt the early morning sun on his face. He felt like a real shit.

When she left the bedroom, that is how she him found him on her patio, shirtless, barefoot, and looking thoroughly miserable. She returned to the bedroom, changed from her see-through, sexy nighty into a fuzzy pink robe and fuzzy slippers. She brought him a cup of hot coffee and waited for him to speak.

Several things were settled. She was and had been using birth control pills since high school. He didn't ask why. She sounded as if children were a long way off if not at all. Asa didn't think about these revelations. He was just relieved. He had seen too many guys stuck in a shotgun marriage or saddled with child support because of an unexpected baby. He did not want that for either of them. Their whole lives were still ahead of them and his graduation was only months away. For him, it would be decision time.

They would continue to have sex, but he refused to move in with her.

She was disappointed. "Why can't you live here?" she whined. You could quit the job at the shop. Think how much time we could have right here."

He said, "no." But she was thinking about their whole relationship. She was not ready to lose him. She discovered with Asa she could not use sex as leverage and that hadn't happened with other lovers.

Graduation was only a few months away. He would be making decisions that might or might not include her. In the back of her head, she heard Aunt Maud at the Christmas party, "He's a keeper if you can hold onto him." Peggy intended to but she had to have a plan.

Chapter Thirty-nine

Tiajana

In Wyoming spring was beginning to tease. The day had been a hard one and Harlan sat in his recliner with his head back and his eyes closed. He and Lillian were talking about Asa. "Asa's graduation is fast approaching. I think we should select a graduation gift," suggested Lillian.

Thinking about it for a minute Harlan said, "When he comes home he will need a new horse. He would probably like to select it himself." Lillian liked Harlan's idea and she told him so.

Warming up to the thought that their oldest son would be coming home Lillian said, "We could give him a big welcome home party." From the expression on Lillian's face, Harlan knew his wife was already considering the names for the guest list and possible menus. He loved her for her thoughtfulness, and he hoped she was not going to be disappointed. Harlan stopped talking and listened. Even here in the main house he thought he heard Charlie yell.

While Harlan and Lillian were discussing Asa, down in the cottage where he and Molly had settled after their marriage, Charlie was really worried. He held a cold cloth to Molly's head as she threw up again.

He kept asking, "Should I call Mom? Should I call the doctor? Are you all right?' She took the cloth from his hand and motioned him out of the bathroom. She freshened up and decided it was time to tell her husband they were having a baby.

Returning to the living room, she sat down on his lap, laid her head on his shoulder, and whispered, "I'm pregnant." He was blank. "Charlie, we are having a baby." Charlie let out a whoop. Harlan was right. He had heard Charlie yell.

Asa studied harder for the upcoming finals so when Peggy said she had access to a beach house up in Malibu for spring break he was pleased. They both needed time off. It was a great week. Sand, surf, good food and shopping for her plus their sex was no longer combat. He put off any thoughts about what he would do once he was finished with school.

At the end of the week when he returned to his apartment, there was a letter from Charlie.

He and Molly were expecting their first child. Charlie and Harlan were having the second story of the house remodeled. The upstairs would be for Molly, Charlie, the baby, and any future children while downstairs, the in-law's quarters would be expanded for Lillian and Harlan.

Charlie was going to be a father. Asa thought about his parents becoming grand parents. "Well, hot damn!" he exclaimed. "I will be Uncle Asa." He was pleased. Peggy said, "That's nice." with out much enthusiasm.

June finally arrived and Asa graduated. He was happy and relieved to have it all behind him. He did not want a party even though Peggy offered. Before leaving his apartment for celebration dinner with the Connors, his parents called. He could tell they were very happy for him and very proud. After saying good-bye, he thought there were things unsaid. He was right.

"He didn't say anything about coming home asked Charlie?" Charlie could see his parents' disappointment. Charlie felt it also and Molly sensed his. She had never met Asa but some times she wondered if he was a jerk.

Melissa had gone to extra effort for dinner. Served on the patio the setting and the food were excellent and the evening was pleasant. Peggy's father seemed to be a little friendlier and Asa thought that he probably expected Asa to talk about his plans. He hadn't thought about any plans. He ought to and should have. He promised himself he would. Too many people wanted to know what he was going to do next. Some of those people deserved an answer.

Returning to Wyoming and working, the ranch with Charlie had always been his dream and that really had not changed. But just where did Peggy fit in or did she? Later in the week Peggy casually said, "Some of our friends are planning on a beach party Friday night. We're invited. Want to go?"

Thinking that he had earned a little celebration, he said, "Sure." He loved the beach. He didn't inquire about who the friends were. The evening was perfect; moonlight, good surf, plenty of food and a lot of booze. It was not a large gathering, but still he did not know all the people. He recognized Manny Blue and some of his regular crowd.

Someone mentioned Asa had just graduated and the party suddenly seemed to be in his honor. Drinks were passed around. Toasts were offered, and he was congratulated. As the evening progressed several bonfires were lit. Somewhere someone was playing a guitar. He was happy sitting in the beach chair, watching the surf and Peggy flitting around the crowd. He was having a good time and so was she.

By nine o'clock some couples had left while others drifted away to find a private sand dune. He could smell weed. The music was slow and soft and several couples were dancing on the wet, hard sand left by the retreating tide. Peggy handed him her glass. "Here, taste this."

"What is it? He didn't want any more beer."

"Lemon-aid." He drank most of it. "Let's dance," she invited.

He enjoyed dancing with her even though she was a little short in his arms. She looked particularly pretty this evening but her perfume was beginning to bother him, "Is that one of your regular perfumes?" He asked. He thought it was making him sick.

"U-hm . . ." she purred in his ear. He was alarmed. He felt truly ill.

"I think I want . . ." He never finished the sentence. Instead, he found himself sitting on the sand staring at her kneecaps.

"Peggy?" He looked up at her. There was no surprise or concern on her face only a slight smile. A warning bell was going of in his head. Now he saw three more sets of kneecaps. Looking up again, he saw one set belonged to Manny Blue.

"Jeeze, Asa. Can't hold all the graduation booze?" The warning bell sounded again and then he knew. Not booze, he had been given a drug of some sort.

"Peggy?" Asa couldn't see her; his vision was not normal now. Manny and his buddies pulled Asa up off the sand and trundled him back to a beach chair. Peggy was there. She patted his hand.

"What you need is a nice cup of coffee," she said brightly. He didn't want coffee. He wanted to go to a hospital and take care of whatever was pumping through his veins and into his brain. The whole beach had a cotton candy effect to it. No matter how hard he tried to talk it didn't work. He could more or less understand the conversation that seemed to come from all directions "Tijuana. Chorizo and eggs. Tequila. He just wanted to go home.

Instead he was dumped into the back seat of Manny's convertible, one of Manny's big bruiser friends on either side of him. Peggy was in the front seat and Manny was driving. The car radio was too loud. He dozed only to awake when someone jammed a pair of sunglasses on his face. Slowly he reasoned that was pretty stupid. It was nighttime. He was only slightly aware when they crossed the border into Mexico.

Asa dozed off again only to be awakened and hustled out of the car with a lot of help into what he thought might be an office. Not much light. Peggy was by his side. Everything was fuzzy. A man in a white shirt read something in Spanish. Asa's Spanish was good but these words meant nothing to him. Several people slapped him on the back. Peggy kissed him. Once back in the car, a bottle of Tequila was passed around. He didn't want any but some went down his throat anyway. He felt sick again but after a bit it didn't really matter.

Chapter Forty

The Morning After

That was all he would remember until he woke up in bed the next morning. He understood it was Peggy's bed. He knew he was wearing his briefs and nothing else. He wondered if Peggy was all right. He did not open his eyes right away. When he tried, the light hurt too much. He closed his eyes. Never had he experienced such a head ach. He raised his left hand to shade the glare from his eyes. Damn, how he hated those fluffy pink curtains. That was when he saw the ring finger of his left hand. He was wearing a cheap Mexican sliver wedding band. The whole night came flooding back. He knew for sure he and Peggy were married. For the first time in years, he wanted to cry. This was not the way it was supposed to happen. They had never talked bout marriage. It was not the way it was supposed to be. He started swearing but stopped. It made his head hurt.

Peggy must have heard him and came in and sat on the edge of the bed. "Feeling better? You really tied one on last night. I'd say this is one hell of a graduation present." She was wiggling her ring finger with the matching wedding band. Oddly, he thought he would buy her a nice ring as soon as he was able. Right now he wanted to upchuck.

She went back to the living room. He could be sick all he wanted. Manny said he would. She certainly was not going to clean up after him. Later in the evening, Asa had showered, shaved and taken as many aspirin as reasonable. He did some of his best thinking in the shower. He looked as his new wife not even married twenty-four hours and said, "You drugged me."

She laughed lightly and said, "Or course not, you silly. You just had too much to drink." He knew she was lying. She left the room saying, "I'm going to call Mother and Daddy and tell them our good news."

He thought, ""We are starting our married life on a lie."

He closed his eyes and tried not to hear her talking to her father. "Of course I'm happy. Yes, yes, no. This is really what I wanted. Tonight would not be good. We'll come for dinner on Monday." Oh hell, he thought, I have to call home. He wanted to put is head down. He wanted to hit something. It would probably hurt too much.

The first night as Mr. and Mrs. was not like Peggy planned at all. She canceled the dinner reservations she had made several days before. At first, she thought he was angry. Well, she had expected that and assumed he would get over it. Later she realized he was sad and she had never even considered that. Asa was not feeling good still and not talking very much. She panicked when she thought he might think about an annulment.

When it was time for bed she put on her new, sexy, pink, peek-a-boo roses baby-doll nighty. He never noticed. Sitting on what was now his side of the bed he said, "Tomorrow we will go purchase you a proper wedding ring." He clicked out the light, turned his back to her and went to sleep.

Dinner with Melissa and J. J. was uncomfortable, at least for the two men. Melissa had hugged him and made him feel welcome. J. J. was cordial but guarded. The mother and daughter did not notice the distance between Asa and J. J. Peggy flashed her beautiful ring while busily telling her mother what kind of reception she wanted. She even wanted to wear a white gown.

J. J. noticed her ring and thought, "At least he didn't buy her a cheap thing."
In that J. J., was correct. Peggy had picked out an expensive one. Asa paid for it with a check out of his ranch account. That was not how he thought he would ever spend that money.

Driving away from the store she asked, "Where is your ring?"

"We couldn't afford one." Another lie and he planned not to tell her about the ranch money. He would find work, and they would live on what he could make.

After dessert and coffee, J. J. led Asa into the library. It was Christmas all over again. J. J. shut the door. This time he did not offer his new son-in-law a drink nor did he pour one for himself. He stood with his back to Asa, and looked out the windows toward the ocean. Asa said nothing and waited. Turning finally he gave Asa a hard look and said. "I have two requests. Peggy's schooling is paid for till she graduates next spring. I want your promise she will graduate."

"Yes sir" was all Asa said.

"No baby! Don't get her pregnant."

"Yes sir." and Asa meant it.

"What are your plans?"

From Asa's perspective, any plans he had were all shot to hell. Instead he said, "I plan to look for work." Neither man heard Peggy open the door or noticed she was now listening to the conversation.

"You better come work for me." It was more of an order than an offer.

Before Asa could politely refuse, Peggy bounced across the room, threw her arms around her father and said, "Oh, thank you Daddy. We're so happy!"
Asa was not happy. He felt trapped.
As a wedding gift Melissa and J. J. sent them to Acapulco for two days after which Asa was going to work for J. J. Connors Construction. Before they caught the plane for Mexico and their honeymoon Asa called his parents. He couldn't put it off any longer.

Both Harlan and Lillian were on the phone when he told them. He tried to sound positive and upbeat and they tried to match his tone. Asa and his bride were off to Acapulco after which he was going to work for his father-in-law while Peggy completed her last year of school. Asa thought it at least sounded reasonable. They offer him congratulations and told him to have a good time in Mexico.

As soon as the call was over, Lillian found Harlan still standing by the kitchen phone. She let him draw her into the protective circle of his arms where she tired to be quiet. Harlan could tell she was crying. For a moment, he felt very hurt and let down. It all made him feel very old.

Lillian and Harlan may have felt disappointed. Charlie was down right angry. He kicked the corner of the corral, turned to his father and said, "What kind of an ass hole is my brother turning into?" He shut up when he saw the sadness on his father's face.

The honeymoon turned out to be pleasant, mainly because Asa saw Peggy was really happy. He admitted to himself that it made him happy to see her happy. He did love her in a way, he guessed. They were rested and relaxed when they returned home.

Asa cleared out his apartment and resigned his job at the motorcycle shop. He was a little sorry and the shop owner was very sorry. Mr. and Mrs. Bennington were honored at a fine reception hosted by Melissa. The reception included white roses everywhere and a three tiered cake and Peggy happily wore a beautiful white wedding gown. The whole thing made Asa uncomfortable as hell.

Both J. J. and Asa saw that Peggy was happy and that eased the relationship between the two men. Peggy's last year at college would begin in the fall while Asa went to work for his father-in-law.

For Peggy, summer started out on a high note. Following the reception, two of her girlfriend gave showers. Peggy spent several weeks playing with all the wedding gifts and sending out the proper thank you notes. But after that, her summer was different. As a married woman, she didn't fit into her old social world. She was bored. Asa was gone all day. She wanted school to start. She looked forward to her senior year and expected it to be a blast.

Asa was finding his way as the newest employee at J. J. Connor Construction. Asa went to work everyday, fives days a week. He got up at 5:00 a.m. in the morning and fixed his own breakfast.

On the job he had a packed lunch and carried his own coffee thermos just like everyone else. He was never late and didn't leave early. He drove his own old truck and didn't wear Peggy's expensive Christmas watch. He worked at being just another laborer, and he didn't talk about his father-in-law.

He discovered Peggy didn't cook. Any nice meal he had ever eaten at her house had been prepared in Melissa's kitchen and delivered by her housekeeper who also cleaned the bungalow and did the laundry. It was a blow to Peggy and a chuckle to J. J. when Asa firmly said no more dinners and no more housekeepers. The newly married couple ate out often. "Didn't someone give us a waffle iron for our wedding?" he asked one Sunday morning.

"I think so," she said from the bed where she was still under the covers.

Asa had opened several cupboards only to discover they were about as bare as before the wedding.

"Where is it?"

"In the boxes in the garage," her voice was muffled.
"And the blender and the mixer and the popcorn popper?, he asked.
"Same place, Different boxes." As usual they went out to brunch.

Chapter Forty-one

The Man Who Married the Boss's Daughter

Asa was not surprised when J. J. started him out as a laborer. Asa shoveled dirt and rocks and broken concrete and asphalt, or whatever the foreman said. Slowly word went around that Asa Bennington was an all right guy. The word got back to J. J. Also, J. J. moved Asa from one department to another and from one crew to another. Everywhere Asa went he was not just the new man he was "The man who married the boss's daughter." He understood he had to work extra hard just to prove his own worth and he did.

His first at-home project, with the landlord's permission, was to completely strip the pink floral wallpaper from the master bedroom. All the pink froufrou décor when away. Asa even purchased new drapes and a new bedspread. Much to Peggy's, disgust he found and old quilt for the foot of the bed.

If that wasn't bad enough, the wedding present from his family was a small, very well done oil painting of some mountains he call the Peetee's. He hung it in the bedroom. Peggy was miffed because he did it all in one weekend when she decided she needed a treat and left to visit Aunt Maud. It did looked more adult and felt more restful, but she didn't say so.

Asa was working hard. He lost weight and firmed up. He looked good, he was settling into his job. It was as if he had moved into the adult world. She felt left behind.

When Peggy did start her last year at school, she found it had all changed. Asa was tired at night and didn't always want to go to a college activity. For a while, he expected her to have a meal on the table. Well, sometimes she did but they ate a lot of takeout. She felt two things: she wanted college to be over and married life was a not exactly like she thought it would be. She was not the center of his attention.

Things would be better once she graduated. She was sure. She tried to recapture some of their fun by planning special activities for the weekends, but it was not the same as before they were married. The sex was still good but not quite the way it was before, at least for her. Perhaps, for Peggy the chase was over. They were settling in. With her graduation, they would also be celebrating their first anniversary. She knew one thing; she was not about to get pregnant like some of her friends.

Asa knew she was trying to make weekends special for him and he appreciated that. However, it was hard to be excited about going away for the weekend when there were piled up dirty laundry and only cold pizza in the frig. He tried not to comment on the messy house.

Every Thursday evening they had dinner with Melissa and J. J. By the holiday season, Asa and Peggy were looking forward to their first Christmas. Asa also looked forward to the Thursday night dinners with his in-laws. He didn't yet know it but J. J. looked forward to them also. J. J. liked Asa and saw great promise in the young man. Reports from the various foreman and department heads confirmed this. He just hoped his daughter saw what a fine man she had married.

Asa began to notice Peggy's thoughtless remarks such as when he read her the news about Charlie and Molly's new baby girl. Charlie and Molly had named the child Catherine. Peggy said, "Geeze, Asa, can't your family ever pick out new names? Just how many Catherines does that make?

She did not notice his hurt when he answered, "This makes the third Catherine Bennington." He wondered what the baby looked like. It would be several years before he saw that she had the same Bennington blue-black hair as his and brother Charlie's bright blue eyes.

For Christmas, Asa suggested he and Peggy fly home for a snow filled, family holiday. Her answer was a flat "no" along with the slamming of the bedroom door. Instead he purchased a live Christmas tree to replace her aluminum one. At least he could have the scent of pine in the air. He thought about Christmas at home with Santa bringing gifts to little Catherine. He knew his mother would have Grandfather Charlie's old rocking horse next to the tree.

In the spring construction picked up and J. J. sent Asa off to different construction sites. Sometimes Asa wondered if J. J. did that on purpose. It was the subject of another argument. "Tell Daddy you want to stay home," Peggy complained.

"No. No one else can do that," he tried to explain.

"Well then, I'll ask. It was one of her favorite threats.

"Shit, Peggy! I work for your father. You don't, so you don't talk to him about me. Do you understand?" She pouted as usual. It occurred to him he didn't find it cute any more.

Asa was often away and Peggy was alone. She saw graduation coming and just wanted the year to be over so she could move on. She would have been surprised to know these were her husband's exact thoughts this same time last year. This time last year he had plans and decisions to make. She had no idea what she would do once she was out of school. She had no plans.

During spring break, they drove up to Carmel and Monterey. Asa had earned little vacation time he told her. What he didn't tell her was that he was holding some vacation time back for a surprise. They had a good time, but Asa thought some of the old passion was missing. Well they had been married almost a year and in truth it had been a hard year in some ways especially the last few months. With her graduation almost here he felt things would smooth out.

They still had the Thursday night dinners with her parents. Often her husband and her father would disappear into the other room and talk about work. It irritated Peggy. This particular evening and away from Peggy, J. J. said, "It was always her mother's and my plan to give Peggy a new sports car if she managed to graduate. If that is all right with you, we would still like to do it."

Asa laughed easily and said, "I think she will be pleased." He was trying to think of a suitable graduation present, himself.

Peggy did graduate. She was thrilled with the new red sports car from her parents. There was of course a party at the Connor's home, family, close friends, and gifts. At home that night Asa said as his gift, he had saved little vacation. "I'd like to take you back to Acapulco, that little hotel right on the beach. It would be for your graduation and for our first anniversary."

She was very slow to answer while she picked dead leaves off a houseplant. "That's sweet but maybe later in the summer would be better." Asa knew perfectly well that later in summer he wouldn't be able to get time off. He was the bottom of the list when it came to selecting vacation time and he would not go over anyone's head. He wondered just what she might do with her time. He hoped she didn't want to start a family. That thought made him uncomfortable.

Asa hoped his wife might be going to find work, something to put to use her English Literature degree. He took her old MG and his old "junker" truck and traded them both in on a used sedan which neither of them drove. She had her new car, and he now drove a company truck. He was pleased at what he was learning about the construction business. Every so often he got to drive some of the smaller equipment and work on the engines of the bigger stuff. He was having a good time and unknowingly earning a respectable reputation. He had earned his spot. He was liked and respected for himself not because he had married the boss's daughter. Peggy could see that and again his success made her feel alone.

For Asa, her graduation brought one more surprise. As long as Peggy had been in school, she had the use of Melissa's department store charge accounts. That stopped with graduation. She opened her own accounts. The first set of bills was an unwelcome surprise to Asa. "You can't charge like that." "We don't have that kind of money," he explained patiently.

"Ask Daddy for a raise."

"No."

"Then I will." She was surprisingly angry.

"We are married. I am working a decent job for a very decent wage. You want to spend more money, then you go to work. You do not talk to J. J.!" She marched into the house slamming the back door and the bedroom door.

Peggy was at loose ends and did not know what to do with her free time. Everything she had ever enjoyed over her growing-up summers seemed out of place. She did keep in mind what Asa said about finding a job for spending money. It couldn't be just any job and it had to be fun, something where she could shine.

One time Asa suggested they go back to Wyoming. She had yet to meet his family. He was startled when she yelled at him, "I'm not going back to some God forsaken cow farm, ever. Don't ask me again" and she slammed the bedroom door, as she seemed to be doing more often. As always she apologized later, but Asa would remember. He hoped again she would not stop taking her birth control pills.

Chapter Forty-two

Nicolas Zoloft

Peggy felt picked on. To often during Thursday night dinners with her parents one of them asked what she planned to do. What were her plans? Melissa even mentioned some charity organizations that would welcome Peggy. In September, she surprised everyone, including her husband, when she announced she had a job. J. J. saw the look on Asa's face and knew this was news to his son-in-law.

"Yes," she said proudly. "I am going to work at the Book Nook. It's a specially shop that sells old and rare books. She told them the address. Her employer was Mr. Nicolas Zoloft. Asa was thinking it was a start but not much of one. J. J. was thinking the same thing.

Peggy brightened considerably after the first few weeks at the Book Nook. Asa met Zoloft at a tea held at the Book Nook for the purpose of inviting the public in to view some antique books from England. The shop was nice, tastefully done with what appeared to be an upper class clientele. Zoloft, to Asa's surprise, was older than he expected. Zoloft had pale blond hair gone slightly gray. He was very slender and very European including his slight accent and his dress. Asa thought of him as a dandy, but he kept those thoughts to himself. Peggy was almost her old self and that was good.

Asa was even pleased and pleasantly surprised when she announced she was planning on taking a night class . . . Russian literature. It was in preparation for a spring sale of eighteenth century Russian books.

"She is going to take night classes? You're kidding," laughed J. J. when Asa told him. Asa and J. J. had the same opinion about the new job, the Book Nook and it's owner.

"The book store is even paying for her class fees. So I guess I can't complain too much," remarked Asa. J. J. was thinking that all that money he put out for Peggy's education might actually result in something. Unfortunately, it meant Peggy would miss the Thursday dinners with her parents.

Thanksgiving was spent with her parents and Aunt Maud. She and Asa got along very well despite the first meeting. Asa called home and could hear baby Catherine in the background. Peggy actually brought home books to study.

Asa did not mention going to Wyoming for Christmas. They were invited to Zoloft's beach house for a holiday open house. Niki's party, as Peggy now called her employer, conflicted with the Connor's annual Christmas party. Thank goodness was what Asa thought. Baby Catherine was walking. Molly sent pictures. Asa knew Santa Clause would find baby Catherine, and he felt home sick for the first time in a long time. Melissa was not well over the remainder of the holiday so there was no dinner at Peggy's parent's home.

"We can have our own special dinner, just the two of us" was Asa's hopeful suggestion.

"I'm not cooking a prime rib and all the side dishes" was Peggy's sharp reply. They went out as usual and ended up eating Chinese food because nothing else was open with out a confirmed reservation. Asa's fortune cookie read, "A new moon will bring changes. He found himself hoping the cookie would be right."

January brought hard rains, strong winds and unusual fog. "Let me drive you to class tonight," Asa offered. She gave him an unexpected hug. "I know the road by heart so don't worry and you don't have to wait up for me. Besides, we have a guest speaker tonight. The class might run over." She was quickly out the door before he could argue.

Asa settled in with a good book planning to wait up especially after he found her door key on the kitchen counter. She was usually home no later than 10:30 p.m. Asa was so absorbed in his reading that only when he heard a car door did he notice it was 11:30 p.m. He was relieved when he heard a knock at the door. Thank goodness. He already knew she didn't have her key. It was not Peggy at the door.

It was two, very wet, very grim uniformed highway patrol officers. Behind them at the curb was the patrol car. It's red light turned the fog pink. He could hear the windshield wipers slapping. Oddly, it occurred to him he knew how to fix that. The officers were professional in every way.

"Are you Mr. Asa Bennington?
"Yes."
"Is your wife Peggy Connors Bennington?"
"Yes."
"We are sorry to inform you there has been an accident." Nothing he heard was making sense. He heard "wet pavement" "fog," and "blind curve." He snapped back to attention when they said, "Mr. Zoloft had been transported to a hospital. Mrs. Bennington was pronounced dead at the scene. In Asa's mind this was all wrong. She was at school. She would be home any minute. The officers droned on. "The car must have been coming from Mr. Zolofts's beach house. They had to have been traveling at a high rate of speed for the car to hit the guard rail like they did." They told him where he could pick up the wreck of the red sports car. However, the wrecker would not pull it up off the rocks until sometime tomorrow.

At last, Asa saw it all. All the little pieces fell into place. There never were any night classes. All her quirky behavior was so easy to dismiss as Peggy being Peggy. Instead Peggy was having an affair. "That son of a bitch!"

The officers stepped back at the sudden look on Asa's face. One even eased his hand toward his side arm. As quickly as the look came it disappeared. "Do her parents know?" asked Asa.

"No sir. We're going there now."
Wearily Asa said, "I'll tell them. It's better that they hear it from me."
The officers were only too glad to leave. It had been a nasty night. Back in the patrol car one officer said to the other, "You figure the husband knew his wife was screwing around?"
The other officer answered, "I think he figured it out while we were standing there. You see the look on his face?"
"Yeah. I wouldn't be the other guy." Asa stood in the open door a long time unaware that rain was replacing the fog.

Chapter Forty-three

Lost

If the neighbors had even noticed, the patrol car they would no longer think about it. The bungalow lights were out. Asa sat in the dark trying to figure out what he had done wrong. In the end he knew, he had done nothing wrong. He had only wanted to see Peggy happy. In a way he suppose he had loved her. He gave up his dreams and changed his goals. It was not enough. Peggy was Peggy. Asa had been another conquest, project or challenge . . . whatever she called them. He had just lasted longer than the rest. Peggy had moved on. For some reason, he thought about his brother Charlie. He wished Charlie all the happiness in the world Asa called his in-law's house.

J. J. answered the phone as Asa knew he would. "I'm coming to the house."

"What's wrong?" J. J. was alert thinking a job had gone wrong.

Using his father-in-law's given name Asa said, "Jerry, it's bad. It's very bad." Asa hung up the phone before the man could ask any questions. After changing clothes, he picked up his raincoat and headed to what he knew was going to be a sad situation. He drove slowly with the truck windows down. He took in deep, slow breaths of cold camp air. He was for the moment okay. He would sort his own feelings out later.

In front of the house was a car Asa did not recognize. J. J. had the front door open before Asa had the truck stopped. In the house, Asa recognized the owner of the car as Melissa's doctor. He motioned J. J. into the library. The doctor hung back and Asa indicated he should come also. Asa told them all he knew about the accident. He left out the part about Peggy's probable adultery and that it was the graduation gift red sports car in which she died.

He had never seen a man age in front of his eyes, but his father-in-law seemed too. The doctor watched J. J. carefully. J. J. asked a few questions and then with the doctor went up to tell Melissa. Asa stood at the dark windows where he knew the ocean was in view. Asa heard his mother-in-law wail. He didn't know, he could hurt anymore but he did.

Some time later, he heard J. J. tell the doctor good-bye. Returning to the library, J. J. opened a bar Asa never knew existed. He took down two bottles of whiskey and one glass. Sitting in his desk chair, he began to drink. He no longer knew his son-in-law was in the room. Asa left, shutting the door behind him. In the kitchen, he found the coffee pot ready for the coming morning. All he had to do was push the button. He wished that was all he had to do, just push a button and make everything all right again. Even with the time difference it was too early to call his family.

Asa knew at 6:00 a.m. the housekeeper and the cook would arrive. He waited. Maria and Lila were sweet women he had come to know and like and they had known Peggy since she was a toddler. They were family and this was also going to be hard. They always arrived together. They were not surprised to see a light in the kitchen. They were not surprised to smell coffee.

They knew something was wrong when they saw Asa at the kitchen table. He asked them to sit. He took their worn hands in his and told them. Both were good Catholics. They made the sign of the cross and murmured a blessing. Tears rolled down their cheeks. He wanted to cry some more himself, but that could come later.

He let them work through the situation and them continued, "Mr. Connors is in his library. He is getting very drunk. Leave him alone until" . . . until what? Asa didn't know, but the two women did. They nodded their heads in understanding. The cook, Lila was patting his hand.

"Could I ask for some breakfast?" he asked. The ladies smiled at that. Taking care of the family was something they both could do well. Also he added, "I expect there will be lots of people in and out today and we will need food." They knew about that, too.

"We know Mr. Asa." They probably knew better than he did he thought. He looked at his wristwatch, the one Peggy had given him last Christmas. He could call home.

Asa hoped his mother would be the one to answer the phone. Harlan was on his way out of the room when he heard Lillian say, "Asa?"

"Mom?" His voice was raw. "Mom. It's Peggy. She's dead." Again, he related only what they really needed to know. Eventually, his mother asked about the service. He said no decision had been made yet. Both her parents were having a difficult time he added. In truth he hadn't even thought about it. Nobody had thought about it.

He ate his breakfast and called Mrs. Hoskins, J. J.'s office manager. She told him to call Saul Stein, J. J.'s lawyer and friend. Saul told him to call Aunt Maud. That was when Asa learned that Saul and Maud were the silent partners in J. J.'s company. Two hours later the Mrs. Hoskins, Maud, and Saul sat in the dinning room and took care of the newspapers, the funeral, the cemetery, and the interment. From time to time, they heard the sound of breaking glass coming from the library. About noon, Maud told Asa to go to bed. Asa and Peggy had often used one of the guest bedrooms upstairs as they sometimes stayed over. He fell into bed, clothes, and all.

Early the next morning he showered, shaved, and went downstairs. The house was quiet. The library door still remained shut. Saul was asleep in a one of the big wing backed chair. He awoke when he heard Asa. Asa motioned to the shut door. "He still in there?"

Saul nodded yes. "I haven't hear any breaking glass for a while." Asa offered the lawyer a drink even though he did not want one. Saul didn't want one either. Asa was hungry. "How about something to eat?" Saul eased out of his seat, and they headed for the kitchen. They picked at the various dishes in the refrigerator then sat down at the breakfast nook table where they ate in comfortable silence.

Asa pushed his empty plate away, leaned his head against the wall and with his eyes closed he said, "Saul, What's left to do?"

"Two things. We need to get that car to a junk yard. I don't think J. J. needs to see it," replied Saul. Asa agreed. Saul paused before going on. "The coroner's office will not release the body to the mortuary till there is a positive ID. Asa opened his eyes.

"Shit!"

"I'll go if you like," offered Saul.

"No, she was my wife," Asa said aloud but thought, "For better or for worse" and said, "I'll go. You want to go home? I'll take a turn on the sofa."

Saul left and Asa dozed on the sofa till Aunt Maud retuned. "I'll stay here. I imagine you have things to take care of. Besides he can be an ass hole when he's drunk she said nodding at the closed doors.

Taking care of the car took longer than Asa expected. It was a little after noon when he arrived at the coroner's office. Even then they had to go find somebody to take care of Asa's business. Peggy's face was unmarked which surprised Asa. It was the rest of her body that had sustained massive trauma according to the report. The man droned on about the cause of death, certainly instant because of the steering wheel not to mention the impact of the car landing on the rocks and of course there was no possibility of saving the baby. Asa choked down his surprise.

He left the office with Peggy's personal effects and the truth of the man's last statement. He drove to a small beach and watched the waves for a long time. He reread his copy of the accident. Peggy was pregnant. His baby? He would never know. Maybe that was better.

The personal effects consisted of her handbag and some items from the car's glove box. In the bottom of the bag along with spare change and breath mints, he found Peggy's wedding ring. He stared at the ring. It was the beautiful diamond ring he had given her to replace the cheap Mexican silver band.

Seeing the beach was deserted he walked slowly to the water's edge and threw the ring as far as he could into the cresting waves. Except for her wallet, he dumped her handbag in the trash. Asa hated California.

J. J. stayed drunk for three days. When he emerged from the library Asa thought he looked like hell warmed over and told him so. "That's about how I feel. I would like you to walk down to the beach with me." They sat on a patch of beach grass where Asa remembered he and Peggy had made love one moonlight night. "Two questions, Asa." J. J. spoke slowly choosing his words, "Was my daughter having an affair with that bastard?"

No use lying. "I believe so" was Asa' answer. They both watched the waves slide up on the sand and only to slip back into the sea. "Well, I guess Peggy was Peggy but you were the best thing that ever happen to her." Silence. "What's happened since I have been . . . er indisposed?"

Asa told him what arrangements had been made and then said, "Jerry you need to clean up and go to your wife. She needs you right now."

"You giving me orders, son?"

"Yes, I guess I am," replied Asa with the affection he felt for his father-in-law.

"Well, help this old man up, then." J. J. was smiling a little.

Flowers, letters, cards . . . all were arriving at the house. The doctor advised against Melissa trying to attend the services. Father and son-in-law managed to get thought the day. Now J. J. was upstairs with Melissa. Only Mrs. Hoskins and Asa were downstairs. "We ought to get rid of these flowers," remarked Asa.

The office manager agreed but thought there were a couple of arrangements Asa might want to keep. She pointed out a bouquet of tiny pink rose buds sent by the housekeeper and the cook. The other flowers were from his family. He kept the tiny roses. All the rest went to one of the local hospitals.

Chapter Forty-four

Going Home

It was late summer before J. J. was effectively back in control of his business. For those months from the outside everything moved smoothly but only because Asa, Saul, and Maud were handling things. J. J. was thankful, and he told Asa so one evening as they sat on the shady patio sipping drinks. J. J. didn't drink very much anymore. "Asa, Saul, and Maud, and I have been talking over some company plans. We are all in agreement. We would like to offer you a partnership." J. J. was pleased with the surprised look on Asa's face.

Asa was careful how he chose his words, "I don't think so."

J. J. was not surprised and said, "You're leaving aren't you?"

"Yes sir."

"Going Home?"

"Not directly. I thought I would drive up the West Coast. Maybe see a little of Canada."

J. J. looked hard at Asa. "You're lying to me, son."

Asa gave J. J. a crooked smile. "If anyone ever asks that's what I told you."

Asa was gone inside a month. Lillian was counting the days to when she might start watching for her son. His father was not so sure.

Asa had told everyone he was heading north. He did drive north up Highway 1. Somewhere in the Bay Area, he turned east. In a small central valley farm town, he traded the car for a nondescript pickup truck. He stopped shaving. He wore a tractor supply baseball cap. He look liked any other hard working local. He attracted no attention. He drove south toward Bakersfield but his destination was San Diego.

Very early, one peaceful Sunday morning he drove slowly by the Book Nook and shot out every window starting a fire. Driving on at an acceptable speed, he pulled to the side of the road to let the emergency vehicles rush by.

Monday morning Saul and J. J. were having breakfast together. Saul's morning paper was folded back to show the photo of the burned out Book Nook.
"Our boy?" commented Saul.

"Wouldn't be surprised," answered J. J. Both men smiled.

Saul added, "Guess the fire department found more than burned books. Appears that Mr. Zoloft was dealing in more than rare reading material."
After shooting out the Book Nook windows, Asa drove east into Arizona.
He began drifting across the American southwest. He cowboyed until each employer found out how good he was and offered him a permanent position. Asa moved on. He worked as a mechanic and again moved on. He even worked in a beer bar where he didn't need a ball bat behind the bar if trouble broke out. He seldom called home.

It was after Christmas that Lillian decided to open Asa's bank statements. She thought at least from the canceled checks she could tell where he was. Asa had not written one check since leaving Southern California. "I just want to know where he is," she told Harlan. Lately she looked tired. Not knowing about Asa was hard on both parents, but Lillian seemed to be having a more difficult time. Maybe that's what mothers did.

Between jobs again, Asa was driving nowhere in particular. It might have been spring, but a light snow dusted the low Arizona hills to the east and it was so cold he was surprised to see a lone man walking beside the highway. The walker was an elderly Indian man. Asa stopped the pickup. Opening the passenger door, the old man asked Asa, "You got any place to go?"

"No sir," replied Asa.

"Good," and the old man climbed slowly into Asa's pickup. A small amount of blood trickled from under the man's worn coat sleeve.

"First-Aid kit in the glove compartment," offered Asa. The old man shook his head no. Several miles down the road, then he broke the silence by saying turn here. Asa did as the man requested and following an almost invisible track, they eventually arrived at a collection of buildings that had seen better days. At the sound of the truck in the yard, dogs barked. The door to what appeared to be the living space opened and a young man appeared. Despite his arm being in a cast, he carried a ready rifle. That was how Asa met John Young Bear and his grandfather.

"I need work," stated Asa.

"Can't pay you," said John.
If you can feed me and I can put down my bedroll, I'd like to stay. Nothing was discussed. Grandpa was nodding yes. They gave Asa a place to sleep and fed him.

John had a broken arm, was a little younger than Asa and was having trouble keeping up with the place. Grandfather was probably in his sixties but looked older. The blood on his arm had come from someone setting his dog on him. John explained, "Those people don't like sheep or sheep herders. They give us a hard time whenever they can."

The old man was a tribal elder and a respected shaman, but he said very little most of the time. Asa decided when Grandpa did speak it was worth listening. John watched as Asa repaired their old jeep and the pump on the windmill. John had spent time in Korea and needed to talk about it. Asa understood and listened.

For each job Asa did, he said he needed some particular tools. He went into town purchased tools along with beans, coffee, sugar, and occasionally chocolate and tobacco.
"You wanted by the law?" Grandfather asked one day.

"No sir."

"But you are running away from something?" questioned the old man. "A woman?" Asa thought about that. Maybe he was but he didn't comment.

After the many repairs were completed, Asa quietly added the new tools to the bin in the work shed. Asa would learn to at least tolerate sheep and eat mutton as prepared by Grandfather. Enough chilies and onion could make anything taste better. After seeing Asa handle a horse, John kidded Asa about being a cowman through and through. Asa knew it was a compliment.

John's arm was out of the cast but stiff. Asa correctly judged that who ever set it hadn't done the best job, but John felt sure he could go look for work pretty soon. It appeared that things were finally turning around for John and his grandfather. That evening the three men sat outside by a small fire, watched the stars and made small talk. Grandfather told stories and as soon as he discovered Asa liked to hear his stories he talked more often. "Maybe that is because your great grandmother was an Indian and your grandmother was Mexican," teased John.

They all stopped talking when they heard the racing engine. "Somebody is drunk," said John.

"Coming down your road, too" added Asa. Softly, Asa moved into the shadows. He was right. It was a pick up truck and the occupants were drunk. They pulled to a dusty stop in front of the fire and stumbled out of the cab. One of them carried a rifle.

"Well, lookie what we got here. A couple of stinking sheepers," sneered the one with the gun. He raised the rifle and took aim at Grandfather's old sheep dog. He never saw Asa. The drunk found himself on the ground and knew for sure his wrist was broken and his gun was gone. Now the rifle was in the hands of a man he hadn't seen.

The man had cold, gray eyes and the gun was aimed at almost point blank range at him and his drunken friends. Despite the snap and crackle of the small fire, no one could miss the sound of the hammer being cocked. The other two drunks sobered up quite quickly with the unwelcome change of events.

The man with the broken wrist tried not to make too much noise but he hurt. Asa's look and voice scared the shit out of them. "Get your asses out of here or by the count of three I'll kill you where you stand. Don't dig up the road on your way out and don't ever come back. I'll be waiting for you."

They could not leave fast enough, and they didn't tear up the road either. Once Asa could no longer hear the truck, he handed John the rifle. "Guess you have a new gun."

"Probably won't take it into town any time soon," remarked John. He was still a little surprised at what he had just seen.

Grandfather had been silent up till now. "Guess this means you like my dog."

"Surely do, Grandfather, surely do," said Asa with a satisfied smile.

Several mornings later Asa noticed the wind now had a bite to it and the scent of sage conflicted with Grandfathers pipe. In the high country above the ranch, Asa thought the Aspens would be turning color. Asa and Grandfather were sitting on the south side of the house trying to soak up what warmth there was in the sunshine. The old sheep dog sat as close to Asa as she could, leaning into Asa's leg. Grandfather always thought that particular dog was a good judge of character.

Grandfather took a deep draw on his pipe and said, "You need to go home." Asa knew it was finally time and he was ready. Grandfather was right. No long drawn out good-byes. Asa left as simply as he had come. Just as he was about to climb into his pickup, the old man handed him a spectacular turquoise ring. Asa started to protest but saw John Little Bear shake his head. Asa accepted the gift.

At the first pay phone, he came to Asa stopped and called the ranch. A woman's voice he didn't recognize answered. "This is Asa," he said. "Who's this?"

"I'm Molly." Before Asa could say anything she continued, "Your mother is ill, very ill. You're needed here at home."

"I'll be there in two days," was all he said and hung up the receiver.

"Didn't he tell you where he was?" asked Charlie for the third time.

"No," she repeated, "Just said he would be here in two days."

"Should we tell Mama?" Charlie asked his father.

"I think not, just incase he doesn't come," was Harlan's answer. Molly thought it was one of the saddest things she had ever heard.

Asa made the trip in eighteen hours arriving at the ranch late in the morning. As Charlie often did, he had taken Harlan on some made up errand just to get him out of the house for a break. Molly was alone when she saw the pick up coming down the ranch road. The driver parked as if he knew the driveway.

"This has to be Asa," thought Molly. She watched him get out of the truck. He didn't look like anything she had expected and he definitely did not look like Charlie. She met him on the porch. "Asa?" he nodded.

"Molly." He knew who she was. In the kitchen, he stopped. Everything was different. Well, the house had been remodeled several times since he left. "Tell me about my mother."

"You want it straight?"

""Yes," he answered.

"She has cancer. It's terminal. The doctor says probably two weeks at the most is all she has. Asa looked as stricken as Charlie had when he first heard the news. In some way, the brothers did look alike.
"Do you want to see her? She'll be awake. She has a nurse with her."

"I want to clean up." He was rubbing the dark stubble on his chin.

"Come with me. I'll show you to your room."

The whole up stairs was new. He glanced at what must be Charlie and Molly's room. Next they passed what had to be the baby's room. Asa stopped.

"Baby Catherine's?"

"Yes, she's napping, but do you want to see her?"

The baby was not asleep. Molly noticed that Asa sucked in his breath when he first saw her. Little Catherine had the same jet-black hair as Asa. The baby looked back at her Uncle Asa with Charlie and Harlan's bright blue eyes. Catherine produced a very big yawn and held out her arms to Molly who picked her up and showed Asa to his room. "That's the bath. Your towels are the green ones. We'll be downstairs."

Showered, shaved, and almost dressed, Asa heard a knock on his door.

"Asa, it's Charlie."

"Come on in." The two brothers, now grown men, eyed each other. Charlie saw the rib cage scar from the long ago camping trip to the Sandies. He knew he was going to cry. It was little brother and big brother all over again. They embraced and slapped each other on the back.

Harlan looked at the man coming down the stairs toward him. It was not the Asa he remembered until Asa smiled. Asa extended his hand and Harlan pulled him into a hug that lasted long enough for the two men to regain their composure. "Tell me about Mom." They did. It was just as Molly had told him.

"I'll tell her your home," said Harlan. At that moment, Catherine toddled up and took Asa's hand.
"Want to come see my Grammy?"

"Yes, I do."
Lillian Penrose Bennington died three days later. She passed so peacefully even the nurse was not sure when it happened. Later in the day, Charlie and Asa stood outside looking at the pastures that were greening up with spring grass. "Mother picked out the casket. She wrote everything out. No funeral. A private burial up on the hill. No flowers," related Charlie.

Her wishes were carried out just as she wished. On that weekend, many Silver Bend clergymen asked for a prayer or hymn in remembrance of Lillian Bennington.

The day of her interment was cold and windy. The family was seated near the grave as one of the friends chosen by Lillian spoke. Catherine wiggled out of Molly's lap and went to where Asa was seated on the other side of Harlan. She tapped him on the knee. He handed his cowboy hat to Harlan and picked her up, snuggled her into his lap and wrapped his coat around her little bare knees. Molly slipped her hand into Charlie's. Harlan thought, "Lillian, I hope you can see this."
That afternoon Asa was going through the stack of cards that came with the many floral arrangements. He studied one and asked, "Who is S. Hathaway?"
Both Harlan and Charlie answered, "Stub Hathaway?"
"Is he still around?" asked Asa.
"Yeah, he is. Still up on his place. Runs a few head of scrub cattle. Stays drunk most of the time."

"You think he would send flowers?"

"Not likely," was Harlan's observation thinking back to when Stub showed up at the EOR. with his poor frighten young wife so long ago. Asa dropped the card into an envelope with the rest.

Several days later Catherine and the three adults were eating supper when Catherine said brightly, "Where did Grammy go?" It was a question Molly had been dreading.

Asa folded his napkin, scooted back his chair and said to Catherine, "Your Grammy has gone on a long journey. Everyone has a journey. Come in the living room with me and I will tell you all about it."

"What is he talking about?" Molly asked her husband and her father-in-law who was smiling for the first time in several days.

It was Harlan who answered. "Asa is telling Catherine the same story I told Asa and Charlie about their grandparents' deaths and my father told me about my grandparents. The story about the journey that comes after this life.

Chapter Forty-five

At Home

Asa stayed. He moved into the stone cottage. He and Charlie slipped into the easy companionship they had always enjoyed. Molly noticed that Charlie was not as tired because Asa was taking up the workload that Harlan had not really been able to do. Those in the community who hoped for a fight or a contest between the Bennington brothers were disappointed. For a while, Asa did his own cooking and kept to himself. He did not want to interfere in the family's life just because he suddenly showed up after all these years.

"Asa, come to the house. Take your meals with us," said Molly. Asa was not yet sure how his sister-in-law felt about him and he didn't want to cause problem. She saw his doubt. "Asa it would please your father and Charlie . . . and me."

"Me too. Me too," piped up Catherine.

In September, it was time for EOR. Harlan said he and the baby would be just fine alone for the evening. Molly, Charlie, and Asa should attend. Asa was reluctant. He really hadn't moved back into the social life of the community yet.

"He should come. It will be a good opportunity for him to meet all the neighbors and our friends" was Molly's suggestion.

Charlie was unsure. "He doesn't know anyone. I mean he doesn't even know anyone to invite. I mean like a date." Charlie was floundering "He is so . . . reserved."

"Charlie, have you really looked at your brother? He is a very handsome man. He is wealthy. He is half owner of one of the best ranches in the county, he is very polite and he is single. Do you honestly think he won't have some one to dine with or dance with? Molly was right, especially as soon as the single ladies and a few of the married ones in the community discovered that Asa Bennington could dance and dance well.

"Damn, you were sure right about that. Asa will have to beat the women off with a stick and he doesn't even know it," was Charlie's comment to Molly after they came home from the party.

About six months after losing Lillian, Charlie found Harlan on the floor of his bedroom when he didn't appear for breakfast. Slight stroke was the doctor's opinion. Asa moved from the cottage and bunked in with his father.

Harlan never fell again, but he also was not the same. They saw he was slipping away slowly. For Christmas, Molly did not try to make it Lillian's Christmas but concentrated on Catherine. After the holiday was over, Charlie gave her a big hug and said, "Thank you for making Christmas easy for Dad and special for the rest of us all at the same time."

Harlan died just after Valentines Day. Like Lillian, he passed softly but because of his position in the community the family decided to have a memorial service in town.

There was no church big enough to hold the number of expected people so the service was held in the old Silver Bend Miner's Hall, a historical building built in Silver Bend's brief silver mining period. Too many people wanted to speak, so as not to hurt any feelings only Asa and Charlie had comments. The Silver Bend Banner paid a nice tribute to Harlan and also Lillian followed by the complete history of the Double B Ranch. The family received condolences from several state officials.

Harlan was laid to rest next to Lillian in the family cemetery. The digging was hard because the ground was frozen and it began to snow as soon as he was buried. It snowed for two days. Asa and Charlie thought it was appropriate.

The snow that fell on Harlan's grave also covered the body of Stub Hathaway. A traveling encyclopedia salesman found the frozen body a week later. Hathaway's death was in the newspaper's obituary column. No next of kin were mentioned. For a while, there was speculation about what might happen to the Hathaway place but even that died down for lack of information.

Chapter Forty-six

Joanna Monroe

The horse stamped her hoof and blew. Asa roused himself from all the old memories . . . too many memories, so long ago. How long had he sat there? The afternoon shadows were longer now. Asa scratched his bearded chin. Growing a full, old-fashioned beard for the OER was beginning to feel like a stupid idea. He needed to clean up if he was going to make amends with his sister-in-law and meet her friend. He eased the horse down the slope and home. Charlie was in the barn when Asa arrived. "You okay?" Charlie asked.

Yeah. Sorry I've been such an ass."

Charlie went on. "Molly's friend is a nice lady, really."

"What's her name again?"

"Joanna Monroe."

Asa decided this whole damn thing started in February. Molly was reading one of her quilting magazines. Molly had learned quilting from their mother and was now an accomplished quilter in her own right. She looked up and announced, "In April I want to go to Denver and attend a quilters' retreat" Both men were surprised, especially Charlie.

His wife only did things that were related to him, to their daughter, Catherine, or the ranch in that order. Asa knew he was in there somewhere, just not sure at what level.

April did come and Molly did fly to Denver to attend the retreat. The two brothers decided they did not like being bachelors. They missed Molly and her cooking. None of the other members in Molly's quilt group could go, so Molly knew she would have a roommate, a quilter from another state probably.

330 Donna Bender Hood

That same February in Anchortown, California, Joanna Monroe read the same information in the same quilt magazine about the Quilters' Rocky Mountain Retreat and decided she would like to attend. If Asa and Charlie were surprised by Molly's plan, Joanna's daughter, Susan, was very unhappy about the idea.

"Mom, you just can't go flying off to God knows where." she said over the phone. Susan was five hours away so she and her mother talked by phone often.

"Why?" asked her mother.

"Because you're too . . ." Susan stopped.

Joanna finished the sentence for her, "Because I'm to old? Susan, I am not that old. I am only going to Colorado, not the end of the earth." Susan argued right up to the morning Joanna flew out of Sacramento for Denver. A quilter from Wyoming was to be her roommate. That is how Joanna Monroe met Molly Bennington. They would become fast friends for the rest of their lives.

Joanna knew Molly lived on a ranch with her husband and his older widowed brother. Molly and Charlie had a daughter Catherine who was out of school and working as a home interior decorator in Casper, Wyoming.

In turn, Molly learned that Joanna had lost her husband to an aneurism just over three years ago. Joanna still lived in the same house. She gardened. She had a cat. She quilted, belonged to a local quilt group just as Molly did and one day a week she read books to children at the small local library. Joanna had a daughter, Susan. Susan was happily married with a one-year-old baby. Joanna also had a son, Bruce Jr. Bruce Jr. was the sadness in Joanna's heart. After graduating from college, he just dropped out of sight.

Sometimes she and Bruce Sr. received a card from some odd place. When Joanna's husband was dying, Bruce Jr. had suddenly shown up at the hospital and asked to be left alone with his father. After which, he hugged his mother and left with out a word. Just before her husband died, he took hold of Joanna's hand and said, "We don't have to worry about our son. He's okay." Not till the coming Christmas would Joanna learn what that meant.

Both Molly and Joanna returned to their respective homes and families excited about their week of quilting classes and speakers and their newfound friend. In May, Molly told Charlie and he told Asa that Molly was inviting her California friend to come stay at the ranch for EOR. Looking back, Asa knew that was when he began to feel grumpy about Molly's guest.

On Joanna's part, she was only too happy to accept the invitation despite Susan's protests, Sacramento to Denver; Denver to Cheyenne, and a short hop to Layton. Molly was waiting at the arrival gate. In the parking lot, Molly stowed the luggage in a station wagon with the Bennington name and Joanna guessed the ranch's brand painted on the door. They drove out of Layton, through ranch and farm country, Molly chitchatting all the way. Molly finally turned onto the ranch road under a broad and rustic sign that read "Bennington Ranch 1868." The ranch was big, and the ranch road long. Molly drove around the front drive so Joanna could see the house. It's been remodeled so many times it does not look like much." Joanna thought, "It does looks old and the wrap around porch looks inviting."

Molly parked by the back gate and they both watched a small, white puffball of a dog bouncing up and down inside the fence. In the way of an introduction Molly said, "That's Kiki." Joanna knew the story of Kiki.

Several years ago, going out to the highway mailbox one frosty morning, the brother-in-law found a box of abandon puppies. They were all dead except one. He put the small shivering animal inside his shirt while he buried the others. The dog became his. Kiki liked people but she loved Asa.

Asa and Charlie were trying to put a small engine back together when Charlie looked out the shop window and said, "They're-home." Asa smashed his thumb and swore. Charlie wondered about his brother. He must have gotten up and the wrong side of the bed and was still there. The station wagon stopped at the gate. Charlie wiped his hands on a rag. "Let's go meet them." Asa didn't say a thing and he didn't move either.

Shrugging his shoulders, Charlie went out to make Molly's friend welcome. Asa watched from the shop shadows. Charlie limped across the drive. Asa could not hear the words but knew by the body language that Charlie was being his most charming self. That man could charm a bird off a fence post, but some times he just didn't know when to stop.

Molly walked Joanna through the house . . . maybe ugly on the outside but wonderful on the inside was Joanna's immediate impression. She saw a great kitchen, a formal dinning room with an old cherry table and china hutch and old paintings on the wall. The living room was big with comfortable seating; two large windows facing the mountains and flanked by a river stone fireplace. A stereo and a television completed the room. "This is wonderful," complimented Joanna

Before she and Molly started up the stairs Molly pointed down the hall saying, it led to the ranch office and her brother-in-law's private quarters. Upstairs Joanna's room was very cozy complete with a quilt on the wall. The quilt was very old with the batting showing through in some places. The binding was ragged. Joanna recognized the pattern as Ohio Rose. A newer quilt, probably one of Molly's, lay across the bottom of the bed. A small bath completed Joanna's home for the next seven days. She knew she would be very comfortable, and she already felt very welcome.

However, dinner was a little odd. The table was set for four, but the brother-in-law did not appear. Because the whole guest thing irritated Asa, he had avoided dinner and gone down to the bunkhouse and eaten with the ranch hands. The Bennington brothers were always welcome. Most of the hands thought the brothers were good employers and the ranch was a good place to work.

After dinner, a poker game was suggested. The ranch foreman did not play but liked to watch. He knew Asa Bennington's poker playing reputation. The boss man could have taken everyone's paycheck, but he didn't. He controlled the game and lost just enough to make it a pleasant evening for everyone.

That was Monday. On Tuesday, quilters from all over the valley descended on the ranch to meet Molly's friend and enjoy a day of quilting. Both Charlie and Asa made themselves scarce till the ladies left in the late afternoon. Again at dinner the table was set for four and again Molly's brother-in-law did not appear. Joanna could tell that Molly was not happy.

Later that night Charlie was already in bed reading a book. Molly was putting cold cream on her face, "You better tell Asa to be at dinner or else," Molly said her voice a little louder than usual.

Charlie moved the book so she could not see his smile. "Or else what?" he asked.
"Tell him I'll stop cooking for him and he can do his own laundry." Charlie knew his wife was ticked off. He delivered the message to Asa the following morning. While Charlie was delivering Molly's message Asa watched Molly show her friend around the yard. The California woman had a camera and seemed to take pictures of everything, wild flowers and weeds and a knot in the barn siding. Even this irritated him.
"Okay, he would attend dinner, but he didn't have to like it."

The brother-in-law was nothing Joanna could have ever imagined. He didn't resemble Charlie at all and he was not old like she expected. Charlie was a square, solid man with light brown hair, and merry blue eyes. Asa Bennington was taller. He was lean, almost hard looking, she thought. He had a full black beard. Both the beard and his hair looked like he had not seen a barber in a long time.

It was his eyes that stopped her, gray, cold, almost flat. There was no welcome in those eyes. Out of respect for Molly and Charlie she ignored the man's rudeness. During dinner, he was almost quiet and excused himself as soon as the meal was finished. Joanna did not see the look Molly leveled at Asa but he did. If looks could kill, he was dead on the spot. Molly also looked hurt. He began to feel a little guilty and that was why on Thursday morning he rode his horse out to where he and Charlie repaired the fence. Asa needed to think things over.

That evening when Asa appeared for dinner, he was a different man and he had made up with his sister-in-law. Joanna was confused. The man was pleasant, almost charming. He might be good looking if not for the scraggy beard. Joanna thought maybe he had some sort of personality disorder. She wondered if she should ask Molly, but decided against it.

Friday was a busy day for everyone. Bob Drake brought over and set up his big mobile bar-B-Q. Charlie and Asa knew people would come to EOR just because Bob was cooking. He was a master at the Bar-B-Q. The rental company delivered the tables and the port-ta-potties. By evening, a little excitement was settling in. Dinner was fun. While they ate, Asa looked over Joanna Monroe from California. She was nice looking. He liked the laugh lines around her eyes. In fact he liked her laugh.

Asa and Charlie made both women laugh over stories about past parties. Molly added some stories of her own. "Who will take care of Kiki with all these people here" asked Joanna. Asa was pleased that she thought about the welfare of the little dog. Asa had pushed his chair away from the table and now the happy dog was sitting in his lap. Kiki knew she was the subject of the conversation, and her stub of a tail was beating as fast as it go could go.

Charlie answered Joanna's question, "Unfortunately you can't always tell who will show up at this event. The front door will be locked as well as the office door. We will put up a kiddy gate, and Kiki will have the run of the house. If anyone tries to go past the gate Kiki will attack." Everyone laughed and Kiki wiggled her whole rear end.

Each of them understood the party was the following evening and not surprised when Molly issued strict orders. "We will all be dressed and in the kitchen by 3:00 p.m." Charlie thought that was a little early but he didn't argue.

After dinner, Molly and Joanna went to the stone cottage down by the creek. It was now Molly's quilt studio. When Joanna learned that many people dressed in period costume for the party she knew the black velvet cocktail pants and low cut Casmir sweater she packed at the last minute were not appropriate. She and Molly finished the quilted vest they had been working on. From Molly's scrap fabric, they had selected fabric in black and gray and peach. They stitched a fast pattern called Flying Geese paired with Four Patch quilt blocks. Molly declared it was perfect and Joanna hoped so. Molly, she knew, was wearing a pink and white square dance dress that had belonged to Charlie and Asa's mother. Returning to the house Joanna thought her friend looked tired, but why not so was she. This EOR was a big event.

Chapter Forty-seven

EOR

Molly and Joanna were already downstairs. Molly's hair was done up and in it was clipped a white rose from her garden. Charlie was the next to appear. His shirt was an old fashion white ruffled one topped off with a bolo tie. He wore an orange and gold brocade vest set off with a gold watch chain across his middle. "It belonged to my grandfather." He declared proudly when Joanna complimented him.

"I don't know if you look like an old time banker or a saloon hall gambler," she kidded and he laughed warmly.

Asa arrived and she caught her breath. Smart slacks just like Charlie's, a white shirt with small pin tucks, a black string tie and an old frock coat probably the real thing from the looks of the frayed cuffs. His only jewelry was a beautiful turquoise ring. It was his face that stopped her. The scraggy beard was gone. In its place was a well-trimmed beard. He was handsome she thought. Why hadn't she noticed that before she wondered? When he smiled, he was even a little sexy. Both men wore black cowboy hats with silver concho hatbands and identical black cowboy boots with silver tips on the toes. The boots were custom made and on the tops tooled into the fine quality leather was the double "B" brand.

If Joanna was looking at Asa, he was looking at her. Dark gray levis, a cream-colored blouse out of some sort of silky material and the vest he knew she and Molly had made for the occasion. She wore a little extra makeup for the evening and long silver earrings. Asa thought he liked what he saw. The lady had class. His grumpy feeling of the last few days was completely gone. It was going to be a good evening all around he thought.

As usual, Joanna had her camera and ushered them all out onto the back steps where she took photos. Asa picked up Kiki. It was a nice picture. White dog against the black coat, besides, he was a handsome man and distant blue gray mountains in the distance provided a perfect background.

Molly said, "Here they come." Both Asa and Kiki turned to look down the ranch road in the direction of the first guests. Joanna took one more photo. It was going to be a perfect picture with Asa and his dog turned and looking away into the distance. The friends and neighbors were arriving and the party began.

Cars, trucks, one tractor, and a Model T brought the guests. They came with covered dishes, salads, home made breads, casseroles and slow cookers, with ice tea, lemonaid, and beer and liquor. The foods were put in the refrigerator, or the oven or plugged in as needed. Soft drinks went one place, and the liquor and beer went to the make shift bar. The aroma of roasting meat tantalized everyone. Joanna and Molly were busy even with the help of the other women. When she could, Joanna watched Asa and Charlie. If it had been a convention, she thought you could say the two brothers were working the room . . . a handshake here, a pat on the back there, a proper kiss on the cheek and a good laugh at something said. She observed that both brothers were respected and well liked and thoroughly enjoying themselves. Everyone was relaxed and having a good time.

She was refilling the lemonade when Asa come up and filled his glass. "Not drinking?" she asked.

"Short straw," he replied. Later Molly explained. "At some of the old parties things often got a little rough. Grandfather Bennington decided when our ranch hosted the activity he would not drink. Every Bennington host since then has done the same. Besides, Asa drew the short straw. He has to give the welcoming speech." She added with a chuckle. "Probably a good thing, too. My husband does not know how to give a short speech." Then she was gone, greeting newcomers and doing everything that needed doing.

Many of the guests were dressed in honor of the old days. There were also the latest fashions in western wear and even a few Hawaiian shirts. Some of the women Molly knew from the quilting day. She saw Granny Hayes sitting in her wheel chair. With Granny was her grand daughter-in-law, Annie. Annie was married to Mick. He had been the high school football star. She was the head cheerleader. It was supposed to be a marriage made in heaven. Now, Annie had two children and was pretty sure a third was on the way. As far as Annie was concerned, being married to Mick was like having another child to deal with. She told Granny Hays "I'm having my tubes tied."

Joanna joined Annie and Granny Hayes just as a bight blue Corvette purred into a parking space too small for anything else. The driver got out of the car carrying a giant bag of potato chips. The woman fascinated Joanna. The woman's pants were just little to tight. Her blouse just a little to low cut. Long, bottle, blond hair blew in the breeze. Many men took a long look. "That's Tina," remarked Granny.

Tina dropped her chips on a table and made her way to the bar all the time scanning the crowd. "Watch this." directed Granny. Drink in hand Tina made her way toward Asa who was in deep conversation with some of the other valley ranchers. They may have seen her coming, but ignored her because they knew what was about to happen. Coming up a little behind Asa, she surprised him. Wrapping her free hand around his neck she pulled down his head and planted a deep kiss directly on his mouth and then released him. Granny laughed. Joanna's mouth dropped open. "Yep, Tina set her cap for that man as soon as he came home."

Annie added, "So did every other woman in the valley." "He is polite to her like he is to every other lady but she hasn't given up even now." By now Asa had handed Tina off to a group of grinning cowboys. He turned in Joanna's direction, took a handkerchief from his pocket and wiped off Tina's bright red lipstick. Asa winked at Joanna.

The dinner bell sounded. Everyone knew it meant the Bar-B-Q was ready and dinner was about to begin. Asa stepped up on a hay bale platform. He raised his glass in a toast, "To family, to good neighbors, to good friends both old and new." Joanna found herself hoping he meant her. A local pastor who was wise enough to offer a short blessing followed Asa. The guests moved onto the waiting abundance of foods. Asa approached Joanna and offered his arm. "Be my guest?" he invited.

Conversation died down a little as the meal progressed. An occasional loud laugh came from the bar area. Some people were drinking their dinner. Desserts and coffee followed and the conversation picked up. Some of the Sunday churchgoers and couples with small children were starting to go home and a small western band was beginning to tune up.

As Joanna helped with the clean up, she and Molly paused to watch the dancing. The line dancing was interesting. Both Asa and Charlie, despite his limp, were very good. There was not that much clean up at the moment and Joanna wondered why Molly was not dancing. After a break, the band resumed and Asa approached them. He held his hand out to Joanna. "Dance with me" was all he said.

Granny Hayes watched Asa Bennington and the Molly's friend move around the floor. "They look good together," she thought. "Maybe, just maybe there is a little spark there and neither of them knows it yet." They did look good together. They were both a little disappointed when the set ended. Asa took Joanna back to where he had found her. "Save the last dance for me?" he said and went back to attend to the departing guests.

Granny was not the only one watching the couple. Jake Ludlow watched from the bar area. He thought the California woman was a looker. He decided he would have himself a little turn around the dance floor with Molly's friend. When Ludlow approached her, Joanna had no reason to say no. Many men had asked her to dance this evening. He was a heavyset man wearing a leather jacket with a lot of fringe.

Once on the floor she knew she had made a mistake. Probably he had had too much to drink. He was pulling her close, too close. She knew he was trying to rub himself against her. When she tried to pull away, he pretended that someone bumped into him. He stomped down hard on her foot. "Sorry there, little lady." He didn't sound sincere. When the dance was over she tried not to limp.

Some time later the band was playing "Good Night Ladies" signifying the dancing was about to come to an end. Asa stood beside her, holding out his hand. Sore foot or no sore foot she wanted to dance with him again. Once he took her in his arms, he noticed her limp. "What happened to you?"

"See the big man at the bar with the fringe jacket? He stepped on my foot."

Asa looked at the bar and saw Jake Ludlow. Joanna felt Asa stiffened and knew he was lost in thought or old memories.

Chapter Forty-eight

Winnie Ludlow

Asa was lost in thought, thinking back six year's ago. He was on his way home from one of the private high stakes poker games held a few times a year by Judge Barns. It was invitation only and all the players were good. The judge had an out of town guest that was supposed to be a good player. The guest was good and Asa had to play smart to win but he did, US$3,000 smart. The judge thought it funny when he gave Asa an old Christmas stocking in which to take home his winnings. Since Asa had had a few drinks, he was driving on one of the back roads when he saw what he thought were garbage bags along the side of the road. "Damn" he said out loud. He hated people that threw their trash on the roadside.

He braked hard. "Holy shit!" That was not a pile of garbage bags. Asa backed up and looked around the area. He clicked off the truck radio and removed his pistol from the glove compartment. He jacked cartage into the chamber but left it on safety. Checking the surroundings one more time, he got out of the pickup. Asa approached slowly. It was the body of a woman. She was alive. He could hear her moaning.

Even with a black eye and a bloody split lip, he knew he was looking at Winnie Ludlow, Jake Ludlow's wife. Everyone knew Jake used his fists on his wife. The sheriff wanted to stop going out to their house when the neighbors called because poor Winnie would never file a complaint. Now Asa was looking at her cowering on the ground. The way she was holding her side he wondered if she had broken ribs.

It was difficult to get her into the truck. She was afraid of him, didn't want him to touch her but she was hurting. She had no choice but to let Asa help her. Once inside she sat as close to the passenger door as she could "You need medical attention." She shook her head no. I'll take you to the clinic." She shook her head no.

"Take you home?"

This time she spoke "I'm never going back, never. Take me to the interstate I'll hitch a ride."

Asa thought over the situation. It was late at night. He was carrying a loaded gun. He had $3,000 stuffed in a Christmas stocking under his seat. In the cab with him was another man's battered, beaten wife. It was not the worst situation he had ever been in but it wasn't good either.

He had the beginning of an idea. "Winnie. Winnie, Look at me!" She turned her face toward him. "Are you positive you don't want to go back?" "Never," she said and he thought she meant it. He went on. "I have a friend. She helps people like you."

"What do you mean like me?"

"She helps women who have husbands like Jake," he explained.

"This friend, she will help me?"

"I believe so" and he hoped that would turn out to be the truth.

Winnie remained quiet for a little and than said, "What is this lady's name?"

"Her name is Mary Redwing."

"Is she Indian?"

"Yes, is that a problem?"

"Might be a problem for Jake but not for me. Where is this lady friend?

"In Montana" he answered. They drove all night and part of the next day.

He called the ranch, telling Charlie he might be gone a couple of days. Charlie respected and trusted his brother so he didn't ask any questions. Asa couldn't let anyone see Winnie. He brought her wet paper towels from the men's room so she could try and clean up a little. He had to find out of the way gas stations where she could use the restroom without being seen. He offered her coffee or soup or hot chocolate or a burger. Winnie said it all made her feel sick. In the late afternoon Asa found a pay phone and called the old number that was still in head, hoping it was still the right number. Maybe Mary was married. Maybe some guy would answer and not be happy that an old boy friend was calling.

Mary did answer. Asa told her the whole story and she was not surprised that Asa was helping some one in need. Mary Redwing ran a safe house for battered women. She gave Asa the address and directions. Pulling into the drive of the big house where Mary had her office and clinic, Winnie only noticed the flowerbeds and the nice lawn and not the security cameras. Mary was on the steps waiting.

She looked older Asa thought. "Well," Asa thought. "He probably did too. He remembered their affair. In the end, she could not give up the safe house and he would not give up the ranch. They parted reluctantly as friends. Inside Mary pointed Asa to her office and gently helped Winnie into another room. He selected the most comfortable chair, put up his feet and was asleep instantly.

Sometime later, he awoke to find Mary seated behind her desk studying him. "Damn," she thought. He still made her heart skip a beat. After years of seeing, her mother abused by her father and then his trying to do the same to her, Mary Redwing knew she had made the right choice but she would always wonder what life with Asa Bennington might have been like.

"How's Mrs. Ludlow?" he asked.

"Besides what you could see, badly bruised ribs. According to her, he kicked her a couple of times after he pulled her out of his car and she is pregnant."

"Ah shit," he commented. Mary didn't say anything. Asa stood up slowly. Lack of sleep was catching up with him. "You think she'll stay?" Asa asked.

Mary nodded. "Because of the baby, I don't think she'll go back."

"Wait here. I have something I want to give you." He went out to his truck. Returning to the office, Asa handed her the Christmas stocking containing his poker winnings. "You sure?" Mary said after she saw the money. "Yes, I'm sure."

"Mary, I need some sleep." She could see that for herself. She entertained the idea of inviting him home to her bed but said instead, "When you drove into town you passed a fishing lake." He remembered. "That's my brother's place. He has a couple of cabins in the back. I'll call him. Two days later, when Asa returned home, the big gossip in town was that Winnie Ludlow had finally run away from Jake. Jake was telling everyone he figured she hitched a ride and went south maybe Layton or even Cheyenne.

Whatever memory had taken him away, Asa never missed a dance step. He apologized to Joanna for making her dance when her foot which was obviously hurting her. He helped her off the dance floor, eased her into a chair and went to stand with Charlie as more guests departed. The party was over. Joanna didn't stay in her chair as much as she wanted to. She knew Molly would need help. Joanna limped toward the kitchen.

At the bar, Ludlow and his new drinking buddies were tossing down the last free drinks of the evening. He watched Asa. "I hate that SOB" The other men followed his glance.

"Not one you want to tangle with," remarked one of the other drinkers. "That Bennington and my brother went at it a few years back. My brother had to have his jaw wired shut. When he could talk said he never saw anyone move that fast or hit that hard."

The guests were all gone. Charlie and Asa had shut the ranch road gate and music drifted up from the bunkhouse. The brothers leaned on the corral fence counting the shooting stars. "Think Mom and Dad would have liked the party?" Charlie asked. "Yes, it was a nice evening all around," answered Asa, but he was remembering just how good Joanna felt in his arms. It was a pleasant thought.

Charlie yawned and said, "I'm turning in." His brother followed him into the house. They were surprised to see Molly and Joanna attacking a sink full of dirty pots and pans. Charlie kissed his wife, thought about kissing her friend but didn't and told everybody good night. Asa also said good night and followed Charlie out of the kitchen. Molly and Joanna were left to finish up. Through the steam billowing up from the sink Joanna looked at her friend. Seeing Molly's tired face Joanna told Molly, "Go on up to bed. I can finish these few things." Surprisingly, Molly didn't argue.

In his bedroom, Asa pulled of his boots and put on his favorite moccasins, hung up the old coat, removed his tie and started to take off his shirt. He wasn't sleepy. A quiet nightcap on the porch with Kiki sounded good and a pleasant ending to a very nice evening. "Come on pooch," he said and gathered up the happy little dog.

Asa walked softly and avoided the kitchen where he could still hear the rattle of pots and pans. All the left over liquor was on the dining room table. He poured a glass of good whisky. On the porch, he put his feet on the banister and let Kiki have his lap. The little mutt gave a big sigh. He sipped the fine liquor very slowly and thought about the evening. The moon was out. Only a few headlights could be seen on the old road to the west. All was quiet except for the kitchen.

Molly and Joanna had worked hard, very hard, he thought. Each year the event was bigger and took more effort. Asa had to admit that having Joanna here to help Molly had turned out to be a good thing. They both deserved a big thank you. He would suggest to Charlie that maybe they should give Molly and Joanna a bouquet of flowers or something in the way of appreciation.

Perhaps they would also like to sit a bit on the moon lit porch. He decided to invite them to join him. Putting down the disappointed dog, he walked softly toward the kitchen. To his surprise, only Joanna was there finishing up the last pot. He leaned against the door jam and watched her. She was limping more. She closed the dishwasher, started it running, hung up the towels and turned. She gave a gasp. "I didn't know you were there."

He apologized, "I came to ask you and Molly to join me on the porch."

"Molly seemed very tired. I talked her in to going up to bed."

"Well, it's a very nice evening out there," He glanced toward the porch, held up his glass and nodded. She had believed she was alone. She had pushed the start button on the dishwasher turned to leave the kitchen. He was there, standing in the doorway, leaning in the doorway with a drink in hand. She thought he had been watching her and she wondered for how long. Joanna acknowledged his apology. She debated about his offer but then moved past him toward the table. He made just enough room for her to go by. She smelled like soapsuds. Looking over the selection of drink possibilities, she picked a nice Irish Cream.

However, before she could open the bottle and pour, he took the glass from her hand. He could tell she was trying not to limp but not doing very good job of it. "Go find a chair and put your foot up. I'll bring your drink." He poured her drink and only added ice to his. When he returned to the porch, she had removed her shoes and was rubbing her foot. A bruise was already visible. In answer to his question about ice for her foot, she said she would take some up when she went up to bed. Kiki was resting her head on Joanna's shoe he noticed.

They sat in comfortable silence for a while. He could tell she was savoring the smooth drink. She broke the quiet by saying "Can I ask a personal question?" He was suspicious when people started a sentence that way. Usually, it was something personal about his life and none of their business but he nodded yes. Her question caught him off guard. "Is Molly okay?

"I think so. Why."

"She seems too tired. We're all tried I suppose but," Joanna's voice trailed off, her concern evident.

"I'll ask Charlie tomorrow."

They watched the vehicle lights on the old road. "Where does that road go?" she asked.

He explained. "It is an old state highway, not much used now because of the new interstate. It goes up into the foothill, past the Sandies, winds around in the mountains and eventually ties into a main road."

"What are the Sandies?" was her next question."

"Have you ever been to Utah's Zion National Park?" She had. "The Sandies are a series of box canyons that look similar to the sandstone formations in Zion. Mostly sand, snakes, cactus, and prickle bushes with a couple of well-hidden deep trout pools."

She smiled. "I bet you and Charlie know exactly where those pools are" and he told her about the camping trip and the spear throwing accident.
More headlights went up the road.
Somewhere a coyote barked. "Coyote" he explained.
"I have them at home, also." This surprised him. He assumed she had a nice apartment in the city.
"Where do you live?"
"The community is named Anchortown. It is located in the Sierra Nevada foothill north of Sacramento. An old gold mining community, it was founded by two sailors." She went on to explain. "In the gold rush days, sailors often jumped ship in San Francisco and headed for the gold fields. These two didn't do well at finding gold. Nearly starved to death the first winter according to the local history. By spring they had only enough gold to buy a wagon and team which they built into a freight business and eventually the town."

They continued to talk and watched the stars come out. She told him briefly about her late husband and about Susan and Bruce Jr. He could tell she was sad about Bruce Jr. and how he seemed to have alienated himself from the family, which angered Susan a great deal. "We had a good marriage but we married too young and the babies came to soon. The first years were hard," she concluded." She didn't ask about his marriage and he didn't mention it.

Asa related that during Catherine's growing up years he would leave the ranch for ten to fourteen days every year so Molly, Charlie, and their daughter could be a family without him hanging around. "Where did you go?" she asked.

"Deep sea fishing with my former father-in-law in Baja, salmon fishing is Alaska, hunting in Canada, two Cattleman's Association meetings one in Chicago, one in Dallas. I have friends in Arizona. We rafted the Colorado River and camped in the Grand Canyon several times. Las Vegas a couple of times."

"You went to Las Vegas by yourself? She asked. Asa knew by the expression on her face she had embarrassed herself with that question.

He decided not to cut her any slack, gave her wolfish grin and said, "No, not always," which was true.

Still embarrassed, she changed the subject by commenting about the increase of traffic on the old road. He had noticed it also. The headlights seem to be moving at a greater rate of speed. He thought he saw flashing red lights, emergency vehicles possibly. They both could hear the thin wail of a siren. She said, "That's not good is it?"

"No, it's not," he replied. She thanked him for the nightcap. Easing the sleeping dog off her shoe she said good night and took her glass to the kitchen. He heard her take ice out of the refrigerator. The house was quiet. He watched the distant road for a little while then he too called it a night.

Chapter Forty-nine

The Sandies

He had been asleep for maybe three or four hours when the phone rang. He picked it up just before Charlie did. It was sheriff McNabb. "Accident in the Sandies . . . truck over the side. The deputies had a hard time getting to the wreck. When they got, there the cab was empty. Lots of broken glass and by the smell of it, some of the glass was broken booze bottles. There was lot of blood. "We figure they are trying to hike out and will go down hill. They should come out on your property."

This was not the first time for this kind of call and both Asa and Charlie knew the drill. "Who was in the car?"

"Two people, the new kid from the feed and grain."

"The one with the tattoos on his knuckles?" asked Charlie.

"That's the one replied," the sheriff "and his girl friend. Her name is Bunny Parker." Asa didn't know either youngster.

"Drugs?' asked Asa. "The mom says no."

"What were they wearing?"

"The mom thinks the kid was in jeans and Bunny was wearing jeans and a bright yellow jacket." The bright yellow jack might give them a break.

"We'll get a couple more hours of sleep. By the time, we can load up it will nearly be sunrise. We'll on our way," said Charlie and they all hung up.

Later Asa would call the bunkhouse and tell them which truck, which horse trailer and which mounts. Molly would brew coffee and make sandwiches. They took rifles, side arms, rope, blankets, an extensive first aid kit, and a couple of walkie talkies. They would eat fried egg sandwiches in the cab while they drove north toward the entrance of the Sandies. When they departed, there was a little light in the east. It was cold. Both Asa and Charlie knew that the Sandies heated up like an oven. By 10:00 a.m., it would be hot as hell and measurable for the injured kids on foot, especially if they didn't have water. In this particular case, they probably didn't have water and were hung over besides. All this Joanna learned when she came down for breakfast.

By the time, the Bennington Brothers arrived at where they wanted to leave the truck, they had decided on which canyons each one would search and how long they would search till they would meet up. If they had not found the kids, they would have to move to a different spot and check in with the sheriff. Hopefully, he might have good news if they didn't.

Now it was past 10:00 a.m. And it was hot. Asa only had an hour and then he would have to backtrack and meet Charlie. His shirt stuck to his back. He wished he had taken time to shave off the damn beard from the party the night before. Asa had hoped he would find the kids before now and that maybe Charlie was having better luck. His horse shied and sidestepped. Asa looked again at a patch of bushes. He had found Bunny Parker and he might have missed her if it were not for his horse. No yellow jacket on Bunny.

She was wearing some sort of camouflage shorts and a short-sleeved shirt. Her arms and legs were covered with cuts. A big cut on her forehead was still oozing blood. Her right ankle didn't look quite right and if all that were not enough she was lying in a big patch of poison ivy.
"Shit."
He could tell she was breathing. He rolled down his sleeves and put on gloves. He stomped down as much poison ivy as he could, making a lot of noise. He didn't want to frighten her. She hadn't moved.

"Miss. Parker! Miss Parker!" He touched her arm. She came up screaming. She hit him as hard as she could with a rock catching him on his side. He pinned her to the ground. All the fight went out of her and she started to cry. "Miss Parker, Bunny," he said louder. "My name is Asa Bennington. We've been searching for you. My brother is looking for your friend."

Her eyes were dilated. Drugs? Alcohol? Shock . . . all of the above? Asa couldn't tell, but he had one hell of time getting her on the horse and keeping her in the saddle until he could find Charlie. Bunny Parker was no lightweight and not very helpful.

Charlie let the sheriff know where they would come up out of the canyons onto the road above so the ambulance could meet them. Over Bunny's head, Asa mouthed the words "Boy friend?' Charlie shook his head no. Coming out on the top first, Charlie saw the ambulance and then the TV news truck. "Oh hell."

He recognized the perky TV newswoman, Barbara Nash. She had a microphone in the sheriff's face. McNabb was wearing his official face and patiently not answering her questions. "No, he would not release any names. Yes, there was one fatality so far. He would not comment on the cause of the accident." When Nash saw Charlie come out on the road, she tried to shift her attention in his direction only to have Charlie maneuver his horse so that the cameraman had a good shot of the horse's rear. Barbara Nash very much wanted to be a newswoman, a top newswoman. Right now she saw this bit of news slipping away all because of a damn horse's ass and she didn't mean the four legged kind either.

Charlie's move allowed Asa to take Bunny directly to the waiting ambulance and the EMTs. Barbara Nair still saw a story unfolding but still couldn't get around the damn horse. Forgetting her mike was on she said to McNabb, "Who the hell are those two?"
Nash was a pain in the ass and McNabb was pleased to see her frustration. "Just a couple of good old boys," he answered.

"Who are they and where did they come from?" she continued.

"Out there," the sheriff waved in the general direction of Nebraska.

"You know sheriff," she had forgotten his name. "You are a real shit."

Giving her his best political smile he said, "And the same to you, young lady."

Walking past Charlie, McNabb flashed him a thumbs up which the TV crew couldn't miss. The crew didn't like working with Barbara Nash, and they were trying their best to look serious. "I'll call you later to make out my report. You two better get the hell out of here," McNabb looked back at the reporter. "And thanks, again," was all the sheriff said.

Asa was grateful to Charlie for making a path and very pleased to have the medics take Bunny off his hands. Asa had seen the TV crew and wanted no part of an interview. Before the ambulance left Asa said to one of the guys. "They might want to know at the hospital she was passed out in a patch of poison ivy. She's most likely covered with the stuff."

"Oh, hell," muttered one of the medics. He was the one who inserted the IV.

Asa and Charlie did just what the sheriff suggested. Charlie had already started back down the trail. As Asa followed, he looked directly at the pissed off reporter. He gave her his best smile. She mouthed "You bastard." He tipped his hat and eased his horse over the embankment and out of sight.

It was after noon when they arrived back at their truck and trailer. Asa knew that Charlie's hip was hurting so he loaded the horses and offered to drive home. Charlie noticed as Asa loaded the horses he was favoring his left side. "What happened to you?"

"She hit me! She hit me with a big, damn rock." Charlie wanted to laugh but he was too tired and his hip did hurt.

Asa drove them home. They pulled into the yard and ranch hands came to take care of the horses, the truck and the trailer. Molly watched as Charlie limped toward the house. "Too much dancing last night and too much riding today," she thought. Once in the house Asa and Charlie related the rescue of Bunny Parker. Charlie made a point of telling how she clobbered his brother with a rock. Asa pulled up his shirt so Molly and Joanna could see the starting bruise. From the looks on both women's faces, he decided that had not been a smart thing to do. Molly hustled Charlie upstairs for aspirin and a hot shower.

He watched his sister-in-law fuss over his brother and wished he had someone to do the same for him. He hadn't thought that in a long time. With only he and Joanna in the kitchen, Asa realized how dirty he was. He snagged two cold beers from the frig and headed for the shower as Charlie had done. "Guess I had better do the same," he apologized. He suspected he had blood and he supposed poison ivy all over his clothes. He did, but she still thought he was interesting and was not even aware she was watching him disappear down the hallway.

In his apartment, he snapped the cap off the beer and downed half the bottle all at once. He turned the shower water on as hot as it would go, pulled off his clothes very carefully and stepped into the steamy water. Letting the hot water sluice over his tired body, he wondered what it would be like to have Joanna Monroe in a shower. "Shit, Bennington, you're such a jerk sometimes!" he thought to himself. Still . . . it was something to think about.

Monday afternoon when the men emerged from their long deserved sleep, the ranch was back to normal. Asa was clean-shaven and Joanna was right. He was a very good-looking man. The evening was pleasant with talk of the party, and it's success but everyone was tired. Molly looked pale. Joanna had to face the fact it was time to go home and she mentioned that to Molly she would book her homeward flights the next day. In the privacy of their bedroom, Molly told Charlie that Joanna had decided it was time to return home. "I think I'm going to miss her," he said.

You aren't the only one."

"Oh, I know you will. She is a good friend. I'm glad you invited her."

"Not me, Charlie', she jabbed him in the ribs. "Your brother."

"Asa?" Charlie would think on that.

Chapter Fifty

Snow in September

Breakfast was leisurely. Molly and Joanna were alone in the kitchen. Molly was taking last night's dishes out of the dishwasher. Joanna looked up when she heard Molly gasp. Joanna watched as Molly dropped all the dishes, doubled over and slumped to the floor where she curled into a ball and grabbed her mid section. "Get Charlie," Molly moaned.

Joanna bolted to the back door, threw it open with such a bang that Asa and Charlie turned around to look. Kiki was barking. Joanna yelled at Charlie and Asa. "Come quick, its Molly!" Asa reached the door first but he stepped aside to let Charlie go to his wife.

"Oh Charlie, it hurts so bad." was all Molly could say. Asa was dialing 911. It seemed the call was taking to long. Asa looked at Molly and said loud enough to get her attention, "Molly, can you get into the car?" She was looking marginally better. Charlie was turning into a basket case. Molly nodded yes. Asa said something into the receiver then hung up the phone. "We're going to meet the ambulance at Four Corners. He moved quickly out of the door to go bring the car to the back gate.

Joanna said, "Charlie where is her purse? Molly's purse . . . for insurance cards? Charlie looked blank.
"In our bedroom." It was Molly who answered the question. Upstairs, Joanna couldn't find the bag at first. "This too, was taking too long," she thought. When she finally did return to the downstairs, the men had Molly in the back seat of the car where she was curled up on Charlie's lap. He was holding her hand and his color was worse than hers. Asa was in the driver's

351

seat. Without thinking, Joanna opened the passenger door and tossed in the handbag on the passenger seat. She shut the door. Asa drove away, speeding down the ranch road.

Joanna watched the car drive away in a cloud of dust. Kiki's yapping brought her back to reality. Except for the unhappy dog, she was alone. They had driven off and left her there. A dust devil kicked up and hid the ranch road for moment then it moved on. She continued to look down the road even though it was empty. She felt cold. She looked north toward the Petees.

Up over the mountains huge lead colored clouds were building. Laundry on the clothesline snapped in the wind. She looked one more time down the empty road and decided she had better take the wash off the line before it blew off.

In the house, she swept up the broken dishes dropped by Molly. She finished cleaning up the kitchen. She had a cup of coffee. Kiki followed her from room to room. She turned the TV on. She turned the TV off. She waited. The house was big, empty and she felt very alone.

About noon the telephone rang, she snatched it up. Asa was apologizing before she could say hello. Interrupting him she said, "What about Molly?"

"Gall bladder, they think. "She admitted she has been in pain but had put off going to the doctor. Depending on the X-rays probably surgery tomorrow morning."

"And Charlie? She asked.
Asa laughed a little. "I think the nurses are ready to give him a tranquilizer." He turned serious. "Listen to me. According to the weather reports there is an early winter storm headed our way. Go through the house. Make sure all the windows are shut. If you can, please bring in some firewood." He told her what cabinets held the emergency lights in case of power failure. Her heart was dropping. She did not want to spend the night alone. He continued. "Charlie is staying at the hospital. I should be home before 6:00 p.m." She suddenly felt much better.

His tone of voice changed. He sounded almost lighthearted. "Be prepared. I'm going to fix dinner!"
"You cook?"
"Yes, I have a specialty," he teased. She felt a whole lot better.

She did as he asked and worked her way through the house looking for open windows. Until now, she had never had any reason to be in the office. Turning on the lights, she stopped. At the far end of the room hung a large map of the ranch, she thought. It was old looking with fancy script and gold leaf artwork. Two desks faced each other. There were filing cabinets, books, and ledgers. On one wall behind one desk hung certificates and awards. On the opposite wall hung antique guns.

It was the wall over the small sofa that gave her pause. She understood she was looking at a collection of family pictures. Looking back at her were all the generations of the Benningtons. The top left picture was an old, small, grainy back, and white. It appeared to have been torn in half. Only the picture of a sitting woman remained. Joanna guessed this woman was the first Catherine in the family. She saw the wild twins that never wanted any part of the ranch. Great grand parents standing proudly next to old cars. The photos changed from black and white to color. Grandparents, Asa and Charlie's parents, standing with young Asa and baby Charlie. Molly and Charlie's daughter, the third Catherine Bennington smiled down at her. The wall ended with an official photo of a young Asa in his Marine Corp uniform and Molly and Charlie and their daughter in her graduation robes. Joanna turned out the light and shut the door. The last room was Asa's, which she knew was originally the private in-law quarters for his parents.

It was more than a room. A comfortable living room with a fireplace. A private outside entrance; windows facing north. One was open. She closed it and looked around. Shelves of books lined the walls. A stereo set. She examined the music . . . all types of music. On one wall, she saw a Navajo rug. There were some pottery pieces and a few baskets. His dresser was not neat but not messy either. In one corner of the bookshelf was a small photo of a petite, pixie faced young woman. Palm trees stood in the background. The long dead wife she guessed. A room off to the side held a king-sized bed, above which hung another old quilt. The big bed was an unmade mess with a pair of moccasins on the floor next to Kiki's doggy bed. A beautifully tiled man sized bathroom completed the quarters. Lavender soap. He used lavender soap. All very comfortable. Very private. She felt she was intruding.

She carried in firewood. She changed Kiki's water dish. She finally ran out of things to do to keep herself busy. Well, if he thought the power would go off that could mean no hot water so she took a shower. She changed clothes three times. Reasoning that he said dinner was his specialty, she settled on the velvet cocktail pants and the Casmir sweater. It was now dreary and rainy outside with an occasional gust of wind. The lights did flicker making 6:00 p.m. seem a long way off.

Once Asa hung up from Joanna he called the ranch foreman, told him about Molly and Charlie. He told the foreman, he was renting a car and planned to be back home no later than 6:30 p.m. They talked about the stock and the possible coming storm. Once that call was concluded he picked up his rental, stopped at the grocery store and made one more stop for the specialty he had promised Joanna. Asa headed toward the ranch and home.

Once on the highway, he began to think about Joanna and the coming evening. What did he expect from her? Ever since Saturday night thoughts of her had been floating through his mind. He was like any normal man. The sight of a fine looking woman pleased him. Some how she was different. She was on his mind a lot and yes he did want to invite her into his bed.

He had not had a woman in his life since the affair with Mary Redwing. He was considering proposing to Mary when she told him about the job offer in Montana. Instead she asked him to come with her. That was followed by several bitter arguments and in the end they both knew it would never work. In hind site, it was all probably for the best. After that he hadn't bothered to date. In a small town like Silver Bend, it was too hard and Layton was too far way. He stayed content with the ranch and the family, but every now and then watching Charlie and Molly he knew his life was not truly complete.

Now, seemingly out of nowhere, Joanna Monroe was very much apart of his thoughts. She was making him ach and making things complicated. Besides the sex, there seemed to be something else. He tried concentrating on the wet road. He was forty-five minutes from home.

It was dark now and looking out the rain-slicked window the only thing Joanna could see was her own refection. She saw a reasonably attractive woman who had taken good care of her self. She also saw a woman whose life had been comfortable, ordered and calm until Asa Bennington danced into her life on Saturday night. Now, and she had to be honest, she was thinking about what it would be like to go to bed with the man. Was there more than just physical attraction? If so? Then what? She had been secure in her widowhood. Now things were complicated in ways she would never have expected.

Asa was back by 5:30 p.m. Kiki heard a strange car and growled. The growls turned to joyful barks accompanied by much tail wagging. Joanna opened the back door. Asa hurried up the back steps. He was rain soaked.

He handed her two bouquets of flowers. "From me and Charlie," he said. He looked contrite.

You didn't have to do that," she said as she accepted the flowers.

"Yes. We did," he said solemnly. "When Molly realized we left you behind she raised holy hell with us." He went back out to the car retuning with an assortment of bags. He set one over to the side. "You don't look in this one." Two others he placed on the table. He pointed, "There's a bottle of wine it that one. Pour, while I change into dry clothes." He left but came back with his wet shirt in his hand. "Would you preheat the oven to four hundred?" As he walked back down the hall, Joanna thought she knew what he was preparing for dinner. She poured two glasses of red wine and waited.

In his room, Asa peeled off the rest of his wet clothes. He took a fast shower and did quick shave. He laid a fire and lit it and made the bed, folding the top sheet down neatly and fluffing the pillows. He dropped Peggy's photo in a drawer. Wearing his moccasins, old jeans and a soft flannel shirt open at the neck and the sleeves rolled up he went into the living room and put more wood on that fire also.

She heard him and brought in his glass. He lit candles saying it was just in case the power went out. When the buzzer on the stove indicated the oven was hot he made her stay in the living room. Returning shortly, he cleared the magazines from the coffee table and placed napkins, plates and forks and a single flower in a jelly glass in front of her. "Dinner in twenty minutes he announced."

He sat opposite her. He sipped his wine, put his head back and closed his eyes for a moment "Tired?' she asked.

"Yes. Molly scared the hell out of me. As I said on the phone, the doctor says she has been in pain for quite a while. She told him she was planning on making an appointment."

In the kitchen, the oven timer sounded. He smiled his big loopy smile and announced, "Be prepared to dine! He returned with a huge pizza and a small plate of dog treats for Kiki. "She isn't allowed to have pizza," he explained.

They sipped the wine, enjoyed the pizza and each other's company. When neither of them could eat another bite, Asa told her to relax and he took the dirty dishes and the left over pizza back to the kitchen where he dumped the dirty dished into the sink an shoved the pizza into the refrigerator. Outside the yard light was still on. He saw large goose feather snow fakes float slowly down to the deepening snow already on the ground.

As she waited for him to come back, again she looked at her refection in the dark windows. And again she saw an attractive woman, a grandmother no less. She had to admit she was wondering what to say if the handsome, sexy thoughtful, sweet man in the kitchen invited her into his bed. Her answer surprised her. It would be "yes."

"Penny for your thoughts?
"Just seeing if I could see the rain." It was a fib. She was thinking how pleased she was that she never stopped taking her birth control pills, not that she thought she would ever need them.

"I have something I want to show you," he said and stepped toward the front door. Wondering if that was an opening line and just exactly what he was planning to show her, she did as he asked. "Close your eyes." She did. She heard the door open and felt the instant cold from outside. With his hands on her shoulders, he guided her onto the front porch, "You can look now."

New, pristine snow coated every leaf, every twig, and every blade of grass and even the few late blooming roses. Huge flakes drifted down from the black night sky. It was beautiful and she told him so.

He was standing behind her. Very slowly he wrapped his arms around her, their bodies not quit touching. Lifting her hair away from the nape of her neck he brushed her neck with his lips. He could feel her quiver. He thought she was beginning to lean into him. The kitchen phone rang "Bloody hell," he muttered in her hair. "It has to be Charlie."
Thinking the same thought, she said, "It could be Charlie. Go answer it."

Alone in the living room, she turned out the porch light and locked the door. Looking at her reflection in the dark window. She thought again, "Do I want to go to bed with the man? Her answer was still "Yes." She followed him into the kitchen. It was Charlie. Asa gave her thumbs up sign to let her know nothing was wrong. Charlie seemed to be asking all sorts of question and Asa patiently answered, "Yes, Not bad. I'll check. We had soup." Asa rolled his eyes at the ceiling.
Then, his eyes widen. Joanna was opening the top buttons on her sweater in a way that left no mistake about her invitation. He couldn't get rid of Charlie fast enough. Flicking off the light he walked around the table toward her. He took her in his arms and hers went around his neck. This time there was no space between their bodies. They kissed long and deep. He unhooked her bra, secretly pleased that he remembered how the damn things worked. He held one of her breasts in each hand and thumbed her nipples. In his ear so

he could feel her breath she said, "My bed or yours?" He leaned back and laughed richly. "Oh lady! I've wanted you in my bed since Saturday night."

By the time, they reached his room he had shed his shirt and started to unbutton his jeans but stopped to put a new log into the fireplace. Sounding very irritated she said, "What's this?" Earlier in the day, she had seen his messy, unmade bed. Now it was perfectly turned down with the pillows waiting. He turned, worried at the tone of her voice and looked at where she was pointing. She was not doing well at hiding her smile. He attempted to look guilty. "Well Joanna, you can't blame a man for hoping." He crossed to her and pulled her willing body against his. She could feel his hardness. "Take me to your bed, Asa.

He did. Their lovemaking was not wild or hasty but deliberate, fulfilling and sure. He caressed every special place on her body. She tasted his tongue. The fire died down and so did their hunger for each other. He knew she was asleep nestled as close to him as she could. The only sound in the room was from Kiki in her dog bed in the corner. Kiki was snoring. All was good in her little world. Asa slept. All was good in his world, too.

He woke first. His hand was asleep. He eased his arm out from under Joanna's head just in time to answer the phone on the first ring. It was Charlie. The surgery had gone well. He was going to stay in town. Probably, Molly would come home on Saturday or maybe even Monday. Asa was hoping Monday.

In answer to Charlie's last question Asa said, "Oh, we're making out just fine." Neither Charlie nor Asa caught the double meaning in his words but Joanna did and buried her giggles in his pillow. Replacing the receiver, Asa said, "What?"

"Think about what you said just now to your brother."

He figured it out and smiled himself. "I can't tell a lie to my brother" and he eased back into bed with her. They had three more days to themselves. They made the most of it before Charlie brought Molly home. The day before Molly came home, all the snow disappeared. Joanna stayed five days after that to help. For Asa and Joanna it was hard to act normal. They found themselves sneaking around like a pair of teenagers.

It only took Molly a day to see the difference her brother-in-law and her best friend and to guess what had gone on while she was in the hospital. Molly was happy. She hoped it would turn into something special for both of them. They deserved it.

Joanna could no longer ignore the fact that she could probably go home. Molly was moving around more and more and feeling guilty for all Joanna's work.

One afternoon Charlie was off somewhere and Molly was asleep upstairs. Joanna was cleaning up the last of the lunch dishes and thinking about what to prepare for dinner. Asa came up behind her, put his arms around her and said, "Don't fix dinner tonight. I want to take you out, just the two of us."

"Can we do that? I know what Molly has to eat but what about Charlie's dinner?"

Asa swayed the two of them gently to some music coming from the radio. "We will go a little early and bring him a take out plate."

About 4:00 p.m. Asa announced, "I want to take Joanna to Chico's tonight."

Charlie brightened up and asked, "What time shall we leave?"

Molly watched the disappointment flit across Asa's face. She looked at Charlie and said, "Maybe they can bring you a plate. I'm not sure I want to be alone yet." Molly gave Asa such a big smile he realized she knew and he didn't care.

Asa and Joanna left with Charlie's order. Seemed Charlie knew the menu by heart. "Well he should," commented Asa. "Chico's is the best Mexican food for fifty miles around." Joanna was not impressed when she saw the building. It looked like a run down beer bar with fake cactus in the one window. The once red door was faded and the Chico's sign hung crooked.

Reading her mind. Asa explained. "Bob and May Mercado are the best when it comes to their menu and the food preparation. You'll see." Inside it was clean and bright but funky. Joanna thought the large, smoked stained, adobe fireplace was probably used in the winter. One wall was all out of state license plates. The face of the small bar and the back bar were done in pecky cedar. The rest of the décor consisted of red, white, and green paper place mats, a few pots of cactus and some hand painted Mexican pottery.

Asa selected one of the high back red leather booths near the back. He waited until Joanna was seated and then slid in opposite her. May waved at Asa from the kitchen and Bob quickly appeared at the table to shake hands with Asa and take their order. Asa introduced Joanna as Molly's friend from California and Bob inquired about Molly's health.

Joanna ordered a norteno and ice tea. Asa asked for his usual and a Dos Eqexs beer. When the beer arrived, Asa downed half of it in one long slow swallow. Joanna watched. Putting down his bottle, he asked "What?"

"You could do a beer commercial," she laughed.

Asa looked very serious. "It is Bob's secret how he keeps his beer so cold. You don't like beer," he asked.

"Only the top three or four swallows when it is really cold and fizzy," she answered.

Taking her hand in his across, the table he said as seriously as he could, "You can have the top of my beer any time." They were unaware they were being observed.

Edna Norris was picking up her to-go order when she noticed Asa Bennington in the back booth with a woman she could not see. "He was holding the woman's hand and really talking," she reported over the phone to several of her friends. "He looked very serious. Probably had too much to drink. There was beer on the table." Had Asa ever heard the gossip, he would have laughed.

The following day, Joanna could not ignore the fact there was no reason for her not to return to California. Her reservations were for tomorrow morning. Molly had already gone up to bed and Joanna went up stairs to pack. Asa and Charlie were watching boxing on TV. It didn't take long to complete the packing. Joanna was not ready for bed. She didn't want to watch boxing. Her life had been very organized and predictable till she came here. Now . . . she didn't know. Going downstairs and quietly out the back door, she sat with Kiki on the back steps. It was almost as if Kiki felt her sadness. The dog snuggled into her lap. Absently she rubbed the small dog's soft ears.

Charlie fell asleep in his chair. The boxing was dull and Asa went to the kitchen for a drink of water. He saw Joanna on the steps. He thought she might be crying. Joining her, he sat on a step below her so he could see her face. Just as he had the night of their first lovemaking he said, "Penny for your thoughts?" A half moon was just peeking over the trees.

"Just thinking about going home" was her answer.

"You don't have to go," he suggested.

"Yes I do."

"Just what the hell do you have to go home for?" he blurted out. He knew immediately how bad it sounded. He regretted opening his mouth. She stood up and turning away from him walked into the house banging the door behind her.

"Bennington, you are such a ass, sometimes," he thought.

In the kitchen she stopped. Why was she so angry, so hurt? Just because he had put into words the exact thoughts she was trying to ignore. She had been rude. She poured two glasses of whiskey and returned to the steps. Sitting down beside him, she said, "I'm sorry. I was rude."

"And I have a big mouth," he said.

"You are right, you know. Just what do I have at home?" she said with a sigh. "What are we going to do?" Neither one of them answered the question because neither one of them had an answer.

The next morning she said good-bye to Charlie and Molly trying not to cry and Asa drove her to the Layton airport. After they left Charlie asked Molly, "Why didn't we go to the airport too?"

"Oh Charlie. Those two are falling in love and they don't even know it yet. They don't want company," Molly added. Charlie looked pleasantly surprised.

Chapter Fifty-one

CALIFORNIA

Her return flights seem to take forever. She had a slight shock when she read the total of her airport long term parking ticket. Sacramento was hot with the usual late summer weather. Everything was brown and dry. She stopped at the grocery store. She stopped and let the neighbor know she was home. It was late afternoon when she parked her car in her own garage. She was home. Her cat, Mr. Finch, pouted and purred both at the same time. The yard didn't look bad; a few tomatoes still clung to the vines. She sat on her patio and thought about Molly, Charlie and especially Asa. Her life was turned upside down. She had to call her daughter Susan. It was a long call after which Susan said to her husband, "Mom sounds different."
"Different in what way?"
"She sounds younger."
Joanna saved the best call for last. She called Asa.

Later, as she was unpacking her clothes a small box with a bow fell out of her folded sweater. Opening it she bean to cry. Tucked into the cotton was a small, sterling silver charm, a cowboy hat. She called Asa again.

They talked once a week, sometimes more often. Each of them had new thoughts to sort through. Joanna's life was not the only one turned upside down. Halloween came and went. Joanna found she had more decisions to make regarding her future and if it was to be with Asa. She went to Susan's for Thanksgiving. Susan had to accept the fact that her mother was in love with this Asa person. Looking at her mother, who was putting the finishing touches on the turkey gravy, Susan said, "Mother, What if he asks you to marry him? What are you going to say?"

362 | Donna Bender Hood

"I don't know."

"But, you think he will ask?"

"Yes, I think he will."

Catherine came home to the ranch for Thanksgiving. Normally her daughter did not come home for this holiday but for Christmas instead. Molly wondered what was up. Catherine had happy news. She had found her special someone. She was sure he would propose on Christmas Eve. The conversation wandered off to love and marriage in general. Catherine asked, "Do you think Uncle Asa will propose to Joanna Monroe?"

"We hope so."

"Did uncle Asa ever have someone special after he came back to the ranch?

Molly watched Catherine's eyes light up when she answered her daughter's question "One or two."

"Who? Tell me who."

"No. That's for him to say if he chooses." Molly could see Catherine's disappointment so she added, "When your uncle came back to the ranch and finally settled in, probably every single lady (a few married ones too) within fifty miles looked his way especially after they discovered he can dance."

"Uncle Asa can dance?" After all these years and she was just finding this out.

"Yes, he is very good." At dinner that night Catherine said to her Uncle, "Mom says you can dance. Asa gave Molly an amused look. "Will you dance with me?"

"Lady Catherine" Asa's pet name for his niece, "I will dance with you at your wedding. That's a promise." He thought about a wedding for himself. If he asked Joanna would she accept?

Later in the week, Charlie asked Asa, "What are you going to send Joanna for Christmas?"

"I still have a few old friends from my time in the military. I have an idea. I'm going to make a few phone calls and see if I can find out what happened to Joanna's son, Bruce Jr. The answer to his inquiries came back in a matter of days. Bruce was in government service; a quite behind the scenes special national security group. Bruce was well. He was healthy. He was happy. His superiors respected him.

That information was only for Joanna, and he included it in a big fancy Christmas card and added, "My Christmas wish for you is happiness now and always." He signed it, "Love, Asa." She wished it could be so.

A few weeks later, Asa and Charlie were in the jeep coming home with the fresh Christmas tree. It was as perfect as they could fine and hoped it would pass Molly's inspection. Asa was driving. He was preoccupied and seemed to be hitting every rut and bump in the road. Charlie couldn't stand it and blurted out, "Why don't you just ask her to marry you?"

"I think I will." Charlie nearly fell out of the jeep.

"You going out to the coast for Christmas then?"

"No," Asa replied. "She and her family have Christmas traditions. I would make it uncomfortable besides he added. I want her all to myself. I'll go for Valentines Day." Charlie didn't know his brother was a romantic, but then maybe it took the right woman.

Catherine called her parents Christmas morning. Russ, her young man had proposed. After congratulating her daughter Molly said, "You won't be the only one making wedding plans. Your Uncle Asa is flying to California in February and is finally asking Joanna to marry him." Catherine let out a happy whoop. Joanna didn't find out about Asa's coming to California till they talked on New Year's Eve. Hanging up, he was not so sure she sounded pleased but she didn't say don't come either.

He spent two days in Cheyenne looking for the perfect ring. Returning to the ranch, Asa could hardly wait to show his selection to Molly and Charlie. Molly's reaction was just what Asa hoped Joanna's would be. Molly said softy, "Oh, Asa. It's beautiful." Charlie noticed his wife was all teary. "Well," he thought. "Asa would be away for Valentines Day. He and Molly would have the house to themselves." Charlie decided he might just surprise Molly with a few diamonds of her own.

The wranglers referred to Asa and Charlie as Big Boss Brother and Little boss Brother not because Asa had more authority. In that he and Charlie were equal. The nicknames came about just because Asa was taller. Even before Asa left, the rumor was that Big Boss Brother was going out to the West Coast and propose marriage to the pretty lady who had been the ranch guest at last year's EOR.

February 12, Asa stepped off the plane in Sacramento with the ring safely at the bottom of his carry-on. She was waiting for him and couldn't miss him. He was carrying a huge red, heart-shaped candy box. Her car was small for his tall frame. The weather was wet and windy. It took over two hours to reach her house. He admitted he was curious about her home.

It was neat, clean as he expected and he decided charming . . . nice cozy kitchen, dining room with an oak table and buffet that she said had belonged to her mother and would some day go to Susan, and a generous living room with a wood burning stove. She introduced Asa to Mr. Finch. "You named your cat after a bird?"

"The name came with the cat" was her explanation. Down the hall, she showed him the guest room. "You're in here." She saw a look of disappointment sweep across his face.
"Or," pointing to the master bedroom "in here if you want."
"I want" is all he said. Her bedroom was a pale icy blue. Over the bed were perfectly matted and framed close up photos of blue and lavender flowers.

"Your photos?" he asked.

She nodded. "I took them at the ranch in September." The bedspread was a dark blue and a white, lavender and blue quilt was folded at the foot of the bed. White plantation shutters covered the doors leading to a nice deck in better weather. She showed him which bathroom sink was his. Back in the bedroom, he saw his picture on her bedside table. It was he and Kiki the night of the EOR.

He could smell something was cooking in the kitchen. Right now, he was hungry but not for food and neither was she. He took her in his arms. Suspended from a fine silver chain around her neck he found his silver cowboy hat charm nestled between her breasts.

They spent the next day just happy to be together and alone. It was wet, rainy and windy . . . perfect weather for staying inside. She had reservations for dinner out Valentines evening which had cleared and there were stars the sky. The two of them looked just like any other couple sharing a romantic evening.

He would propose tonight. In preparation, Asa shooed Mr. Finch off the sofa and put music on the stereo. When Joanna came into the living room, he was tapping his foot. She knew him well enough now to know he was about to say something he felt was important. She suspected what was coming and she knew what she would say. He patted the seat beside him. Kicking of her shoes, she curled up next to him. She did love him.

"Joanna, marry me." He opened his hand and she saw in his palm, the lovely engagement ring. She slipped it on her finger. It was a little big. She took it off her finger, and laid it back in his palm and closed his fingers over it. "I can't."

"Why? What the . . . ?" She placed her fingers over his lips and shushed him. She spoke slowly "As much as I want to marry you I can't. I am being treated for cancer."

He had gone over every possible reason why she might not accept his proposal but this was not one of them. She told him the entire story. She had already undergone one surgery. Radiation was not an option because of the tumor's location. She was on a new drug. The doctors would not know any thing for sure till May or maybe June.

"When did you find out?" was his next question.

"In October."

Why didn't you tell me?" He was very hurt.

"Don't you see? She was trying not to cry. "Every time we talked, you treated me like I was normal. No questions about medication. Did I have a temperature? Was I getting enough rest? Was I eating right? I needed to feel like we had a future. I needed that from you and only you." He put the ring back in his pocket and held her close as if wanting to transfer his health to her. He wanted to be angry at someone or something. He wanted to cry, too.

The flight back to Wyoming seemed never ending. The Denver airport was jammed because Chicago and Atlanta had weather problems. In Cheyenne, his flight to Layton was canceled. He called the ranch. "I'm renting a car and driving. It will probably be midnight before I'm home." He hung up.

"Charlie, I think something is very wrong," Molly said to her husband.

February slowly turned into March. It was a hard spring for cattle ranchers . . . too much snow melting too fast. Flooding followed by more snow and late freezing weather. The word was out. The California woman had apparently turned down the Big Boss Brother's proposal at least for now. Big Boss, who usually was easy to work with, was now "hell on wheels." Everyone gave Asa a wide berth. Those men that had to work with him did so quietly and efficiently but couldn't fault Asa because he worked himself harder than anyone else. Trying to pull a stubborn calf out of the creek, Charlie pulled a muscle in his back. Charlie was grumpy.

Molly was worn out taking care of Charlie. Asa was just plain pissed off at the rain, the cows, at Charlie, at himself, at everyone except Joanna.

April was a little better. Catherine brought Russ home for Easter. Young Russell Brickman seemed like a fine young man. Charlie was reluctant to admit that Russ might be good enough for his only daughter. The two young people were clearly in love, which depressed Asa, and for that he felt guilty. Asa made a point of taking some of Charlie's chores so he and Molly could spend as much time as possible with Catherine and Russ. His niece had big plans for the fall wedding.

Asa and Joanna talked every week. He told her a little about Catherine and Russ all their plans and hoped the news was not as depressing for Joanna as it was for him. He asked no health questions, and she volunteered no information. They did not discuss the future. It was hard to keep a conversation going sometimes. Molly talked to Joanna also but if Joanna was telling Molly anything Molly was keeping quiet. Even this year's high calf count did not improve Asa's out look on the future. For the first time in a very long time, the ranch was not the main thing on Asa's mind. Life was so damn hard!

Asa was muddy, cold and tired. The weather had turned back to winter and made it hard on animals and men alike. He was beginning to think he hated cows. For the third time today, Asa was pulling off his irrigation boots when Molly said, "Joanna called. She asked that you call her back."

His heart sank and for the first time since Valentines Day he felt real dread. She answered on his first ring. "Come back with your ring if you still want to marry me."
"You're cured?" he asked. He hadn't crossed his fingers since he was a kid, but they were crossed now.
"I'm in what they call remission. I can have my life back"
Hopefully he said, "No more doctors?"
There will always be check-ups with blood work which can be done just as well in Wyoming as here and I have to take very good care of myself," she added.
"I'd like to be in charge of that last part, the taking care of you part."
"I'd like that too," he heard her say and uncrossed his fingers.

He was in California two days later. This time he rented a car, stopping on the way to her house for champagne and a dozen long stemmed red roses. She must have been watching for him because when he drove in she was standing in the driveway waiting.

Chapter Fifty-two

Pizza Again

Roger Smith had been driving this particular UPS route for several years, and he liked this little mountain community of Anchortown well enough that he was thinking about suggesting to his wife they move here. You got to know the people on your route. Right now he was going to Joanna Monroe's home.

Never in all his time of delivering boxes to her house had any of them been addressed to a Mr. Monroe. He was totally surprised to see this woman, he assumed had no man in her life, wrapped in the arms of a tall man wearing cowboy boots. Even at this distance, he saw it was a passionate embrace. He dropped off his delivery and on the way back down her drive he looked in his side mirror. The couple had the car trunk open. The man was handing Joanna a big bouquet of flowers. Yes, Roger Smith would tell his wife about this community.

The first thing Asa did was to slip his ring back on her finger. It fit. She had regained a little weight. They spent three days making plans. Joanna talked to Molly. Joanna talked to Susan. Molly and Susan talked to each other. So many plans.

They wanted to marry in July in Carmel. Molly and Charlie would come to California. No honeymoon, at least not right away. The newlyweds would come back to Joanna's house and decide the final plans for moving Joanna to Wyoming?

It was a friend of Susan's that led them to the final wedding plans. Susan announced to her mother. "I couldn't wait to talk to you so I confirmed everything. "It is a B&B just outside of Carmel. Located on an old ranch and it has a chapel . . . you know for weddings. I made reservations for you and . . . Asa, Molly, Charlie and David and me. We will leave the baby with his mother." Joanna related this to Molly. Molly and Susan talked many more times.

"You know, my love, you are not the only one making big plans," Asa said to Joanna. "I have already talked with Charlie about a building site. I am going to build you a house."

"Us," she corrected him.

It was not going to be as big as the old main house but big enough for company especially Susan and her family, once in a while. It would be beautiful. Situated on a small slope, he decided it would be a split-level. Their bedroom would occupy the top floor. It would face north with a grand view of the mountains. When they grew too old for steps, they could move downstairs to one of the nice guest bedrooms and the guests could have the upstairs.

The kitchen had to face east to catch the morning sun. Molly offered to share her quilt studio, but Asa though Joanna should have her own. The house had to come first, however. Asa drew pictures and made notes of all his ideas and asked her endless questions about what she might like. He had a whole folder to take back with him. He reminded Joanna of a small boy with a new set of building blocks. Asa was no small boy, and he was talking about large hand hewn beams to grace the exposed beam ceiling in the living room. When she asked if she could have slate floors like the main house he answered, "You can have anything you want." It was a matter of speculation about how well Kiki and Mr. Finch might get along.

Right now he was waking up very slowly in Joanna's bed. Sleeping in for Asa was a rarity. His face was against her pillow, and he caught the essence of her perfume from the night before. Lazily he turned over and stretched his naked body beneath her pale blue sheets. Joanna was standing in the hall doorway watching him. Wearing a pale yellow caftan that covered her body completely except for her bare feet, Asa felt a stir of desire. She was carrying a tray. He could smell the coffee and maybe muffins.
"Muffins?" he asked.
"Blueberry on the deck when you are ready," she answered as she went out onto the sunlit deck outside her bedroom. He put on his pants and joined her.

She was sitting in a chair with her bare feet on a footstool, the coffee tray positioned between them and his chair angled so he could use the footstool if he pleased. They ate their muffins, drank their coffee, and played footsie. They could hear the geese on the neighbor's pond.

He was tapping his foot. She waited. "You know even if I can get the permits, find an architect and a contractor we will be very lucky if the house is finished by next summer. So . . . the question is where do we live to start with?" She waited. "I was thinking about asking Molly to let us have the cottage."

"You mean her quilt studio?" Joanna was dismayed at his suggestion. He nodded his head yes. She shook her head no.

"Can't we just live in your quarters?" she asked.

"You would be willing?"

"I am, if you are."

Any remaining plans could wait; he was leaving tomorrow. "How about a movie and then I think you should fix dinner," she suggested.

"You want me to fix a dinner?" He was surprised.

"Yes, you know, your specialty, take and bake pizza . . . like the night of the snowstorm. We'll pick one up on the way home." Before they left for the movie, she set the kitchen table with a red and white checked tablecloth, candles, and flowers. Two glasses and a bottle of wine sat on the counter. It was a warm afternoon, and she made Mr. Finch go outside.

They took her car, but he drove. She knew the location of the movie complex, and the pizzeria and he wanted to learn his way around. The movie was titled, "Close Encounters of a Third Kind." They both liked the film. Asa particularly enjoyed the way the big space ship arrived. The musical score was great.

The take and bake pizza was on the back seat, and they were headed home for his last evening. The both could smell the pizza even through the plastic wrap. For such a beautiful afternoon, there was very little traffic. They were heading east, and Asa was driving and talking about both house plans and honeymooning in Hawaii. She was having trouble keeping up with all his ideas. An older, big, black car ahead of them seemed to be having a problem. It was going rather slow and was weaving from side to side. Joanna was looking at the names on a list to receive wedding announcements.

"Do you really know someone named John Young Bear?"

"When he didn't answer and she looked up, puzzled."

"Joanna, write down the license number of that car ahead of us." She did.

In the rear view mirror, Asa could see a second car coming up behind them already signaling to pass. The thing he did not want to happen did happen.

The car from the rear passed them just as the one in front veered into the passing lane. They collided with a screech of grinding metal and sparks. Joanna didn't know she screamed. She had never seen a real car accident. In lurid fascination, she watched the passing vehicle roll over several times into the center divider heading toward the oncoming lanes where an eighteen-wheeler was rolling toward the scene on the other side. She didn't see the first car speed away.

In the west bound lane Raul Mendoza was one happy man. He inserted a Freddy Fender tape into the big rig's tape deck and hummed along. After driving truck for over thirty years he was retiring. This was his last run. On the seat beside him was an envelope of $100 dollar bills. For six years, he had been keeping as much money out of his pay envelope as his wife wouldn't notice and putting it a secret account in a Reno bank. How to give her the money was the question bouncing around in his head. He wanted her to buy some real fancy clothes. They would go to Las Vegas till the cash ran out.

Because this morning he had stopped at the bank and closed out the account was the reason he was about six hours behind his regular schedule. To make up time, he was highballing down off Donner Summit toward Sacramento. He knew the California Highway Patrol frowned on such driving, but the roadway was surprising empty. In the eastbound lane all the traffic, he saw couple of passing cars.

That was when he saw two of the cars collide causing one to spin out of control into the center divider and toward him. He swore in both Spanish and English. He leaned on his air horn. As he blew by the wreck, he saw a man trying to help the driver. Raul thought he saw the flames on the under side of the car. He called for anyone listening on his CB.

In one fluid motion, Asa had pulled off onto the shoulder, turned on the emergency blinkers and was out of the car. "Stay here." He had run toward the damaged vehicle, which had come to rest just short of the fast lane westbound traffic.

As the big semi roared by, Joanna could see Asa's hair blow in the draft of the passing truck as he worked at opening the driver's door. She could also see flames licking at the under side of the car.

"Noooooo!" He could not hear her.

Finally, Asa was able to wrench the door open where a young woman sat in shock. She was not even trying to move. She's old enough to have a baby in the car he thought.

"Are you alone?" No answer. He repeated his question.

"Yes"

"No one else in the car?"

No, just me"

You need to get out now! Are you hurt? Asa could smell smoke and comprehended there was fire somewhere.

"I think I'm okay," but she didn't move.

"The car is going to blow up! Move now." He didn't know if that was the truth, but it might make her move. He intended to slap her if she didn't respond to his command. She began to move slowly. Maybe she smelled the smoke because all of a sudden she was making an effort. Together they ran from the smoldering vehicle. It was making a ticking sound as metal heated up.

Raul Mendoza had been able to bring his rig to a stop and was now running back toward the struggling couple with his fire extinguisher. Asa pushed the girl into a slight indentation in the ground and fell on top of her. A fireball erupted into the air. A whoosh of hot air knocked Raul backward after it rolled over Asa and the girl. Joanna could see nothing because of the black smoke. She could hear sirens. They sounded to far away.

Emergency personal did arrive. The girl was going to be very sore. She had dirt in her hair and refused to go to the hospital until she fainted. Then she agreed. Raul, Asa, and even Joanna were interviewed and questioned. Asa answered all the routine questions.

"We sure thank you for your help Mr. Bennington. You too Mrs. Bennington." Joanna couldn't smile at his mistake, because she was trying to keep her lip from trembling.

Aside to Asa, one of the officers remarked, "Damn it! I hate these hit and run accidents." It was the moment Asa had been waiting for.

"We wrote down the license number. Would you like it?"

The officer brightened considerably. "I sure as hell would."

The excitement was over. Asa got back into their car, held out his hand to Joanna and put his head back. He took a deep breath. "Are you all right?" he asked her before she could ask him.

"I will be. The question is, are you okay?" she replied.

I think I am a little singed. She looked at the hair on the back of his head.

"You are," she told him. He started the car and headed for home.

Finally, they were home. She was carrying the pizza and following him into the house. "Oh, Asa," she exclaimed.

"What?'

"Your shirt is all . . . sort of melted." In the bathroom, she helped him out of the ruined polyester shirt. His back was not burned but very red and a little tender. He moved carefully and slept on his side most of the night. In the morning, he had to return to Wyoming. The flights were going to be uncomfortable to say the least. The flight time did go by fast. He had lots of plans to think about.

In June when it was time to move the herds again, Charlie thought Asa might not want to go. It was something they had always enjoyed doing together, but Asa's life was about to change. Asa did want to go and Charlie was pleased even if the only thing Asa talked about was the new house.

Almost back to the main house, Asa wanted to stop at his chosen building site. Charlie liked to see his brother so happy and wondered if he was this goofy when he was preparing to marry Molly. Later arriving at the house, they both saw the dark car with tinted windows parked at the front gate.

"Do you know who that is?"

Asa didn't. "Looks government to me."

"You go take care of it then," suggested Charlie.

A young man got out of the car as Asa approached. Asa was reasonably sure who he was looking at.

"Asa Bennington?" the young man asked.

"Yes"

"I'm Bruce Monroe." Asa was correct. He was looking at Joanna's son.

"I understand you did some checking up on me," Bruce said. Asa nodded.

"What did you tell my mother?"

"That you are well. You are happy and you are working in the government."

"What did she say?" Bruce wanted to know.

"I was not there. I sent the information in my Christmas card. It was my gift to her. She thanked me. I do believe she was happy and very relieved."

Bruce was silent. He appeared to be thinking something over then he said, "I did some checking up on you and I want to talk to you about the wedding." Asa tensed.

From the garage where he had parked the truck, Charlie observed Asa and the stranger. He saw his brother tense up then slowly relax and a big smile spread across his face. He saw the two men shake hands, and the stranger got back in his car and drove off. Even after Charlie inquired about the man, Asa only grinned and said, "You'll see."

Joanna called Susan and invited her to bring the baby and come for a week to help her select a wedding gown. "A real, traditional, white wedding gown?" asked Susan.

"No. I think I want something in lavender or maybe pale violet . . . a little old fashioned, I think. I'm going to ask Asa and Charlie to wear their cowboy hats and boots. Susan wasn't to sure about that idea but she could tell her mother was very happy.

"Mom. Where you and dad really happy?"

"Yes, we were. We made some early mistakes and it was hard but yes we were happy. I'm just surprised I have found love twice. Some woman don't even find it once."

Asa was packing for what he felt would be his last trip to California at least as a single man. Charlie knocked n the door and entered the room. "Did Molly tell you that Stan Kenner wants to see us in town tomorrow at 9:15 a.m."

"Yes she did. Kenner is a real estate man. What does he want with us?"

"I can't think of any reason."

The following morning they arrived exactly on time but there was a woman in Kenner's office already. He motioned them in anyway.

"Gentleman, Let me introduce Mrs. Jerome Crocker." The name meant nothing to either Charlie or Asa. The woman was older than Asa, attractive, and very well dressed.

"Asa. Charlie." Neither of you know me but I used to be married to Stub Hathaway. Your parents knew me as Spoonetta Hathaway."

"You sent flowers when our mother died," interrupted Asa.

"Yes, I did. Lillian Bennington was the first person to ever show me a kindness. I never forgot your mother even after I ran away from Stub."

Spoonetta Hathaway Crocker continued, "You know . . . he beat me till I lost the baby which was, in retrospect, a blessing I suppose." She paused. "I have had a very fine life despite the way it started out, but before my husband and I leave for our new home in Hawaii I am getting even with Stub once and for all. I am selling you the Hathaway land for $1 if you still want it." Both Charlie and Asa reached for their wallets.

Kenner knew the Bennington Brothers would want the Hathaway place. As far as he was concerned that piece of land should always have belonged to the Double B and Kenner had the papers ready. Asa and Charlie thanked the widow Hathaway or Mrs. Crocker or whatever her name was, said their good-byes and walked out of the office with straight faces. As soon as they were out of sight from the real estate office, they broke into sidesplitting laughter and slapped each other on the back. A passing pedestrian didn't know who they were and thought they might be drunk.

Chapter Fifty-three

The Wedding

Two days before the wedding, Asa flew to Sacramento. Joanna picked him up. Her house was surprisingly empty, and there were packed boxes in the guest rooms. She had been busy. Mr. Finch wound himself around Asa's leg. "Have you given any thought about how you are going to send Mr. Finch to the ranch?" asked Asa.

"I truly think he is too old to adjust to ranch life. The neighbor that cares for him when I am gone wants to adopt him." It was a good solution.

"Tell me our plans again," asked Asa.

"Day after tomorrow we drive to Carmel where we meet Molly and Charlie and Susan and her husband. We all have a nice dinner together. We are all at this same bed-and-breakfast that Susan assures me is perfect. The wedding is the next day at 11:00 a.m. in the little chapel on the B & B property. The proprietor, a Mrs. Chase, has made the arrangements for a justice of the peace. There is a lunch for all of us after the ceremony. Susan and David have to leave right after the lunch. Molly and Charlie are going sight seeing. You and I are alone till the next morning when we meet Charlie and Molly for a good-bye breakfast"

"Okay" was all he said then added, "I suppose you won't let me sleep with you the night before the wedding?

"Absolutely not. You are bunking in with Charlie. Molly is in my room." Asa tried to look pained.

As Molly had requested, arrangements of purple iris and daises spilled over on the small stone alter. Susan, as matron of honor, carried white roses and iris and would proceed down the isle ahead of Joanna to where Asa and Charlie would be waiting. Mrs. Chase was a little confused when Molly, the red headed sister-in-law, requested that Mrs. Chase stop Joanna outside the door to the chapel for just a minute or two.

The justice of the peace was a nice old man that had performed many weddings in his day and thought he had seen it all. He thought this groom and best man were a cut above some of the people he had married. Maybe they were wearing cowboy boots and hats but they sure as heck were not drug store cowboys. He rather liked the way this was turning out until the bride was late, entering the chapel; she was on the arm of a strange man. Tears were streaming down her face. The bride's daughter looked at her mother and began to cry also. The groom was smiling broadly and the best man seemed very confused.

For the organist, the ceremony started just like any other wedding. Susan entered the chapel and walked down the isle just as they had practiced. It was then things changed. The door in the back closed softly. The organist was used to wedding glitches. She continued to play, waiting for the doors to reopen and the bride start toward the wedding party. Behind the closed doors, Joanna didn't understand why Mrs. Chase asked her to stop.

"Mom," looking off to the side she saw her son, Bruce. He was wearing a purple iris in his buttonhole. He offered his arm. "May I walk you down the isle?" After that everything went as planned. The luncheon, served outside under a huge old tree, was perfect probably because Molly had arranged it, as a surprise without telling Joanna. Bruce could stay for lunch. Asa and Molly and Charlie wandered through the old garden to give Joanna, Susan, and Bruce some time alone.

In the way of conversation, Charlie reminded Asa, "We will meet you for breakfast in the morning. Molly and I are checking out and driving up to San Francisco, spending two nights and then flying home from there."

Good-byes and hugs all around. Susan whispered in her mother's ear, "You know Mom, he is a fox." Susan was tickled at her mother's blush. Then, Bruce and Susan and her husband were gone along with Charlie and Molly. Asa and Joanna were alone. It felt good. "Well, Mrs. Bennington, what would you like to do?"

Let's change clothes and go to the beach." They walked the beach hand in hand. They sat on a rock so that she could snuggle up next to him and he could put his arms around her and pull her close. She could feel his heart beating. They ate crab sandwiches while they watched the fog roll in.

"Did you give Charlie a gift for being your best man," Joanna asked.

"Yes. I did." She could tell Asa was pleased. "Charlie has been looking at a very fine saddle for sometime now. If Molly had wanted it, he would have bought it immediately but he wouldn't spend the money on himself. It will be at the ranch when they arrive home. What did you give Susan?"

"My old wedding rings. She is going to save them for the baby."

A foghorn sounded somewhere. When he felt her begin to shiver he said, "Let's go home"

"Home is Wyoming but the bed-and-breakfast will do nicely tonight."

Back in their room, he thought about making love to her, after all it was their wedding night but all of a sudden it was enough to have her so near and knowing they didn't have to say good-bye anymore.

He was just about to drift off to sleep when Joanna said, "Susan called you a fox."

"A what?"

"A fox. She said you are a fox"

"Well. For some one who is a married woman, a mother and my step daughter, I'm not sure that is proper."

"It's okay? Besides I agree with her." He pulled her gently into the curve of his body. The last thing she remembered hearing was his contented sigh.

Back in Wyoming at last, they moved into the big house with Molly and Charlie. Some of Joanna's possessions went into storage and packing boxes were stacked in the barn. Ground was broken for the new house. Sitting on old lawn chairs, the four of them toasted with champagne. The newest Mr. and Mrs. Bennington went camping at Lake Peetee, but Asa couldn't persuade Joanna to swim naked until the last day.

"EOR is next week," Joanna mentioned. Are we dressing in costume this year?"

"I don't think so and I am not growing a beard either" was his answer. "But I do think you need a proper pair of boots."

"What if I can't walk in cowboy boots?" she asked.

He was puzzled. "What do you mean?"

"Not everyone can walk in cowboy boots. Some people walk as if their back or maybe their feet hurt," she explained.

"These will be very good custom boots. You will do just fine and your feet won't hurt either." Thinking about it he added, "Won't have them in time for EOR." Joanna was happy to wear exactly what she wore the previous year.

EOR day was hot for September so the evening was going to be pleasant. The two brothers and their wives drove to the hosting ranch together. The evening was fine until near the end. Molly and Joanna were off somewhere so Asa and Charlie walked to the makeshift bar for the last drink of the evening. Standing at one end of the bar was Jake Ludlow.

He watched the Bennington Brothers approach. "Well, if it isn't the super trooper." Asa and Charlie both understood this was in reference to the article in the silver Bend Banner about Asa helping rescue the California highway crash victim in the spring. The article went on the say how Asa's turning in the license number resulted in the driver being in jail and awaiting trial. The whole article embarrassed Asa. In truth, it was the headline that pissed him off. Molly sent a copy of the article to Joanna who laughed at the headline, "Local Rancher Corrals Crook."

Charlie and Asa acknowledged Jake pleasantly and had just asked for their drinks when Jake said loud enough for others to hear, "Had to marry the bitch and bring her back here." Charlie knew what was going to happen. He stepped back out of the way and so did everyone else.

Asa placed his glass on the bar. He had wanted to punch Jake Luldlow for a long time and that time was now. Asa planted his feet. He doubled up both fists. His left fist landed solidly in Ludlow's beer belly followed by his right, which landed squarely on Ludlow's jaw as he sagged from the first blow. Bystanders flinched at what they heard the sound of breaking bone.

Charlie reasoned Asa had done enough damage and moved to Asa's side incase the Bennington temper took over. In a quiet and clam voice Charlie said. "Don't put your boots to him, Asa. Ludlow has had enough." Asa really wanted to kick the downed man. He didn't. He took several deep breaths instead and thanked Charlie. The bartender was an older man. He wrapped ice in a towel, handed it to Asa for his hands and said, "Nice left, Mr. Bennington."

Asa's smile was crooked. "Damn. I didn't remember it hurt that much. It did feel good, though." Both Asa and Charlie thought that neither Molly nor Joanna had seen the altercation, but they were wrong.

At home in the little apartment, Joanna handed Asa some more ice. "You hit Jake Ludlow, didn't you?"

"I did"

"Why?"

"He said something he shouldn't have."

"What?"

"That, my love, you don't need to know." There was a slight edge to Asa's voice. Joanna could guess what Ludlow said and didn't need to hear it from her husband she decided.

Upstairs, Molly had just asked Charlie the same question. In reply Charlie said, "Jake made a crude remark about Joanna."

Molly could guess and closed the conversation by saying, "I am surprised that some one hasn't hit Ludlow before now."

November brought Catherine's wedding. For Molly and Catherine, planning the wedding had been difficult. Russ' parents were divorced and used the wedding to snip at each other. Joanna suspected that Molly and Charlie were spending a lot of money on this wedding, and they were not complaining. They liked Catherine's young man, and she was their only daughter.

Catherine had very definite ideas. The wedding was in the fall and Catherine chose autumn colors. The three brides maids would wear very simple gowns in pale shades of yellow and orange and peach with a long scarf in a fall leaf print draped over one shoulder and fastened on the opposite hip. Molly was not sure about this but only said so to Joanna. The best men, Russ and Charlie, were to wear tuxedos with cummerbunds and bow ties made from the same fabric as the scarves being worn by the brides maids.

Charlie said absolutely not. He would not wear a "flowered" bow tie. It didn't make it any better when Catherine said the pattern was not flowers but fall leaves. "No" was her father's last word and she conceded. Asa was on Charlie's side and was relieved when Catherine told him he only had to wear a peach rose in his buttonhole.

One day out in the barn alone with Asa, Charlie commented, "You can't believe how much this wedding is costing." He added, "Not that I'm complaining." Asa knew because Joanna had told him.

"Well, brother, Catherine is the only child this ranch has and she is my niece. Joanna and I wouldn't mind paying for something . . . say as another wedding gift. Hell, the ranch could pay for some of it. You know our auditor is always telling us to do something we can charge to public relations. Seeing Catherine happy is damn good PR if you ask me."

Charlie smiled at his big brother. "I'll mention it to Molly."

Molly and Charlie drove to Casper early and Asa and Joanna followed a few days later. On the road Joanna commented, "It looks like Catherine got her wish."

"How is that?" Asa asked.

"Catherine wanted this wedding to be about fall and the fall colors. Just look at the mountainsides. The trees still have lots of fall leaves. It is beautiful. Now if it just doesn't snow."

Despite the forecast of snow, the wedding day dawned clear and sunny. Catherine with her art talent and with Molly's help had made the church and the reception beautiful. Catherine was a radiant bride. Russ was handsome and clearly nervous. The rural mountain church with the big glass window looking out on the hillside was packed. Charlie walked Catherine down the isle. When he retuned to the pew and Molly, Asa could see tears streaming down his brother's face. Asa reflected that Charlie always cried at important occasions.

Joanna thought how at her wedding there were only eight people and that was if you counted the justice of the peace. She hoped that Catherine and Russ would be as happy as she and Asa were. When she began to sniffle Asa handed her his clean handkerchief just as Charlie handed his to Molly.

Catherine had selected the Paint Brush Inn for a sit down dinner to be followed by dancing to DJ music. The inn was modeled on the famous old national park inns with huge timbers and much beautiful wood. Much of the artwork consisted of paintings of the beautiful western flower from which the inn took its name.

The bride and groom and both sets of parents sat at a head table. Asa was very relived he and Joanna did not have to sit there also although Catherine had suggested they should. Neither Asa nor Joanna thought very highly of Russ's parents. When Asa started calling them the Bickering Brickmans the name stuck. As Asa so bluntly put it to Charlie one time, "Such a nice young man should not have such ass hole parents." Charlie couldn't agree more. More than one time the Brickmans had reduced Molly to tears while trying to make the wedding plans. Russ had even apologized for them.

Unfortunately, the couple began to live up to the nickname as soon as they were seated next to their son. Even before the church service, Asa could smell liquor on Bill Brickman's breath. Now he sat next to Russ and flirted with someone out of Asa's range of vision. Fortunately right after the dinner and before the speeches, toasts and the cake the two Brickmans disappeared into the bar. Some how Russ must have clued in the MC because when it was Bill Brickman's time to toast the couple the MC just skipped over him. Most of the guests never noticed.

The toasts were made and Joann was relieved that most of them were in good taste. The beautiful cake was amazing. Catherine had refused to tell Molly anything about it. Three tiers with all white frosting, it was designed to look like a crazy quilt pattern detailed right down the traditional quilt embroidery stitches. The only color on the cake was topper, a small bouquet of real roses in fall colors.

Catherine removed the bouquet from the vase hidden in the cake and asked Molly to come forward. Presenting the flowers to Molly Catherine said, "Thank you, Mom." Asa was not the only man handing his wife another handkerchief.

Once the cake was done, there was a brief break while the D. J. set up his equipment. Catherine and Russ danced first. Asa was beginning to wonder if he might run out of handkerchiefs. What was it about weddings that made women all soppy? Russ handed Catherine off to Charlie. Secretly Catherine had been taking dance lessons and Charlie had his instructions. He was to hand his daughter off to her uncle, which Charlie did.

"Uncle Asa, you promised to dance with me at my wedding."

"Indeed I did, Lady Catherine." Asa bowed deeply, offered his arm to Catherine and escorted her onto the center of the dance floor. He was tall handsome man in formal wear with black hair to match that of the lovely young bride. If it were not for Charlie's happy blue eyes, they could have been father and daughter. That comparison had been made through the years and Asa felt a little sad he would never dance with a daughter of his own at her wedding.

They made a perfect picture. Guests began to watch and moved off to the side to give the couple space. Some even clapped as uncle and niece whirled elegantly around the floor. Charlie's chest puffed out. Molly and Joanna cried again. Asa smiled down at his niece, and Russ was just a little intimidated by the whole Bennington family.

As the evening progressed both Asa and Joanna thought the D. J. had just the right mix of music. In their six months of marriage, she had learned to dance with him and it was something they both enjoyed. The newly weds had left about an hour ago. The Bickering Brickmans had managed to miss that also because they continued to sit in the bar and argue. The party was beginning to thin out.

During the evening, Asa thought the D. J. had played some Nitty Gritty Dirt Band and when he asked, the D. J. confirmed this. It pleased him that people actually noticed what he played. "Do you take requests?' asked Asa.

"I'd be happy to."

Nitty Gritty Dirt Band "Make a Little Magic" was Asa's request.

The D. J. looked through his files and said, "One request before yours."

But Asa was not finished. "Do you take dedications?"

Normally he didn't. It could get out of control but for this man, obviously a member of the wedding party he decided he would.

"It's for Joanna," Asa told him.

Asa and Joanna were on the dance floor when the D. J. announced, "This is for Joanna." The music floated over them, and she buried her head on his shoulder both embarrassed and pleased. She listened to the words and when he pulled her tight against him she felt the hardness of his desire.

Leaning back a little so she could look up at him she said, "You aren't thinking about that big, empty, king-sized bed back in our room are you?"

Laughing now he answered, "You know me to well."

"That's not hard," she replied.

"The hell it's not," he said pulling her close again. They both laughed at the double meaning of their private conversation. Loud voices came from the bar area. "Is that the Brickmans, again?" She nodded.

Let's pick up Charlie and Molly and head for the hotel.

In the lobby of the hotel, Asa stepped to the desk and ordered champagne and two glasses sent to their suite. The deskman's eyebrows went up just a fraction at the label of champagne Asa ordered. Finally alone in their room Asa striped off his coat, threw it on a chair and took off his tie. Joanna was carefully folding her wrap when he took her in his arms and kissed her soundly. He pushed her away gently. "Now you have to go sit in that chair over there." He motioned to the big easy chair by the little fireplace.

Perplexed, she watched him go into the bedroom where she saw him fumble around in his suite case. He returned with a small package.

"Here." Opening the box she saw the most beautiful diamond earrings she had ever seen.

"Oh, Asa," was all Joanna could say.

"Charlie picked out a different pair for Molly. We just wanted you two to know how much we appreciated all the work you both went to for the wedding." Joanna looked at the earring for a moment longer than jumped up.

"Okay, it is you turn to sit in the chair." That was not what he had planned to do. After he was seated, she also went into the bedroom and returned with a wrapped gift.

"For you," she laughed. "And Charlie is receiving one also."

He could tell it was a book. However, he was not prepared to find leather bound copy of his mother's Layton County and Bennington family journals complete with area photos he suspected Joanna had taken. The champagne arrived. It was a perfect ending to a perfect day.

Asa and Joanna took over a week to return home. They enjoyed Yellowstone with snow. They took as much time as they could just so Charlie and Molly could also have some time alone after the hustle and bustle of Catherine's wedding.

Christmas followed Thanksgiving. Asa took Joanna out in search of the perfect tree. Russ and Catherine came home to help ring in the New Year. They had good news. Russ had been accepted into a prestigious law firm. The holidays were good, but wistfully Joanna very much wanted to have their house completed and she understood nothing was going to happen until the snow stopped falling. Winter changed to spring and construction was under way and by their first anniversary she could set up a card table in the unfinished dining room. Asa grilled hot dogs. Molly provided a salad. Asa promised a proper meal as soon as they were settled in, probably some time in September he hoped. They all hoped.

Chapter Fifty-four

All the Benningtons at Home

He was right about a September move in. EOR was a week away.

"Would you mind not going?" Joanna asked.

"No, I guess not. Why?" Asa was tired and dirty from working on the new driveway. He and Charlie had been on the tractors all day. He figured Charlie was already down at the main house in a nice hot shower. He and Joanna were still living in the private quarters in the main house and the arrangement was getting old. Right now, he and Joanna were sitting in their new kitchen. The last fourteen months had not been that bad, but he was ready for his own house, with his own wife in their own bedroom and their own bed and nobody else around. He knew Joanna felt the same way. Probably, so did Charlie and Molly.

Joanna walked in back of where Asa was sitting in one of the old lawn chairs She dug her elbows into the places along his shoulder muscles she knew needed the most attention. He let her work her magic on his tired body and then said, "You don't have any regrets about marring me?

"Yes. I do." She could feel him try not to tense so she worked her thumbs into his stiff neck. "I'm sorry that some how we couldn't have met sooner." She could feel some of his tension easing.

Returning to her original question about the EOR, Joanna continued. "The last of the furniture is supposed to arrive on Friday. That includes our bed. I think by Saturday night we could be moved in. I mean completely moved in."

"In that case I don't want to go to this year's EOR. I want to stay home with you . . . and only you . . . at last," he said with a sigh.

Even though Joanna made their apologies to this year's EOR hostess, she still sent an angel food cake with Molly. The morning of EOR Joanna handed the cake to Molly. "I think is amusing that the first thing I cook in my new oven is a cake I am sending to EOR and we are not even attending." Molly chuckled and agreed.

Joanna and Asa looked forward to their first night in their beautiful new home. He grilled steaks. She prepared his favorite pasta salad with a side of fresh sliced pineapple. They sat on the not quite finished patio, sipped wine they had saved for the occasion and watched the stars come out. He put down his empty glass and stood up. "We have a lot of work to do," he commented.
"Tonight?"
"Yes. Which room in the house do you want to make love in first?" He was pleased. He could still make her blush, sometimes.
September quickly turned into October, which turned into November.
Molly waited for Joanna to invite them for Thanksgiving, thinking that Joanna would want to host the first holiday in the new house. After no invitation came, Molly said she would cook the turkey. Joanna was relieved. She was not feeling well at all. In fact she had a doctor appointment for the week right after New Years.

Asa even offered to fly Susan and her family to the ranch for Christmas. Reluctantly Joanna extended the invitation. "Oh Mom, We can't. We have reservations at Disneyland." Joanna was relieved. "Mom, is everything okay?
"Yes. Everything is fine." Susan didn't think so. Asa thought Joanna didn't seem to enjoy their first Christmas in the new house as much as he thought she would. She seemed to just go through the motions. She seemed preoccupied. He inquired a few times only to have her say everything was fine. Like Susan, he didn't think so.

Asa let Joanna out of the car at the doctor's office front door. "I'll go get coffee. I'll be back and have the car warm by the time you are out," he said. He watched her walk away from the car and disappeared into the building. At the Honey Bear Cafe, he wanted to drink his coffee alone so he sat in a booth toward the back. He was worried about Joanna.
He quickly had company. One of the newer deputies placed an order to go, spotted Asa and walked back to join him while the order was prepared. "Guess you heard about Jake Ludlow?" Asa hadn't. "Must have been driving drunk again. Drove off the Old Mine Rd. into a deep ditch. Snow plow found the truck this morning."
"Dead?" asked Asa.

"Yeah. Don't know if the accident killed him or the cold. Seems the big question is what to do with his house, his tractors and his bank account. Guess he had a wife once but no one knows what happened to her." The deputy picked up his sandwich and left Asa to his thoughts. Asa finished his coffee and outside the cafe he saw the Ludlow article on the front page of the Silver Bend Banner. Asa purchased a copy of the paper. He would send the article to Mary Redwing. She would know what to do with it if anything.

The doctor asked Joanna all the usual questions. He gave her the usual office examinations. He gave no hint about what might be wrong. Ordering some lab work, he told her to come back in two weeks. Then, he was gone to his next patient. Joanna thought it was a very long two weeks. Asa thought so too. He pushed the idea of her cancer returning into the back of his mind and he didn't mention Jake Ludlow's death.

On the day of the return visit Joanna heart dropped when the receptionist showed her into the doctor's office and not one of the examination rooms. Dr. Trotter huffed into the room. He was running late. "Morning Joanna."

He read through her file, shut it and folded his hands on the desk in front of him.

She couldn't wait. "Is the cancer back?"

"Is that what you think? Good grief! You're not sick. Joanna, you are pregnant!"

"Pregnant??" she repeated.

"Yes. Due in May is my guess at this time. You didn't plan this?"

"No. I've been taking my pills. We felt we were to old to start a family."

The doctor started to make a joke about aggressive sperm. Instead he said, "Any birth control pill only offers about 99 percent protection. As far as your being too old, your age will just mean we will take a few extra precautions, but I see no reason why you can't have a normal pregnancy and have a healthy baby." He gave her papers to read and told her when to make the next appointment.

On the way out, she stopped in the lady's room. She splashed cold water on her face and looked at herself in the mirror. How was she going to tell her husband? In the car, he said. "Well?"

"Everything is just fine. Really fine." He saw the worry and the strain were gone. This deserved a celebration.

"Early dinner in town? Italian? Mexican? Ribs? Chinese?"

"Let's take Chinese home." She knew where there was a bottle of cold champagne. It was a good thing they went home. The snow was falling thick and fast.

She put the food in the oven to reheat and changed into a soft lounge robe. In the living room, she placed the tray, the champagne and the glasses on the coffee table. She flicked off the TV. "I have a toast to propose." She poured carefully. "To us." He wondered just what the hell she was up to but he could tell she was very happy. She sipped. He sipped. "And to our baby." He choked spiting champagne down the front of his shirt.

He was totally blank. "Asa, I'm pregnant." She watched the emotion play across his face . . . surprise, joy, pleasure and then concern.

He turned serious. "What about you?" "She told him everything," the doctor said.

"Damn! I designed the house all wrong." He commented. They didn't tell the rest of the family till after Valentine's Day.

She felt fine into the last of February and so was curious why that month's examination took a lot longer than the previous ones. As soon as you're dressed, "we need to have a little chat," was what Dr. Trotter said as he left the room. She tried not to feel the beginning of dread in the pit of her stomach.

Once Asa had adjusted to the idea of being a father, he had been walking on air. She didn't want anything to go wrong, not now. As Charlie remarked to Molly, "You would think that my brother was the only expectant father on the planet." Apparently, Charlie had forgotten just how excited and goofy he had been while they waited for Catherine.

Again Joanna was sitting in the doctor's office. He looked across the desk at her. He put his elbows on the desk and tented his fingers, "I am referring you to a specialist." She was trying hard to hold back tears. "Joanna, I hear two very strong heart beats. "I believe you are carrying twins."

As he always did when she returned, Asa had the engine running so she would be warm. "Well?"

She took his hand and placed it on her protruding belly. "Would you believe there are two babies in there?"

"Asa?"

"Asa, we hare having twins." It was only the second time in their married life she had seen him speechless.

When he did speak it was to say, "Damn!" He said it very softly. He remained silent all the way home while she explained everything about the new doctor and that the birth would be at the hospital in Layton because it would probably be by cesarean. "We have to pick more names, don't we?" he commented.

Dr. Moss was a nice man. After more examinations, he confirmed everything Dr. Trotter had suspected. The May date was set, and there was not much to do except wait. Joanna continued to expand. Asa was dismayed at her increasing size.

May came very slowly. The surgery date was just two weeks away. It couldn't come soon enough as far as Asa was concerned. He understood his wife felt miserable, and he was correct. Her mid-section was so big. Her feet and ankles were swollen. No matter if she sat or lay down there was not one comfortable position. They were sleeping downstairs in separate beds because she was so big and clumsy. "I can't believe I did that to you," he said and then was sorry he said it.

"Well, you did," she snapped and waddled toward the bathroom.

Joanna was immediately sorry she snapped at him. He was so patient. It seemed to her all she did was snap at everyone and then apologize. Back from the bathroom, she eased down into her big chair across from where Asa sat reading about irrigation. He set his book aside. Rising from his chair, he went to stand behind her. With his gentle thumbs he softly rubbed the kinks out of her neck. She sighed. I'm sorry I was rude . . . again"

"No matter. You're worth it," he answered.

"I really want my body back. I am tired of sharing it with two other people." She knew he would be smiling at her remark.

"When I have it back I want a real hug from you." She was too round for real hugs and he missed them too.

Later that night Asa awoke with a start. He seemed to be doing that more and more often. Quietly he walked around the house making sure everything was in order. Through the trees he could see the outside yard light at the main house. Everything appeared to be okay. At the door to Joanna's room he paused. The nightlight created a soft glow. He watched her sleep. At least she was getting some rest. He wondered again about these last, almost nine months.

Sure making a baby was a very pleasurable thing, especially with the love of your life. However, pregnancy was whole different matter, especially toward the end. He and Joanna would be responsible for two babies, two little people who hopefully would grow into healthy, happy, competent individuals. He and Joanna were committed for the rest of their lives. He was pleased but in a little awe of the prospect. Asa wished he had talked to his father and mother more about their lives and their early years.

The surgery date came. It was a beautiful spring day. Asa watched his wife flinch as he drove to the hospital. He didn't know if it was winter potholes or the babies punching and kicking in their confined space. They were allowed to have dinner together in her room after which he went to his lonely hotel. He didn't want to go to the bar. He tried watching TV. He thought about calling home. In the end, he went to bed and stared at the ceiling. This time tomorrow he would be a father.

Morning finally arrived and Asa visited with Joanna briefly. He was somewhat comforted to see they had given her something and she was resting. A quick kiss and she was going down the hall and he was being ordered to the waiting room. He knew the expected hours allotted for the surgery. He watched the clock. Maybe the clock hands were stuck. He was the oldest man in the room. Other fathers-to-be assumed he probably had been through this before. He waited. He wanted to thump on the clock to make it move.

"Mr. Bennington." The nurse calling his name startled him. She reminded him of a drill sergeant he once had. "Your wife and babies are doing fine."

Several other men in the room heard the word "babies." Someone slapped him on the back and said, "Way to go old man."

The drill sergeant nurse continued, "You can see them in just a few minutes," she said nothing more but started down the hall expecting him to follow.

"What did she have? What did we have?" he corrected. Asa needed to hustle to keep up with the nurse.

The woman stopped so suddenly Asa almost ran into to her. She had a smug expression on her face.

"Mrs. Bennington told me not to tell you." Before Asa could reply to that she continued. "Where are her flowers? You didn't bring your wife flowers?"

"Shit," he muttered as he followed her down the hall. "Shit. Shit. Shit" The drill sergeant nurse smiled to herself knowing the handsome, first time father would arrive tomorrow with a huge bouquet. Stopping at a closed door, she commanded. "Wait here."

The door opened and a young nurse motioned him in. Joanna was propped up in bed. Her hair had been fixed. Maybe just a little makeup. She was wearing a fancy, quilted bed jacket, a gift from Molly. Joanna looked beautiful. On each side of her, wrapped in soft, pale yellow blankets he saw tiny pink, no red faces. One baby was asleep. The other, he thought, might be looking at him. "Come meet your family Mr. Bennington."

Taking a deep breath he said almost in a whisper, "What do we have?"

"You will have to come take a peek for yourself, Mr. Bennington," and she smiled.

THE END